THE SHAMAN'S BONES

Books by James D. Doss

The Shaman Sings
The Shaman Laughs
The Shaman's Bones

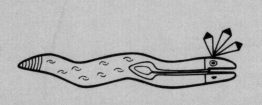

THE SHAMAN'S BONES

James D. Doss

AVON BOOKS NEW YORK

AVON BOOKS
A division of
The Hearst Corporation
1350 Avenue of the Americas
New York, New York 10019

Library of Congress Cataloging in Publication Data:
Doss, James D.
    The shaman's bones / by James D. Doss.—1st ed.
        p.   cm.
    I. Title.
PS3554.075S49   1997   96-52148
813'.54—dc21   CIP

First Avon Books Printing: September 1997

AVON TRADEMARK REG. U.S. PAT. OFF. AND IN OTHER COUNTRIES, MARCA REGISTRADA, HECHO EN U.S.A.

Printed in the U.S.A.

FIRST EDITION

RRD-H   10 9 8 7 6 5 4 3 2 1

✦

For Dick Hutson
and
Fr. Richard J. Anderson

The Harpy styles a nest of broken bone,
remains of corpses eaten as her prey.
She sleeps by day and flies by night alone
upon her raven wings of silk moiré.
　　　　　　—Gene W. Taylor
　　　　　　　From *Out of the Night*

❖

/pit<u>u</u>ku=pɨ/ liked to have gifts left at his home . . .
shamans whose power came from him would leave gifts,
preferably beads or rings, at the hole supposed
to be the entrance to his home.
　　　　　　—Anne M. Smith
　　　　　　　Ethnography of the Northern Utes

THE SHAMAN'S BONES

CHAPTER 1

Southern Ute Reservation
At the mouth of *Cañón del Espíritu*

*T*he golden eye closes softly . . . day's farewell is a sly wink on the horizon.
Now it begins.

Upon the crests of barren mesas, shadow-streams flow slowly over the amber
sands. With all the stealth of serpents, these dismal currents slip silently over
basalt boulders, slither among clusters of yucca spears . . . one darkling reaches
out with velvet fingers to stroke the gaunt limbs of a dwarf oak; another paints
ghostly images on a cracked wall of stone.

This is but a prelude to true night, when black tides spill over towering cliffs
to flood the deep channels of meandering canyons. The oldest among the People
whisper tales of serpentine creatures that swim in these ebony rivers—the elders
chant guttural, monotone hymns to keep these dark spirits at bay.

A powdery blue mist swirls about the squat figures sitting on the summit of
Three Sisters Mesa. The sandstone sisters bow their heads under the stars . . .
and sigh . . . and sleep an eternal sleep.

But not everyone rests so well on this night. Sleep—if it can be called sleep—
comes with shivers and groans. Dreams—if they can be called dreams—invoke
shifting, amorphous shapes . . . muttering, mocking voices . . . pale, gaunt
hands that beckon. And on occasion—cold fingers caress the dreamers and
bring them gasping from their almost-sleep.

These dreadful apparitions are, of course, delusions. Images inspired by un-

healthy imaginations . . . by troublesome bits of food that lie undigested in the gut. They are twilight's lies . . . wicked tricks played by shadows . . . midnight's hollow deceptions. They are mere fantasies.

Except . . . when they are not.

Daisy Perika has eaten a delicious bowl of greasy posole on this particular evening, and now a growling stomach interferes with her need for rest. While a tilted cusp of moon drifts across a crystalline sky, the Ute woman rolls over in her little bed, and groans. Daisy is not awake; neither does she sleep. The old shaman drifts in that chartless sea that separates this land of ordinary consciousness from that distant shore of honest slumber.

Though her eyes are closed, she can see her surroundings with a terrible clarity. Troubling apparitions flit before the weary woman. Dreams. Half dreams.

And visions.

She stands alone on a flat, lifeless plain of flinty pebbles . . . under a mottled gray sky that knows neither moon nor star. There is a sudden rolling, rumbling of dark clouds that live and breathe . . . a crackling snap of bluish flame as thin fingers of lightning reach for her.

But it is not electric fire that touches the dreamer . . . a warm, heavy liquid rains from the sky, pelting her upturned face with a crimson pox. She licks a drop from her lips; it tastes of salt . . . she shudders and spits it from her mouth. Now the scarlet deluge is hail . . . it hammers on her head . . . and hands . . . and feet.

A rapping-tapping . . . a ringing-pinging . . .

She pleads to the Great Mysterious One to make it stop . . . the repellent shower subsides.

But now an abominable thing approaches the shaman . . . floating, twisting, tumbling in the tortured eddies of the night—like a rotten log caught in the current of a swift stream. It slows . . . hangs above her . . . suspended as if from invisible wires for the dreamer's close inspection. It is a dead thing. A blackened, frozen carcass . . . an eyeless corpse.

And this is only the beginning.

☼ Ignacio, Colorado ☼
The following day

Scott Parris turned the blunt nose of the old Volvo into the graveled parking lot. By the time he'd slammed the door, Charlie Moon was waiting in the entrance of the Southern Ute Police Station. Moon's coarse black hair brushed against the cedar crossbeam above the six-foot-eight-inch doorway.

Parris shook his friend's outstretched hand. "Headed down here as soon as I got your message."

The Ute policeman glanced up at the midday sky. A red-tailed hawk circled low. Looking for lunch, he figured.

Parris squinted at the hawk, then at the Ute. "What's up, Charlie?"

Moon's smile was a wary one. "Come inside, pardner."

Daisy Perika was sitting quietly in Charlie Moon's office, her wrinkled hands resting in her lap. She was waiting patiently for the lawmen. Much of her life had been spent waiting, and it did not bother the old woman.

Her nephew appeared in the doorway. "Scott's here," Moon said.

Granite Creek's chief of police, a six-footer with broad shoulders, was dwarfed by the big Ute. The soft-spoken *matukach* removed his battered felt hat and nodded in a gesture of respect. "Mrs. Perika."

"Sit down," the old woman ordered, as if Charlie's office were hers to rule. By common consent, it was.

Both men sat; Moon on his oak desk, Parris on an uncomfortable wooden chair, painted a dull green. Government surplus or a BIA castoff, he guessed.

Daisy Perika sat with her eyes closed, as if calling up some lost memory.

Parris glanced uncertainly at Moon; the Ute policeman's face was unreadable. He turned his attention to the old woman.

She opened her eyes and stared at his chest. As if she could see his heart thumping inside his rib cage.

The silence was difficult for the white man. "How've you been, Mrs. Perika?"

"Knee's been hurting some. And my back. But I'm better now."

Parris grinned. "Glad to hear it. That you're better, I mean."

Once more, she lapsed into silence.

Parris waited. When she was ready to speak, she would.

Daisy Perika cleared her throat, and directed her words to the *matukach*. "I asked Charlie to call you. To get you to come down here to the reservation." She sighed. "I'm too old to travel all the way up to Granite Creek. Besides, that mountain air is too cold for my bones."

Parris nodded expectantly; his smile had been replaced by a nervous tic that jerked at the left side of his mouth.

Charlie Moon smiled thinly; the troublesome old woman had refused to say a word about what was bothering her until the *matukach* policeman arrived. He hoped this wouldn't be too embarrassing.

3

"Last night I didn't sleep too good." Daisy rubbed at her eyes. "And I had me a dream."

Charlie Moon rolled his eyes and looked up at the buzzing fluorescent lamp on the plastered ceiling. Aunt Daisy had insisted that Scott Parris drive almost a hundred miles to hear about a dream! It was a good thing the *matukach* policeman was a patient man. And fond of this peculiar old woman.

She cut her eyes at Moon. "And this dream, it showed me something that is going to happen," she said firmly. "Something bad."

The lawmen waited while she gathered her thoughts. Such visions were sacred, and meant primarily for the enlightenment of the dreamer. The old shaman would tell the policemen only the essentials.

Daisy looked down at the faded blue print dress draped over her arthritic knees, and felt somewhat foolish. It had all seemed so real, so important. "There was blood . . . it fell like out of the sky . . . like rain." Now she glared at Charlie Moon, as if daring him to dispute her. "There was a . . . a dead person . . . with no eyes. And I heard a funny sound. Like this." She picked up a ballpoint pen off Moon's desk and tapped it hard against an aluminum coffee mug. Ping . . . ping . . . ping . . . The old woman paused and looked accusingly at the mug. "No," she said thoughtfully, "that's not quite what it was like."

Parris glanced at Moon.

The Ute was looking down at his oversized rawhide boots. This was damned embarrassing.

"That's all," the old woman said in a weary voice. She wanted to go home. Her feet were cold, and she heard a faint ringing in her ears.

Parris got up from his chair; he squatted beside the old woman. He had come to understand her, as a son understands his mother. "This vision . . . what does it mean?"

She blinked owlishly at him, then looked up at her big nephew. She could sense that Charlie Moon, despite his outward composure, was uneasy. Her nephew tried so hard to be a modern man, to think like the *matukach*. But in his soul he was still a Ute. "Some who are of the People, and some who are not of the People, will die. And—" her voice was a hoarse whisper "—they won't die easy."

Moon got off the desk and shoved his thumbs under his heavy gun belt. He went to the window and looked at the sky. There was no sign of the red-tailed hawk, but a pair of acrobatic black grackles chased a hapless raven. A single leaf-shaped cloud floated on the westerly currents.

The old woman's tone, as she spoke to Parris, was almost apologetic. "I don't think you or Charlie can keep any of this from happening, but I thought I should tell you."

Parris frowned and put his hand over hers. "Do you know who will die?"

She enjoyed the warmth of his hand. "No. I could not see their faces."

Faces. This made it real. Parris felt his skin prickle. "Where will this happen . . . when?"

Daisy Perika leaned close to the *matukach*. She jerked her thumb over her shoulder, like a hitchhiker. "It'll start up there, to the north . . . where the wind always blows cold." The shaman closed her eyes tightly. "And it won't be long in coming."

☼ Angel's Café ☼

A gusty September wind flung a mixture of chalk-dry dust and yellowed cottonwood leaves against the steamy window of the restaurant. Charlie Moon watched the dead leaves and was reminded of the approach of winter. It was time to haul firewood from the mountains. A cord of piñon would be just the thing.

Scott Parris watched a thin blond waitress pour decaf coffee into his cup. He glanced across the table at the big Ute policeman. "What d'you think?"

Moon, having already put away his pot roast and boiled potatoes, had skewered a quarter of an apple pie with his fork and was sawing at it with one of Angel's dull knives. "Don't know what to think." He kept his eye on the pie. "You know how Aunt Daisy is. She gets these funny notions sometimes, and won't let me alone." He put a forkful into his mouth. "Mmmm," he said.

Troubles might come, Parris noted enviously, but Charlie Moon rarely lost his appetite. Or gained a pound. Damned annoying, that's what it was.

Moon sawed at another megabite of pie. The Ute knew his *matukach* friend took Aunt Daisy's visions very seriously. They were much alike, this white man and the old woman. "Sorry I brought you all the way down here for something like this."

"No problem," Parris said. "It's a relief to get away from the station for a few hours." He took a sip of the decaffeinated coffee, then added "nondairy coffee whitener" from a plastic dispenser and artificial sweetener from an inch-square paper envelope.

Moon swallowed the last bite of pie, a half cup of heavily sugared coffee, then looked over his cup at Scott Parris. "I recall you're going to the Baja next week."

"Yeah. Deep-sea fishing." Two wonderful weeks. "And you should be going with me."

"I'd like that," the Ute said wistfully. "But I'm down to a couple of days vacation." Moon, who was sinking all his salary into his never-ending home construction effort, couldn't afford the price of the airline fare. If Scott knew this, he'd buy the tickets himself. Even if he had to borrow the money. And claim they were bonus miles that hadn't cost him a dime. That just wouldn't do. If he could beat his friend out of the money in a few hands of poker . . . well, that was another thing altogether.

"Well, I'll miss you," Parris said. Too bad Moon didn't save up his vacation.

The Ute waved at Angel, who brought another slab of pie and the coffeepot. "You oughta take Sweet Thing along."

"Thing's pretty busy with her work. And—" Parris smiled faintly "—Anne says she doesn't care much for the odor of fish."

Though he'd never met a pie he didn't like, the Ute inspected this new offering and found it satisfactory. "She must've been joking."

"Don't think so. She said that fish stink. And they're slimy." Women were strange and mysterious creatures.

"You oughta ask that pretty woman to marry you. Then you could honeymoon down in Baja—she might turn into a fisherman herself."

"I don't know . . ." Parris began. On the couple of occasions he'd even hinted at marriage, Anne had gotten nervous. Changed the subject.

Scott Parris stared longingly at the Ute's pie and wondered whether Angel stocked any low-fat desserts. With artificial sweetener. Fat chance.

✿

When he was barely west of Pagosa Springs, Scott Parris pulled off Route 160 at a plush golf resort. He found a public telephone under a tall spruce. Parris stood in the enclosure and stared at the instrument. And listened to the muttering voices of his conflicting thoughts. Finally the chief of police picked up the telephone. He hesitated, grunted, and placed it back on the chrome hanger.

He closed his eyes and pictured the triangular sail of the fishing boat, the salt breeze, fresh fish roasting over an open campfire. It was a fuzzy picture . . . slipping away.

Parris grabbed the telephone receiver again, knowing what he must do. His stomach churned. He pressed O, waited for the operator, and gave her the number in Granite Creek. He listened, then jammed an assortment of coins in the slot.

A woman's voice answered on the second ring. "Worldwide Travel."

"Hi." He identified himself. "About my airline tickets for Baja California . . . yeah, Santa Rosalia . . . and the hotel reservation . . ." He paused, remembering the shimmering blue-green waters. Black fins cutting the surface, the nylon line slicing the water. The solitude, and incomparable peace. But it was not like he had a choice. Not really. Not a year earlier, he'd learned the hard way—a warning from Daisy Perika was not to be taken lightly.

The travel agent was tapping impatiently on her telephone receiver with a long plastic fingernail. Tic. tic. tic. "Are you there, Mr. Parris?"

He closed his eyes and was almost surprised when he heard his voice. "The whole trip. Cancel everything."

Now he heard the measured sound of tap-tapping on her computer keyboard.

"Hotel's no problem, Mr. Parris. But you'll lose about three hundred and twenty-some dollars on the plane tickets," she reminded him. "Those were a special purchase."

"Oh shoot," he muttered. Childishly he kicked at the telephone booth, cracking the thin fiberglass sheet.

The travel agent was startled. "What was that noise?"

"What noise?" His big toe throbbed.

"You sure you want to cancel those tickets?"

"Do it." He gritted his teeth.

"Consider it done." The travel agent sighed. "Too bad. Something come up?"

"Yeah," he said into the mouthpiece. "Something came up."

Scott Parris hung up the phone and limped off toward the parking lot. He stopped by the old Volvo, shaded his eyes with one hand, and squinted toward the western horizon. The pale sun sinking into the blue mists had the warm patina of a polished disk of bone. Heavy clouds drifted in from the northwest; the smell of rain was a sweet perfume. The air was comfortably warm, almost balmy.

He shivered.

CHAPTER 2

Utah, Uintah and Ouray Reservation
Sarah Frank's bedroom

The end of this day approaches . . . the western sky is a dusky gray hue, streaked with sooty smudges.

Sarah is not afraid. This child fears neither the night nor those shadowy things that scuttle about and mutter unintelligible threats under the cloak of darkness.

It was not always so. Before her third birthday, she had been frightened by many ordinary things.

The unexpected sound, the sudden movement, the unfamiliar form.

It might be the droning whine of a blue horsefly humming by her nose. The gray sagebrush lizard darting along an unpainted pine rafter over her bed. An eight-eyed topaz spider dancing upside down on an invisible web. The sudden crack of summer lightning, a crooked finger of fire touching the bristlecone pine by her bedroom window. Even the soft woolly worm, with sixty-six stubby legs treading upon her white cotton stocking. This would send the child clutching breathlessly at her mother's skirts.

But most of all, Sarah had dreaded the night and those nameless things that lurked in the darkness. It would begin at dusk with the haunting call of the horned owl, or the dry chirp of the Mormon cricket. Then . . . there was the gloom of her little bedroom, which had been a walk-in pantry before her father had rented the small house. Here Sarah would watch misty shadows shimmering on the cracked plaster wall. She would hear small voices whisper warnings at the foot of her bed, and call upon her mother. After Mary Frank had kissed Sarah and left the room, the child would huddle under the quilt and repeat the memorized prayer over and over.

> *"Now I lay me down to sleep*
> *I pray the Lord my soul to keep . . ."*

It had been almost two years earlier, on the evening before her third birthday. Shortly after her mother had tucked the covers under her feet, kissed her on the nose, and left the bedside. Sarah had dutifully recited the "Now I Lay Me Down to Sleep" a dozen times. The child knew that praying was asking God for something, but she wasn't so sure what she was asking for. Sarah had no idea what her soul was or how it would help her if God agreed to keep it. And keep it where? In a cigar box hidden in a dark closet? In an empty jelly jar upon some dusty shelf?

Then, as she huddled under the covers in a cramped fetal position, Sarah had remembered her exasperated father's words. It was on that very day, when she had hung on his trouser leg and whined for attention because Mommy was busy in the kitchen. She had leaned backwards, stuck her tongue out, and made a noise at him. "Aaaaaaahhh . . . mmmaaahhhhh." Sarah recalled that she had been very young then, and silly.

"Lissen, bunny." This was what Provo Frank called his little darling. "When you've got somethin' on your mind, don't beat around the bush about it. Just say what you want!"

She hadn't understood the part about beating around a bush; she'd never do such a dumb thing anyway. But the last statement had been clear enough.

"I wanna . . . I wanna . . . ummmm . . . sit in your lap . . . Dad-deeeee."

"Okay, sure." He had picked her up and she had leaned against his chest while he finished reading the newspaper. Daddy had even read the funnies to her. Charlie Brown and Lucy and Snoopy. And Dilbert with the turned-up tie and his chubby pooch, Dogbert. It was that simple; she had asked to sit in his lap—he had granted her request.

That was the lesson she had learned on that day. You must tell big people *exactly* what you wanted. They didn't seem to know what she needed. This seemed odd, because Sarah often knew what her parents were feeling. The anger . . . the fears . . . the longings. Sometimes she knew what they were about to say. But it had been a lesson well learned.

So later that night, the child had made a specific request. Sarah had asked God for a birthday present. For someone to come and sit by her all night while she slept.

The response to honest prayer may be subtle and unobtrusive, indeed may go almost unnoticed. And be a long time coming. Or the answer may be sudden and dramatic, like a flash of lightning bridging heaven to earth. But such childlike prayers are always heard. And requests are granted with the same divine extravagance that has sown the sweet brilliance of countless galaxies across this endless sea of space and time. Worlds and dangers and blessings beyond counting.

As the innocent waited expectantly for the heavenly guardian to appear at her bedside, she fell into a deep, dreamless slumber.

Later on that same night, the child had opened her eyes. Sarah may have been dreaming. She may have been awake. But it seemed that morning had surely come—a warm light had flooded her little bedroom, lighting every dark corner. The tiny girl had rubbed her brown eyes and blinked in the multicolored brightness . . . and seen her lovely visitors. The child had tried to count them on her fingers, but it was not possible.

There were more than ten.

✧

The twilight is thick around the house where the child lives; it flows like a fog over the low hills, settling into the shallow valleys. If you step outside, you can taste it. More than that, you can feel it . . . roll up little bits of it between your finger and thumb.

Tonight, as the sun sets, Mary Frank vainly seeks comfort by switching on every light in the little house. As the outer darkness gathers, Mary's chatter at her Ute husband becomes rapid, her laughter is quick and contrived. And she is startled by the thirsty lilac branch brushing against a windowpane, alarmed by the least breath of desert air kissing the nape of her neck.

Mary rubs her palms together; she watches the darkness gather at the window. She also watches her husband watch television. Provo Frank is absorbed by a rerun of *The X-Files* on a snowy screen; he yawns intermittently. In between yawns, he sucks on an amber bottle of Corona beer. He pauses in the middle of a swallow, cocks his head to listen. The Ute's hearing is uncannily sharp. He mutters to his wife: "Sounds like the little bunny wants her momma."

Now Mary hears the urgent call of a small voice. Filled with an unaccountable fear, the young mother launches herself from the couch and hurries to her daughter's bedroom, pushing away absurd visions of rattlesnakes under the bed, of crimson rashes on soft skin, of vile kidnappers lurking at the window. She yanks a cotton string to switch on the bare sixty-watt bulb that dangles from the ceiling. Weak with relief to find her child safe, the mother exhales and whispers a prayer of gratitude.

"Momma . . ."

Mary Frank puts her hands on her hips. She fakes a stern glare at the tiny girl who is propped up on her elbows, blinking at the bright light. The kitten sleeps near the bed, in a cardboard shoe box lined with an old dishrag.

"What is it this time, Sarah?"

"Water," the child murmurs with a yawn. "My kitty is thirsty."

Mary Frank sighs and shakes her head. But she is the child's mother. She goes to fetch the water.

❂

The sliver of moon sent a silver shaft through the windowpane to illuminate the face of the child. Its light, like the night air that drifted through a crack under the sill, was frigid.

Mary Frank knelt by the side of the bed and smiled at her daughter. Sarah sipped from the mug of water, hand-pumped and icy cold from the shallow well under the kitchen floor. The child seemed especially tiny on the feather mattress, but her eyes were large and luminous in the half-light.

Sarah looked up at the shadowy form of her mother, outlined by flickering blue illumination from the television screen in the next room. The child blinked; she was fascinated by the dancing particles of dust illuminated by this dim wedge of light that glowed through the doorway.

Her mother whispered, "It's way past time you were asleep."

The tiny animal sleeping in the shoe box by the child's bed made a slight gasping sound.

Sarah leaned and put her hand on the warm fur; she could feel a ripple of delicate ribs as the creature breathed. "Mr. Zigzag . . . are you all right?"

The skinny kitten, half-wrapped in the ragged dish towel, was unaware of her light caress.

Mary smiled. "It's nothing to worry about. He's just having a dream."

Kittens, of course, do dream their peculiar dreams. They dream dreams of other kittens to play with, of yipping puppies to hiss at, of tasty sardines to eat, of fat green grasshoppers to chase, and quite often they have nighttime visions of human beings. But upon occasion, they encounter unfamiliar, frightful creatures. Such imaginary beasts, of course, are well equipped with pointed tooth and hooked claw . . . and these dreams are terrifying. Sometimes the dreaming kitten's heart will stop beating. Forever.

This kitten's legs jerked spasmodically, then moved in rhythm as if the fragile creature were running. Running away. The human beings in the bedroom could not have imagined the kitten's strange experience in the dark world of feline dreams.

"Your kitty is fine." Mary brushed a wisp of black hair away from her daughter's face. "You must close your eyes. Right now."

"But I'm not tired, Mommy." The little girl yawned.

"It is a good thing—to sleep." Mary's own sleep had lately been troubled. She kissed her daughter on the forehead. "Remember where good little girls go when they sleep?"

Sarah smiled. "Yes, Mommy . . ." She quoted her mother's words with robotic precision: "When they sleep, *good* little girls go to visit with the angels." Now the child added her own fancy: "And they have a picnic with the angels. And smell the pretty flowers, and play with yellow butterflies in the grassy meadow."

"Yes. Angels . . . flowers . . . butterflies. Now, close your eyes."

In truth, Sarah had not seen the angels since that night before her third birthday. But the child could close her eyes and pretend that they were near. When she pretended very hard, it seemed that she could almost see them. And sometimes when she slept, Sarah would have childish visions of sweet outings with the angels. The little girl would dream of picnics in lush valleys . . . of pink sugar cakes and orange sherbet . . . of flitting golden butterflies and little birds that sang the sweetest songs.

Mary Frank was in no hurry to leave the bedside and go to her husband, who waited anxiously, drumming his fingers on the kitchen table. Provo had finally lost interest in the television drama and was eager to tell his wife more about his fantastic scheme. Typical of a Ute, she thought. He would talk about his plan endlessly, as if enough words could convince her that no harm could come of it. Good fortune would come to the family, he insisted. And to the People. *His* people, of course.

Her knees ached from kneeling; Mary sat down on the cold linoleum. The woman of the Tohono O'otam leaned her elbows on the bed. She cupped her chin in one hand and lightly touched her daughter's forehead with the other. Mary sang the old lullaby in a gentle whisper:

> *"Hush, my child*
> *Lie still and slumber*
> *Holy angels guard thy bed*
> *Heavenly blessings without number*
> *Gently fall upon thy head."*

The child's tiny fist rubbed at her eyes. Now she was blinking, but straining hard to resist the elastic pull of sleep.

Mary pulled the worn cotton blanket up to Sarah's chin. "Say your prayers."

The child's lips moved.

> *"Now I lay me down to sleep*
> *I pray the Lord my soul to keep."*

Her mother had never taught her the final words of this prayer. But now the young woman said the words in her heart. For her daughter. And for herself.

> *If I should die before I wake . . .*

She swallowed hard . . .

> *I pray the Lord my soul to take.*

Mary waited. For one minute. Two.

Finally Sarah's eyes were shut. Her shallow breathing became regular. Only then did Mary Frank leave the child's bedside and go into the kitchen where her husband waited. First she would listen. Then perhaps she could talk him out of this folly he was set on.

She knew better, of course.

✪ Colorado, Southern Ute Reservation ✪

In a few beats of her heart, it would be midnight. Daisy Perika was near enough to sleep that her limbs were becoming heavy, her breathing slow and labored.

In her dream the old shaman walked along the rocky bank of the Piños; the gentle breeze was sweet with the fragrance of wild asters. Her feet trod upon a worn path, and the path led to a quiet refuge. The cemetery. Daisy entered the place, shaded by great cottonwood and mountain ash, where the bones of many of the People rested.

The dreamer paused, sniffed at the crisp morning air. There was something more here than the scent of the flowers, of grass, even of the river itself. Yes. It was freshly turned earth. The shaman walked slowly to the edge of the little cemetery, to a spot under the outstretched limb of a small ash. Daisy Perika stood over the new grave. She puzzled at what she saw, why she had been brought to this place. It must be important, but there was nothing so unusual here . . . just a grave waiting for a tenant.

And then the shaman noticed . . . this was a very *small* grave.

CHAPTER 3

Northeast Utah

The worn tires of the old car whined on the lukewarm blacktop. Mary Frank wanted to look back, but could not. Everything behind them seemed a part of some distant, fading lifetime. Fort Duchesne, that sweet oasis of cottonwood trees and waving grass. The Ute tribal complex near Bottle Hollow, where she had a good job in the visitor reception center. And their small home, a government-issue box of plywood, aluminum siding, and faulty plumbing. She was filled with a desperate longing, a bittersweet nostalgia for that which was lost. These things were all barely a half dozen miles behind them, but already their reality seemed to have been swallowed up in the past, like yellowed photographs in an old family album. Familiar, yet foreign. And somehow . . . *never to be seen again.*

The young woman shuddered and shrugged off these foolish, neurotic imaginings. They would have their annual vacation, visit her husband's old friends on the Southern Ute Reservation in Colorado. Then the little Frank family would return to their home in Utah. Mary glanced at the man she loved, who steered with two fingers on the wheel. Provo had an abundance of confidence. And an inexhaustible supply of enthusiasm for the future. He would not understand these worries that bedeviled her; he might even try to laugh them away. Whenever he did that, she wanted to choke him. Mary bit her lip and squinted through the sandblasted windshield at the vast landscape cleaved by the shining strip of US Route

40. The passing tourist might see only the security of the paved highway across the lonely desolation of the Uintah Basin. This woman of the Tohono O'otam saw a vast ocean of red soil, pockmarked by floating clumps of sage and saltbush. She glanced toward the south. A pair of angular limestone escarpments were cast adrift among the bluish waves of twilight. For a terrifying moment Mary was uncertain—was the old Jeep moving eastward along Route 40 . . . or were these gaunt white craft sailing westward across a rolling, bloodred sea?

Sarah Frank was sitting cross-legged in the rear seat, half-wrapped in a thin cotton blanket. She stared with childish rapture at the crimson sunset framed in the dust-streaked rear window of the Wagoneer. She whispered to her kitten. "See, Mr. Zigzag, it'll be night soon." Sarah hugged the warm animal close to her neck and affected a delicious shudder. "When it's real dark, the booger-man'll come out to get you!" She giggled; the kitten licked her ear with a sandpaper tongue.

The voices of her parents droned in the front seat; she turned to listen and held the kitten up so it could listen too. They were talking about taking a different route on this trip to southern Colorado.

Sarah could hear the tension of excitement in Daddy's voice; he was moving his fingertip along a map her mother held under the glove compartment light. "We'll take a left on 191 at Vernal." Vernal! That was the town where the big brick building was. Inside were bones of dinosaurs. And just outside the brick building, standing very still in the grass under a tree, was the hairy elephant with the great sweep of white tusks . . . waiting for some careless child to come too close. Someday, Sarah promised herself, when she was big, she would summon up all her courage, and touch the great beast's matted leg.

The voices of her parents intruded once more into Sarah's consciousness. Mommy seemed worried.

"I don't know, it's so far out of the way." Mommy worried about lots of things. "What will Sarah and I do while you go on your . . . your visit?" It sounded better to call it a "visit."

"You and the bunny rabbit—" Provo Frank nodded backwards toward Sarah "—can stay in Bitter Springs for a day or two."

She put her hand on his knee. "And you?"

"You know I've got some business to do. A man to meet."

An anxious look spread over Mary's dark features. "And then . . . ?"

"I'll go to the place where he lives," he said with an air of mystery, "to somewhere east of Eden."

Daddy laughed at this and Mommy shook her head, but Sarah didn't know why. Grown-ups were beyond understanding.

They passed a lone horseman on the shoulder of the road. Sarah waved. The rider waved back; the horse tossed its head.

"Daddy," the child squealed, "you know what I want for my birthday next month, when I'm five years old?" It was always best to tell Daddy what you wanted. Mommy always said we can't afford it or we have no place to keep it or it'll eat us out of house and home or wait until you're older, Sarah.

"Hmmmm . . ." Provo scratched his head thoughtfully and grinned at the reflection of his daughter in the rearview mirror. "Let me look between your ears and see if I can figure it out." There was a long pause as he squinted with great concentration. "It's pretty blamed dark there inside your head, lots of little gears and cogwheels turning. But wait a minute. Now I see something hairy . . . has four legs . . . a tail . . . and it smells bad. Could it be a billy goat?"

"No," she shrieked impatiently, "it's not a billy goat!"

"Well . . ." He scratched at his head. "Is it maybe . . . a horse?"

"Daddy," she giggled, "how did you know? But I don't want a great big horse. I want a little horse. White with brown spots. With big eyes and a tail that swishes and swats horseflies." She whispered into the kitten's ear. "You can ride on him too, Mr. Zigzag."

Provo chuckled. "No problem, sweetheart. How about a saddle with Mexican silver?"

"I won't need a saddle," she said with that perfect confidence known only by children, "just a pretty blue blanket on his back." Sarah rubbed her little fingertip along the crooked white mark on the black kitten's head. "With white zigzags." Sarah closed her eyes . . . she could see the dancing pony. And the blue blanket with white zigzags.

Her father sighed, as if a blanket were far more expensive than a saddle with Mexican silver. "Well, a blanket it is, then."

"Don't tease her." Mary frowned and slapped her husband on the arm. "You know how she is; now we'll never hear the end of it."

The young Ute man laughed out loud. "Maybe I'm not teasing." He had big plans. "Maybe—" he winked slyly at his wife "—things are gonna be better for us." If he pulled it off, he would be a big hero with the People. They would move down to Ignacio. There would be, at the very least, a steady job with the tribe. As time went by, there would be promotions. He lost himself in this fantasy. Someday, after a long while, he might even be elected tribal chairman. Provo Frank's wide face broke out in an infectious grin. Mary leaned against his shoulder and sighed. The good woman closed her eyes and prayed for her husband's safety.

Sarah, satisfied with her maneuver, turned away to watch the last smear of crimson on the western horizon.

"Neola . . . Tabiona . . . Altonah . . . Bluebell," the child sang softly to her kitten, "Upalco . . . Altamont . . . Spring Glen . . . When . . . when . . . oh, when will I see you again?"

The names of the Utah towns were pretty, like the alternating yellow and purple glass beads strung on her necklace. But when would she come back to see them again? Sarah closed her eyes tightly and tried to see her future. At first she saw only blackness, with tiny dots of flickering white lights. Gradually the child saw the familiar little window . . . and the curtain parting between today and tomorrow. Tomorrow morning, she saw herself sitting cross-legged, on a big bed with a thick orange quilt. She saw Mommy, bobby pins clenched in her teeth, combing her long black hair. This made the child smile. Then it was night . . . then another day. She saw Daddy; he was very happy . . . and Mommy was angry with Daddy. There were shouts . . . and Daddy's curses . . . and Mommy's tears. She tried to see the following day. Maybe they would be in Ignacio then. Maybe she would get to see Aunt Daisy. Aunt Daisy wasn't really her aunt, but Sarah pretended that she was. She tried hard to see what Mommy and Daddy were doing on the second day. The child was puzzled . . . all was darkness, as if a black velvet curtain had been drawn across the small window she looked through.

❖

The golden eagle circled, its hungry yellow-flecked eyes focused on the crest of the reddish mesa where the occasional small mammal darted among the junipers. The magnificent bird caught a thermal, soared upward, then folded its wings. *Kwana-ci* dived over the wide canyon to an altitude that was just above the crest of the mesa, then spread its wings to glide toward the brownish-red cliff. The bird flapped its wings three times to gain altitude. Focused on the center of predator's retinas was a small gray form that moved in the shadow of a long-dead ponderosa log.

It seemed that the fate of the rabbit was sealed, but at the last moment the eagle was startled by the shrill cry that came from very near.

Kwana-ci caught a strong thermal and soared high over the mesa. The cottontail would live another day.

But for another harmless creature, time was running short.

❖ Bitter Springs, Wyoming ❖
The City Limits Motel

Sarah sat cross-legged on the green carpet in front of the snowy television screen, munching on a cheese and mayonnaise sandwich. There was a game show on the TV. The pretty lady with long yellow hair was spinning a large red and black wheel. The wheel had words and numbers on it, but Sarah could not read the words or the big numbers—she had only memorized one through ten. And zero, but that didn't count, because zero meant nothing at all. Zero was a funny number; if you had zero gumdrops, you had no gumdrops at all. But Mommy had told her that if you put a one and a zero together, that was ten, as many finger as on her hands or toes on her feet. It made little sense, but that was the way most grown-up things were. Mommy was walking back and forth, stopping sometimes to stare out the motel room window. When Mommy wasn't looking, Sarah tore a strip of processed cheese off the sandwich and gave it to Mr. Zigzag. The kitten lapped happily at the sticky white mayonnaise, then daintily bit off small chunks of cheese. Finally Mommy sat down on the bed and picked up a tattered magazine. Then she dropped the magazine and went to the bathroom and started to comb her long black hair and fix it with bobby pins.

Just outside, above the persistent hum of the wind in the eaves, there was the sound of tires crunching on gravel and the familiar chugging of the old brown car that Daddy drove. Sarah jumped up and ran to the motel window, but she could not quite see above the varnished wooden sill. She jumped up and down and when her head bobbed above the sill, Sarah could see Daddy getting out of the car. Mommy ran to the window; she had some black bobby pins still clenched between her teeth.

"Oh, thank God," Mary Frank muttered through the bobby pins.

Sarah put the cheese sandwich on the floor, then clapped her hands. The child scooped the black kitten off the worn carpet and whispered into his ear. "Daddy is back, Mr. Zigzag. Now everything will be alright again." The kitten, who flicked his tickled ear, seemed not to care in the least that Daddy had returned. Sarah waited near the door. When it opened, Daddy came in grinning. Mommy was not smiling. Daddy picked Sarah up and gave her a big hug. "How is Daddy's little bunny?" She squealed and laughed. Daddy sat her on the bed, but she slid off and went to hug his leg.

Daddy tried to hug Mommy. But she backed away and said something. Daddy got very quiet. Then Mommy yelled at him, and he yelled back, and there were more shouts.

Sarah backed away; she sat down on the floor, in front of the big black television, and held her little hands over her ears. She watched someone win a pretty red car and tried to think only about the car and how happy the television people were. She wondered how they made the people and the car small enough to get them inside the television box. Her world was filled with such mysteries. The child heard only scraps of the harsh words that passed between Mommy and Daddy.

". . . about time you got back . . ."

"But I saw him . . . got what I wanted . . . We'll be out of here tonight."

"Not till you pay the bill, we won't . . . check was no good . . . My Visa card was refused at the convenience store . . . We've been sitting here eating cold sandwiches and drinking water . . . The motel manager wants cash. She'll call the law if you try to sneak away."

"Dammit, woman, I told you to . . . I'll make it good . . . A couple of phone calls and . . ."

"Don't you dare swear in front of Sarah . . . My father was right about you . . . always got either a dirty word or a beer bottle in your mouth . . ."

"Well, you and your Papago pappy can just kiss my . . ."

And then Daddy slammed the door and was gone. Mommy went in the bathroom to weep.

Sarah wiped away her own tears. But at least it was quiet now. The child only wanted to go to sleep. And escape.

☼ The Pynk Garter Saloon ☼

The angry young man buttoned his thin denim jacket, pulled on a pair of unlined leather gloves, and spat a Ute curse against the icy wind. He wasn't quite sure what this curse meant, but it was a fine mouth-filling oath that he'd often heard his grandmother use when her husband came home drunk, when a lamb died, or when she dropped an egg on the floor. He swore again, this time in English, at his hardheaded Papago wife, and then once more just for the hell of it. Provo Frank was feeling just a tad better; the cold air sliced at his lungs, but it also made him feel alive. Like a man who wouldn't be pushed around by his wife. He paused in the parking lot to get his bearings. The motel was situated just south of the first interstate exit for Bitter Springs, a spread-out high-plains town that didn't actually begin until a good piece to the east. Immediately to the south of the motel, there was a long rocky ridge; on its crest were a handful of stunted, wind-tortured piñon, the only trees within miles. Unless somebody had planted a pine in Bitter Springs. To the south of this ridge, there was nothing but barren, wind-dried land. To the north, it wasn't much better. There was nothing to see but a long rolling plain that would eventually connect to the Wind River Range. Provo suddenly felt lonely, and wished he could go back inside the motel room. But he couldn't face Mary's wrath, not just yet.

Not without some liquid fortification.

His Jeep Wagoneer was the only car in the lot. Except for the old Cadillac convertible that belonged to that sour bitch in the motel office. He swore again, this time at the nit-picking motel manager who'd gotten so hot about the rubber check. Then once more at his wife. "Dumb-assed woman," he muttered into the wind. She should have put her tribal paycheck into the checking account before they left Bottle Hollow, then the check he wrote wouldn't of bounced. Hardheaded, know-it-all Papago woman. Just like her pinch-faced father, that's what she was. He turned, squinting into the wind. The City Limits Motel was actually a half mile outside the city limits of Bitter Springs, Wyoming. He could see a soft glow of light off to the east. Provo wanted a drink, and he wanted it bad. He thought about driving into town, but when he was angry, he liked to work it off with a hard walk. He turned to the west and looked past the convenience store that had turned down Mary's Visa card. He already knew they didn't carry liquor. Yesterday morning when he'd got here, he'd gone inside to pick up a six-pack of Coors, and they said they didn't have a liquor license. Stupid squirrel-brains. What kind of a dump didn't even sell beer and still called itself a "convenience" store? Ought to be some kind of law against it—wrongful advertising or false labeling or something like that. But Provo remembered that there was a bar of some sort to the west, about two hundred yards past the convenience store. It had been closed when he'd stopped by yesterday, but that'd been well before noon, and it was almost dark now. He leaned against the stiff wind and trudged to the north side of the motel parking lot; he could see a neon sign sputtering and winking on a tall pole in front of the bar. The Ute pointed his face westward, toward the beckoning pink and blue flashes, and after a few dozen paces he could just make out the sign. A blue neon leg with a high-heel shoe was kicking back and forth. When he was much closer he could see a flashing pink bow on the thigh of the shapely leg. The illuminated script below the leg said Pynk Garter Saloon.

Cute.

Some mom-and-pop operation, most likely. And they'll want to talk about the weather and such. Well, he thought glumly, it'd have to do. He pulled off his right glove with his teeth, then felt in his pocket and found a few quarters.

The wind, which had shifted, was at his back now . . . helping him along . . . urging him on this path.

✧

The bar, like the motel, was almost deserted. The room was a long dark rectangle, illuminated by a single row of sixty-watt track lights over the bar, which neatly divided off a third of the cavernlike interior. A dozen battered wooden tables were scattered about; walnut-stained booths lined the wall opposite the bar. At the narrow end of the saloon were three doors. One was marked DAGWOOD, another BLONDIE. An artist with more enthusiasm than talent had painted pastel likenesses of those ageless, happy cartoon characters on the rest-room doors. Provo disapproved of such foolishness. A third door was painted with one word—PRIVATE.

At first the Ute thought he was alone with the overweight white man whose whole attention was focused on a greasy cheeseburger that sizzled on a crusty grill behind the bar. The short-order cook, who began to slice a large white onion with a gleaming Bowie knife, didn't bother to look up and acknowledge the presence of this prospective customer. Provo stood uncertainly, wondering whether he should return to the motel. He could stop by the convenience store, buy some Fritos and soft drinks. Mary would be feeling better by the time he got back; they could talk things out . . . then go to bed . . . Sarah would be sound asleep and . . . Yes . . . maybe he'd just go back to his wife . . .

Bam! The wind slammed the door behind him.

There was an almost feline movement in a dark corner near the door that was marked PRIVATE. A woman, also a *matukach*, got up from a table where she'd been working at a crossword puzzle in the dim light. As tall as Provo, she had slender muscular arms, and shoulders that were broad for a woman. Her shining hair, black as his own, was done up in a single braid, much like the Ute's. Her skin was milky white. This was not a woman who exposed herself to the Wyoming sun and wind. Her hips shifted under the black satin dress as she slowly made her way behind the bar. Not your regular mom-and-pop, Provo thought. But at least it was warm inside. Fatty didn't look like he'd talk a man to death, and the woman in black wasn't hard to look at. Provo could smell the sweet, musky aroma of whiskey. The Ute's spirits began to rise.

The woman lit a long filtered cigarette and placed it between her painted lips. "What'll it be?" she said past the bobbling cigarette.

Provo parked his butt on a stool. "So. How long you worked here?"

"I own the place."

"Oh," he said.

She leaned her sharp elbows on the bar and blew a small puff of smoke in his face. "I'm Lizzie Pynk." She said it like he'd have heard the name.

"Oh," Provo said, recalling the name of the joint, "like a pink garter."

"I wear a pink garter on one leg." She smiled. "Want to guess which leg, cowboy? It'll cost you twenty bucks to see if you're right."

Provo grinned crookedly. "Later, maybe."

The woman in the black dress jerked her shoulder sideways to indicate the bartender-cook. "That's Sam."

"Well," Provo said with a poker face, "I can see how it works. Mr. Personality draws the customers in—and you do all the real grunt work here."

It seemed that Fat Sam rolled one bloodshot eyeball at the customer, and kept the other focused on his work. The heavy man was slicing a hamburger bun with the Bowie knife; the heavy blade was razor-sharp.

Lizzie laughed. "You're cute. So what'll ya have?"

"Gimme a Coors." Provo felt in his jeans for the quarters.

The wind, which had shifted to the north, shook the wooden structure. Windows rattled like chattering teeth. Lizzie didn't seem to notice. "You got it, cowboy. For a new customer, first drink's always on the house."

"Then make it whiskey." The Ute grinned. Yessir, this was one first-class establishment.

Lizzie Pynk reached behind the counter for a dusty bottle; she poured a full measure into a shot glass.

Fat Sam snapped off a quarter of the greasy cheeseburger and began to exercise the heavy muscles in his jaw. Now both of his eyes were focused on the customer.

The Ute tossed back the whiskey and enjoyed the instant surge of warmth in his belly. Provo Frank promised himself to remember this place. Yessir. Anytime he was in the neighborhood, he'd stop at the Pynk Garter Saloon.

But the Ute would never pass this way again.

CHAPTER 4

Mary Frank's eyes were dry now. She had used two pillows to prop her daughter up on one of the beds; the black kitten was snuggled against the child's neck. Sarah watched the television, but her eyes were sleepy.

The little girl turned to look up at her mother, and was pleased. Mommy had put on her prettiest red dress! That meant that she and Daddy wouldn't be mad anymore when Daddy came back. They would hug, and kiss, and whisper, and laugh. And then they'd say, "Sarah, it's time you went to bed." And pretty soon they'd turn all the lights out. Sarah whispered in Mr. Zigzag's ear and told him that everything would be alright now. The kitten seemed to understand; he licked at the child's chin with his sandpaper tongue.

The Papago woman turned away from the child and pulled the curtain aside. The sunset was no more than a whitish smudge on the horizon; a bank of low clouds was rolling in from the north. The wind, which had been steady, was now sighing and moaning in gusts. Like a woman in labor, she thought. Mary could hear a sharp pelting of sleet against the motel window, but she could not see the ice particles. The Wagoneer was still the only tourist car in the motel parking lot; Provo must have walked to the bar up the road. Well, he didn't have much cash, so he couldn't get very drunk. That this was the most positive view she could take of the situation suddenly hit the Papago woman, in an almost physical sense, in the pit of her stomach. What had become of her life? Daddy had been right. She'd been a fool to marry this big-talking, do-nothing Ute. Mary turned and looked at the little figure on the bed. Sarah's eyes were closing and then opening, valiantly attempting to fight off the inevitable victory of sleep. The wife and mother considered leaving her husband to start a new life . . . but there was little Sarah, who loved her father . . . so she'd just have to make the best of it. At least for a while. Maybe when the child was a little older . . . She turned back to the window and shrugged off the thought of leaving Provo.

He'd be back soon, anyway. Pretending nothing bad had happened between them. His mood would be softened by the alcohol, his mouth telling her he'd take care of the motel bill tomorrow, his restless hands reaching out hopefully, then touching her. He'd be wanting to go to bed, of course. Despite her cold fury with her irresponsible husband, Mary smiled. Provo wasn't the best man a woman could have.

But he wasn't the worst, either.

✧

Lizzie Pynk poured the second shot.

This one wasn't on the house. Provo took off his hat and ran his finger under the damp sweatband. Aha—there it was. He unfolded the one-hundred-dollar bill and dropped it on the bar with the casual air of a high roller.

Lizzie held the greenback between two scarlet fingernails, turning it over twice. It looked like the McCoy, all right. Interesting. "So what line of work you in, cowboy?"

Provo was about to say, "I do some carpenter work," but that didn't sound quite good enough. The shabby Pynk Garter Saloon was glowing with the sweet fire of the whiskey in his belly; the reasonably attractive woman was beginning to look like one of those perfect ladies on the covers of the magazines he saw at the supermarket checkout counter. "Jewelry," he said. "I distribute a line of wholesale jewelry."

"Jewelry," she said, as if the subject bored her. "What kind?"

"Best kind," he said defensively. "Got a case of silver and turquoise in my car. Handmade. Navajo. Zuni. Finest quality." "Finest quality" was a phrase he'd heard on the radio just this morning, on the long drive back from the old man's shack. Provo tried to remember what the advertisement was pushing. Mobile homes, maybe. Or was it pork sausage? In the Wagoneer, he did have a cardboard box of trinkets. The "silver" was nickel or chrome plating over brass. The "turquoise" was fragment rejects from a factory in Juárez, or a cheap look-alike mineral from a quarry in Thailand.

Lizzie found a cotton cloth and polished a beer glass. "Sounds like expensive stuff."

"Damn right." Provo tossed back the shot of whiskey and paused to enjoy the lingering warmth as it went down. "The best is always expensive."

"You travel a lot, then?" She pulled the dark braid over her shoulder and began to play with it. It reminded the Ute of a black snake.

"Sure," he said with the assurance of an old pro. "You got to go where the customers are. Denver. Chicago. Miami." From time to time Provo pitched his cheap Mexican knockoffs at flea markets in Arizona and New Mexico. Paleface tourists from Ohio and Michigan bought it by the pound.

"You must be staying over at the City Limits, then." She had watched the man arrive from the window by her table; he'd walked in, and the City Limits was the only motel within two miles.

"Yeah."

"It's slow this time of year. I guess you have the place pretty much to yourself."

He nodded. "Coulda had any room I wanted."

"Traveling alone?"

"Yeah. Alone."

"Sounds lonesome."

"Excuse me. Got to go relieve myself." He slid off the stool and looked around uncertainly.

Lizzie smiled. She pointed toward the door with the inane Dagwood profile.

☼

His visit to the Dagwood rest room completed, Provo returned to his stool. There was a full shot glass on the bar in front of him; he looked around for the pretty woman.

The fat man spoke for the first time. "That one's on the house."

He squinted to focus on the amber liquid in the shot glass. "What's this?"

"Our best stuff." He winked. "Put lead in your pencil."

"Oh." Provo blinked. "Where's . . . whatzername . . . Lizzie?"

Fat Sam nodded toward the door with the small metal sign that said PRIVATE.

The wind was howling now; the frame building shuddered in the high gusts.

"Damned wind," the Ute muttered.

"We could get blowed clean away," the bartender said. "Happens ever so often."

"No shit," Provo said drunkenly. The fat man wanted to talk now—

he was even smiling. Provo had liked him better when he kept his mouth shut.

"Sure," Fat Sam said without a hint of a smile. "Two years ago this place was up in Washington state, smack in the middle of New Princeton."

"Never heard of any Princeton." Provo took a sip of the drink.

"Well, New Princeton's a fine town. Did a fair business with the lake fishermen. Then a big storm blew in from the west." The bartender waved his arms. "Wind plucked this place up like fuzz on a dandelion. Blowed us all the way over to Bozeman, Montana."

"Bozeman, huh? Must've been better for business."

"You'd have thought so," Fat Sam said thoughtfully, "but that wind set us down on a vacant lot in a Mormon neighborhood. Right next door to one of their churches. Way the zoning laws was set up, we couldn't sell no liquor atall. And Mormons aren't fond of strong drink, anyhows."

"Tough break for you," the Ute said.

"You got that right. But come November the twelfth, there was a big norther blew in from Alberta, picked us up, brought us down here by Bitter Springs."

Provo looked around himself at the empty bar. "Looks like pretty slim pickin's around here too."

Fat Sam nodded. "Yeah. But I expect business'll pick up when summer comes."

The Ute looked out a window into the darkness that seemed to go on forever. "When does summer come around here?" He drained the shot glass.

"Fourth of July, they say. Generally lasts until the sixth."

Provo had lost the thread of the conversation. That last drink was a real slammer. His belly, which had been warmed by the first few shots of whiskey, was hot now, and his head was thumping inside. Dumb thing to do, he thought, drinking raw whiskey on an empty stomach. He put his hat on to shade his eyes from the blaze of the sixty-watt track lights, and fumbled in his coat pocket for the pack of cigarettes. This reminded him about the business he'd come all the way up to Wyoming for in the fist place. He'd located the old man. And now he had what he wanted! His dumb-assed wife, with all her worrisome talk about bounced checks and unpaid bills, had almost made him forget about it.

He had to squint his eyes to see the bartender. "I need to make a phone call."

Fat Sam pointed to a dark corner near the entrance. "Pay phone's over there."

Provo got up and headed toward the booth. This was going to be a private conversation, with a very important man. He leaned against the varnished paneling and pulled the door shut. A light came on, and it was impossible to see into the dim space of the Pynk Garter Saloon. He could have been floating in space, far from the earth, far even from any star. Provo found a quarter and dropped it in the slot. He dialed the long-distance operator and waited impatiently.

✷ Ignacio, Colorado ✷
Southern Ute Tribal Headquarters

Austin Sweetwater, who had the appearance of a great sleepy toad, sat behind his massive oak desk and glared sullenly at the impertinent girl from the *Southern Ute Drum*. For half an hour the journalist had been asking annoying questions, like
   "What have you accomplished in your first term, Mr. Chairman?"
      and
   "What do you think your chances of reelection are, Mr. Chairman?"
      and
   "What do you think about your opponent's growing popularity, Mr. Chairman?"
      and
   "To what do you attribute your steady decline in the polls, Mr. Chairman?"
   He had felt compelled to answer her pointless questions patiently, but through gritting teeth, because he knew everything he said would be in the newspaper next week. Damn newspaper. If there was any way, he'd shut the troublesome rag down after he was reelected. But the bespectacled girl's pouty little mouth was moving again, her black ballpoint pen poised like a dagger over his heart.
   "Mr. Chairman, what do you think about your opponent's charge that you are . . ." She hesitated, cleared her throat, and started again. "That when it comes to issues important to the tribe, you are both ignorant and apathetic?"
   "Dammit." He slammed his palm on the desk. "I don't *know* and I don't *care!*" Ha. Let 'em print that.
   The chairman, puzzled by the annoying girl's sudden smile, was relieved to hear the telephone ring. He snatched the receiver, wondering who would be calling tribal headquarters long after normal working hours.

✷

His long-distance call completed, Provo slammed the instrument into the plastic receptacle and pushed the folded Plexiglas door open. The overhead light in the booth went out, and he could see into the dim cavern of the saloon. *The Ute astronaut returns from deepest space to the Pink Planet, to do battle with the Pig-Faced Man for the favors of the Spider Woman. Why am I thinking such stupid crap? Must be pretty damn drunk.*

But this didn't feel like a normal drunk. His mind was sharp as a razor, crystal-clear. He could remember all the jokes he'd ever heard, every sight he'd ever seen, every place he'd ever been. There was no stumble in his gait as he approached the bar; his eyes were clear. And he felt like telling the truth.

"I'm actually a carpenter," he said to the bartender.

"An honest trade. Want another drink?"

"In a minute, maybe."

Provo looked around for the woman. He wanted to tell her his best jokes. "When's she comin' back?"

Fat Sam nodded to indicate the closed door. "When she's finished with some paperwork . . ."

Provo leaned forward. "When you got six lawyers buried up to their necks in sand, what've you got?"

The fat bartender shrugged. "Search me."

"Not enough sand." Provo's laugh was interrupted by a minor choking fit. His throat was very dry. And the light from the sixty-watt bulbs was hurting his eyes. He pulled the hat brim down over his forehead.

Fat Sam smiled. "That's a good one, cowboy." *Heard it six times this month.*

"I'm not a cowboy. I'm a Native American. A Ute. Cowboys and Indians are natural enemies, as you oughta know if you ever watched any John Wayne movies."

"I sure miss the Duke," Fat Sam observed solemnly. His eyes were suddenly moist.

"Me too," Provo said. "*True Grit*—that was my favorite."

The bartender wiped halfheartedly at a wet beer glass. "But them old cowboy times is long gone."

Provo got off the stool and fumbled with the buttons on his jacket.

"Hey," Fat Sam said, "Lizzie said to wait. Said she'd fix you something real special . . ."

The Ute was stomping toward the door.

Provo had forgotten about Lizzie. A feeling of uneasiness was spreading through every muscle, every fiber in his body. Something was wrong— terribly wrong. And then he thought of his wife. His dumb-assed, bull-headed Papago wife. But he knew just what she needed.

Fat Sam waved. "Hey . . . wait a minute, buddy." But it was too late. The door slammed and the man was gone. Like he'd never been.

The Ute had walked a dozen paces before he realized that a heavy, wet snow was falling. He pushed his collar up. Before he faced Mary, he'd want another drink. He thought about turning around, heading back to the Pynk Garter Saloon. Then he remembered the stash. He had a half pint of belly warmer stashed in the Wagoneer. Where Mary would never find it. With this comforting thought in mind, Provo set his course toward the motel parking lot. And the Jeep. And most of all, toward the half-pint. There was one minor problem that gnawed at him. He couldn't remember exactly where he'd hidden the damn thing in the car!

It seemed a small decision—going to find a half-pint of cheap whiskey hidden inside a cluttered Jeep Wagoneer.

It wasn't.

❖

Mary Frank stood like a sentinel at the motel room window. The snow was falling in great sheets. The flakes were the size of quarters, making a splotchy, wet paste against the glass. The cheap motel had no lights to illuminate the parking lot, and she could barely see the form of the Wagoneer parked a few yards from the door. The snow was covering the old automobile's thin brown paint, the grease spots on the hood, the rust on the fenders. Fresh icing on an old cake. Soon the car would be pretty.

Her daughter's voice interrupted this reverie. "What are you looking at, Mommy?"

"The car."

"Why?"

"Because . . ." But someone was approaching through the swirls of snow. Pausing by the Wagoneer. Opening the unlocked rear door. Inside now . . . bending over the back of the rear seat . . . the dome light provided a slight illumination. Mary sighed. Her husband was looking for the half-pint of whiskey he'd hidden in the spare-tire compartment. The Papago woman had found the half-pint when she was packing the car for the family vacation. She'd emptied the whiskey onto the driveway and thrown the bottle into the trash.

Mary turned to look at her tiny daughter, dwarfed by the bed. Sarah was straining to hold her eyes open. "Daddy's in the car, sweetie. I'm going to run outside for a second . . . to talk to him." With this farewell, she closed the door.

The moaning of the frigid wind should cover any noise, but it was the searcher's nature to be as silent as possible. The contents of the old

Wagoneer were tossed about in a bitter frustration that was rapidly building toward anger. A cardboard box was dumped on the rear seat. Nothing
in there but clothing . . . a tattered coloring book . . . a box of Kitty
Kat food. Stiff fingers, numbed by the cold, fumbled with the latch on
the black toolbox . . . But wait.

There was a thin blade of light from the motel door . . . the sound of
hurried footsteps crunching on the gravel.

Sarah was lost in a deep sleep. The dreamer was riding a pretty spotted
pony . . . instead of a leather saddle, she sat on a fine blue blanket
decorated with white zigzags.

The kitten was not asleep. Mr Zigzag heard the startling sounds from
outside—a shrill cry, followed by a sharp curse. The tiny animal abandoned the warm comfort of the bed and the child. The kitten climbed
to the back of a stuffed chair sitting by the window, and perched there
to look outside. Eyes wide. Ears pricked.

There was a dull thump. Then silence.

The hair on the kitten's neck bristled; the animal scampered back to
the bed and snuggled close to the little girl. The kitten mewed pitifully,
even licked Sarah's chin. But the child did not awaken.

Minutes later, the kitten's keen ears picked up a most unnatural series
of reports. The distant tattoo was faint, but each sound was quite distinct.
Almost as if someone was firing a gun. But these were not gunshots. It
would have been far better if they were.

They were . . . a rapping-tapping . . . a ringing-pinging.

۞

The child muttered sleepily when her father rushed into the motel room
and scooped her up in his arms. If Mr. Zigzag had not been held tightly
in the girl's hands, the kitten would surely have been left behind.

CHAPTER 5

Leadville, Colorado

Sarah stretched, and yawned. Mr. Zigzag was in her lap when she sat up in the front seat of the Wagoneer. The little girl looked around. This was where Mommy always sat, right next to Daddy. She pressed her nose against the glass. Daddy was outside, putting gasoline into the tank. He paid a woman at a little window and then got in the car. He gave Sarah a small carton of milk and a chocolate cupcake with a curly line of white sugar icing on the top.

"Where are we, Daddy?"

"Leadville." Like it would matter to a girl that wasn't yet five years old. But Sarah always wanted to know the names of places she visited. And she always remembered them later.

She stood up and looked over into the back seat. It was a real mess, she thought, stuff scattered all over the place. Mommy won't like this. She looked out the window. Mommy must be in the ladies' room.

Provo Frank found his keys, then cranked the Wagoneer's V-8 engine. It rattled, coughed, then roared to life, and he pulled away from the pumps.

"Wait, Mommy isn't back yet!"

Her father set his jaw, said nothing.

"Daddeeeee—wait for Mommy!"

"Mommy's gone."

"Gone where?"

Females, even little ones, were always asking questions. Hard questions. He tried to ignore his daughter.

"Gone *where*, Daddy?" There was alarm in her voice.

Provo hesitated. "Back to Arizona. To Ak Chin."

"Why?"

He swallowed hard. "Her daddy's sick. She's gone to take care of him."

"When'll she come back?"

"Don't know. Eat your cake, dammit."

Sarah mimicked her mother's firm tone. "You are not supposed to use bad words in front of a little girl." She tore the cellophane off the chocolate cake and took a small bite. It was very good.

"Damn," he muttered, but under his breath.

Her Papago grandpa loved Sarah, so he would get better real fast if she was with him. "Why didn't Mommy take me to help her take care of Grandpa?"

He glanced at the rearview mirror. A black and white police cruiser was three lengths behind him. Provo lifted his foot off the accelerator and gripped the wheel with white knuckles. "I don't know why. Now, shut up and drink your milk."

"I can't drink any milk if my mouth is shut." She poured some milk from the carton into her palm and allowed Mr. Zigzag to lap it up.

"Oh shit," he said, and for the fist time since he was six years old—when his beagle puppy got run over by the gravel truck—Provo Frank wanted to cry.

✿ Bitter Springs, Wyoming ✿

Sergeant Harry MacFie was rolling west on the interstate, but his mind was on the long day ahead. First, check out the pissant complaint from the fleabag motel. Then, drive three hours to Cheyenne for a meeting with DEA agents who were coordinating an effort to, in their bullshit bureaucrat talk, "establish a correlation matrix" of illegal drug outlets in Wyoming and Idaho. Today's DEA cops, in MacFie's view, were of two types. Type One were smart-assed college kids who thought they could solve crimes with their laptop computers. Type Two were forty-year-old adolescents with fuzzy beards and dirty jeans. Hell-for-leather undercover cowboys whose chances were maybe fifty-fifty of living long enough to see their grandchildren. Though he'd never admit it, the middle-aged policeman envied these fellows who, at least, were trying like hell to do something important with their lives.

Sergeant Harry MacFie, by contrast, was starting his day by going to meet a sour old woman with a rummy husband who had maybe a teaspoonful of brains between his ears. Nuts. What a pissant job. He should, he mused, have been at least a lieutenant by now, even a captain. And would've, but for what the management in the Wyoming Highway Patrol referred to as "MacFie's bad attitude." Well, what'd they know? Damn bunch of stuffed-shirt desk cops.

He had left the residential section of Bitter Springs behind, and was in the sparse region where the south side of the four-lane was dotted with a few double-wide mobile homes and a range of business establishments, from the gleaming to the ratty-looking. The policeman passed the Ford dealership with its long row of gleaming new pickup trucks, a failed Mom's Family Restaurant with plywood nailed over the windows, Toby's RV Service and Sales, and more of the like. The morning sun was already well over the horizon, warming his freckled neck through the rear window of the Ford Crown Victoria. MacFie hadn't had his breakfast yet, hadn't even had a cup of decent coffee, and the empty feeling in his stomach did not improve the doleful Scot's mood. If the damn City Limits Motel had been built a few hundred yards to the east, then the Bitter Springs town police would have jurisdiction and he wouldn't be bothered with this nonsense. Sergeant MacFie had ten patrolmen under his supervision; he could have sent any one of them. But this was, at least, an excuse to get out and move around. As long as you kept moving, you didn't die.

MacFie idly wondered whether the city council would move to annex this west section. He hoped so. It'd save him a lot of pissant calls from these whining, pissant motel owners. He nosed the big Ford onto the exit ramp and looped around under the four-lane to the south. The frontage road was the sad remnant of the two-lane highway that had served this part of Wyoming before the days of the interstates. Maintenance now was limited to patching only those potholes that were big enough to throw a full-grown boar hog into.

The highway patrolman, not eager to confront the wrath of the salty old woman who managed the City Limits Motel, drove west for a short distance and turned in to the parking lot of the Pynk Garter Saloon. The neon leg was still up there, kicking rhythmically at batting moths. The eyesore of a building was, at this hour of the morning, tightly shut. He circled the Pynk Garter slowly, routinely surveying the windows, the doors, searching for any sign of a forced entry.

Harry repeated this routine survey at the Texaco station, waving at the young woman behind the cash register. Sometimes folks wouldn't realize for a week or more that a rear window had been broken, or an unused door jimmied. But everything looked pretty tight.

He sighed with resignation and headed east up the frontage road, turning in to the graveled parking lot at the City Limits Motel. The word VACANCY was painted onto the wooden sign, with no ready means to alter this hopeful invitation. MacFie doubted that the old motel had ever been filled with customers. Sensible tourists preferred to stop in town. Aggie's old Cadillac convertible was parked out front, so that meant she was at home. Aggie never let her husband drive the Caddy since Billy'd taken to drinking.

He got out of the black-and-white and looked around, pretending not to notice the scowling face of Aggie Stymes framed in the office window. Her old man would be in the back room with his pet bird, watching the television screen. Aggie kept the books and cleaned up the rooms; Billy Stymes soaked up a couple of six-packs a day and didn't miss his soaps and game shows. The Stymeses, never known for their winning personalities, had gone particularly sullen on MacFie after an investigation a half dozen years ago, when a tourist family from Oregon claimed somebody had stolen some valuables out of their room. It had been a nasty affair, but with insufficient evidence to charge anybody with anything. The missing camera and pearl necklace had magically appeared in the tourists' room after MacFie had shown up. The policeman figured Aggie had found the stuff and returned it. Oddly, she'd seemed to take more offense than her sullen husband at the lawman's probing questions. There had been an underlying tension between MacFie and the Stymeses since that incident, but when there was a problem, Aggie generally called the highway patrol. The county sheriff, a former rodeo cowboy who was more interested in his budding country-western singing career than being a lawman, wouldn't bother with what he called "Aggie's chickenshit complaints."

Aggie Stymes' face had disappeared into the dark recesses of the office; she didn't open the door until he had knocked twice. When she did show up, the elderly woman's wrinkled face was hard and impassive under her short-cut hair—much like the angular granite outcropping under the tufts of grass on the windswept ridge behind the motel. MacFie tipped his battered hat and smiled as best as he could. He knew that a warm smile unnerved the sour old woman. "Top o' the mornin' to you, Miz Stymes."

She grunted, mumbled something that might have been an obscene observation about his mother and birth control, then stepped aside so he could enter.

MacFie's sharp blue eyes took in the scant details of the Spartan office. A flaked Formica-topped counter with Aggie's oak swivel chair behind it. On the counter, a plastic machine with a slot for processing credit cards, an electronic cash register, a pale yellow telephone with a couple of dozen buttons. A bound registration book for guests. The calendar on the wall behind Aggie was three years old. Maybe she kept it because she liked the picture—a cluster of royal palms, dark volcanic sands, pale blue waters. It looked like a beach somewhere in the warm waters of the South Pacific.

Aggie took a Camel cigarette from a crumpled pack; she jammed it into a convenient slot where two front teeth were missing. She didn't light the cigarette—just let it dangle.

MacFie looked over her scruffy gray head into the back room. Billy was back there in his usual spot, hunched forward on the couch. Bleary eyes glued to the TV. But he was sipping at a mug of coffee. MacFie was surprised to learn that the old rummy drank coffee, and it made the lawman yearn for a cup of his own. Aggie had a percolator on a small table behind her. Next to it, there was a box of fresh doughnuts from the Early Riser Bakery. All these goodies were behind the counter, of course. The City Limits Motel did not offer any fringe benefits to its few customers. A wisp of steam curled out of the glass percolator; MacFie sniffed. "Coffee," he muttered. "Smell's good."

Aggie ignored the hint. "I expect you're here on account of my call yesterday." She emphasized the "yesterday."

The officer nodded, but he was still gazing hopefully at the coffeepot. "Cold morning out there."

She took the cigarette out of her gums, rolled it between her fingers, then pointed it at the policeman. "Sure as hell took you long enough to get here, MacFie."

"I was detained for a few minutes," he said. "We had us a bank robbery, two kidnappings, and a mass murder over in Bitter Springs. And if that wasn't enough, we had us a parking violation to boot."

Aggie's face was like stone. Either she didn't hear him or she didn't know he was joking. "Like I told your dispatcher, I had another drive-off night before last. Third one this year."

He closed his eyes and sighed. "So what's the tab?"

She pulled her bifocals over her ears and squinted at a bill. "Two adults, one child. Three nights at forty-two per night. With taxes, that comes to one hundred and thirty-eight dollars and fifty-two cents."

MacFie fumbled around in his jacket pocket until he found a small notebook and a stubby lead pencil. He licked the pencil tip. "Description?"

Aggie shrugged. "Man was dark-skinned. Young, thirtyish. Wore a pig-tail." She grinned maliciously. "Taller than you, I'd say." It was an ill-kept secret that MacFie wore special boots that added a couple of inches to his height.

He felt his face getting warm. Damn this smart-assed old woman. "What about the others?"

35

"Woman. Dark hair . . . his wife, I suppose." She gave MacFie a funny look, then glanced quickly toward the hulking form of her husband. "Sort of pretty if you like the skinny type. And a little girl." Aggie started to say "cute," but didn't. She jammed the Camel back between the gap in her teeth and felt in her apron pocket for the plastic lighter.

"So how'd he pay?"

"Personal check." Aggie flicked the button on the cheap lighter, got a wavering yellow flame on the third try, and touched it to the tip of the cigarette. She inhaled gratefully, then blew smoke at the policeman's face. "His check wasn't worth a jug of spit."

He looked up and his blue eyes twinkled. Maybe Aggie was getting careless. More likely, she wasn't in the office when the fellow showed up, and old Billy had taken the check. "You accepted an out-of-state personal check?"

"It's my business, Harry, and I'll run it how I please." She ran her index finger along a jagged crack in the Formica and looked so pitiful that he almost felt sorry for her. "I got the bank to make a call the next day after they got here; there wasn't enough in their account to buy a box of doughnuts."

This reference to doughnuts pained MacFie. With some effort, he averted his gaze from the pot of steaming coffee, the box of glazed doughnuts. Probably the coffee was as bitter as Aggie's heart, and the doughnuts as hard. "Give me whatever documentation you got on these people."

Aggie was prepared; she'd been through this drill before. She pushed a manila envelope across the table to MacFie. He unbuttoned the brass clasp. There were a half dozen flimsy papers inside, paper-clipped together. He removed the offending check. Provo and Mary Frank were the names on the light blue paper. Vehicle was a '76 Wagoneer. License plate number was Utah. Address was Bottle Hollow, Utah. That was on the Uintah-Ouray reservation. So the man was most likely a Ute. It'd be a good idea to alert the Indian police departments on the three Ute reservations. Two of them were in southern Colorado. And he had a buddy down there. Charlie Moon. Good fellow.

The amount on the check was for one hundred dollars. He frowned across the counter at the old woman. "This was for a deposit?"

"Yeah. Said he didn't know how long they'd be staying."

"They leave anything in the room?" MacFie noticed Billy Stymes look up momentarily from the TV.

"Lots of stuff," Aggie said quickly. Almost unconsciously, she cut her eyes toward the darkened room where her husband sat, then back at the state cop's poker face. "But nothing worth anything. If there was," she added pointedly, "I'd confiscate it against the money they owe me. That's my legal right."

"Which room were they in?"

"Unit eleven," Aggie said. "A real nice room."

"Gimme a key."

She did, then grinned crookedly. "You want a cuppa coffee?"

"No," he lied. "I'm already coffeed up." But the lawman left the motel office without slamming the door.

"Unit eleven," Billy Stymes said to his wife, "has always been a bad-luck room for us." He pushed a half dozen grapes into his mouth and chewed.

The raven flew down from its dowel-rod perch over the television set; it lighted on the man's round shoulder.

"Hello, Billy," the raven croaked.

"Hello, Petey," the heavyset man said. Billy picked a grape from the bunch and held it gingerly, by the stem. "Have yourself a snack."

The raven raised its head, gulped three times, and swallowed the grape.

Billy raised his voice and repeated his observation. "Eleven," he said, "it's been a hard-luck room for us."

Aggie turned to glare at her husband. "What'n hell you jabberin' about, Billy?"

He shook an imaginary pair of dice in his hand. "One-One. Snake-eyes," he explained. "Bad luck." He flushed red under her stare and turned away, but Billy still felt her hard gaze. It prickled on the back of his neck. He didn't look up. "I sure do need a drink," he said in a tone intended to provoke pity.

It didn't.

"Black coffee," she said spitefully. "That's all you'll get to drink till you learn to do as I say. And quit feeding that damn bird grapes. You know how much a pound those grapes cost me?"

He put his hand in his shirt pocket and removed a delicate ring.

Aggie squinted; the cigarette dangled from her bluish lips. "What's that?"

"Silver and turquoise," he said, rubbing it with a dirty finger. "Pretty. I thought you'd like it."

Her voice was deadly calm. "Where'd you get that, Billy?"

He hung his head and muttered, "Found it."

"Found it where?" She grabbed the ring from his hand.

Billy clamped his mouth shut.

"Where?"

"Outside."

"Where outside?"

"In the parking lot."

She slipped the ring into her apron pocket. "It's a cheap trinket, you damned fool—not worth a jug of spit!"

The raven flew back to the safety of the perch. "Jug of spit," the bird croaked happily.

Billy did what he always did when it was necessary to escape the dreary reality of his life. He concentrated his full attention on the flickering television screen. A pretty blond woman, dressed only in a satin slip, was sitting at a vanity. She was carefully applying a scarlet lipstick to her perfect, full lips. A man's leering face appeared at the window behind the pretty lady. The woman saw the intruder's reflection in the mirror; she began to scream.

The big man's body shuddered; he pressed the selector button on the remote and flicked through four channels. The screen he stopped at was a Roadrunner cartoon. The skinny coyote was strapping Acme rocket shoes to his feet. Billy chuckled. "Attaboy, ol' dog. Go get 'im, Rover." Billy turned his head and looked at Aggie's plump behind. "I don't much like Harry MacFie snoopin' round here alla time," he said. "I hope he gets what's comin' to 'im."

Aggie, who was painting her fingernails, didn't pay any attention to her husband. Billy hadn't said anything in ten years that was worth listening to.

CHAPTER 6

Southern Ute Reservation, *Cañón del Espíritu*

The sun had fallen behind the mesa, and with the gathering twilight came a sweet coolness that refreshed her.

The Ute woman had been a long time in the Canyon of the Spirits, and was pleased to see her little trailer home nestled among the trees in the broad valley. Daisy Perika left the cotton sack by the foot of the steps and leaned her pointed digging stick against the porch; tomorrow she would spread the stuff out in the sun to dry. The shaman had gathered *yerba del buey*, alum root, yarrow, woundwort, and more. After three days, she would grind some roots into a fine powder. Some of the leaves, she would boil. She'd do the final mixing with a dash of salt, a dab of blue cooking clay, a pinch of soot from blackened juniper twig. A little of this, a little of that . . . These would make fine medicines to cure bleeding, headaches, upset stomach, aching joints, influenza, diarrhea . . . all sorts of common ailments. And what she didn't use, Daisy would sell to the distributor of herbs who showed up at the yearly powwow in Ignacio.

The old woman climbed to the top of the porch, groaning with each step. She untied her scarf, turned the knob on the door—and stepped over the threshold into the darkness of her kitchen. That was when she heard the sound. A very slight sound, as if someone or . . . some*thing* . . . close to her . . . had moved. Daisy fumbled in her purse for a tiny flashlight attached to a key ring. Her hand trembled as she pushed the flashlight switch with an arthritic thumb. When she did this, several things happened, almost at the same time.

At a point less than three feet above the floor, a pair of yellow eyes reflected the tiny beam of light. The eyes blinked. Then moved toward her. Quickly.

She screamed. "No . . . Ahhh . . . Get away!" The old woman instinctively backed through the open door. She tripped on a shoelace and fell backward onto the porch, arms flailing in a vain attempt to grasp onto something. "Ahhhh . . . Hiiieeeee!" It was as if someone had struck her on the back with the two-by-six boards that were assembled to make the floor of the porch. "Oooohhh . . . dear God . . ." Dazed, she prayed that her back was not broken. Now something furry was on her face, licking her nose. The old woman tried to scream, but the fall had driven the wind from her lungs. Go away, she prayed silently, go away. The thing licked at her lips; its tongue felt like coarse sandpaper. Please go away. Oh, please, God, have mercy on a poor old woman, take this devil away from my home. She finally found her voice in a hoarse whisper. "Oh no . . . no . . . please . . . away."

A small, hollow voice came from the darkness. "It's us, Aunt Daisy. We're only a little girl and a kitty." The child's voice assumed a comforting tone. "You don't have to be afraid." The kitten, apparently quite satisfied with its work, bounded into the doorway and was scooped up by a small pair of hands.

Daisy struggled to assimilate this news; she also attempted to regain some shred of her lost dignity. "Sarah . . . Sarah Frank?" She raised herself to one elbow. "Why're you hiding in the dark? Trying to scare an old woman to death?"

"My kitty was sleeping. He woke up when he heard the door open."

Daisy took some time to absorb this, then she felt the pain. "Damn," the shaman said bitterly as she rubbed her hand on a sore hip, "I think I broke my ass."

"You shouldn't say bad words in front of a little girl."

"I'm an old woman," Daisy gasped, "and I'll say any words I want. Besides," she added reasonably, "when you've been scared half to death, the rules are different."

The child held the kitten out, like an offering. "This is Mr.—"

"Aaaggghhh," the old woman said, and waved her hand in rude dismissal.

The child's voice betrayed her astonishment. "Don't you like little kittens?"

"I like 'em just fine," Daisy rattled, "had two of 'em for breakfast this very morning. Fried crispy. With brown gravy." She tried to imagine something more gruesome to add, but the fall had dulled her natural eloquence.

The child clutched the kitten close to her neck and whispered into its ear. "Don't be scared, Mr. Zigzag, she's just teasing . . . I think."

Daisy groaned, then snapped at the unwelcome visitor. "So what're you doing here?"

Sarah summoned up her courage and spoke to the old woman. "Daddy said we must stay with you . . . for a little while." Daddy had also said, "You take good care of Aunt Daisy." Grown-ups always said things like that. The little voice, close to tears, quavered. "But if you don't want us, we'll go away."

Daisy grasped a vertical support on the porch railing and blinked at her visitors. "Come out here . . . where I can see you better."

Sarah stepped onto the porch, but hesitantly. She did not release the kitten.

Daisy sat up and tried to focus.

The tiny girl wore a navy-blue cotton dress with white polka dots. And a white lace collar. The dress went almost to her ankles. A clever mother had evidently made a long garment that the girl could "grow into." Her hair was long and dark as midnight, her eyes darker still.

"And this thing." The old woman pointed at the animal. "What's its name?"

"This is Mr. Zigzag Frank." She kissed the kitten on the face and returned it to her shoulder.

"Niaaaooow!" Mr. Zigzag said to no one in particular.

Daisy Perika struggled to get to her feet; her ears were ringing. She glared at the kitten. "Hello yourself, Mr. Ragbag."

"It's Mr. *Zigzag*."

Daisy barely heard the indignant correction; her thoughts were focused on the Frank family. Provo Frank's father was a second or third cousin from Daisy's father's side of the family. And Provo had married himself a Tohono O'otam woman from Ak Chin, way down in Arizona, almost to Mexico. Those "Bean People" were a peculiar outfit. The Ute woman was suspicious of anyone who could survive the searing desert heat. Or want to. Maybe their brains were fried and they didn't know any better. Daisy used the porch railing to aid her in staying upright. She hoped Charlie Moon wouldn't marry one of them desert Indians. The children from such a union might be peculiar. Maybe they would lie out in the sun, on hot rocks. Like lizards. Daisy eyed Sarah suspiciously.

She blinked at the child. "How'd you get here?"

"We came in Daddy's car." The little girl's voice had a faraway quality. Sarah stroked the kitten.

"That's very interesting. I'd like to hear lots more about it." Daisy's sarcasm was lost on the child. "But where'd your folks go after they dropped you off here?" She could think of a couple of choice places to recommend, but the testy old woman had already been reminded that she must not use bad language in front of a little girl.

"Mommy didn't come with us—Daddy says she's gone to be with Grandpa in Ak Chin, 'cause he's sick. Daddy didn't say where he was going." Maybe back to Bottle Hollow. Maybe to Neola or Tabiona. Or Altonah or Bluebell.

"Hmmmph. Did he leave you any money?"

The child shook her head glumly.

"Hmmm . . . Ragbag the cat . . . he got any money?"

"Kitties," Sarah explained patiently, "don't *ever* have money."

"An' why is that?"

" 'Cause they don't have any way to carry it. Like a purse."

Daisy sighed. So. Another mouth to feed. Or, if you counted the ratty-looking little cat, two more mouths to feed. Well, she would manage somehow. There was a big can of rice stored in the closet, along with a burlap bag of dried pinto beans. Anyway, this child wasn't bigger than a minute. And the cat. What was it Homer Tonompicket said about that skinny pig he kept in his backyard? Daisy remembered: "Root, hog . . . or die." Well, that runty cat could root around till it found some grasshoppers and lizards.

"Oooohhhh," Daisy groaned as she rubbed her buttock. "I think I broke my . . . my axle." She fairly spat the words at the child. "My *rear* axle."

✸ Ignacio, Colorado ✸
SUPD

Chief of Police Roy Severo found Charlie Moon by the coffeepot. The small man looked dwarfish by the tall, broad-shouldered frame of Moon. "You know Peter Frank's boy, don't you?"

Moon took a sip of sweetened coffee from a black mug painted with a yellow slice of moon. "Provo? I see him every year or so, when he brings his family to Ignacio." Moon and Provo Frank had grown up together on the southern reservation, gone to high school together, even done some serious drinking together. Until Moon gave up the bottle and went off to college, then to fight in Desert Storm.

"That's the one." The chief waved a smudged sheet of paper up under his subordinate's nose. "Looks like he's passed some bad paper again."

Charlie Moon accepted the notice and read it over his coffee mug. As he read the first half of the page, the coffee took on a bitter taste.

WYHP BULLETIN 0997-221
DIST = ALLPD/7S + UTE RES (UINTAH/OURAY+UTE MNTN+SOUTHERN UTE)

WANTED FOR QUESTIONING RE BAD CHECK [$100.00] PASSED @ CITY LIMITS MOTEL, BITTER CREEK, WY: PROVO FRANK. (W-MARY/D-SARAH).
RESIDENCE: BOTTLE HOLLOW, UT.
OCCUPATION: UNKNOWN
CURRENT EMPLOYMENT: UNKNOWN
SS#: TO FOLLOW
REF SGT. HARRY MACFIE = WYHP = BITTER SPRINGS WY

Harry MacFie's telephone and fax number were at the bottom of the page. Moon folded the paper carefully and put it into his shirt pocket. "I know this MacFie."

Roy Severo raised an eyebrow. "How's that?"

Moon grinned. "Picked him up at the casino . . . last January, I think. Held him in the jug for a couple of hours."

Severo looked at the coffeepot, then away. He was already high-strung, and caffeine just kept him awake at night. "Was he drunk?"

"Nope. Just highly annoyed at some fellow who puked on his new shirt. Harry broke up a window frame. And some glass."

"Last I heard, breakin' a window ain't exactly a jailin' offense."

"Well," Moon said, "it was on account of *how* he broke the window."

Severo's face was showing his agitation with this overgrown, slow-talking man. "Well, how'd he break it?"

"That fella that puked on him—MacFie pitched him right through the window."

Now Severo laughed.

"After he cooled off, I bought him some breakfast over at Angel's. And sent him on his way."

The chief nodded. "Anything on his record from the arrest?"

Moon drained the mug. "Wasn't exactly an arrest. More like we loaned him a cell so's he could rest for a while."

So there would be nothing on the cop's record. "Courtesy to a fellow officer, eh?" Severo wasn't sure he approved of such bending of the law.

Moon refilled the black moon-mug from the one-gallon stainless steel can. "I don't expect MacFie's forgot about it."

Severo shrugged. Having a friend among the Wyoming Highway Patrol wouldn't hurt. "What're you gonna do about Provo?"

Moon looked over the smaller man's head toward an enlarged photograph of Rolling Thunder, the tribe's almost-famous bull buffalo. "Nothin'. Just wait to see if he shows up on the reservation. If he does, I'll have a talk with him." Maybe help him straighten this thing out.

✧ Cañón del Espíritu ✧

The child walked beside the old woman, who was poking at the ground with a sharpened stick. "This root," Daisy said as she pried a twisted yellow tuber from the sandy loam, "is good for bleeding. And for warts."

"Daddy has a big wart," Sarah said. "It's on his thumb."

"Hah." Daisy wanted to say, "Your daddy *is* a big wart." But she didn't.

Sarah gasped as a fuzzy spider scuttled near her shoe; she stomped on it. "Nasty bug!"

The old woman groaned. "You shouldn't ever kill a spider."

"Why?"

" 'Cause he has plenty of relatives who'll come and bite you."

"Ooooh—I'm sorry, Aunt Daisy." Sarah looked uneasily around her feet, expecting an imminent attack.

"Never mind. I know how to fix it." Daisy used her digging stick to draw a circle around the dead spider. This done, she told the child exactly what to say.

Sarah bent over the circle and spoke to the dead creature. "A Navajo killed you. Send your family to bite the Navajos." She looked up at the old woman. "Did I do it right?"

"Perfect," the shaman said. This child, though woefully ignorant, had potential.

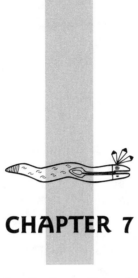

CHAPTER 7

Granite Creek, Colorado

Scott Parris looked across his desk at the young woman with the blond hair and the thin, hopeful face. She was maybe ninety pounds soaking wet. If she had heavy boots on. Alicia Martin wasn't exactly pretty, but she was good to look at because she was young and full of hope. And spunk. Ms. Martin was, according to her application, a mere twenty-three years old. Just last month, she'd graduated from the police academy class in Phoenix. Grades were fair to good. Having completed her three days of orientation supervised by the able Lieutenant Leggett, Alicia was ready to begin her first day as a trainee-officer with the Granite Creek Police Department. If she got through the first ninety days, she'd be a regular cop. With the privilege of risking her life daily, directing traffic in snow-storms, and suffering obscene gestures from teenage hoods. All for the princely starting pay of seven dollars and fifty cents per hour.

Alicia stared expectantly at Chief Parris, who seemed almost embar-rassed. This, she realized, was a shy man who was ill at ease around women. Word was the chief didn't put up with any nonsense, and he could get mad enough to bite tenpenny nails in half. But this man had a reputation for being fair to a fault. Yes. A woman would get a square deal on this force. That was one of the reasons she'd picked this particular small town in Colorado to begin her career. Finally he looked directly at her. Alicia smiled, and as she had anticipated, he blushed and looked back at the ballpoint pen he was playing with. He wasn't bad-looking, for such an old guy. He must be forty, at least.

Scott Parris cleared his throat, then began his set speech for trainee-officers. "Thing is, Officer Martin, we always start our new employees out kind of slow and easy."

"As long as you don't give me meter-maid duties." She'd meant it as a joke.

Now his face turned beet-red. "Actually, checking the parking meters is the responsibility of our department, and I—"

"Oh, it's all right," she said, "I don't mind doing almost anything just as long as it's not permanent. Well, I didn't exactly mean permanent, you know." She clamped her mouth shut. *I am such a chatterbox.*

"Today Lieutenant Leggett will assign you a specific section of town to patrol. Your duties will be to observe and report. If you see anything that looks like serious trouble, you'll be expected to—"

"Do I get a car?" She didn't want to ride around on one of those dumb bicycles. It was . . . well, it was undignified.

Parris grinned and relaxed. "You won't need a black-and-white today, Officer Martin. I've asked Leggett to assign you to the downtown beat. It's all within eight blocks of the station. So you'll—"

"Great," she interrupted. "That'll do fine." A *beat*. It sounded so old-fashioned. But the chief was an old cop, from Chicago. A beat, no less. *Mom will be so proud!*

She was standing at attention. Looking damn spiffy in her spit-polished black shoes, navy slacks with a razor-edge crease, and light blue shirt with a silver shield over her left breast. The black automatic pistol holstered on her belt seemed incongruous on the small, slender figure. He wondered why she hadn't selected something smaller. Like a .38-caliber snub-nosed revolver. Probably because it would seem like a "woman's gun." Parris still carried a small .38 in a shoulder holster under his left armpit. No matter what they said, automatics would, sooner or later, jam on you. And then you'd wish you had a reliable firearm.

The chief of police sighed. "That is all, Officer Martin. Report to Lieutenant Leggett."

Alicia's back went ramrod-straight. He hoped she wasn't going to salute.

Fifteen minutes later, Parris stood beside Lieutenant Leggett. They watched Officer Trainee Alicia Martin march briskly away from the station entrance, past a half dozen black-and-whites parked at the curb. She was heading down Front Street toward Main. Her Glock nine-millimeter pistol hung snugly on her right hip, a portable Motorola radio transmitter on her left. She had an ugly black baton gripped lightly in her delicate hand. The blond ponytail bobbed as she walked. No, she was not exactly pretty, but she was cute. Too damn cute to go out there and face . . . face whatever. The chief did not look at the lieutenant when he spoke. "You think she'll be alright? I mean . . . she's just so . . . so *small.*"

"Size isn't everything, sir. Officer Martin's got a lot of moxie."

Parris' response was glum. "I don't want my inexperienced officers to have moxie. I want them to be damn careful."

Leggett smothered a smile. The chief worried about all his officers. Even the hardheads, like Eddie Knox. Like an old hen with chicks. "She'll do fine, sir."

But Scott Parris, still uneasy after his eerie visit with Daisy Perika, felt a coldness inside. The old Ute woman's words echoed in his mind. Blood. Falling like rain . . . there were clouds sliding off Salt Mountain. Rolling clouds. Wet clouds, with a faint reddish tinge.

The chief of police turned and frowned at the lieutenant. "Just the same, I want somebody to keep an eye on Officer Martin for a few days. But they'd best not let her know . . . "

"Good as done, sir." Leggett, who had anticipated this order, had already dispatched Eddie "Rocks" Knox. Rocks had a wooden leg, but if there was trouble, the dour old cop was hell on wheels. Leggett wondered why the boss was so itchy, why he was expecting something to go wrong out there. But Leggett had learned that when Chief Parris got into one of his nervous moods, something interesting usually happened.

✪

This was, just possibly, the happiest day of Alicia Martin's life. She was a real cop, in a lovely little town in the southern Rockies. The day itself was perfect. Lovely clouds, anchored on Salt Mountain like great ocean liners, hung over the valley. A glint of late morning sun touched the golden cross on the peak of the steeple of St. Mark's Presbyterian Church. A swallow darted by, landing on the outstretched limb of an aspen. She had dutifully checked the parking meters, dropping her own nickels into a couple that had red flags up. She'd smiled at an old man struggling along with a walker, and stopped traffic so he could cross over to the Corner Drug Store on Silver Street. A small girl with a lollipop in her mouth had stopped to stare at the police officer. Alicia wanted to polish the silver shield on her blouse, but resisted this temptation. Someone might be watching. Oddly, though she saw no one there, she did feel "watched." Alicia put this down to a slight state of nerves. This was, after all, her first day alone on what the old man called the "beat." Damn, that sounded fine!

She turned onto Spruce and walked slowly toward Third. Officer Trainee Alicia Martin passed a dry cleaner's. A convenience store. A drive-in hamburger restaurant littered with paper cartons and other junk. She stopped long enough to pick up a half dozen bits of debris and dump them in a waste can. An officer of the law must set a good example. The only notice she got was from a pimple-faced adolescent who leered and said something about a "pistol-packin' momma." Alicia, who was a good-natured person, smiled sweetly at the youth and went on her way.

The battered Jeep Wagoneer was parked in front of the Philly Bar and Grille, a dark, seedy hangout for unhappy men who started drinking well before noon. Something clicked in Alicia's memory of this morning's briefing. The Wagoneer was old enough to be a '76. And it was brown. With Utah plates. She removed a small pad from her hip pocket and checked the notes she'd made two hours earlier. Her heart raced when she saw that the number on the plate matched the six digits recorded in her neat hand. She squinted at the notes by the license number.

Provo Frank. Bad check/motel/WY. (Ute)

Well, it wasn't much. Not like she'd spotted a bank robber's car, or even a stolen vehicle. The man had written a check, and there had been insufficient funds in his account. It happened to all of us, sooner or later. And he might not even know that the check had bounced. Still, this was a coup of sorts—Chief Parris and oh-so-perfect Lieutenant Leggett would be impressed!

She would do this by the book. Alicia removed the Motorola radio from the canvas holster on her left hip and pressed the button. "Base, this is Officer Martin. I'm outside the Philly Bar and Grille."

Clara Tavishuts' voice barked in her ear. "Ten-four. What is your report?"

Alicia hesitated. "I have a brown Jeep Wagoneer. Utah plates." She read the license number of the plate and enunciated each syllable as she passed it on to the dispatcher. "We had a notice that—"

There was a burst of static. "Ten-four, Officer Martin. I'll get back to you on that. We have an accident with injuries out on the four-lane."

"Roger." Alicia slipped the radio back into the fabric holster and sighed. She stood awkwardly outside the Philly Bar and Grille, waiting. A minute dragged by. She started to radio the dispatcher again, but decided that would not be quite the professional thing to do. But should she stand here all day, waiting for headquarters to get the lead out?

Eddie "Rocks" Knox sat sullenly in his aged Dodge pickup; he would collect twenty-four cents per mile for using his personal vehicle for this dandy assignment. But he'd be lucky to collect fifty cents today, because she was on foot patrol. Follow the kiddy cop around town all day and make sure she don't stub her little toe. Dammit. Eddie was only happy when he had something to be displeased with, and today was just super. Now the little blond girl was standing outside the Philly Bar. He'd listened to her call, but didn't know why she was so interested in the old Jeep Wagoneer. During this morning's briefing, Eddie "Rocks" Knox had devoted all his attention to a sugar-coated jelly doughnut. He'd heard something about some Ute who'd passed bad paper up in Wyoming. Who the hell cared for such bullshit anyway?

She'd stuck the Motorola handset back onto her belt, and now she was fidgeting. Just like a woman. Probably she needed to go pee. Women's bladders, Eddie knew from experience with his wife, were way too small. So they had to go pee every ten minutes.

Yep. Now little miss Blondie was going into the Philly Bar. Probably to use the ladies' facility. But something gnawed at the stump where the titanium prosthesis was strapped to his knee. Now he could feel the toes on his phantom foot. The toes that weren't there were itching. That wasn't a good sign. If this little girl broke her fingernail and ol' Eddie Knox wasn't right there to dry her tears, why, Chief Parris would just throw himself a fit. Glumly Eddie dismounted from the three-quarter-ton pickup and sauntered along the bricked sidewalk toward the Philly Bar and Grille. He was in plainclothes, just so she wouldn't know someone was riding herd on her.

Alicia pushed the door open and walked into a dank atmosphere, sour with the smell of stale beer and urine. It was a dump. She paused, removed her dark glasses, and looked around the place. It wasn't much. The only window was up front, and that was dominated by a greasy red neon sign that merely said Coors. In a Colorado tavern, that was a sufficient advertisement. To her left, a long bar ran the length of the shotgun building. There were no stools; this was strictly a stand-up joint. On a shelf behind the bar, a small television was tuned to the Sports Channel. The Cubs were losing to someone. There were no tables, but the right wall was lined with booths. Except for the bartender, the place seemed empty. A pale, gaunt man stood behind the bar, watching the baseball game. Somebody slid into second base on his face and the bartender laughed.

Alicia approached the bar, irritated that her palms were suddenly cold. "Morning."

The tall bartender nodded politely, but did not speak.

She blinked again at the booths. "You don't seem to have any customers."

"Just one." He nodded toward the small door in the rear that was labeled MEN.

"Could you give me a description?"

The bartender shrugged. "Young man. Dark complexion. Got hisself a pigtail."

"Could he be a Native American?"

"Could be a Chinaman for all I know."

At this point, the restroom door opened. A man emerged. He stopped in midstride when he saw the police officer.

He fit the general description. Alicia smiled.

Provo Frank did not notice this friendly gesture. He did notice the club in her hand. And the pistol on her belt.

"Sir, are you the owner of the Jeep Wagoneer parked at the curb?"

He hesitated. "I don't own no car." He glanced over his shoulder, at a rear door with a red EXIT sign. It must lead to the alley. When he looked back, the skinny lady cop was walking toward him; her right hand seemed to be touching the holster that held the gun. Provo backed up. One step. Two. She kept coming.

"Sir, may I see some identification?"

Almost without willing it, Provo Frank snatched a beer bottle off the counter.

Alicia froze. With her left hand, she was raising the baton to protect herself. The reaction was just a fraction of a second late; she felt the bottle smash into her face. The young woman barely felt the hardwood floor when it came up to smack into the back of her head. Then all was blackness.

When the bartender bolted from the front door, waving his thin arms, Eddie "Rocks" Knox was ten yards down the street. Leaning on the trunk of an oak, picking his teeth with a sharpened matchstick. "Help . . . she's hurt bad," he screamed at anyone who might hear, "get some help!"

Provo Frank ran up the graveled alley, then cut across a lawn of freshly cut grass surrounding an 1880s three-story Victorian home. A bulldog barked and nipped ineffectively at his heels. The terrified Ute ran wildly. Maybe there were other police nearby, maybe they would shoot him down—now that he'd hit the lady cop. He sprinted down the street, checking parked cars as he went. All were locked. He spotted a pickup. It was not locked. And the keys were in the ignition!

Despite his wooden leg, Eddie was inside the Philly Bar and Grille in ten seconds flat. The young woman was on the filthy floor, flat on her back.

Her face was mashed and bloody. She was twitching, making soft mewing sounds, like a small animal. Like not-quite-finished roadkill. Eddie ordered the hysterical bartender to place the 911 call, then kneeled to administer first aid to the fallen officer. The woman had a pulse; bleeding wasn't too serious. That was about all the good news there was. He browbeat the shaken barman into giving him a rough description of the "suspect." Knox used the fallen officer's Motorola transceiver to call in a report on the man with the pigtail. The one-legged cop was thinking about chasing after Alicia's assailant when he heard the low wail of the ambulance siren.

Eddie stumbled outside the bar to meet the paramedics. Chief Parris' Volvo, far ahead of the ambulance, was turning the corner on two wheels. Eddie "Rocks" Knox was afraid of no man. But he had failed in his assigned duty, and the chief would be breathing fire. Instinctively he thought of escape. Eddie looked up the street toward where he'd left his big Dodge pickup.

It was gone.

❖

The chief of police stood just outside Officer Trainee Alicia Martin's cubicle. Parris didn't look toward the bed, where the young woman was connected to humming machines with yellow rubber tubes and insulated copper wires. Nourishment mixed with analgesic and antibiotics dripped from the IV into her punctured vein. The electrocardiogram made its pulsating spiked traces and beeped monotonously, like an out-of-tune cricket. Her head was bandaged up so that only mouth and nostrils were exposed. Intensive-care nurses wearing serious expressions scurried about. Officer Eddie Knox stood nearby.

Knox was looking at his shoes. The chief hadn't said a word to him. Not a word. And Knox was terribly ashamed that he'd not protected the young woman. If only the boss would give him a good cussing out, that'd be a lot better. Damn the man anyhow.

Lieutenant Leggett entered the Intensive Care Unit, nodding politely at the head nurse, who was annoyed at the crowd of cops underfoot.

Parris didn't look at Leggett either. Through thin lips, he said two words. "Tell me."

Leggett stood beside his chief and began his recitation. "FBI report came in ten minutes ago. Prints on the broken beer bottle are positive matches to military files. Suspect is one Mr. Provo Frank, of Bottle Hollow, Utah. We've put an APB out on . . . " He hesitated, not wanting to say, "Eddie's pickup." "On the stolen vehicle. No reports so far. He's already wanted in Wyoming for passing a bad check. Skipped from a motel in Bitter Springs."

The chief had clenched his big hands into white-knuckled fists. "Tell me about the car he left behind."

"It's an old Wagoneer. I've made a detailed list of the contents." He passed a thick sheaf of stapled papers to the chief.

Parris scanned the list and, despite his grim mood, almost grinned. The pedantic Leggett was thorough to the point of being comic. There were typewritten itemizations of Dentine gum wrappers, six peanuts, one cashew, eight bobby pins, and it went on. A half case of Quaker State 10W-30. "That old rattletrap must burn a lot of oil."

"It's pretty much a clunker, alright," Leggett said. "Leaks oil from the crankcase. Already dripped a puddle in the city garage. Muffler's pretty well shot too, and the shocks are gone." Leggett glanced slyly at Knox. "Guess he did need some new wheels."

Knox growled. Smart-assed kid, that's what Leggett was.

Parris turned to the second page. "This jewelry . . . it worth much?"

Leggett shook his head. "Nossir. Cheap stuff."

Parris turned to the third page and found the list of tools. An asterisk was placed by each item that was engraved with the initials PF.

One wood saw*
One hacksaw, three spare blades
Two pairs long-nose pliers
One pair wire cutters*
One pair gasoline pliers
One set wrenches, English
One set wrenches, metric
Two Craftsman adjustable wrenches, one 6" one 10"*
One tin snip*
One bolt cutter*
One copper-tubing flaring tool*
One 80 W soldering iron
One roll solder
Six screwdrivers (four standard blade, two Phillips)
Two wood chisels, one metal chisel
One carpenter's square
Three metal punches
Two steel measuring tapes (20' and 50')
One spirit level*
One wood plane*
One three-foot crowbar
One eighteen-inch crowbar

There was also an inventory of standard nails, roofing nails, carpenter's staples, wood and metal screws of various sizes, baling wire, rolls of tape, paintbrushes, and more of the like. Something about the list of tools was peculiar, but Parris couldn't quite put his finger on it. Parris returned the list to Leggett. "Anything interesting about the Frank vehicle?"

"Well, there are several dark spots, on the rear seat and floor. And on the back of the front seat."

Parris turned and glared at him. "Spots?"

Leggett looked thoughtful. "Blood, I'd say. Splattered. I've taken photographs. And removed some samples for forensics."

Parris was about to comment when Alicia's surgeon entered the Intensive Care Unit. "What's the verdict?"

The physician was a round-faced jolly man, who wore a perpetual smile. He glanced toward Alicia's bed, then lowered his voice. "Oh, she'll survive."

Parris' tone was hopeful. "Then she'll be okay?"

"Okay?" The surgeon rubbed at his sleepy eyes. "Not for a while. And her recovery won't be easy. Poor thing'll be eating through a straw for a month. Maybe two."

"She'll be in pain, then?"

The surgeon rubbed his hands together, as if they were cold. "This young lady will have to endure several more operations to repair the extensive damage to her jawbone and teeth. After that, she'll need a good plastic surgeon. I daresay she'll . . . uhh . . . suffer considerable discomfort. For quite some time. I assume she has sufficient insurance . . ."

Parris closed his eyes and ground his teeth. "Thank you."

The surgeon sensed that he was an outsider among this grim little tribe of lawmen; he excused himself and hurried away.

Parris' face was without expression, his voice soft, almost gentle. "Lieutenant—issue this notice to every member of the department. Without provocation, Mr. Provo Frank has assaulted one of my officers. He is to be considered extremely dangerous. I do not intend to have another officer injured by this . . . this suspect." He turned his head, to look Leggett square in the eye. "Do I make myself perfectly clear?"

Leggett started to quote the "book" to his boss, but he saw something cold and ruthless in the chief's eyes. He swallowed hard. "Yes, sir."

Eddie "Rocks" Knox also understood, and was immensely pleased. When they got this mean-assed bastard in their sights, they would take him down. The chief was an out-of-towner, a damned easterner from Chicago. But in spite of this, he was a stand-up guy. Tears of gratitude filled Eddie's eyes; he rubbed the bone handle of his .357 Magnum.

James D. Doss

✪ The Sugar Bowl Café ✪

Scott Parris sat across the table from his sweetheart. There were two mugs of steaming coffee between them. And more than that.

The chief of police had been out of bed before the sun came up, and midnight wasn't far off. He'd been exhausted until Anne had showed up in her little blue Miata. Now it was like always. There wasn't a tired bone in his body. Parris felt half his age. He felt like dancing. And he couldn't take his eyes off her face. Her face. In her best days, Elizabeth Taylor should've had a face like this. Waves of strawberry hair fell over her shoulders.

Anne took a tentative sip of her coffee, made a funny face, then stirred in half a packet of artificial sweetener. "It's terrible about that young woman."

"The man who did it is a Ute. I'll check with Charlie Moon; maybe he'll have a line on the bast . . . on the suspect." Parris wrapped his big hands around his coffee mug. It had been almost two years since he'd met Anne. In the police station. Sitting on that ugly green couch. Looking like a million bucks. No . . . her value had inflated since then. Make that ten million bucks.

Scott Parris cleared his throat.

She raised an eyebrow. *Yes,* her eyes said, *what's on your mind?*

He scratched at his chin. "You know . . ."

"Yes," her soft red lips said, "what's on your mind?"

He felt a strange sensation in the pit of his stomach. No. It wasn't strange. It was his old companion, the one who was always waiting just behind him. Fear.

"Anne . . ."

She reached across the red checkered oilcloth and touched his hand. Like a mother comforting a little boy. "Yes?"

"I . . . uh . . . got something for you."

She clasped her hands in delight. "A present?"

"Yeah." He fumbled in his jacket pocket, found it, then placed his hand over hers.

She withdrew her hand and stared at the small box. "Oh my . . ."

"Open it."

She did. "A ring."

"Yeah." He grinned like a little boy.

"A diamond ring. It's . . . it's beautiful."

"Yeah." He'd be making payments for eighteen months.

Her smile seemed oddly forced; a shadow passed across her face.

"If it isn't the one you want . . . well, we can go back to the jeweler's and you can pick one out."

Anne closed the velvet box. She frowned at her coffee. She poured half-and-half from a miniature crockery pitcher and stirred the milky swirl until the liquid was neither black nor white. Like his world—where everything was some indeterminate shade of gray. Being a policeman, he noticed little things. Like the fact that Anne Foster never used cream in her coffee.

"Anything you want to say?"

She wouldn't meet his eyes. "This is so . . . just so sweet of you . . . I just don't know what to say."

"I guess you already said it." He was achingly tired, to his marrow. And older than his years. He got up from his chair and dropped a couple of crumpled dollar bills on the checkered oilcloth.

She still didn't look up.

He rubbed a hand through his hair, which felt thin. Half a step before bald. "Guess I need to get some sleep." Old men needed their rest.

Now she looked at him. Her lovely face was drawn. Haunted. "You've had a hard day, Scott."

Anne hadn't call him "Scotty." He mumbled a good night, then turned on his heel and left the Sugar Bowl Café. His legs were numb, he didn't feel his feet hitting the floor. A small voice told him this: he'd just left the best part of his life behind. And he didn't know why.

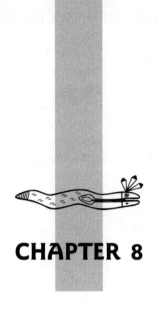

CHAPTER 8

Moon considered Scott Parris, who was riding in the Blazer next to him. It was funny. This *matukach*, like most of his kind, normally talked a blue streak. Well, not exactly a blue streak, but Parris generally grunted or said something every minute or so just to keep the silence at bay. For a taciturn Ute, that counted as a blue streak. Today the white man had not said a word since they'd left Ignacio. It could only be one thing. There was, after all, only one issue in Parris' life that would bring on this silent, reflective mood.

The Ute decided to go fishing.

"So," Moon said, "how's Anne doing these days?"

Parris grunted and looked out the Blazer window at nothing at all.

Moon remained silent for another mile, which amounted to another minute.

"So," Moon said, "how's Anne doing these days?"

"I thought," Parris grumped, "you'd never ask." He reached into his coat pocket and produced a folded envelope. He passed it over to Charlie Moon. "This was delivered to my office this morning. Along with an engagement ring I gave her last night."

The Ute pulled off onto the grassy shoulder of Route 151. He removed a single sheet of thin blue stationery from the envelope. At the top was the reproduction of a single red rose, and the name printed in large flowing script was Anne Foster. The Ute read the brief note.

Scott—
I'm sorry about last night. Can we talk?
Love you,
Anne

"Women," the Ute said sagely, "are hard to understand."

"Tell me about it."

This glum *matukach* sounded like he was about ready to cash in his chips and pull the sod over his chin. Moon dropped the note back into the envelope and passed it back to Parris. "So what're you gonna do, pardner?" The Ute cranked the engine and checked the rearview mirror before he pulled onto the highway.

"Do? I don't know." Scott Parris placed the envelope on the dashboard and stared at it. As if it were a poisonous snake, ready to fang him. In the heart. He turned to frown at the Ute, who was concentrating on the ribbon of oil-streaked pavement in front of the Blazer.

"Charlie?"

"Yeah?"

"Anne and me, we get along fine. Been seeing each other for a long time now. Why doesn't she want to marry me?"

"Why don't you ask her?"

Parris groaned. Served him right. Ask a damn fool question, get a damn fool answer.

Daisy Perika was washing the breakfast dishes when she heard the faint sound of an automobile approaching. She opened the little window over the sink and turned her best ear to listen.

Sarah looked up from her seat at the kitchen table, where she was finishing a small glass of milk. "Somebody coming, Aunt Daisy?"

Mr. Zigzag was on the floor, nibbling daintily at a small crust of lard biscuit clenched between his black paws.

The old woman closed her eyes and listened more intently. The rumbling sound was unmistakable. "It's Charlie. My big nephew." There was a ring of pride in her voice. "He's an important man . . . a big-shot policeman for the tribe." Charlie was driving a little faster than usual. Maybe it was about something important. Without a telephone, and with no more than a couple of visitors a week, a lot happened in Ignacio that she didn't hear about until it was old news.

Daisy dried her wrinkled hands on a frayed dish towel; she glanced at the child, who was rubbing the kitten's arched back. "You stay inside with that animal. I'll go out to meet Charlie."

The old woman made her way carefully down the porch steps; she waited several paces from the trailer. Without knowing how she knew, the shaman knew that whatever Charlie had to say, it would not be something for the child's ears. And Daisy also knew that Scott Parris would be in the Blazer with Charlie. In a dream last night, she had seen both of them coming down the lane.

Charlie Moon wasn't surprised. "There she is. Waiting for us."

"You think she'll know something about this Provo Frank?"

"Maybe. When he was a kid and got into trouble, he liked to hide out in *Cañón del Espíritu*. Aunt Daisy would give him food. She'd let him sleep in her trailer if it was too cold outside. But this was where he always headed."

"If he's here, Charlie . . . well, you know what he did to that young woman cop I hired."

Moon glanced across the Blazer at his grim-faced friend. Parris had blood in his eye. "If Provo's here, pardner, he's in my jurisdiction. I'll arrest him."

Parris didn't respond to this. His greatest desire was to break every bone in the man's face. Just for a start.

Moon braked the Blazer in the dirt lane that led to Daisy's trailer. The old woman stood still as a fence post, her arms folded. Waiting. The Ute policeman got out and took a quick look at the damp clay in her lane. There were familiar week-old tracks made by Gorman Sweetwater's pickup. But no trace of the mud tires on the pickup Provo had stolen from Eddie Knox.

Parris removed his hat and smiled at the old woman. "Mornin', Mrs. Perika."

Daisy nodded. "So the trouble I dreamed about. It's started."

Parris looked quickly at Moon, who avoided his friend's glance. "Well, we've had some trouble, alright. But I don't know if it's what you were expecting."

She raised her hand to protect her eyes from a sudden beam of sunlight that flashed through a break in the clouds. "Why'd you come out here to see me?"

Moon glanced at the trailer. For an instant he saw a face at the window. Nothing there now. If Provo was inside . . . The Ute's hand moved slightly closer to his holstered revolver. He didn't look at Parris as he spoke softly. "Somebody's inside, Scott. Move behind the car." Parris didn't give any outward evidence that he'd heard the Ute's instruction, but he ambled around the Blazer, kicking lazily at the tires. When he was behind the police car, he reached under his jacket for the .38.

Daisy, who hadn't heard Moon's words to his partner, watched all this with an expression of mild puzzlement. "What's goin' on, Charlie?"

Moon didn't look toward the trailer. "We're looking for Provo Frank. I want you to tell me straight—is he hiding out in your trailer?"

Daisy looked uncertainly at Parris, who was checking the cylinder on his .38. "No. But he left his little daughter here—her and her mangy little cat. Almost scared me into my grave, she did!"

Moon grinned. "It's okay, Scott. He's not here."

Parris holstered his .38 and left the protection of the Blazer. "You sure?"

"It was Provo's daughter," the Ute policeman said. "She's inside."

"If it's all the same to you two," Daisy said, "I'd just as soon nobody else knew the child was here with me."

Moon glanced toward the trailer. "For now, it's nobody's business." The less talk about him on the reservation, the more likely Provo would come back for his kid.

Parris leaned forward, his face close to Daisy's. "This Provo Frank, he darn near killed one of my officers up in Granite Creek. A young lady. Smashed her face up pretty bad."

Daisy knotted her brows. "That don't sound like Provo—he was always a nice little boy."

Moon frowned. "He's not a little boy anymore. If you know where he is, you'd best tell me."

Daisy hesitated, looking from one lawman's hard face to the other.

Her Ute nephew nodded toward his partner. "Scott and his friends are pretty upset. Just like I'd be if somebody came onto the reservation and beat up on one of our young women. If they catch Provo, I expect they'll kill him."

Significantly, Parris did not respond to this comment.

Daisy understood. It would be far better for the young man if Charlie arrested him on the reservation. "I can't help you. I never saw him. And the child don't know nothing either."

Moon glanced at the trailer. "Where's Mary Frank?"

Daisy shrugged. "In Arizona, down at Ak Chin, I guess."

"How do you know?" Parris asked.

"Well, that's what Provo told his little girl. When she woke up in the car, her momma wasn't with 'em. Her daddy told her that Mary went off on a bus, to take care of her father. I guess the old Papago is sick with something or other."

Moon turned and walked toward the Blazer. In a moment he had dispatcher Nancy Beyal on the radio. He gave her a set of instructions and waited until she patched him through. He chatted for a couple of minutes and then signed off.

Parris and Daisy had waited in tense silence while Moon made the call. The Ute slammed the Blazer door. "I talked to the Papago police in Ak Chin. Mary's father is healthy as a horse. In fact, he and his wife left on a vacation to see their son in Alaska. They're planning on coming back by way of California. Mary's mother always wanted to see Mickey Mouse in the flesh, so they're gonna stop off at Disneyland."

"So Provo lied to his daughter," Parris said.

Moon frowned. "Looks that way. But why?"

"Men," Daisy observed sagely, "don't need any big reason to lie. It comes natural to 'em."

"Could be," Moon said, "they had a spat about something. Mary may have just got on a bus and took off."

Parris wasn't buying this. "And left her daughter behind? I don't think so."

Daisy nodded in agreement. "No. I know Mary Frank pretty well. She'd never go off and leave her daughter. Not if she had anything to say about it."

At this comment, Parris stared hard at Charlie Moon. The Ute understood what his partner was saying with that silent look. "Thing is—" he directed his words to Daisy "—Scott's men found some blood in the old Wagoneer that Provo abandoned up in Granite Creek. FBI did some checking and found out that Mary gave blood at the Uintah-Ouray reservation last August. The blood in the car matches her type."

Daisy glanced toward the trailer, then at her big nephew. "Maybe Mary cut herself while she was in the car," she said hopefully. "I'm all the time cutting my hand on a tin can lid or with a knife."

"The blood," Parris said evenly, "was splattered about. A forensics expert from Denver says the pattern is consistent with blood ejected from an impact wound. The victim was probably standing very close to the rear door of the Wagoneer, which was open."

Daisy looked at Moon for a translation.

"It looks like somebody who was in or close to the Wagoneer got hit pretty hard," the Ute said. "The person whose blood was splattered around inside the car had the same blood type as Mary Frank. And now Mary is missing. Provo left Wyoming in a big hurry. And he's lied to Sarah about where Mary's supposed to be."

Daisy stood very still for a long time. And very silent. Finally she spoke. Almost in a whisper. "You want to talk to the little girl?"

Moon looked uneasily at Parris.

The *matukach* policeman hesitated; he wasn't eager to interview a little girl, not yet five years old, whose mother was missing. And whose father he very much wanted to kill. No, it didn't feel quite right.

"I guess we might as well do it," the Ute policeman said glumly.

They sat around the kitchen table. As soon as he'd seen the child, his intense hatred of Provo Frank began to cool. Despite what the bastard had done to Alicia, Scott Parris knew he couldn't break all the bones in the man's body. No, he could do no such thing to little Sarah's father. An arm or a leg maybe. And only if it was necessary to make an arrest.

Daisy poured coffee for the men; the child had a can of Pepsi.

Mr. Zigzag lapped happily at a dish of milk.

"So," Moon said, "did you have a nice vacation?"

Sarah nodded solemnly. "It was pretty nice. We went to a town called Bitter Creek. And stayed at a nice motel, while Daddy went away."

"How long was your daddy gone?"

"Oh, about one night. But almost two whole days. Mommy was *really* worried."

"Did your daddy say where he was going?"

She nodded. "To visit a funny old man. Daddy had a picture of him that he'd cut out of a newspaper."

"We didn't find anything like that in the Wagoneer," Parris said to Moon. "He must still have it on him."

Moon leaned close to the child. "Do you remember what the old man in the picture looked like?"

"Well, I guess he was awfully old." She looked at the Ute woman. "Almost as old as Aunt Daisy."

Daisy raised an eyebrow at the child. Parris hid a smile with a cough. Moon chuckled. "I guess he must have been about two hundred years old, then."

The old woman frowned at her nephew and muttered something he could not make out.

The child nodded. "And he had a mark over his eye, right here." She used her finger to draw an arc over her left eye.

Daisy frowned; this sounded familiar, but she couldn't quite remember why.

"Well," Moon said, "that's something to go on. Maybe we'll give it to the Wyoming police and see if they can learn who Provo went up there to visit with. It might help us figure out what his plans are."

"Daddy was going to meet the old man in a supermarket. Would it help," Sarah asked, "if I told you his name?"

For the first time since Alicia's assault, Parris laughed. "Yes, young lady. That'd help a lot."

"Daddy called him Blue Cup."

Daisy, who had been hunched forward in her straight-back chair, sat upright with a jerk. "Blue Cup?"

Moon frowned at his aunt. "Could it be that fellow who left Ignacio a long time ago? He'd be pretty old by now."

Daisy looked doubtful. "I thought he was dead." She turned to the child. "Why did your Daddy go to see this Blue Cup fellow?"

Sarah shrugged. "To get something from him, I think." She took a gulp of Pepsi, then bit a chunk off an Oreo cookie.

Moon leaned his elbows on the table, his hands clasped as if in prayer. "Sarah, I want you to tell us exactly what happened after your daddy got back to the motel. After he'd been off to visit Blue Cup."

She closed her eyes tightly, trying to remember. "Well, he was really happy. Daddy said he'd got what he went for, but Mommy was mad at him about his check and us being all by ourselves with nothing to eat but cheese sandwiches. They yelled a lot and I didn't want to hear it, so I put my hands over my ears and watched the TV." She looked shyly up at Scott Parris. "Do you like *Wheel of Fortune?*"

He smiled. "I think I've watched it a time or two."

"Well, I watched TV while they fussed. Then Daddy left. He banged the door real hard. Mommy went in the bathroom and cried. I cried some too. Then Mommy came and stood by the window. She was watching Daddy's car. The last thing I remember was Mommy said Daddy had come back, that he was in the car and she was going outside to talk with him. Then I guess I went back to sleep. I remember that Daddy came in and picked me up off the bed; he put me and Mr. Zigzag in the car and I went to sleep. I don't remember much until I woke up in the car with Daddy. It was light outside and Daddy said we were in Leadville."

"And where was your mommy, when you woke up in the car?"

Sarah shrugged again. "She was gone. Daddy said she had gone to Arizona, to take care of her daddy." She looked at the kitten, and her lower lip quivered. "I don't know why Mommy didn't take me with her."

❖

Scott Parris was silent while the Ute negotiated the rutted dirt road that led away from the mouth of *Cañón del Espíritu* toward the county-maintained gravel road. When they were on the blacktop of Route 151, the *matukach* lawman spoke. "This Provo Frank has assaulted one of my officers. Bashed her face in, for no reason at all. And ten to one, something real bad has happened to that little girl's mother."

Moon grunted. "There's a fine Mexican restaurant at Arboles. You want to stop for some burritos?"

"We've got to find this guy, Charlie. Nail his ass to the barn door."

"You like your burritos with red or green chile?"

"We could drive up to Wyoming. Talk to the highway patrol sergeant who put out the notice. Maybe even look up this old Blue Cup dude. Find out what Mr. Provo Frank was up to."

"I kind of prefer green myself." The Ute passed a slow tourist, who was intimidated by the SUPD Blazer. "Sometimes the red's too hot."

"Think you can get permission from Chief Severo to make the trip?"

"Maybe." Moon grinned at his friend. "You think we'd have time to drop a line in the Wind River? I hear they've got some whopper rainbows up there."

Parris pretended not to hear the Ute. "Guess I'll have red on my burrito. For some reason, green chile always makes me think of spinach."

"Ol' Popeye always ate his spinach," Moon observed. "And he was one hell of a sailor man. He always whipped that great big guy."

Parris chuckled. "Whatever you say, Bluto."

CHAPTER 9

Bitter Springs, Wyoming

Daphne was drying glasses with a greasy white cloth when, out of the corner of her eye, she noticed the Volvo pull to a stop in front of the First Chance Café. She thought it was significant that the two big men parked next to Harry's black-and-white, then had a long look at it. Their exhaled breath was frosty in the early morning chill, the wind whipped at their jackets. She watched them push through the heavy doors, then pause to sniff at the pleasant odors of bacon and sausage. These two fellows looked like they'd driven all night. They would be hungry, and a big meal usually meant a big tip.

She rewarded them with a smile that was genuinely cheerful. "What'll you have, gents? Coffee for starters?" She hoped they didn't ask for decaf. Only wimps and old ladies drank decaf, and neither class was good tippers. "We got a special on the biscuit-and-gravy plate with three eggs."

The very tall, dark one sat down on a stool in front of her and pushed his black Stetson back a notch. "That'll do for an appetizer, young lady. Then we'll have us some breakfast."

Daphne, who was no longer young and had never been a lady, raised a penciled eyebrow and put her hands on her hips in a gesture she thought seductive. "Now, you, honey, you're *my* kind of man." The waitress glanced around at the empty restaurant and performed a slight, comic bow to her prospective customers. "I'm Daphne, and I'll be your waitperson this mornin'.'" She pointed to the red name tag on her collar. "They call me Daffy."

"Well," Charlie Moon said with a straight face, "don't you pay no attention to 'em. You seem right as rain to me." He looked toward his "pardner" for confirmation of this diagnosis. Scott Parris nodded his solemn agreement.

Daphne slapped her thigh and haw-hawed. "You must be that Injun feller Harry told me was comin' all the way here to see him. Harry said you was a card."

Moon admitted that he was, indeed, "that Injun feller."

Scott Parris blinked sleepily and ordered dry toast and black coffee.

The waitress's tone expressed her disapproval. "That's *all?*"

Parris grudgingly allowed as how maybe he could eat one scrambled egg.

Daphne, who knew a man this size couldn't last until lunch on just one egg, wrote "2 SE" on her order pad.

Moon made a decision for the special. With four fried eggs, over easy. And home fries. And extra biscuits, and heavy on the gravy. And a chicken-fried steak on the side.

Daphne grinned, exposing a mouthful of large teeth; she shouted the orders toward a long rectangular opening behind the counter. A small man's bald head popped up in the window. Gumpy began the ritual that was hidden from the customers. With his right hand he broke a half dozen eggs onto the sizzling griddle. With his left he dropped sliced bread into the toaster and slid a pan of "made from scratch" biscuits into a preheated oven.

The Ute turned slightly on the stool and looked over his shoulder. "Them Harry's wheels parked outside?"

"Yes, them's his, alright. He's been waitin' for you boys, honey. Harry's sittin' back there on the throne, prob'ly readin' his *Wall Street Journal.*"

At that moment Harry MacFie emerged from the door marked MEN. He grunted as he fastened the silver buckle on his heavy gun belt over a hint of middle-aged belly. "Well, what've we got here? I do declare, it looks like Ossifer Charlie Moon."

Parris turned on his stool and blinked. MacFie was about five ten, clad in a tan uniform. The lawman's skin was pale and weathered, like cracked eggshell. Orange freckles dotted his round face, and were scattered like a pox over his thick neck and under the blond hair on his heavy forearms. His eyes were bright blue, and piercingly clear.

Among the Shoshone, it was rumored that this lawman's blue eyes had extraordinary powers. No one could see so far . . . or see things that were so small.

The Ute introduced Parris, who shook the Wyoming policeman's sun-burned hand.

Harry MacFie straddled a stool and pushed his shiny belt buckle against the counter. "Daffy, get my fellow officers whatsoever they want." He nodded nonchalantly toward the Ute. "Charlie will pay."

"The wind," Parris muttered almost to himself, "it always blow like this?"

Moon poured sugar into his black coffee. "They don't call it wind up here till it's over thirty-five miles an hour."

MacFie looked out the window, squinted, and judged the wind velocity from the angle of a flimsy Russian olive that leaned hard to the east. About twenty-five miles an hour, he thought, maybe just a tad more.

Parris rubbed his hands together, then wrapped them around the hot coffee mug. "It's not winter yet, but it feels cold enough to snow." The worst coldness came from inside.

MacFie swallowed a grin and a gulp of steaming coffee. "In these parts, it can snow any day of the year, and does." He scratched at the stubble of beard on his chin. "Five years ago, it was on the Fourth of July, I was over to Rawlins to pick up a prisoner from the sheriff. Well, I can tell you, by noon we had us a regular blizzard. Five or six inches of powder on the level, two or three feet in the drifts." He saw a doubtful look pass over Parris' face, and quickly rose to the challenge. "And most summers it never does get warm enough to melt the snow. The wind . . ." He paused and listened to the tempest whistling and moaning over the pitched roof of the restaurant. ". . . the wind just plumb wears it out."

Daphne swiped at the spotty countertop with a greasy rag and nodded. "That's the honest truth. It's from the wind blowin' the snow on the rocks, I guess. By mid-May the flakes is like cornmeal, by June it's about like face powder, by the first of July it's ground down to almost nothing at all. Just little white specks mixed with the dust so's you don't hardly notice it."

MacFie nodded his approval and reminded himself to leave Daffy a dollar tip today. He ordered the Rancher's Breakfast with scrambled eggs and pork sausage. And buttered toast.

Scott Parris ate his toast in moody silence while the happy Ute and the Wyoming cop exchanged lively accounts about the weather in Wyoming and southern Colorado. His thoughts were not on the weather; the sweet picture of a redheaded woman was sharply focused in his mind's eye. He wondered whether Anne was having breakfast. Whether she had brushed her hair.

"Over at the Riverton airport," MacFie said after a gulp of scalding coffee, "they use a twelve-foot logging chain for a windsock. When that chain's pretty near straight out, the control tower orders them planes to head into the wind and it takes about a half hour to land. But when that ol' chain snaps and plum blows away to Nebraska, and it happened twice last year, why, we send them jet planes down to land in Denver, 'cause you never have no real winds in Colorado."

"Well," the Ute said dryly, "I'd have to admit one thing. The wind sure has picked up here in the past few minutes."

"I hate to interrupt all this creative lying," Parris said amiably, "but we drove all the way up here to do some police work."

MacFie slapped the countertop. "Right you are, my good man." He winked at Daphne. "Let's leave this five-star restaurant and this beautiful woman and go outside into the harsh weather."

They followed MacFie's big Ford black-and-white along the four-lane that sliced through the dry heart of Bitter Springs. As they left the western edge of town, the landscape became bleak to the Ute, who was accustomed to the sweet land between the Animas and the Piedra. Parris was also affected; the stark nothingness reminded him of his own emptiness. He wondered where Anne Foster was right now. What she was doing.

They pulled to a stop in front of the City Limits Motel. Parris looked over the cinder-block building at the long, rocky ridge. This north side was streaked with windswept snow, spotted with dried tufts of buffalo grass, a half dozen stunted piñon trees. A godforsaken place, he thought. The motel had a couple of customers. Both of the vans had California plates. Probably they were traveling together.

Aggie's Cadillac convertible was parked outside the office. So she'd be inside at the reception desk. Or cleaning up the rooms.

The Colorado lawmen joined MacFie; the Wyoming policeman was leaning on the fender of his dust-streaked Ford. He grabbed his hat to save it from a sudden gust of wind; Moon and Parris copied this precaution.

"From what we've learned from the little girl," Moon said, "her mom and dad had a big fight. Mr. Frank left. To get himself a drink, I imagine."

"He could've driven into town," MacFie said. "But right over there's the closest place he could've gone to." The highway patrolman pointed west, toward the Pynk Garter Saloon.

"He didn't use his automobile," Parris said. "Sarah Frank said her mom was waiting by the window. According to the kid, Mrs. Frank was watching the Wagoneer when she saw her husband return. Evidently he got inside the car. Maybe for shelter from the snowstorm. She went outside to have a talk with him. The girl went to sleep after that. Next thing she knows, her father picks her up and drives away. They're all the way down to Leadville before she wakes up and finds out her mother isn't in

67

the car. Provo tells the kid that her momma's taken a bus to Arizona to take care of her sick father. That turns out to be a bald-faced lie. After he assaulted one of my officers and stole a pickup truck, we confiscated the Wagoneer and found blood splattered in the back seat and on the door. Blood type matches Mrs. Frank."

The Wyoming policeman shook his head. "That don't sound good. I had no idea this was anything more than a bad check. Although—" he scratched at his sunburned neck "—It did seem odd, they way they ske-daddled and left so much of their clothes and stuff in the motel room."

Parris glanced quickly at his Ute friend. "They leave any men's clothes behind?"

MacFie frowned. "Now that you mention it, what was left was mostly women's things. I guess he took his own stuff with him."

A dark expression crept over Moon's face. "So he left Mary's clothes behind?"

"And a bunch of cosmetics, hairpins, a hairbrush . . . you know, wom-en's stuff."

"Sounds like he knew she wouldn't be needing it anymore," Parris said. "Is the family's property still in the motel room?"

"Nope. I had no idea this was going to turn out to be an important investigation. Aggie made me clean it out. I got it all boxed up, stored over at my office."

"Who's Aggie?" Moon asked.

MacFie nodded toward the office. "The City Limits Motel is owned by Aggie and Billy Stymes. Aggie runs the place. Mostly all Billy does is drink beer and watch TV. And feed grapes to his raven."

Moon looked toward the motel office. "He keeps a raven for a pet?"

MacFie nodded. "Yeah. And Billy's kind of an odd bird himself. Few years back, he was accused of thievin' by some guests. But the missing stuff turned up and I didn't have no case against him."

"What was he accused of stealing?" Parris asked.

"Camera, as I recall. And a pearl necklace. But the tourists went back to their room after they went to file a complaint with the town police, and the stuff was there. Town cops turned it over to us state boys, 'cause the City Limits Motel ain't quite inside the city limits, if you see what I mean."

Parris buttoned his jacket around his neck. "Any complaints about Billy since then?"

"Nary a one. I figure he's pretty harmless."

"Maybe," Moon said, "somebody else was out by the car. When Mary Frank thought she was going to see her husband. Maybe she surprised somebody . . . and got hurt."

"If it happened like that," MacFie asked reasonably, "why would Mr. Frank run away? Why wouldn't he report it?"

The Ute had no answer for that.

"We have to bunk somewhere tonight," Parris said to Moon. "You want to get a couple of rooms here?" It looked inexpensive. Cheap, actually.

The Ute nodded. "Anyplace is fine with me, pardner. I'm so tired I could sleep on a pile of rocks."

MacFie slapped Moon on the back. "First I'll introduce you to Aggie. Billy won't come away from his TV. Then we'll walk over to the Pynk Garter and find out if Mr. Frank had himself a drink that night."

"Provo," Moon said sadly, "never had just *one* drink."

The interview with Aggie Stymes had been short and fruitless. Well, almost fruitless. They'd had the opportunity to watch Billy Stymes feed seedless grapes to the talking raven. The sly bird had cocked its head at Moon and squawked: "Way to go, cowboy. Where is it? Where is it?"

MacFie, who loved to hear the bird talk, had offered the raven a bite of his Snickers candy bar.

Billy, who apparently considered such food unsuitable for his precious raven, had hustled the bird off into his bedroom. Aggie had sullenly answered questions about the Frank family. She'd not been pleased that they had a daughter. "Rather not have guests with kids," she'd said as she inhaled lungfuls of cigarette smoke. "The little snots generally leave a mess for me to clean up."

The Colorado lawmen were happy to leave the dank air of the motel office. Billy and Aggie Stymes, MacFie observed upon leaving, were not exactly your "Ozzie and Harriet" family. Because MacFie loathed walking, they drove the short distance to the saloon.

MacFie led the way to a booth. It was a Saturday, and business in the Pynk Garter Saloon was brisk. The clientele, MacFie observed, was mostly young and unwashed. Mostly from the town, although some of the faces were unfamiliar to the Wyoming lawman. The presence of the highway patrolman noticeably quieted the murmur of the crowd.

MacFie grinned sideways at his friends. "This remind you of an old movie?"

"Yeah," Parris said. "Except the saloon usually gets quiet when the bad guys come in."

"As far as this bunch of yahoos is concerned," MacFie said proudly, "I am the number-one bad guy."

A slender woman in black got up from a table in a dark corner; her hips swayed as she walked toward their booth. Parris noticed the some-what muscular arms, the broad shoulders. He wondered idly whether this woman was taking some kind of male hormones. But when she got close, he realized that this was a very feminine creature.

Her eyes quickly appraised the newcomers, but she spoke to the highway patrol officer. "Hi, MacFie."

"Hi yourself, Lizzie. These are my buddies from down in Colorado." He nodded toward each man. "Charlie Moon and Scott Parris."

"Cops," she said with a slight grimace.

"How'd you know?" Parris asked.

"Birds of a feather. Nobody but another cop would hang out with MacFie." She put her hands on her hips. "You guys here for business or pleasure?"

MacFie grinned at his companions. "A little of both. I'll have a Coors. What about you guys?"

"I'll have a Pepsi," Moon said.

"Pepsi for me too," Parris said. "But make it a diet. No caffeine."

"Jeepers," Lizzie said with a little laugh, "MacFie is consorting with a couple of Mormons."

The big Ute was staring at the woman's black skirt. It was slit on both sides to an interesting location. About three inches above the knee.

She could read his simple mind. Lizzie put her slender hand on Moon's big paw. "You're wondering," she said softly, "about the name of this place. And whether I'm wearing a pink garter."

Moon nodded dumbly.

MacFie was grinning ear to ear; Parris blushed for his friend.

"Well, I am," Lizzie whispered in Moon's ear. "The question is—on which leg?" Very slowly, the woman began to lift the skirt. One inch. Then two.

The Ute was transfixed. MacFie had lost his grin, Parris was bug-eyed.

She dropped the skirt. "Put a twenty on the table," she said to Moon. "You guess which leg's got the pink garter, you get a free look. If you're wrong, I keep the twenty."

Moon grinned boyishly at the proprietor of the Pynk Garter Saloon. "How do I know I can trust you? You could claim I guessed wrong and keep my money."

"Shame on you for not trusting me." She tugged playfully at his ear. "Tell you what, honey. If you guess wrong, you get to see the *black* garter."

Moon was thinking about it . . . but this was such a *public* place.

Lizzie caressed his cheek with the tips of her fingers. "I love big, shy men." She turned to the local cop. "But I don't cotton to little redheaded woodpeckers. You don't come around except you intend to harass me, MacFie."

With some effort, the Scotsman pulled his stare away from the long, provocative slit in her black skirt. She'd put him in a bad mood. "Tuesday night, last week," he barked. "A man by the name of Provo Frank walked up here from the City Limits Motel. Had himself a few, then went back to the motel. Left without paying his bill." It was a shot in the dark, but if he'd asked her whether Frank had been in the place, she'd have denied it. Lizzie didn't like cops in her joint. Except, maybe, for this big Ute. MacFie felt a mild surge of jealousy.

Lizzie's face went flat, like her dark eyes. "If you know all of that, what do you want from me?"

"Wanted you to tell us what you could about this fellow." MacFie smiled and tried to sound reasonable. "What he had to drink. What he had to say. Anything you can remember."

Lizzie shrugged. "I don't remember anybody like that."

"Like what?" MacFie asked. His tone was still friendly, but there was a cold glint in his blue eyes.

"Like . . . whatever you said. A young fellow with . . . I don't remember."

"I never told you he was young, Lizzie. Never told you anything except that he was a man. Now, how can you be so damn sure you don't remember him?"

"I just figured, with so many customers . . ."

"It was on a Tuesday night, Lizzie. This place is quiet as a tomb on a Tuesday. If you had five customers, I'll eat my hat."

Her eyes were darting from one lawman's face to another. Why had MacFie brought in out-of-state cops? And the biggest one was dark, like the man they were asking about. "I just can't remember everyone who comes in here, MacFie. They all look pretty much alike. Maybe," she said, "if you had a picture . . ."

Moon pulled a half dozen photos from his jacket pocket. Three were of Mary Frank. The woman said she didn't recognize them. He gave her a picture from Provo's high school yearbook. It was fifteen years old, but still a good likeness. Provo was a man who didn't age all that quickly.

Lizzie cocked her head and seemed to be trying to remember. "Could be he came in. But I'm not sure what night it was. Maybe Sam will remember."

MacFie nodded. "Let's ask him."

Lizzie jerked her head at Sam; he hiked up his red suspenders with his thumbs and ambled around from behind the bar.

He didn't look at the lawmen. "What's up, Lizzie?" He slung a wet bar towel over his shoulder.

She put the picture in his hand. "MacFie wants to know whether somebody looking like this guy came in last week. On a Tuesday night. He looks familiar, but I'm not sure."

Sam studied the photograph. "This could be a guy . . . Yeah, I think it's him. Liked his Coors."

"How many beers he have?" Moon asked.

Fat Sam caught a meaningful look from Lizzie. "Just one."

Moon's eyes narrowed. Since he was fifteen years old, Provo Frank never had just *one* beer. And since he was twenty-one, he'd preferred hard liquor.

MacFie was pleased. "Now, that's good, Sam. What else do you remember?"

The fat bartender closed his eyes in concentration, evidently straining to recall that Tuesday evening. "Well, the wind was blowing pretty hard. We talked some . . . about the weather. Sports, maybe, I'm not sure. He wasn't much of a talker. Didn't stay long. I guess he must have left a little after dark."

The conversation was interrupted by a muscular young man with a fuzzy beard. He sidled up to Lizzie and put his hand on her hip. "Hiya, honey. You with anybody?"

She smiled coldly at the out-of-towner. "I own the place, sonny. Now, get your hand off my behind."

Sam showed no interest in the youth; a slow grin was spreading across Harry MacFie's freckled face. Moon and Parris were rising from their seats in the booth, but the drunk seemed unaware of this dual menace.

"Relax, fellows. I can handle this little boy." Lizzie smiled sweetly at the bearded man. "One last chance, Gomer. Unless you're a lizard and can grow yourself a new paw, move it."

He let his hand drop down to her thigh. The young man opened his mouth to say something clever, but the words never passed his lips. It happened so fast that the lawmen would argue later about exactly how she did it. The result, however, was not in dispute. In a flash, Lizzie had the bearded drunk by the forearm; his wrist was pressed against the small of his back. Simultaneously her left hand made a small, knotty fist and rammed hard against his kidney. He slumped to the floor with a groan; his head made a hard thump on the varnished hardwood. Lizzie, her fist poised, waited a moment in case he attempted to get up. He didn't.

"You think we should lend a hand?" Moon muttered to Parris.

"She seems to be doing alright," the Granite Creek lawman said.

"Oh, I ain't worried about *her*. I'm concerned about that poor feller on the floor." The Ute chuckled. "I figure maybe the two of us could hold her offa him. And if MacFie ain't afraid to take her on, why, the three of us would have an even chance of fightin' her to a draw."

"Include me out," MacFie said with upraised palms.

Sam, who seemed unmoved by the incident, grabbed the drunk by the collar. He dragged the limp body to the door and tossed it into the parking lot. All in a night's work. A couple of sheepish buddies eased the groaning man into the back of a Toyota pickup and threw a dirty horse blanket over him. They revved the little four-cylinder engine and, to prove their manhood, left a spray of airborne gravel in the pickup's wake.

Moon and Parris watched from their seats in the booth.

"Now, that," Moon said with genuine appreciation, "is some kind of woman."

"Lizzie," MacFie agreed thoughtfully, "she's not your everyday female." No, but she was a woman that he'd like to know more about. A lot more.

At sundown Moon and Parris stood outside the City Limits Motel with MacFie. The lawman zipped his leather jacket against the frigid wind, which had shifted to the southwest. "Well, whaddayou boys want to do tomorrow morning?"

"Let's meet for breakfast," Moon said.

MacFie looked toward the east. "Same place as this morning?"

"It'll do," the Ute said. He liked the waitress. And the large helpings.

The Wyoming policeman nodded; he looked sideways at his big Ford; the engine was idling. He longed for the warmth inside. "What then?"

"Then," Parris said, "we'd like to have a talk with this old Ute fellow that Provo Frank came up here to visit."

"Blue Cup," MacFie said glumly. "Yeah. I know where he lives."

Scott Parris leaned on the counter and eyed the sullen woman until her rude stare wavered. He glanced at the varnished pine slab mounted on the paneled wall behind her. On the board was a row of heavy, blackened nails. Except for the room Moon had rented, each nail held three keys. Parris asked for the room the Frank family had occupied. He watched the woman's slack jaw stiffen.

Aggie Stymes remembered her oafish husband's superstitious pronouncement about Unit 11. Snake-eyes, he'd said. A hard-luck room. She hesitated momentarily, then relented. Aggie grunted as the office door closed behind the Colorado man.

Maybe, Parris thought as he turned the key in the tarnished brass lock, he'd find something helpful . . . some little trace of this family left behind.

A cursory search revealed nothing of the Franks in the shabby motel room.

He sat down on the bed, exhausted. On this particular night, the lawman would sleep well enough. But soon he *would* find something the Franks had left behind. Something awful. Something precious. Then his weary soul would long for rest.

And find none.

CHAPTER 10

Saturday evening

For an instant the scarlet sun rests on a shimmering blue pedestal . . . a flat-topped mountain called Crowheart Butte by the Shoshone. When the earth has rotated for another two minutes and eight seconds, this nearest star will vanish behind the scarlet horizon.

✦

In this canyon of many colors, near the Wind River reservation of the Shoshone, the old shack leans comfortably against the massive trunk of a bent cottonwood that trembles and rattles as it dies a slow death. Parked beside the hut, shaded under the tired branches of the tree, is an antique U.S. Army Jeep.

The dwelling has a single door, mounted on rusted hinges. There is no window.

Inside the crude log cabin, the furnishings are sparse and selected for utility. A fifty-gallon drum set on cinder blocks by the north wall serves as a makeshift furnace and an oven to roast quail and cottontail. Smoke is vented sideways; the sooty stovepipe points like a cannon barrel through a mud-plastered hole sawed in the log wall. A rusty kerosene lantern hangs by a twisted copper wire from a dark ceiling where patient spiders cast their lacy nets for unwary blue bottlefly and frogeye moth.

On the north wall is a rude shelf; on this shelf are a few books. The most read book is a worn paperback copy of *Black Elk Speaks*. There are leather-bound volumes of Poe, Kipling, and volume II of *The Pocket University*, a small book about great journeys. There is a copy of *Mahler—His Life and His Music*. One book is displayed quite prominently. It is a hiker's guide to Wyoming's Wind River Range. The aged occupant of the cabin has no need of such a guide; he knows the sunlit trails of these rugged mountains far better than he knows the winding pathways of his soul. But he had to have this particular book because the author's picture is on the cover—she is exceptionally pretty. She is a *matukach*, but something about her . . . the smile . . . the eyes . . . reminds the old man of someone . . . a pretty Ute girl who had melted his heart. But that was decades ago. Another lifetime. There are no framed photographs of relatives on the shelf—there is no family that the occupant cares to remember. There is no calendar on the wall—for this old Ute, April is the Moon of Grass Is Tender; November, the Moon of Dead Leaves Falling. It is enough.

A redwood picnic table dominates the middle of the room. The centerpiece of the table is a green Coleman camper's stove. On the two-burner stove is a blackened iron skillet and a well-smoked coffeepot. A place is set at the table for the occupant: a thin china plate painted in the Japanese style with fantastically delicate songbirds, an enameled tin cup, a meager assortment of steel flatware. Every implement is clean and tidy and serves its purpose.

The only nod to modern civilization is a portable radio, and this device is always tuned to the same FM station in Riverton. When the batteries have sufficient charge, the cabin is filled with strains of flute and violin and piano. Galway . . . Menuhin . . . Rubinstein.

Mounted on the rear wall is a shelf. Mounted upon the wall above the shelf is a wooden crucifix; the wooden cross is surrounded by an eclectic assembly of religious objects. Under the altar-shelf is a simple bed made of unpainted pine boards. On this wooden structure is a lumpy homemade mattress—it is a yellowed cotton sheet that has been stitched around its edges to make a rectangular sack. Inside the mattress, making their bivouac in sheaves of dried buffalo grass, are an army of black fleas, a regiment of juniper mites, and battalions of other microscopic creatures that have not been named by humankind.

Stretched across the grass tick is the thin, almost emaciated body of an elderly man. His coarse hair is spread like a black fan on the crude mattress; the soles of his thin feet are caked with the orange dust of this canyon called Cradle of Rainbow Lizard.

The insects who live in the mattress do not dare to come out to nibble at his skin. An orange digger wasp whines its meandering way near to hover menacingly over his forehead—and is momentarily tempted. But the wary insect circles twice around his face, then makes a droning retreat to a dark sanctuary among the rafters.

This is no ordinary man.

The Ute shaman's eyes are tightly closed, his thin blue lips barely parted, his wrinkled hands folded carefully across a hairless chest. If the breath of life does flow through the old man's lungs . . . it is not revealed by the slightest motion of his rib cage.

But, despite appearances, Blue Cup is not dead.

Neither does he sleep.

But dream—if it can be called dreaming . . . this he does.

In his vision, the shaman sees three men. They will visit him when the sun is high over the dark profile of Crowheart Butte. Two of the men are *matukach*; the smallest of the pale men is known to him. This is the lawman with the clear blue eyes that have the power to see farther than the eyes of ordinary men. The other *matukach* is a stranger . . . but a man to be reckoned with. This man can hear what others do not hear . . . the voices of the spirits.

The third man, the very large one . . . he is one of the People!

The shaman feels a peculiar buzzing sensation at his throat, as if a great horsefly rests on his neck and hums its brutish insect song. Now an oppressive weight—like a great hand—seems to press the old man against the thin mattress. There is a ripping sensation as the shaman's spirit-body departs from its tent of flesh.

The old Ute's lonely spirit drifts always southward . . . to hover above the bright land of his birth . . . to walk through *Cañón del Espíritu* where his mother's bones are buried . . . to taste the sweet waters of the cool rivers. Someday, his spirit sings, the wanderer will return to this place and remain here . . . forever and forever.

But first he must redeem himself with his people.

☼ Sunday, 10:30 A.M. ☼

It had been a bone-jarring drive after they left the blacktop behind. The highway patrol officer had left his black-and-white in Bitter Springs; he'd brought his own "Wyoming Cadillac"—a big four-wheel-drive Chevy pickup—for this foray into the back country. For most of an hour they had followed MacFie's dust over flat, windswept ranchland. The prairies were covered with blue grama grass that was interrupted with occasional tufts of hardy buffalo grass. The latter plant's tiny seeds are concealed inside spiny husks that attach themselves to the bison's shaggy fur. It was a wonderfully symbiotic arrangement for beast and for plant. Everywhere the American buffalo traveled, they had carried the seeds for the creation of lush new pastures.

Now the road slipped off the prairie into a depression bathed in the long shadows of great mesas. It was cooler here, but the winds were not so fierce. Moon stared at talus slopes on each side, these skirts of mammoth mesas that stretched for miles toward the granite peaks. The grasses that had covered the prairie were sparse in this place, but there was no shortage of sagebrush. Nestled against the side of sandstone boulders, occasional clumps of blue columbine displayed a five-petaled white flower above a larger pale purple underblossom. Thick patches of yellow mountain gumweed clung tenaciously to the disturbed soil along the lane.

Scott Parris took his time maneuvering the Volvo around deep ruts and under overhanging branches of hardy juniper and the dry, rustling leaves of Russian olive. MacFie bounced far ahead in his four wheel-drive-pickup; they could see only a remnant of yellow dust hovering over the trail.

As they entered the southern foothills of the Wind River Mountains, the lane was a pair of barely discernible tire tracks. They climbed narrow ridges, crossed dry stream beds. Parris had second thoughts about the wisdom of bringing the Volvo into this wilderness. They should have crowded into the pickup with MacFie. After a half-hour crawl when the Volvo speedometer barely bounced off the zero peg, they seemed to be approaching a wall of solid rock. The road was sandy, but at least there were no ruts. Parris slowed; he carefully nosed the Volvo around a tilted escarpment of basalt and entered the mouth of the multicolored canyon.

Among the many remarkable crevasses in the pleated skirts of the Wind River Range, there is not another quite like this. The remarkable feature is the dazzling multitude of colors. The sand-laden winds have exposed layers of bright hues on the sheer walls of the gorge. Near the top of the cliff, under a few feet of Eocene oil shale, there are three yards of deep blue clay. A sulfurous orange sediment interspersed with a dozen layers of pale yellow bentonite is compressed in the center of the sandwich, a remnant of Cretaceous volcanism to the west. But the most striking structure lies at the bottom of the cliff. More than two hundred feet of fiery red Jurassic sandstone supports the base of the rainbow. This red band, saturated with oxide of iron, appears to be perpetually moist . . . seeping great drops of rusty blood. But, like much that one sees in the Wind River Range, this is an illusion. The crimson sandstone is dry as talcum until late in June, when great booming thunderstorms slip down from the snow-streaked peaks of the Winds. Then underground springs feed moisture into the minute cracks of the red stone and it becomes the primitive artist's crimson palette. The place has that stark, lonely appearance of never having seen the presence of human beings. But appearances are . . . merely appearances.

❖

As the most recent glacier was receding, six families of human beings came into this canyon. They were seeking shelter from the winter gales that howl in the barren foothills of the mountains that would, nine thousand years later, be called the Wind River Range. These hardy people, who had migrated from the endless and dismal pine forests to the north, were in awe of the layered tints of the canyon walls. The oldest woman of the tribe, who had been blind for many years, had seen this wonderful place in a dream. Though she had to be led along the trails with a braided rawhide rope around her waist, the woman had directed her people to this land. Once here, they described the wonderful colors that she would never see with her physical eyes. At first sundown, her agile grandson caught an unusual lizard. He climbed onto her lap and told his grandmother about the colored stripes on the back of these black reptiles that darted among the crevices in the rocky wall, and how these stripes resembled the bright colors on the cliff itself.

She had been told in her dream that a child would reveal the name for the place where her bones would rest forever.

While her grandson still sat on her lap, the old woman pronounced this to be a sacred place. She also gave it a name that would be repeated for millennia. Three days later, she died and was buried under a slab of sandstone on the floor of the canyon. Her bones have long since turned to dust. No one remembers her name. This nomadic tribe of mammoth hunters had no formal name, and their story of courage and hardship is lost in the dark mists of prehistory.

Only two signs remain as evidence that they ever existed.

The most conspicuous was a long, delicately flaked flint spearpoint found by a hiker in a deep wash after an August thunderstorm. The other remnant of the mammoth hunters, a gift of the elder, is the name of this place. A few still remember that this canyon has always been called Cradle of Rainbow Lizard.

The Arapaho and the Bannock shaman would come to this canyon to leave their red handprints on the face of the sandstone boulders, a sign of secret vows. They would call upon the Striped Lizard for power to kill the cruel, fearless Spanish invaders. Much later, they would divine up spells to thwart those slightly mad, foul-smelling, hairy-faced trappers who came for no other purpose than to kill all the beaver. And for making hats!

The fierce Crow warriors would come to mix the iron ochre with cold water from a small spring. They would paint their faces with scarlet stripes before they went to make war against anyone at all, but preferably against the hated Bannock or Shoshone.

The Shoshone, who have a more lurid view of this forbidden site, refused to give voice to the old name. When they refer to it at all, it is in whispers. They call it "a bad place to stay away from."

Blue Cup is a Ute. The *Núuci* are a most practical people, not given to dramatics. He calls this place "home."

❖

Parris was pleased that the road was now a broad, smooth expanse of solid rock. Within a few hundred yards, the lane came to an abrupt end at a cluster of gaunt cottonwoods.

Under their leaves that rattled in the breeze, MacFie was leaning against the tailgate of his dusty pickup. The pale man was idly picking his teeth with a dry piñon needle. Scott Parris pulled the Volvo to a stop behind MacFie's dusty pickup; Charlie Moon was unfolding his long frame from its cramped position before his friend had switched off the ignition.

The cabin was placed on a fingerlike peninsula of the same sandstone that made the road the equal of the best asphalt in Wyoming. Moon was astonished at the beauty of the remarkable natural pavement. The overwhelming impression was of cleanliness; except for an occasional ripple of scarlet, the variegated pink sandstone was without spot or blemish. The cabin was set on a half-acre flat oval of this stone carpet; it was so spotlessly clean that a man felt like he ought to wipe his boot soles off before taking a step. It was as if someone regularly swept the porous sandstone clean. And someone did. The relentless Wyoming winds were still forming the canyon floor, scouring away the sandstone, another millimeter every year. At the edge of this immaculate escarpment, the sandy soil supporting the pines and cottonwood was a brilliant orange-red. Looking at this too long, Moon thought, could hurt a man's eyes.

Scott Parris pushed the Volvo door ajar with his boot and got out to stretch. He stood very still and digested the scene before him. Blue Cup's home was in a wide draw between a pair of low, rock-strewn ridges that supported a scattered forest of thirsty piñon and juniper. Beyond these ridges, the vertical canyon walls were painted with wide bands of moist red, pale yellow, and, near the summit of the mesas, a deep blue. A rocky stream bed supported a trickle of water connecting a few shallow pools. Like turquoise nuggets strung on a necklace. There would be a few hungry trout in those pools, waiting for an unwary insect to touch the surface of the water. Or, Parris mused, a hand-tied fly. His thoughts turned to the fishing rods packed in the Volvo trunk.

Harry MacFie walked toward them slowly; he was bent slightly forward at the waist, like an old man suffering from back pain. The Wyoming highway patrolman had removed his canvas hat and rubbed at a bald spot that was sunburned and peeling. MacFie waved his hat toward the log shack. "Far as I know, guys, this's the dump where Blue Cup hangs his hat." The three men stared at the small cabin. It had a pitched roof of dark pine shingles that had oozed globs of pitch. The structure leaned on a large cottonwood; a stovepipe jutted horizontally from the north wall. A rusty Jeep was parked in the shade of the aged tree, which sighed a death rattle as a breeze pulled at its limbs.

Moon leaned back and stared at the multicolored cliffs. "This place on the Wind River reservation?"

"Nope." MacFie scratched idly at his neck, as if the infestation of orange freckles were crawling on his skin. "National forest land. I think the guv'mint built the cabin for hikers and such." He responded to Moon's raised eyebrows. "Strictly speaking, the old man's a squatter."

"Why haven't the feds evicted him?" Parris asked.

MacFie shrugged. "I heard they've wrote up the papers on him. And warned him to get off." His eyes darted about. "But you know how slow the guv'mint works . . . he'll probably still be here ten years from now."

The Ute studied the cabin's single door. The desiccated wood paneling was decorated with four horizontal lines of black paint over an oval yellow object that might have represented an egg. Moon thumped his knuckles on the door. "Anybody home?"

No answer. Gently he twisted the knob. Locked. He turned his back on the cabin. The man's car was parked outside. He should be somewhere in the neighborhood. "Hallooo," Moon shouted. A hollow imitation of his call echoed back from a distant mesa wall.

Parris pulled the collar of his jacket around his throat. "He could be anywhere out there. Looks like we've missed him." This was a snipe hunt.

Despite the frigid breeze, MacFie wiped perspiration from his face with a wrinkled white handkerchief. "Old Blue Cup—he comes and goes as he pleases."

Moon experienced an uneasy feeling, like a hidden pair of eyes was watching him. He wondered what his friend might sense about this place; Scott Parris couldn't follow a buffalo's trail through mud or smell a dead skunk till he stepped on it, but the *matukach* lawman did have a sense of the unseen. Those dark things that stared at your back and made your skin crawl. This was one reason the white policeman was a favorite of

Aunt Daisy's. Moon looked sideways at Harry MacFie. "Blue Cup . . . he have any friends?"

"He's got this Shoshone sidekick by the name of Noah something or other." The policeman paused and shut his eyes in a vain attempt to remember the name. "Noah . . . Jumping Bird or Hopping Buzzard, something like that. Early thirties, maybe five nine. Deef as a stone since some Judy laid a beer bottle across his head."

"This Noah," Parris asked, "he stay here with Blue Cup?"

"He don't actually live with him, but I've heard that the Shoshone fella watches over the place for Blue Cup. Keeps outsiders from snoopin' around, meddlin' in the old medicine man's business." MacFie scratched enthusiastically at his crotch where it felt like a family of deer ticks had taken up residence. He'd found a blood-gorged tick on his thigh last week, and since that unhappy discovery, it felt as if the wee beasties were all over him. "That Shoshone, now, he's mostly a loner, like the old man. Both of 'em are kinda peculiar."

Peculiar . . . compared to who? Parris wondered.

"Where does the Shoshone live?" Moon asked.

"I hear he bunks out there somewhere." MacFie waved an arm to indicate the general direction of Crowheart Butte. "In a homemade tent, from what they say." He wiped at his brow again, then stuffed the damp handkerchief back into his pocket. "Most folks are scared to come out to this place, 'cause they think that old Blue Cup'll put the Big JuJu on 'em." MacFie blushed. "O'course, it's all bullshit." The Wyoming lawman spat into the dust to express his disdain for such foolishness. But he didn't go near the shack.

Parris frowned at MacFie's gray pallor; a healthy man shouldn't be sweating in this cool weather. "You feel alright?"

The pale man avoided Parris' eyes. "Me?" He forced an unconvincing smile. "I'm fine as frog hair." He felt a mild pain ripple along his left arm.

Moon examined the Jeep; everything about it looked ancient except the new snow tires. Goodyear Wranglers. There was the faded remains of a large white star on the hood. "Looks like army issue, nineteen forties. Haven't seen one of these in years." He glanced at MacFie. "How does he make a living?"

MacFie had found a half-eaten candy bar in his coat pocket; it was rock-hard and decorated with lint. He took a bite. "My old woman," he said between chews, "she cashiers over at the food market in Bitter Creek. Monday afternoons, Blue Cup buys his spuds and beans there. And first of every month the old man cashes one of his guv'mint checks at the store. Military pension or Social Security. Sometimes he has food stamps."

"Well," Parris said, "we've come a long way. Sure wish he was here."

Moon circled the rusty olive-green Jeep; he kneeled and wiped caked dust off the license plate. It was current. He wrote the number on the page of a small notebook.

Parris sniffed at the morning air that had been so sweet; now there was a heaviness about it. He moved close to his friend and lowered his voice so the Wyoming policeman couldn't hear. "Charlie. I got a feeling . . ."

Moon frowned, then nodded almost imperceptibly. "Like somebody's watching?"

Parris suppressed a shudder. "You feel it too?"

"Nah," the Ute said, "Don't feel a thing." But he was watching his friend closely. "I'm not one to point out a man's shortcomings, but you're getting to be kinda spooky . . . sorta like my aunt Daisy."

"You," Parris said with a grin, "are getting to be a real pain in the—"

It seemed to MacFie that the old man simply appeared. Out of nowhere. One moment the three lawmen were alone, then he stood among them. Blue Cup wore his graying hair in a pair of braids that reached to the small of his thin back. The gaunt Ute was dressed in a bright pink shirt and faded jeans; a pair of pointy-toe rawhide boots protruded from the Levi's. He leaned lightly on a knobby mulberry staff.

Charlie Moon was not at all surprised to see the old Ute. "Hello, Grandfather," he said.

Blue Cup appreciated the gesture of respect. He nodded, his dark eyes sweeping across the forms of the lawmen. They were just as he had seen them in his vision. His gaze passed over Sergeant MacFie without particular interest; the blue-eyed Wyoming lawman was a familiar sight around Bitter Springs. The shaman's gaze paused on Scott Parris. Now, this was a very interesting man. A man . . . perhaps . . . who was touched by the Power. His gaze finally rested on Charlie Moon. "You are of the *Núuci?*"

"Yes, Grandfather."

Parris started to speak; he was silenced by an almost imperceptible gesture from Moon.

"If these men were not here," Blue Cup said evenly, "I would ask: who are your people?"

The old man wanted to know the Indian names of Charlie Moon's parents, and it would not be appropriate for the *matukach* to hear such information. Moon walked away several paces, the old Ute at his side. They paused by a fallen ponderosa log, out of earshot of the white men.

"My father was Big Shoes; my mother was Alice Winterheart."

The old man nodded as he remembered. "Of course . . . you are Charlie Moon . . . you are called 'Makes No Tracks.' I have heard about you." He looked up at the man. "You are very tall, like your father. And his father before him. Your mother . . . Lois Winterheart's daughter . . . she was a good woman. Her people were good people." The old man paused, as if thinking about many things. Finally he spoke: "You have come here to see me?"

Moon nodded. "Yes, Grandfather. I have some questions to ask you."

Blue Cup looked away toward the stark, bluish profile of the Wind River Range. The breeze had fallen still. "I am an old man, now. I do as I please." He glanced sharply at Moon. "I may not wish to answer your questions."

"It will be as you wish, Grandfather." This was a stubborn old man. "But we have come a long way. And I need your help."

Blue Cup's eyes softened. "Help?" He could not remember the last time one of the People has asked him for assistance. He was surprised that it made him feel good.

"I am looking for a man . . . one of the People."

The old Ute glanced toward the white lawmen; they were leaning on the brown pickup truck. "Why do you look for this man?"

"He has violated the law . . ."

Blue Cup waved his hand in a gesture of annoyed dismissal. "It does not matter to me that one of the People has violated the white man's law!"

"And if he has also broken the law of the People?" Moon asked softly.

The old Ute shrugged. This son of Big Shoes was a clever young man. And persuasive. "What do you want from me?"

"We have learned that this man came up to Wyoming . . . to see you. I need to talk with you about his visit. Something that you know might help me find him."

The old Ute sat down on the gray-pink bark of the fallen ponderosa. "This looks like a lonesome place . . . but more people come out here to see me than you may think." The old shaman smiled. "So you'll have to tell me the name of this man."

"I'm looking for Provo Frank," the Ute policeman said. "The son of Peter Frank." The policeman saw the muscles tighten in the old man's neck. So. Provo had come to see the old man. "I understand he came here to get something from you."

It was, as a matter of principle, best to have no business with policemen. But this man was one of the People. Word of Charlie Moon's strength and courage had spread far from the Southern Ute Reservation. It would be better to be Moon's friend than his enemy. "I can tell you some things, Makes No Tracks. But not everything . . . some things involve sacred matters."

Moon squatted, facing the old man. "I understand, Grandfather."

Blue Cup stole a quick look at Moon's face. He picked up a dry twig and drew a circle in the sand. "I will tell you some things . . . but first, tell me what you know about this man . . . this Provo Frank . . . about his coming to Wyoming." He drew a deep line diagonally across the circle.

It was not surprising to Moon that this old man was cautious about discussing his business. "I don't know much," the Ute policeman admitted. "Except he came up here to see you. He left his wife and daughter at Bitter Springs. When Provo left the motel, he hadn't paid his bill. Left 'em a bad check."

Blue Cup raised his thin eyebrows in disbelief; the thin pink scar over his left eye was also arched. "You came all the way from Colorado because a Ute owed some money to that pair of weasels?"

"So you know 'em." Moon grinned. "They seemed like a nice enough couple to me."

"Aggie and Billy Stymes." Blue Cup shook his head in disgust. "A couple of bad actors if you ask me." He jerked his head in the direction of Harry MacFie's pickup. "Ask the highway patrolman. He knows all about Aggie and her thieving husband." He stared at Moon through slit lids. "But it seems like a long trip for you, just because of a bad check."

"Provo's bad check was just the start, Grandfather. A few days later, he assaulted a young police officer in Colorado. Broke her face up pretty bad."

"He injured a woman?" The old Ute shook his head. "That is a shameful thing. A man should not fight with a woman." He drew a second line through the circle, making an X in the hoop.

"Provo's wife is missing," Moon said. "Mary Frank may have come to harm also . . . she is a Papago."

"The people you call 'Papago,'" the old Ute said by way of pointed instruction, "are now called by their old name. They are the Tohono O'otam. The Ute are brothers and sisters with the Tohono O'otam, and should call them by their proper name."

Charlie Moon felt his face warm under this gentle rebuke. "This is true, Grandfather. The Tohono O'otam are our brothers and sisters. This is why I must find Provo Frank. It is a matter of tribal honor."

Ahhh . . . this young man was very clever. Blue Cup made a critical decision. He hoped that he would not regret this course of action. "This Provo Frank . . . of course, he did come to see me."

"He came by himself?"

The old man nodded. "In that old Wagoneer."

Moon was pleased with himself. "It would help me to know why he came."

"For the same reason you came out here, son of Big Shoes." The shaman squinted merrily at the policeman. "He wanted something from me."

"Can you tell me what this was?"

The old shaman closed his eyes and rested his chin on a knotted fist. "He wanted the only valuable thing that I possess. He desired the Power." It was what they all wanted. Including the deaf Shoshone, Noah Dancing Crow.

Moon had many questions, but he remained silent. Now was the time for patience.

Eventually the old Ute broke the silence. "He came here, where I live, because he wanted to know the old secrets. He offered me some money." A mixed expression of distaste and amusement spread over the shaman's gaunt features. "He is only a young man, not much more than a boy. I explained to him . . . that such secrets are sacred. They cannot be bought with money."

Moon nodded. Any elder—any keeper of the secrets—would have been insulted by Provo's proposition.

"I told him," Blue Cup continued, "that a man can obtain his portion of the Power only by many years of spiritual quest. He must be clean of mind and body . . . the Sun Dance is a good way to start."

Moon smiled at the thought of Provo Frank attempting the rigorous discipline of the Sun Dance. "What did he say to that?"

The shaman chuckled. "The young man went away . . . very sad. But wiser, I think."

"Surely he didn't go away empty-handed . . . did you give him anything?"

The old man raised his eyebrows. "No—only a thimbleful of wisdom." He cocked his head quizzically at the policeman. "Why do you ask me this question?"

Moon got up and cleared this throat. The old man wasn't going to like this. "When Provo got back to the motel, he was pretty happy. He told his wife that he'd got what he'd gone after."

Blue Cup looked up questioningly at the big policeman. "I thought you said his wife was . . . missing."

This old man's mind was sharp enough. "That's right. I heard this from his daughter. Sarah . . . she remembered how happy her daddy was. What he said to her momma when he got back."

The old man used his mulberry staff to push himself up from the ponderosa log; he turned his face toward the equally stern features of Iron Mesa. "You'd better come with me, Makes No Tracks." The shaman pointed the staff at Parris and MacFie. "Those *matukach* policemen—they must stay here." The old man started off at a brisk pace that was impressive for one of his years.

Moon followed the shaman up a long talus slope composed of crumbling shards of sandstone; he noticed that there was no obvious trail. Probably the clever old man came by a different route every time, to conceal the way to his secret place. The policeman smiled. What Aunt Daisy said was true: old men were much like little boys.

After a fifteen-minute climb, the aged Ute paused and began to remove a cluster of brush from the sheer wall of the sandstone cliff that towered far above them. His work revealed a narrow vertical crack in the wall; it was larger at the bottom, like an inverted V. Or the tooth of a serpent. Blue Cup stood back from the entrance, as if hesitant to discover what was inside. Or what was missing. He nodded to indicate the opening. "You think you can fit yourself in there?"

Moon studied the crack that meandered upwards to become a thin line in the cliff wall. At the bottom it was maybe two feet wide, and it got skinny pretty quick. "Maybe. If I let all my breath out."

The scrawny old man turned sideways and vanished into the side of the cliff. Moon lay on his side and pushed himself through the opening, but not without scratching his new silver belt buckle. When the big man was inside, he discovered that it was impossible to stand upright. The ceiling was nowhere higher than six feet.

The near-darkness was suddenly interrupted by a pale yellow light; the shaman held a cigarette lighter to the wick of a stubby candle. When the wax was burning with a two-inch flame, Blue Cup twisted the base of the candle into the sand at his feet. Moon blinked in the dim, flickering light. The irregular cavern was approximately round, probably formed over aeons by the occasional rainwater dripping from the crack that opened on the mesa top. The ceiling was blackened by the soot of many fires. This shelter had probably been used for thousands of years before Blue Cup had discovered it. On the far wall there was a crude shelf that had been chiseled by the hand of man. The old shaman, who was muttering unintelligibly in the Ute tongue, retrieved a small leather bag from this location. Blue Cup squatted near the candle and untied the parcel. He inspected the contents carefully, naming each object. There were paper-thin sheets of mica . . . a pointed sliver of polished rose quartz . . . a hand-sized shard of red and black pottery (on this surface was the stylized figure of a bird) . . . an amber crystal . . . a beautifully chipped white flint arrowhead . . . the fragile skull of a small rodent . . . and a half dozen black stone beads.

The old man looked up at the policeman and smiled. "It's all here." He began to rewrap the package, to tie the buckskin thongs. "I guess I was worried over nothing."

"Well," Moon said, "I'm glad to hear that Provo didn't take anything. But it's still a puzzle why he was so darned pleased when he got back."

"Wait," the shaman said. "There is one possibility . . . but no." He nodded to himself. "He would not have known where to look." The old man's eyes darted around uncertainly. He opened his mouth, then closed it. "Unless someone . . . a tribal elder maybe . . . told him where such sacred objects are hidden."

"I'll wait outside while you check, Grandfather." The air in this place was suffocating; Moon was eager for any excuse to get into the sunshine.

"No. That is not necessary. You are a man that I trust." On his hands and knees, the shaman crawled to a position that was approximately in the center of the ceremonial cavern. He began to dig in the sand with his hands. Slowly at first. Cautiously, as if the treasure were fragile. Then frantically. After several minutes, he paused. He did not look at the big policeman; his voice was barely above a whisper. "He has taken it."

Moon leaned over beside the old man, whose features seemed to move in the flicker of the candlelight. "Taken what, Grandfather?"

Blue Cup covered his face with his hands. "I cannot tell you."

Moon understood. To give voice to the name of the object was forbidden . . . this could rob it of its power.

The shaman got to his feet; he picked up the flickering candle and held it between his face and the big Ute's. "This Provo Frank, he is a terrible man. A thief. I tell you this, son of Big Shoes . . . I will do everything in my power to help you find this robber. Everything!"

"Sergeant MacFie," Moon said, "told us you had a Shoshone friend. That watched after things for you. Was he supposed to be keeping an eye on this place?"

Blue Cup spat in the red dust. "Noah Dancing Crow," he said bitterly, "is much like the police." He looked at Charlie Moon's face with hard, glittering eyes. "He's always getting in the way—but never there when you need him."

✧

So as not to eat the Scotsman's dust, Scott Parris had kept the Volvo a mile ahead of MacFie's big Chevy pickup. Moon had repeated his conversations with Blue Cup to the *matukach* lawman; Parris had listened without asking questions. It seemed to the Ute that his friend's mind was wandering in other places.

They were halfway back to Bitter Springs when Parris suddenly jammed on the brakes and pulled over to the shoulder. He cut the ignition, got out of the Volvo, and slammed the door. Charlie Moon eased himself out of the sturdy automobile. The Ute had seen the *matukach* behave oddly before. He waited.

Parris jammed his hands into his hip pockets and kicked the Volvo tire rim so hard that he bruised his big toe. Same one he'd hurt weeks earlier on the telephone booth near Pagosa Springs. "Damn, Charlie, I'm blind as a . . . a . . ."

"Bat?" the Ute said helpfully. "Mole?"

Parris limped to the rear of the car and sat down on the trunk. "I mean it was right there in front of me." He glared at Moon, like it was partly the Ute's fault. "Provo Frank is a carpenter, right?"

"Ever since he was about eighteen."

"You remember that list of tools we found in his Wagoneer."

"Well," Moon reminded his friend, "you were supposed to send it to me, but . . ."

"Damn, Charlie, I'm sorry. Soon as we get back to town, I'll call Leggett, get him to make you a copy of the file."

The Ute leaned against the Volvo, and waited.

Parris had calmed somewhat, and lowered his voice. "That carpenter had himself a saw, Charlie. He had a level, a crowbar, wood chisels, a square, tin snips, pliers, punches, tape measures, a wood plane, screwdrivers, a glue gun. He had wood screws. And sheet-metal screws."

"But . . . ?"

"I was so interested in what he *did* have, Charlie, I didn't notice what *wasn't* there! This jackleg carpenter had nails, Charlie. Pounds of nails. Sacks of em. All kinds of damn nails."

Moon waited.

"There was no *hammer* in the Wagoneer, Charlie. And there's blood splattered around inside. Mrs. Frank's blood. The hammer wasn't there because the bastard clubbed his wife to death with it, then ditched it." Parris shook his head in dismay; why had it taken him so long to put two facts together? Advancing age, maybe.

Harry MacFie did, in fact, have extraordinary eyes. From almost a mile away, he'd seen Parris kick the tire. He pulled his Chevy pickup to a stop beside the Volvo and pushed a plastic button to lower the passenger-side window. "What's the problem, boys?" The Wyoming lawman gave the old Volvo a critical look. He'd never drive one of them foreign-made rigs out here where there wasn't hardly nothing but GM and Ford dealers for a hundred miles in any direction. Spare parts, that was always the problem. "You got car trouble? I got some tools behind the seat."

Moon leaned on the pickup and squinted into the cab at the pale man. "My pardner is lookin' for a hammer."

CHAPTER 11

As soon as he could no longer hear the sound of the lawmen's automobiles, Blue Cup lit a match. He put the flame to the whisker of a pine knot. He placed the torch carefully on a pedestal of pink sandstone that stood near the stream. It was a beacon . . . a signal. Maybe the Shoshone watchman was at his campsite on the ridge where he could see both the belly of the canyon and the entrance to the sacred cavern. Maybe Noah Dancing Crow was watching and would see the flame . . . or maybe not.

The aged Ute squatted under the old cottonwood and waited with a patience that was encoded into his genes, a precious heritage from countless ancestors who had survived because they possessed this gift.

Almost an hour passed before he heard the soft padding of the young man's feet on the canyon sands.

Noah Dancing Crow slowed to a respectful walk as he approached the old Ute *bugahant*. He stood expectantly in front of Blue Cup.

The elderly man pointed to a spot two yards in front of him. His Shoshone apprentice squatted and clasped his hands. The deaf man watched the shaman's lips.

There was a very long silence before Blue Cup spoke. Swallows and bats darted overhead, making supper of pixie moths and bottle flies.

"A thief," the shaman said in a monotone, "has violated my sacred place."

Noah's body tensed, but he did not speak.

"This criminal has stolen my most valuable object. An object filled with the Power."

The deaf man suppressed a groan.

"You—" Blue Cup pointed at the young man's bare chest "—are supposed to keep watch for me."

The Shoshone wanted to speak, to explain. But he looked glumly at his master's feet, then at his face.

Normally the Shoshone was full of explanations to justify his failures. The old Ute hated the excuses, but this enigmatic silence annoyed him even more. "Do you have anything to say for yourself?"

Sheepishly Noah shook his head. There was nothing that he wished to say about this calamity. Indeed, there was nothing that *could* be said.

"Then go," the old shaman snapped.

The young man got up, hesitated momentarily, his lips trembling. Then, without uttering a word, the Shoshone vanished into the long shadows of evening.

Blue Cup unlocked the door of his cabin. It was the one place where he could always find solace and comfort—aside from the ceremonial cavern. But now that sacred place had been violated. The cave would have no power until the stolen object was returned.

He lit the Coleman lantern and sat down on a bench at the wooden table; his body was weary.

The old man's thoughts slipped backwards through all the years he had known. The remembrance of his childhood was dim, like the shadow of a ghost in the light of a flickering candle. His memories of that time were always of night. Of a father who drank the amber water that lit a fire in his belly and a glint of madness in his eyes. Of a mother who was there only for a little while . . . then she was buried in her favorite white cotton dress. Of a little sister who died of the measles. Of a darkness that smothered his soul.

But the memories of his early manhood were bright and sharp. Like the sting of the red wasp on his neck. He had wanted, above all things, to become a man who would have the admiration and respect of the *Núuci*. But it was not to be. It was the worst thing that could happen to a man. A picture of the sacred ceremony on Shellhammer Ridge flashed before him. It had been his last act as a part of the Ute community. Now he danced alone, where no man could see, where the women did not sing the tremolo.

For more than half a century, he has been an outcast. In this harsh land where the rain seldom fell except to make a flood. And the long, frigid winters made his bones hurt. The contrast to the beautiful land of the Southern Utes where the soft rains filled many rivers and sweet spring grasses came in April, this was a source of great bitterness to the old man. But this bitterness nourished him. Without it, he would have died many winters ago.

He sighed and pushed himself up from the bench.

The gaunt shaman gathered dry twigs from a cardboard box in the corner of the cabin. He found a book of matches in his shirt pocket, and lit a small fire in his oil-drum stove. As he inhaled the smoke from the flaming piñon, he summoned up the full strength of his bitterness toward the sneaking thief. When the fire was reduced to smoldering rubble, he removed his cowhide boots. Then he took off his cotton shirt and faded jeans. The old shaman used warm ashes to paint dark circles around his eyes and three horizontal lines across the narrow bridge of his nose. He drew a sooty zigzag of lightning on his breastbone. With some reluctance, he repeatedly muttered the Ute word to summon up the power:

Kwasi-ge-ti . . . *Kwasi-ge-ti* . . . *Kwasi-ge-ti* . . .

He waited for several minutes.

Then . . . it came, like a frigid blanket that draped itself over his shoulders. He could feel the very presence of the *Presence*; hear the whispered greeting in his left ear!

Trembling, the shaman stood near the hot coals and urinated upon the embers. An acrid yellow fume billowed up from the remains of the fire. Blue Cup deliberately inhaled the fumes; his nostrils burned as if flames licked at them. The Power did not come without pain. In this choking mist, the shaman clearly saw the man. The face of Provo Frank. The face of the thief. But where was the man? He went to a shelf and opened a small canister that had once held black cough drops; in the container was a small, chalky bone. The bone was from the finger of a human being who had died centuries earlier. An ordinary Ute would not have touched such a thing. There was nothing ordinary about Blue Cup.

The shaman stepped outside the cabin, into the dusty twilight. He coughed and spat to relieve the burning sensation in his throat. He glared at the quarter moon sitting like a plump slice of orange over the rim of the canyon called Cradle of Rainbow Lizard. The shaman raised his left arm and pointed to the west with the chalky human finger bone. Nothing was there. Blue Cup turned slowly counterclockwise, his small bone pointing . . . a compass seeking that which was lost to him. He was pointing to the south, and began to feel a slight buzzing in his fingers. He continued to turn. When the finger bone pointed somewhat east of south, the sensation had ceased. He turned back to the south. The signal was faint . . . and then it was gone.

Now, this was very strange . . . the signal was weak, then gone altogether. It was as if Provo Frank was hidden from his powers. Protected. Shrouded. By some greater source of the Power?

And then Blue Cup remembered the gossip he'd heard from the Southern Ute Reservation. When Provo Frank was a troublesome teenager, he'd stolen something in Ignacio . . . maybe a bicycle . . . the old man could not remember what . . . but the young thief had fled into the wilderness. And had received food and shelter from Daisy Perika—the troublesome woman who had a sizable share of the Power.

Of course. Once more Provo Frank was hiding behind Daisy Perika's skirts—that's where the rascal was! It might eventually be necessary to visit this old woman. But first there was a more powerful magic to attempt. He would go to the great black stone that had fallen from the sky. The stone that had the marks of many powerful men. Blue Cup's lips made a serene smile. Softly he began to hum his favorite melody.

Ode to Joy.

☼ Wyoming, The City Limits Motel ☼
Unit 11

For the second night, Scott Parris stretched out on the lumpy mattress where Mary Frank had slept her last sleep. He rested his head on a pillow filled with walnut-sized chunks of foam rubber.

The policeman had an uneasy sense that he was not alone in the room. He saw nothing in the semidarkness. He heard no sound except the occasional rattle and chatter of the motel's old water pipes. But the presence of Mary Frank was almost palpable.

Though exhausted, he doubted he would sleep well on this night. He closed his eyes and willed his mind to disconnect from the troubles of the day. He imagined himself standing by a stream with his fly rod . . . there was a deep pool where the emerald-green currents eddied around a weathered basalt boulder . . . beneath the surface was a two-pound cutthroat . . . hungry . . . waiting.

In three minutes, he was snoring.

☼ Colorado, Southern Ute Reservation ☼

Daisy Perika lay on her small bed. The child was on a pallet on the floor beside her. Sarah had insisted that Mr. Zigzag must have his own bed, and had given Daisy instructions on how it should be prepared. The little kitten was now sleeping in a shoe box. The cardboard container was lined with one of Daisy's best dishcloths. She knew that she must not spoil the child, but Sarah, at least until things were sorted out, was an orphan. This made the old woman terribly sad. She had lost her own parents when she was not much older than little Sarah.

Finally Daisy drifted off to sleep. At first she slept peacefully without dreaming—without visions from the far places.

But soon, as the old woman's eyes moved under her lids, the dream came . . .

The shaman was not in her bed. Neither was she old. Daisy was a woman of perhaps twenty summers—and she sat just outside her trailer on the wooden porch. She wondered whether her old body was inside, in the small bed—and decided that it must be. This body she occupied was light and strong. And it did not feel the chill breath from the mouth of *Cañón del Espíritu*. She understood that she must wait—something would happen soon.

The shaman perceived the small form when the dwarf was still far away, walking his bowlegged gait through the Canyon of the Spirits. It was strange, his little legs took such short steps—but he moved . . . oh so swiftly! The very fact of his approach was somewhat odd—Daisy almost always went to see the *pitukupf*. Sometimes he would meet her in another place—but never before had he come to her home. This observation was mildly unsettling. Was the *pitukupf* coming to live in her home? Surely not. The little man did not like living anywhere above the surface of the earth.

Daisy sat on the porch step and, with some apprehension, stared at the *pitukupf*. He had a wicker basket, which he set at the foot of the steps. On the basket was a blue cover. The shaman recalled a television program where she had seen a skinny man in a large turban who had sat before just such a basket. When the turbaned man played his flute, an evil-looking snake raised its head from the container and swayed to the rhythm of the music. Daisy prayed silently that the *pitukupf* did not have a serpent in this basket.

She gathered up her courage and spoke: "Hello . . . *mii-pu-ci togo-ci*. I hope you are well."

The *pitukupf* received this greeting with some satisfaction. Long ago, Daisy's grandmother had told her that this particular dwarf was pleased to be greeted as "little grandfather." It was, of course, a mild joke to refer to his health. The dwarf-spirit could no more suffer bad health than the wind could be sick. It was not even certain that one of their kind could die.

The little man sat down behind the basket and sucked on his clay pipe. As usual, he was not in a talkative mood. It was the way of his kind. Unlike human beings, *pitukupf* did not speak unless they had something important to say.

Daisy waited for an appropriate time, then spoke again. "All of the People know that the *pitukupf* who lives in *Cañón del Espíritu* has many wonderful powers." It was a great exaggeration; less than a dozen Utes believed that he existed.

The little man nodded his agreement.

"Among these," Daisy continued somewhat cautiously, "is the power to find someone who cannot be found by human beings." Once, many years ago, when her first husband was alive, the *pitukupf* had told Daisy where to find a child that was lost in a late April blizzard. The boy had been discovered on the bank of the Piños, precisely where the little man had said he would be found. He'd lost several toes to frostbite, but had lived.

Again the *pitukupf* nodded. He blew three perfect smoke rings which rose lazily toward the night sky.

"You know . . . that the daughter of Provo Frank is in my house."

He knew, of course. The little man knew everything that happened in his canyon. Or near it.

"I need to know," she continued, "where the father of this child is. He's in some kind of trouble."

For some unaccountable reason, the dwarf smiled. The *pitukupf* gestured with his scrawny arms as he spoke to the shaman; he spoke in a Ute tongue so archaic that Daisy had to listen closely to understand. He told her that it was not Provo who was in danger.

Daisy shivered, but kept her silence. "Is it . . . Charlie? Or his *matukach* friend?" The little man's face revealed nothing at all. "Is the child in danger?"

Still no response that she could read. The dwarf looked away to the north, and the old woman felt sick at heart. "Tell me, little grandfather, what is in the future? Is it me? Am I to die?"

The dwarf placed one gnarled hand on the blue lid that covered the yellow wicker basket. And . . . oh so slowly . . . he began to remove the lid. Instinctively Daisy leaned backwards. But then the lid was off, and the dwarf waited patiently, puffing on his pipe. Curiosity overcame fear; the old shaman leaned over the container and looked inside. In the dark recesses of the basket, there were many bones. Small ones, large ones. All had been burned. Most were broken into pieces. She wondered: were these the shattered bones of deer? Of elk? Of pig?

The *pitukupf* reached into the basket and removed a small, yellowed tooth.

It was a human molar.

"What does this mean?"

Her question was ignored. But the *pitukupf* spoke to the shaman of an urgent matter. They were to go on a journey. He pointed toward the far lands where the winters are made.

✧ Wyoming, The City Limits Motel ✧
Unit 11

Scott Parris drifted through odd dreams, dredged up from the bottom of the dark pools of his subconscious.

He walked along a crowded beach with his wife; they held hands and enjoyed the warm breeze off a fragrant sea. Helen was wearing a short, yellow cotton skirt over her white swimsuit. She carried a small leather purse in her right hand. A group of teenagers played volleyball. A fat old man under an umbrella smoked a cigar; he was working a crossword puzzle in the *London Times*. A small girl used a rusty toy shovel to dip wet sand into a green plastic bucket, then emptied the bucket and began again. Helen was saying something. She was thirsty.

Did she want a Coke?

Helen raised an eyebrow. Didn't he remember the terrible accident in Canada? It had only been three years ago . . . didn't he realize that she was dead? And buried in a cemetery in Southside Chicago? Dead people, she solemnly informed him, do not drink Cokes. Helen laughed at him, as if it was a terribly funny joke.

Now, as if by some dark magic, his dead wife was dressed in a black velvet dress. Her hair was also coal-black, and done up in a single long braid. Like the strange woman in the Pynk Garter Saloon. All of the people on the beach were dressed in black. He stared . . . were they also dead? The young people abandoned their volleyball game . . . the old man gave up his crossword puzzle . . . the child left her sand bucket and shovel behind. The shadowy ones gathered in a crowd, muttering urgent whispers . . . and beckoned to his wife.

The dark Helen pulled her hand from his and walked away.

He called to her . . . she seemed not to hear.

Now the beach was empty.

He began to weep.

And then the dream was finished.

But another one began . . .

Scott Parris was conscious of two persons in his motel room. It was absurd, almost funny. One was a tiny, rather homely little man; the almost comical figure wore a bright pea-green shirt. And black breeches cut off just below the knees. In his belt there was a flint knife hafted in a wooden handle. A lovely young woman was standing beside the bed. She wore a simple dress, embroidered around the neck and sleeves with tiny blue beads. Like the small man, she wore no shoes. Her face was both wonderfully new to him . . . and yet vaguely familiar, as if they had met in some distant place . . . perhaps in another age. Or in another world. He wanted to reach out and touch her . . . to know that she was real. But his arms were impossibly heavy.

The little man raised his hand and muttered something in short, choppy syllables. The scene became fuzzy . . . the figures began to fade away. Within moments, they would be forgotten.

He seemed to drift, in an infinite, gray sky. Then a brief flash of lightning came from somewhere far away. And touched his mind.

The dreamer was indeed floating, but not in some distant land. He was directly above the City Limits Motel. He could see the long, narrow cinder-block building. And the parking lot. His old Volvo was sitting on the gravel like a fat metallic beetle. The sign on the Pynk Garter Saloon blinked to the west; the shapely neon leg kicked at moths. To his east were the many twinkling lights of Bitter Springs. To the south there was the long, rocky ridge. With tufts of grass, worried by the winds. And a cluster of trees. He understood that he was dreaming . . . but this seemed so real.

He was moving to the south now, as a dry leaf carried aloft by the wind. Above the long ridge. One of the piñons was larger than the others—and separated from their silent company as if shunned by the woody tribe. He did not like this tree. Not at all.

Against his will, he found himself drawn closer to the solitary piñon. He resisted. This slowed his acceleration only slightly.

As he came nearer, he circled the tree . . . like some great bird, he thought. Like a buzzard. The image was a repellent one. He came closer.

And saw.

Scott Parris' body jerked spasmodically; the dreamer flailed his arms across the bed. He opened his mouth to scream, but made nothing more than dry, gasping sounds.

Like a death rattle.

Daisy Perika sat straight up in her bed, clutching a worn quilt to her chest. Something astonishing had just happened . . . something involving the *pitukupf* . . . a basket of bones . . . and a journey to a cold, windy place. It was all jumbled in her head, and the memory was fading fast. Like a dream.

So it must have been just that. A dream best forgotten. Maybe she had gas on her stomach from the tamales she'd warmed up for supper. Or maybe it was the cheddar cheese she'd sprinkled on the tamales. Mexican food would be the death of her. Daisy looked over the edge of the bed. Sarah was sleeping so soundly, as only innocent children can sleep. The kitten, with his shining buttonlike eyes, was staring up at Daisy from his shoe-box bed. Unaccountably, this annoyed the old woman.

She leaned over and fairly hissed at the tiny animal. "Don't look at me, Ragbag. Go to sleep right this minute or I'll . . . I'll tie your tail in a hard knot!"

The kitten curled up in the dish towel and yawned.

Daisy continued to glare at the furry little creature.

Presently Mr. Zigzag closed his eyes.

"Hah," Daisy said with satisfaction. Now that scabby little animal knew who the boss was! The old woman also curled up in her bed. And closed her eyes. But it was a long time before she slept.

A cold, smoky dawn was creeping westward over the frigid Wyoming plains when Moon heard the urgent banging on his door. Only half-awake, he tried to ignore the knocking. Who'd bother him so early in the morning? And then he remembered. Of course. Scott Parris was bunked in room eleven. Just three doors down. Moon groaned and pulled two pillows over his head.

It didn't help.

"Charlie!"

"Go 'way," the Ute growled.

This audible proof that his friend was in the room only encouraged Scott Parris, who dropped a heavy-fisted blow that almost shattered the thin outer paneling on the hollow motel door.

"Aww, shoot," Moon grumped. He got up, rubbed his eyes, stepped into his jeans, pulled on a heavy flannel shirt, and stomped barefooted to the door. The worst part of all would be the white man's smiling face. Parris liked to tell anyone who'd listen that he was a "morning person." Truth was, he was a damned annoying person when a man needed his rest.

But when the Ute opened the door, he was startled at the gray, drawn face of his friend. "What's wrong, pardner?"

Parris glanced over his shoulder toward the parking lot, but didn't speak.

"Come on in." Moon shivered. "Must be below zero, and the wind's blowing."

Parris stepped in like a sleepwalker, his eyes blank.

Moon slammed the door, then sat down on the bed to pull on his wool socks and heavy boots. "You wantin' breakfast already?"

Parris shoved his hands deep into his jacket pockets.

"Let me guess. You couldn't sleep, so you didn't want me to sleep either."

His friend seemed not to hear.

"You know the biggest problem we Utes have with you *matukach*?"

No answer.

"You talk too damn much, that's what. Always yakkity-yak-yak. You just never know when to shut up. All that talkin' gets on my nerves, pardner."

Scott Parris looked at his friend; the eyes of the *matukach* were hard and cold. He turned and opened the door.

Moon, puzzled by Parris' peculiar behavior, was now as silent as his friend. The Ute policeman followed his "pardner" across the edge of the graveled parking lot, around the far end of the City Limits Motel to the rear of the long cinder-block building. Parris paused once, then started tramping through the snow. Straight up the side of the barren ridge. The Ute followed him through the unmarked snow, which was two feet deep in drifts. In places, the relentless winds had cleared the earth of snow and they walked on pebbled yellow clay frozen hard as granite. When they reached the summit, Parris paused. He was immobile for several seconds, as if the thick leather soles of his boots were frozen to the cold ground beneath him.

Moon blew warm breath onto his cold fingers. The Ute was under the impression that his friend was trying to decide which way to go from here.

This was not so. Parris knew exactly where he *had* to go. But he didn't want to. From the motel parking lot, he knew, even a tall man could only see the top few feet of the largest tree on the ridge. From where they stood on the crest of the ridge, a man could see the entire tree. Including the trunk. Especially the trunk. Parris didn't move. He could not will himself to take one step closer . . . not just yet. He raised his arm and pointed a gloved finger toward the largest of the piñons.

The Ute, bemused by this behavior, and still attempting to wash away the dregs of sleep, immediately made his way through the untracked snow toward the tree. When he was within a dozen steps, Moon felt a sudden sense of unease. The Ute paused. He stood very still, his head cocked sideways. He studied the tree. Nothing very remarkable, just an old piñon with a dead top. Probably had taken some lightning strikes, now and again. And then he did notice something a little unusual about this tree. The lowest of the heavy branches were maybe two feet above the ground.

And something about these limbs were not quite right . . . the shape was kind of odd. Something extra was there . . . something that was almost hidden . . . something that was on the other side of the piñon branches. And then Moon knew what it would be. Limbs. And from one of these freeze-dried elbows . . . these pitifully dead limbs . . . hung a shred of scarlet cloth.

It whipped in the wind like a dark funeral pennant.

CHAPTER 12

Harry MacFie, who had taken charge of the investigation, had foolishly tried to drive his Ford black-and-white straight up the side of the ridge from the motel parking lot. He immediately got stuck, fumed, and kicked a small dent in the fender. With the Colorado lawmen as a reluctant audience, MacFie cursed the politicians over in Cheyenne. It'd taken years of pleading to get the tight-fisted bean counters to buy just two four-wheel-drives for the Wyoming Highway Patrol. And both of those were snapped up by the lieutenant responsible for the Jackson Hole district. The Scotsman, still fuming, had walked up the ridge with Moon and Parris, who followed their previous tracks.

The other official vehicles, whose drivers were more cautious than Mac-Fie, had gotten onto the ridge by way of a rutted Jeep track that snaked in from the south off a rancher's graveled road. There were two other highway patrol black-and-whites, several town police, some sheriff's office cops in a new Ford Explorer, and the county medical examiner's big Dodge van. A thin young man who published Bitter Creek's newspaper had caught a ride with one of the town cops. He'd already taken more photographs than the ME, who had used up two rolls of thirty-five-millimeter film. Within a couple of hours, the newspaperman had predicted, there would be reporters in from Casper and Cheyenne. Before dark, the television newsies' helicopters would fly up from Denver.

Scott Parris wondered whether Anne Foster would be covering this lurid homicide for the Granite Creek newspaper. He pushed this thought to the back of his mind, to a dark corner with other old rubbish that was gathering dust.

A forensics technician from Cheyenne was ambling along, sweeping a metal detector over the snow. A highway patrol officer, a slim young woman, was carefully pulling a garden rake through the snow close to the tree. So far they'd found nothing except a badly bent nail. It was five inches long, and had a brown stain of blood on the tip.

The county sheriff showed up in a spotless white Toyota pickup. The former cowboy, who had a slim cigar in his mouth and two pearl-handled pistols slung on his Italian leather gun belt, started asking pointless questions and giving even more pointless instructions. Apart from his own staff, he was ignored.

Scott Parris stood to the north, thirty yards away. He'd never approached the tree, not even walked around to the south side where the frozen corpse was suspended. In his dreams he had already seen the horror that hung on the piñon. One look was enough. More than enough.

Charlie Moon was standing close by his friend. The Ute poured sweet black coffee from a stainless steel thermos into a pint-sized Styrofoam cup. He offered the steaming brew to Parris, who accepted it gratefully but without comment. Parris had said nothing since they'd left the motel at dawn. And the Ute had allowed his friend this gift . . . this cocoon of silence.

The Colorado lawmen watched the circus.

Sergeant Harry MacFie said something extremely rude to the cowboy sheriff, turned on his heel, and stomped his way toward the Colorado lawmen. The Wyoming highway patrolman had a big meal on his plate, maybe the biggest case of his career. MacFie was running on adrenaline. He slapped Parris on the shoulder. "Well, my boy, when you came up with that missing-hammer notion, I knew for sure you was a real cop. But figuring out that the body was stashed up here . . . well, how you did that sure beats me."

Parris didn't answer; his face was sickly pale.

The Wyoming lawman grinned uncertainly and looked at Moon. "He always such a chatterbox?"

"He's only like this before breakfast," the Ute said. "Low blood sugar." Neither of them had had a bite to eat and it was almost noon. But Moon wasn't all that hungry.

The well of MacFie's enthusiasm was bottomless. "You boys want to know the gory details?"

For the first time in hours, Scott Parris spoke. Like he was reading from a written report. "She was struck in the head with a hammer. That happened down at the motel parking lot. Then she was brought up here. She wasn't quite dead yet."

MacFie's mouth was gaped open.

Parris continued in a dry monotone, as if he were dictating a homicide report. "Mrs. Frank's body was . . . was *nailed* to the tree. The nails . . . they're five or six inches long . . . were hammered through her wrists. And her feet. Even one through her neck. Her eyes . . ." His voice was detached, almost clinical. "Her eyes are missing from the sockets."

"Yeah," MacFie said with a quick glance toward the tree, "picked out by buzzards and such, I expect." If the weather had not been so cold, the birds of prey would have had a much more substantial feast. The highway patrolman was disappointed to have his thunder stolen; he turned on the Ute. "You already told him about the nails?" He assumed that the rest was speculation. It was not. "There was somethin' else odd about how the body was—"

"The corpse," Parris said in the monotone, "is upside down."

MacFie fixed his blue eyes on the Ute. "You knew that, Charlie."

"Yeah. But I didn't say nothing to my pardner about that, Harry. And I didn't know about the nails. When I found . . . when Scott showed me where . . . uh . . . she was, I didn't get all that close to the corpse." Even "modern" Utes like Charlie Moon didn't make a practice of getting close to dead bodies. Or mentioning the names of the recently dead. It just wasn't a healthy thing to do. Ghosts would come and haunt you. Even if you didn't believe in ghosts. Didn't matter a damn to them what you believed.

The pale man glared at Scott Parris. "How'd you figure she'd been nailed to the piñon . . . just because Provo's hammer is missing, I s'pose . . . but how'd you know she was feet-up?"

Parris' voice was barely above a whisper. "The hammer'll be found within a few yards of the tree. Under the snow. To the southeast. Twelve, maybe thirteen paces."

MacFie was, for once, at a loss for words. He turned away and retraced his steps toward the grove of gnarled junipers.

The ME was beginning the painful process of removing Mary Frank's frozen corpse from the tree. She used a crowbar to pull the heavy nails from the wood and flesh.

Within moments, MacFie was waving his arms, yelling shrill orders at everybody, directions that were pointedly ignored by most of the town cops. One young officer stopped to listen to the Scotsman's instructions. She took her garden rake to the place where he was pointing. To the southeast. Start at ten paces, he said. She did; her paces were short ones. She started hacking away at the hard crust over the snow.

Charlie Moon waited. The Ute watched the uniformed police officer drag the rake through the crumbling snow. He also watched his "pardner."

Parris turned and stared far away toward the north. At nothing, it seemed to the Ute.

Five minutes later, and less than fifteen yards from the tree, a victorious shout went up from the officer who'd been sifting through the drifted snow with her rusted garden rake. MacFie, followed by the medical examiner, sprinted to the site.

Parris turned to watch, but he seemed oddly disinterested. Like a man watching the replay of an old movie. Moon, despite his curiosity, held his position near his friend.

MacFie, his red hands freshly gloved with surgical rubber, was bagging something. He laughed, shouted something of a congratulatory nature, then slapped the young woman on the back so hard she stumbled. The other officers also laughed, and shook her hand. The uniformed woman (who was just three months away from Tullahoma, Tennessee) beamed, blushed prettily, and said something modest about how "a blind hog had found an acorn."

Harry MacFie stomped through the snow toward the Colorado lawmen, the transparent plastic bag held high, like a feathered stick that had just counted coup on a deadly enemy.

Moon spoke. "It's just what you expected, pardner."

It was, of course, the hammer.

MacFie was short of breath, his face beet-red with exertion. "Well, this does it, boys. It's the claw hammer missing from Provo Frank's tool kit. And there's blood all over the damn thing!"

Moon squinted at the bagged murder weapon. "What makes you so sure it belongs to Provo?"

"Take a gander at this." MacFie pointed a rubber-covered finger at the hardened steel head. A pair of initials were engraved deep into the metal:

PF

"Any prints in the stains?" Moon asked. Provo's prints would, of course, be all over his own hammer, but if his prints were in the blood . . .

"There's some marks, alright . . . like fingers," MacFie said, "but it looks like he had gloves on."

Moon bowed his head and closed his eyes against a sudden gust of wind. He'd wanted to believe that Provo, damn fool that he was, would not have done anything like this. But he was a police officer who depended upon facts, and the evidence was now overwhelming. The mystery was not who'd done the thing, but why.

MacFie's blue eyes were sparkling. He grinned at Scott Parris. "Way I got it figured, boys, I actually got me *two* prime suspects."

Moon looked down at the Scotsman's red face.

"It's either Provo Frank that did the dirty deed, or," he added slyly, "it's the fellow who knew just where the body was. Exactly how it was nailed to a particular tree. And where the murder weapon was dropped." He winked at the big Ute. "Charlie, I hope your buddy has a damn good alibi for the night of the murder." MacFie was determined to goad Parris into explaining his astonishing deductions.

Scott Parris went deathly pale; a woman's body was nailed to a tree. And this man, a sworn officer of the law, was making jokes! A huge pulse of adrenaline surged through the lawman's arteries. He clenched his right hand into a meaty fist. Oh yes. It will be quite satisfying, punching the teeth out of this smart-ass cop's grinning mouth. And if his Wyoming buddies take offense, why, that's even better. Let 'em come . . . I'll just whip the lot of them!

Moon recognized the storm warning; he wrapped his big fingers firmly around his friend's right forearm, cutting off the circulation. "Well, I've had me enough of this cold wind, pardner. Let's go wrap ourselves around some hot breakfast." The Ute grinned at MacFie, who was blissfully unaware of the threat. "Can you do without us, Harry?"

"I'll get by somehow. You boys ooze on over to the First Chance Café. Tell sweet Daffy I said anything you want is on me . . . no, tell her to charge it to the Great State of Wyoming." He slapped Moon on the back. "I'll see you boys there in a half hour or so, and I expect to get the whole lowdown from Sherlock here. I just don't know how he did it, but I sure as hell want some lessons in detectin'!"

The tension drained out of Parris; composure gained the upper hand.

Moon loosened his viselike grip on his friend's arm.

Parris turned away and stumbled down the ridge on feet that were numb from the bitter cold.

Harry MacFie watched them go, the wide grin still on his face. By gosh, these were sure a couple of A-number-one lawmen, and fine fellows to boot! He thought about how they'd soon be heading back to Colorado, and also about how he might never see them again. This brought tears to the sentimental man's blue eyes. The amiable Wyoming highway patrolman would never know how close he'd come to losing a half dozen perfectly sound teeth.

Nor could the Scotsman have known about a fire yet unkindled. Or the sad tune the piper would play.

*   *   *

With her characteristic enthusiasm, Daphne poured great gollops of black coffee. Most of it got into Moon's cup. Word of the corpse hanging on the tree had not yet found its way to the First Chance Café, but the Ute figured the big story was only minutes away.

Scott Parris and Charlie Moon, who had limited themselves to coffee, had just about given up on MacFie. Moon, whose appetite had recovered, was engrossed in the lunch menu when the Wyoming policeman burst through the door, rubbing his chapped red hands. The Scotsman appeared tired, but not at all discouraged. He clapped a paw on Parris' shoulder. "Hello, boys! You save any grits for me?"

Parris barely nodded to acknowledge the man's presence.

Moon used his boot to push a flimsy chair away from the table for the highway patrolman; MacFie plopped himself down and bawled at Daphne. "Bring me a three-egg Mexican omelet, sweetheart. With all the fixin's. And rye toast. And a gallon of black coffee."

Daphne sauntered over, her wide hips swinging (seductively, she thought) under her faded pink uniform. "Gumpy, he don't make no omelets after eleven in the A.M., Harry—you know that."

The pale-faced lawman put his hand on the revolver holstered on his belt and squinted one eye at Daphne (menacingly, he thought). "Does that half-assed little short-order cook know I'm armed and dangerous?"

"Gumpy," she said, "started sharpening his butcher knife when you came in. He said if you mouthed off, somebody would have free sweetbreads for lunch." Daphne grinned and held her fingertip close to her thumb. "Little bitty sweetbreads."

Harry shook his freckled head in feigned dismay, then raised his thick, reddish eyebrows at the lawmen across the table. "As you can see, boys—there ain't much respect for a tin star in this here joint." He turned and smiled sweetly at Daphne. "You may convey this to the chef: Sergeant Major Harold MacFie will be most pleased to have a double cheeseburger and a big bowl of red chile. With beans."

The waitress took a stupendous order from Charlie Moon (she managed to brush her leg against his), a request for a Cobb salad from Scott Parris (she sniffed her displeasure at this choice), then scurried off to shout a shorthand version to old Gumpy, who was five five, one hundred and ten pounds, blind in one eye, and hard of hearing. Gumpy also taught Sunday school to a class of six- and seven-year-olds over at First Methodist. But he did have a butcher knife. It was, indeed, razor-sharp . . . and sweetbreads were his specialty.

"That old cook's a damn lunatic," MacFie muttered darkly. He took off his jacket and draped it over the back of his chair. The battered felt hat stayed on his round head. He rubbed his hands together; his blue eyes darted quickly between Moon and Parris. "Well, boys, let's have it."

Parris ignored him.

"Have what?" Moon said innocently.

"Don't get cute with me, you big smart-assed Injun. You know damn well what I mean." MacFie jerked a thumb at Parris. "How'd your partner do it? How'd he know where that poor woman's body was?" He lowered his voice now. "How'd he know somebody nailed her *upside down* to that piñon tree? And how'd he know where the hammer was at, under knee-deep crusted-over snow?"

Moon grinned. "That's four 'how's,' paleface."

MacFie slapped his hand hard on the table; customers four tables away jumped; a fat lady spilled coffee in her lap and yelped. "Dammit, don't hold out on me! I got a murder case, and paperwork to do—you boys got yourselves a witness who saw the whole thing. That's plain enough." He got halfway up from his chair, leaned on the table with both hands, and glared down at the two big lawmen. "And I damn well mean to know who it is!"

Parris, who seemed unshaken by this display, put his hand over the top of his coffee cup; he watched the steam curl out between his fingers. Presently he looked across the table at MacFie. "I could tell you . . . but it wouldn't help."

MacFie sat down; he raised his hands in a gesture of conciliation. "I'll be the judge of that, Mr. Parris. Alright. I'm listenin'."

Moon leaned back in his chair, ready to enjoy what was coming.

Parris took a deep breath, then exhaled. He fixed his gaze on a greasy light fixture; it dangled from the ceiling on a brass chain, about two yards over MacFie's head. The lamp swung in a slow, pendular motion. Almost hypnotic. But he didn't say a word.

MacFie sat like a statute; only his blue eyes moved. He flicked a quick glance at Parris, then at the big Ute, who was trying not to grin. "Charlie, what's goin' on here?"

"My pardner," the Ute said, "sometimes he has these . . . these hunches."

The Scotsman's lips made a hard, bluish line. Much like the veins standing out on his forehead. "Hunches?"

Moon nodded. "Every once in a while, they're even right." The Ute glanced at his friend. "That's how he made his big reputation."

MacFie's blue eyes fairly glinted with fury. "Okay, you silly sumbitches," he said through clenched teeth, "it's clear enough you got yourselves an eyewitness . . . and for some reason you ain't ready to lay your cards out on the table." He put his chapped hands over his eyes, like he might burst into tears. "If I didn't like you two big clowns so much, so help me, I'd arrest the both of you for . . . for . . ."

"Willful obstruction of justice?" Moon offered helpfully. "Conspiracy to create an impediment to a lawful investigation . . . ?"

"Too many damn syllables," MacFie said helplessly. "How about just 'pissed me off'?"

"Works for me," the Ute said thoughtfully. He raised his coffee cup to Parris. "How about you, pardner?"

"Only one thing matters," Parris said evenly. "Find Provo Frank. Arrest him. Jail him. Try him." He looked coldly at MacFie. "And then . . . hang him high."

"Well," MacFie responded genially, "first we gotta find him, don't we?"

Daphne came by on the run; she slowed just enough to splash coffee in the general vicinity of MacFie's cup, then trotted away to service a table of bearded truck drivers.

MacFie wiped at the spilled coffee with a soggy napkin.

"It looks like Provo had too much to drink, then killed his wife." Moon tapped a spoon thoughtfully against his coffee cup. "But it's kinda peculiar. I've known him since he was a little boy. Even killed a few six-packs with him, back when I was a drinkin' man." Now he frowned. "When Provo got himself liquored up—he'd get quiet. Sentimental. Maybe sing a song. Then go to sleep." The Ute policeman sighed. "I just can't imagine him gettin' wild—and doin' something like . . ."

Harry MacFie was calmer now. "Maybe . . ." the Wyoming lawman said cryptically, "maybe he wasn't on booze, Charlie. Maybe he . . . maybe he'd ingested some drugs." MacFie stirred his bitter coffee; he avoided the questioning gaze of the Colorado policemen.

Something was funny here, Parris thought. The remark was not characteristic of MacFie; he'd said it almost too casually. The man knew something. And why did he say "ingested"? That was sure a two-dollar word in a two-bit mouth, and it suggested that the act of taking the drugs was not voluntary. Why hadn't he said, "Maybe he'd *taken* some drugs?"

The Ute stared out the window. A slender poplar was bending in the wind. "Drugs?" Anything was possible. But that sure didn't sound like Provo. On the other hand, he hadn't been around the man that much in the last four or five years. But surely not *drugs*. Moon spoke softly, without looking at MacFie. "How'd you get the idea Provo Frank might've been under the influence of drugs when he . . . when he killed his wife?"

"Well . . ." MacFie placed a stubby finger on his temple and spoke with exaggerated solemnity. "It was like this, boys. I had me a hunch!" He leaned back in his chair and chuckled with genuine satisfaction.

Parris felt his face drain of blood. It'd been a mistake. Not knocking the smart-assed man's teeth out.

✧

Harry MacFie gazed across his desk at Lizzie Pynk, who was sitting somewhat primly in an uncomfortable wooden chair. Fat Sam was pacing like a caged bear; the bartender reached into his jacket pocket and found a crumpled pack of Lucky Strikes.

"No smoking on the premises," Sergeant MacFie said softly; he nodded to indicate a sign on the wall behind his desk that displayed precisely those same words in four-inch-high letters. Sam grumbled something that was unintelligible and stuffed the Luckies back into his pocket.

If he'd been doing this by the book, he'd have interviewed them separately. Recorded their comments, compared them later. But the lawman rarely did anything by the book. And he preferred to keep this unmatched pair together, so he could watch the little signals that passed between them.

MacFie frowned at the file folder he'd placed strategically on his desk, then looked up at Lizzie. "We're building up considerable information on the Mary Frank homicide, but I need to know *everything* her husband did the day she died. Particularly on that evening." He'd placed the file so the typed label (prepared only this morning) was easily seen.

STATE OF WYOMING
LIQUOR LICENSE REVOCATIONS
CAUSES/FINAL DISPOSITION

Harry had stuffed the folder full of weekly reports on highway patrol vehicle repairs. "It looks like you . . . and Sam here—" he smiled benignly at the fat man "—were the last folks to see Mr. Frank before he went back to the motel. So you can help fill in some blanks. I figure, and I'm speakin' as a friend now—" the policeman glanced meaningfully at the file "—it'd be in your interest to cooperate."

Lizzie tried not to look toward the file folder, but it pulled at her gaze like a magnet tugs at iron filings. She shrugged. "We've already told you. He came in. Had a shot of whiskey. Then he left."

While the pair watched, MacFie made careful notes on the second sheet of a yellow legal pad that he held close to his chest. Like a good poker hand.

2 half gal milk—1/2%
dozen eggs, large
Cokes, diet
hamburger, low fat
potato chips, low salt

He took his time to complete the grocery list, let the top sheet fall over the "notes," then looked up at Sam's round face. "Funny thing, memory." The policeman's blue eyes were like December ice. "At best, it ain't perfect. And as you get older, it gets worse. You say Mr. Frank had a shot of whiskey. Now, when I visited your fine establishment, Sam here, he told me Provo Frank had a beer." MacFie held a single finger up. "One beer." That triggered a memory; MacFie returned to the list.

Coors Lite—six-pack

Fat Sam turned his back on the lawman; he fixed his gaze on a bad watercolor of Dutchman's Mesa.

MacFie grinned at Lizzie. "Now, maybe one of us has a faulty memory." He stared at the fat pinched into little folds above Sam's starched collar; the lawman tapped a ballpoint pen on the knuckles of his left hand.

Tic . . . Tic.

And waited.

Tic . . . Tic . . . Tic.

Lizzie barely smiled; she wanted MacFie to know that she was mildly amused at this sophomoric tactic. But her hands were cold.

Still the plastic cylinder tapped on the hard knuckles.

Tic . . . Tic . . . Tic . . . Tic.

Sam clenched his hands behind his back. He cleared his throat. He unclasped his hands and shoved them in his trouser pockets. The fat bartender found a disk of peppermint in his left pocket, unwrapped it from the cellophane, and popped it into his mouth. He sucked on the hard candy for a few seconds, then began to crunch it between his molars.

Sounds like a hog eating corn, MacFie thought.

Even above this crunching noise from his jaws, Sam could hear the metronome clicking of the ballpoint on MacFie's knuckles. When the taste of peppermint had faded from his tongue, Sam leaned back and forth, shifting his weight from one foot to the other.

The tic-tic sound suddenly stopped; the muscles in Sam's round shoulders went taut.

The silence began to hang heavy; even Lizzie was getting edgy.

A heavy cloud drifted over the afternoon sun and the room darkened.

Sam was suddenly oppressed by a bizarre fantasy. What if Lizzie and the annoying little cop had snuck out of the room. What if he was here all alone . . . and they were out in the hall smirking . . . waiting to see how long he'd stand here? Sam knew this was completely absurd. But the fantasy grew until he could stand it no longer. The bartender slowly rotated his short neck, until he could see over his shoulder. Lizzie was still there . . . and the lawman was behind the desk, his blue eyes glinting at some secret joke.

Once more he began to tap the pen against his knuckles. Slowly.

Tic . . .Tic . . .

Lizzie wanted to say something. She told herself that she wasn't afraid of this little redheaded turd, perched behind his desk like a chubby woodpecker. But when she'd start to open her mouth, some hardwired circuit in her brain just wouldn't let her do it. It was like when you try to take in a breath and swallow at the same time. Can't be done.

MacFie waited. Tapping the ballpoint against the knuckle of his thumb. Slightly faster now . . . the metronome matched the racing heartbeat of the fat man.

Tic. .Tic. .Tic.

Lizzie looked like she was chewing on her tongue. MacFie knew she'd sit there like a brick until the moon came up. But Fat Sam was a nervous type; he'd eventually have to open his mouth.

Faster the metronome. Tic.Tic.Tic.

So suddenly that it unnerved MacFie, Sam turned on his heel and fairly shouted: "Well, maybe he *did* have a shot of whiskey. Maybe more than one!"

MacFie stopped tapping the ballpoint and saw relief spread over the fat man's face. Like butter melting over a hot biscuit, the Scotsman thought. "If you was to make an estimate . . . how *many* drinks more than one?"

Sam looked quickly at Lizzie; she didn't seem to know he was in the room. Or care.

"Shit, Harry, I didn't keep count. Three. Four maybe." Beads of sweat were breaking out on the barman's wrinkled forehead; the fat man's breath came in short pants, like he'd just climbed six flights of stairs.

"Okay. So he tossed a few drinks." MacFie tapped hard on a thumb knuckle, saw the muscles tighten in the fat man's jaw, then let the ballpoint hang in midair. "How'd the alcohol affect him?"

Fat Sam opened his mouth, saw the look darted from Lizzie's cold reptilian eyes, then clamped his gums shut. Again he turned his back on

MacFie. Beat a drum tattoo on your damn knuckles, you smart-assed redheaded Scotchman. I ain't gonna tell you nothing else.

Lizzie knew better. She crossed her legs; the dark skirt pulled well above her knees.

Despite himself, MacFie gawked.

She smiled at the lawman; men were pretty much alike. "Sometimes a customer has a few too many to drink, Harry. We have an insurance problem." She glanced at the menacing folder on MacFie's desk. "If some yahoo leaves my business establishment and ends up in an automobile accident, the aggrieved party might sue me. Put me out of business, even."

His gaze darting quickly between her almost pretty face and her rather nice legs, MacFie nodded dumbly. He was, of course, familiar with the Liquor Dispensers Liability law. He knew about a case just last month in Lander where a man had shut down his bar after he'd lost a ten-million-dollar lawsuit. He'd kept feeding beers to a stupid cowboy until he was cross-eyed-blotto. The drunk had promptly gone out and run down a teenage girl on a bicycle. MacFie breathed deeply, forced himself to keep his gaze on the woman's face, then repeated his earlier question. "How did the alcohol affect Mr. Frank?"

Lizzie shrugged again. "The usual. He got kind of loud." She glanced at Sam, who had his eyes closed. And his mouth. "I had to ask him to leave."

MacFie looked away from the woman; he stared at the back of the fat man's head. Sam felt the gaze, and shuddered.

"Sammy, you have anything else to tell me?"

The bartender didn't respond.

Lizzie spoke, her voice soft and reassuring. "You were going to tell Officer MacFie about the telephone call."

Sam's shoulders drooped in relief. He turned and looked directly at the lawman. "Yeah. Almost forgot." He swallowed and his Adam's apple bobbled. "That Frank guy, he made a phone call. From our pay phone." He found his wallet and produced a folded piece of paper. "You want the number?"

MacFie was wide-eyed. "You got the number he called?"

Lizzie smiled. "No, Chief Inspector MacFie." She spoke carefully, as if to a slow-witted child. "Sam is offering you the number of the public telephone that is located inside the Pynk Garter Saloon." She got up, draped a glistening mink over her broad shoulders, and walked out of MacFie's office. The lawman sat and listened to the sound of her spike heels going down the hall. He was surprised to realize that he missed her. Well, he admitted, he mainly missed her long, milky-white legs.

MacFie had forgotten about the bartender.

Fat Sam scratched at his ample belly; the tail of his white shirt was half-out, hanging over his tight belt. The bartender looked hopefully toward the open door, then at the lawman. He placed the paper with the pay phone number on MacFie's desk.

"Yeah, Sam." Harry sighed. "You can run along with momma."

When he could no longer hear Sam's heavy footsteps in the hall, Mac-Fie picked up his telephone. He punched at the buttons until the bell jangled in Cheyenne. The elderly woman answered after four rings.

He grinned. "Betty darlin'? Yeah, this is Harry MacFie over at Bitter Creek. I need a trace made on a phone call."

She asked for the relevant information, and got it.

MacFie waited, now tapping the ballpoint against the gristly bridge of his sunburnt nose.

Betty tapped three keys to make a computer connection to the long-distance data bank. She waited for the screen prompt, responded to the PASSWORD query, then entered the number of the Pynk Garter public telephone and the date of the call. The response required less than five seconds. There had only been two calls made on the pay telephone that day. The first could be dismissed; it had been made shortly before noon to a residence in Bitter Creek. The second had been made at precisely 8:16 P.M.—to a number in Colorado. Ignacio. She made another query and was given the identity of the subscriber.

MacFie stopped tapping his nose with the ballpoint pen; that instrument was now used to record the information from the helpful lady in Cheyenne. When he had completed his scribbles, he thanked her and hung up. But a sour look shadowed the Wyoming lawman's face. Unless he wanted to drive all the way to southern Colorado and do the questioning himself, he'd have to give this little tidbit to the Ute cop. Charlie Moon, who damn well knew how his partner had come up with all the details about the Mary Frank murder scene. There was an eyewitness, and for some damn reason, they were keeping that source under wraps. Could it have been the Frank child? The grim thought that a little girl had watched her daddy nail her momma to a tree made MacFie shudder.

For a moment the stubborn Scotsman thought about making the trip to Ignacio, rather than sharing this information with Moon. But it was an awful long drive, and anyway he probably wouldn't be able to question this particular bird without the Ute policeman's help. So he'd grit his teeth and pass the information on to Charlie Moon. All the same, it burned MacFie that the Ute policeman and his buddy were holding out on him. Cocky bastards, that's what they were.

The Wyoming highway patrolman should have made the trip south. And stayed in Colorado while the leaves on the aspens turned to flakes of gold, and were carried away on the west winds. It would have been far better.

CHAPTER 13

Ignacio, Colorado
Southern Ute Tribal Headquarters

Charlie Moon, his big hands clasped at the small of his back, stood before the chairman of the Southern Ute tribe.

Austin Sweetwater was completing his first term in office—it had been like a new pair of expensive boots. There was some pride associated with the acquisition, but it still wasn't a good fit. But just like a man couldn't discard a fine pair of boots, Austin would rather limp along than give up the office. The election was only weeks away and he faced a serious challenger. The informal polls taken by the *Southern Ute Drum* showed Martha Tonompicket running slightly ahead of him. The chairman chewed on an unlighted cigar; he paced nervously under the mounted head of the buffalo that was the symbol of the tribe. Finally he removed the cigar from his mouth and glared at the stub as if he didn't recognize the thing.

Charlie Moon suppressed a smile. Austin was a decent enough fellow, but he wasn't cut out to be tribal chairman.

"So," Austin Sweetwater said, "you just got back from Wyoming?"

The Ute policeman nodded.

"The tribe's decided to match the Papagos' reward for the arrest and conviction of the murderer of Mary Frank. It'll be announced in the *Drum* next week."

Nowadays, maybe the chairman was even reading the section of the tribal weekly newspaper entitled "Southern Ute Job Opportunities." At this thought, Moon could not hide a slight smile. "Anyone at all can earn the reward?" Moon asked hopefully. "Does that include employees of the SUPD?"

The chairman's little belly bounced as he chortled his braying donkey laugh. "Dream on, Charlie." Austin looked thoughtfully at the tribal policeman and recalled Moon's Ute name. Makes No Tracks was the source of several legends. Some of them might even be true. But Mary Frank was dead. And Charlie Moon hadn't found Provo Frank. This big fellow was, so everybody said, an unusually good policeman. Moon was also a man you could depend on. If he said he'd do a thing, it was as good as done. But for such a popular man, Charlie Moon was hard to figure. The chairman wondered idly why Moon showed no evidence of political ambition. Probably the man was lazy. Most big people were slow-moving and lazy. Now that he'd placed Moon in a suitable category, he felt better. For Austin Sweetwater, everything had to be in its box. His wife had once told him that he had the soul of an accountant. Austin appreciated what he believed to be a compliment. Accountants who knew the man would have been insulted. Chagrined, even.

Austin jammed the wet cigar between his nicotine-stained teeth and tried again. "Mary Frank's murder . . . Was it . . . ummm . . . as grisly as the papers say?"

Moon was not to be drawn out. "It was bad enough."

The chairman nodded and waved impatiently. "What about Provo?"

Moon feigned an innocent look. "What about him?"

Austin wheeled on the big policeman and looked up at the impassive face. "Where in hell *is* that wife-killer, Charlie?"

"We don't know."

The chairman sat down behind his huge desk. Like a tiny frog peeping over a lily pad, he was overwhelmed by its size. He leaned back and propped his new Tony Lamas on the polished surface. He felt this gesture gave him some psychological advantage over the big policeman, who obviously had insufficient respect for those in high political office. Austin removed the limp cigar from his mouth, ground it out in a gleaming Nambé Ware ashtray, and stuffed it into his jacket pocket.

"Maybe a few minutes before his wife died, Provo Frank made a telephone call to your office." Moon waited.

Austin's eyes widened. "Yeah, he did call a while back. I didn't know it was the same night that . . . ."

"Same night."

The chairman looked at the clock on his desk. Almost time to shut up shop and go home. "You want to know what he had to say?"

"It might be interesting." Moon sat down on the chairman's desk and wondered whether Austin would order him to get off. And whether, if he did, he would. He thought maybe he would. Maybe.

Austin pretended not to notice the bulk of the big Ute on his desk. "Provo, he was babbling a lot. Something about a sacred object he'd got his hands on. He laughed, like maybe he'd been drinking, and the bastard whistled . . . right in my ear." The chairman pulled at his right earlobe.

The policeman's eyebrows raised slightly. "He say anything else?"

"Lemme think." Austin Sweetwater felt in his pocket for the cigar; it crumbled in his fingers. He wiped his hand on his trousers. "Oh yeah. Said he wanted me to call a special council. Elected officers. Tribal elders. The works."

Moon pulled his notebook from his jacket pocket. He found a blank page and scribbled:

Provo F. calls A. Sweetwater—Sacred Object
Whistles—Council/Elders

"And why'd he want to call a council?" It was hard to imagine Provo Frank speaking to a tribal council; he only came to the reservation about once or twice a year and had never shown much interest in tribal affairs.

"Provo, he didn't say. Then there was some static, and the phone crackled a lot. I heard him say something about 'thirty-eight,' and I thought maybe he had himself a pistol. That was when he whistled in my ear. And then he got kind of excited and started yelling about how he'd be a big man now. I figured he was drunk or something, so I hung up and forgot about it."

Yes, Moon thought. Drunk. Or *something*. The Ute policeman wrote "38" in his notebook. He got off the desk, and regretted taking Austin Sweetwater so lightly. "He say anything else?"

Austin was frowning, like a schoolboy considering a tough problem on his algebra exam. "Well, now that you mention it, Charlie, there was one thing that was peculiar."

"Peculiar?"

The chairman looked up and scratched at a loose fold of skin under his chin. "He said that when I called the elders to this meeting, I should make sure that Walks Sleeping showed up. Charlie, that old man's maybe a hundred years old and blind as a mole." And, Austin reminded himself, never votes in tribal elections.

"Walks Sleeping," Moon said almost to himself. Yes. The Ute police-man sorted through his memory of tribal history. Walks Sleeping had been appointed tribal chairman during the year when the elected chairman died after a horse kicked him in the neck. That year had been a bad one for the tribe. Walks Sleeping had served as leader of the Southern Utes for about five months. But then he'd resigned without explanation. It had been a long time ago.

The summer of 1938.

❖

Charlie Moon pulled the Blazer to a halt in the dusty yard. "This is it," he said to Parris. An almost new red Toyota pickup was parked by the old adobe structure, which had a pitched roof of corrugated steel sheets. And windows with wooden frames that wanted paint. At the side of the house, under a blighted long-leaf cottonwood, the rusting hulk of a green 1952 Mercury sat with its tireless rims balanced on cinder blocks.

Moon switched off the ignition and pocketed the keys. He'd heard a few stories about the blind man inside the house. Walks Sleeping had not driven an automobile since the Mercury engine had thrown a rod almost forty years ago. The Toyota pickup belonged to his granddaughter, who was a waitress at Sky Ute Lodge. Little Myra, who weighed maybe ninety-five pounds, was also responsible for taking care of two children. Her baby boy and her grandfather.

It seemed that no one had noticed their arrival.

Scott Parris followed the Ute policeman to the front door; Moon knocked lightly. A white moth fluttered off the sill, but otherwise there was no response. The Ute waited for what seemed a long time to his *matukach* companion, then knocked again. Now there was a sound of soft, unhurried footsteps.

A young barefoot woman opened the door; she leaned to one side to balance a fat, naked baby on her hip. A shapeless gray cotton dress hung over her thin shoulders like a feed sack. The baby raised a tattered teddy bear for the visitors to see. The cotton stuffing was coming out at the neck; the head was hanging by a few brown threads.

The young mother looked up with a slight frown at Moon. She stole a quick glance at the stranger's face; it was partially shadowed by the brim of his battered felt hat. This was a good face. Clear, honest eyes. A mouth that smiled easily, though the man had an aura of shy melancholy. She found the combination appealing. And there was no wedding band on his finger. Nervously Myra twisted a lock of coal-black hair between her fingers. Dammit, why hadn't Charlie called her on the telephone before he brought a good-looking man to visit? She fantasized about punching the Ute policeman in the belly, but knew it wouldn't do any good. Charlie Moon, that hulking giant, just didn't understand *anything* and most likely never would. Men were such . . . such big dopes!

"Myra, this is Scott Parris." The girl ducked her head when the stranger took his hat off; she almost smiled. The cherubic baby grinned and slobbered and solemnly muttered garbled phrases. Having had his say, he immediately lost interest in the visitors and chewed placidly on the teddy bear's black nose.

Charlie Moon looked over her head. "We need to talk to your grandfather."

She pushed the door wide and nodded to indicate that they should enter. They followed the tiny woman, who seemed barely more than a girl, into a rear room that had large windows on three sides. A small fly buzzed back and forth between the screened windows. The light breeze billowing the white cotton curtains was pleasant and added to the tranquil atmosphere of the bedroom. But even with the fresh breeze, and despite the cheerful fluttering of curtains, the chamber was a waiting room for an old man who had an early appointment with death.

The figure in the rocking chair was indeed old, and lean to the point of having a cadaverous appearance, but the silver hair on his head was thick like spring grass. The only sign that he was alive was the rhythmic puffing on the brier pipe hanging from his mouth.

The girl whispered into his ear. He cocked his head sideways and gazed toward the visitors through milky eyes.

"I do not see very good," he croaked, "but I guess the great big one, like a moose, that has to be Charlie Moon." He would, of course, not say Moon's Indian name in front of this *matukach*.

Moon leaned forward and touched the old man's sleeve. "It is me, Grandfather. And this is Scott Parris. He is chief of police at Granite Creek. Scott is," he added significantly, "my friend."

"Hah, everyone has heard about this *matukach* who is a friend of Charlie Moon. I have heard about some of these big things you have done together." It was probably mostly lies, like the brash young men used to tell around the campfire after a big buffalo hunt or a raid against the Cheyenne. The blind man waved his arm. "You might as well sit down."

Myra glanced shyly at Scott Parris, then turned and left the room.

The policemen seated themselves in straight-back wooden chairs.

The old man pointed his pipe stem at Parris. "Does this *matukach* know who I am?"

Moon glanced quickly at his "pardner" and smiled. "He knows that you are old and full of wisdom."

"Then he knows that you are young and full of bullshit." The old man's thin frame shook with silent laughter. "But I *am* old. And simple-minded—so I like to hear such fine things said about me even when they are not true." He exhaled smoke with every word. "So." He turned his face toward Parris. "You are from Granite Creek. My family, we used to camp up there by Salt Mountain during the Moon of Grass Is Tender. It was a very long time ago, when the whites were digging holes into the rocks to get the silver metal. We thought all the *matukach* were crazy." From his amused expression, it was clear that Walks Sleeping had found no reason to alter this opinion.

"Grandfather," Moon said, "we have come to talk with you about some trouble."

There were so many troubles . . . why did the young always wish to remember them? The old man wanted only to forget. And to sleep. He shook his head; a melancholy expression spread from his eyes down to his mouth. "Is this about Peter Frank's son . . . Provo? I heard about what happened to Provo's wife. It was a bad thing."

"Yes," Moon said.

Walks Sleeping looked blankly at the pipe in his wrinkled hand, but he could see only shadows.

"Provo Frank has been up in Wyoming," Moon said. "He has visited Blue Cup."

Walks Sleeping raised his bushy eyebrows in surprise.

"I've heard," the Ute Policeman said cautiously, "that Provo Frank has taken something that belongs to Blue Cup. Something valuable."

"Young men," the old man said, "sometimes do foolish things." How well he remembered his own youth.

"On the same night his wife died," Moon said, "Provo Frank made a phone call to Austin Sweetwater. Once he got to Ignacio, Provo wanted to speak to the tribal council, and the elders. He wanted you to be present, and mentioned something about 'thirty-eight.' Nineteen and thirty-eight was the year you were tribal chairman. Anything you can remember about that year might help me. But," Moon added slyly, "I doubt you'd remember anything about something that happened so long ago."

"Remember," Walks Sleeping said, "remember? Ahhh . . . that is what old men do best." He nodded to affirm this. "Yes . . . we remember. And sometimes—" his voice drifted off into a crackling whisper, "—we try to *not* remember."

The old man paused in his rocking; he allowed his head to rest on a thin pillow that was tied to the back of the chair. Walks Sleeping stared blankly toward a ceiling that he could not see. Remembering. The old man tried to count how many winters it had been since that long-ago summer, when that Sioux fellow had come to Ignacio in his big black Packard. Yes . . . the troubles had begun when Pierced Nose showed up. Maybe he should tell Charlie Moon about the Sioux's visit . . . but it had all gone terribly wrong. One good man had withdrawn from tribal life, living like a man without the People. Another young man had left the tribe entirely. That old trouble . . . it had become a curse that had injured the People for many years. Maybe, if a man talked about it, the curse would return.

Scott Parris shifted his weight; the legs on his chair creaked.

Walks Sleeping was startled; he looked through the cataracts toward the sound. He had forgotten about the white policeman's presence. What Moon wanted to hear about was tribal business. Certainly not meant for the ears of the *matukach* policeman. "I don't know if I can remember."

"There were rumors," Moon said, "about some troubles . . . back in 1938."

Walks Sleeping grinned a toothless grin that Scott Parris found unaccountably comical. "There are always rumors moving among the People like a fever from one sick man's head to another's. These rumors have many parents, and also many children." He closed his eyes and rocked in the chair.

The Ute policeman glanced at Scott Parris, then at the old man. "Grandfather, I need to know whether—"

Walks Sleeping waved impatiently. "Go away now. I am sleepy."

Moon had half expected this. He stood up, towering over the tiny, shriveled figure in the chair. "If you think of anything . . ."

The old man's chin dropped to his chest. Within seconds, he was snoring.

Moon got up and glanced toward the granddaughter, who was standing in the bedroom doorway. The fat baby seemed grafted to her hip; he was happily sucking on a bottle of cold milk. The tot was now clad in a tiny blue and white sailor suit. A half-pint baseball cap was askew on his spherical head; it was emblazoned with the words "Go Broncos." The tattered teddy bear had been replaced with a rubber duck, and the baby's face had a mildly sullen expression.

Myra Cornstone was still barefoot, but she had changed into a cheerful print dress: pink flowers on a light blue background. Her raven-black hair had been brushed until it glistened.

She glanced quickly at Scott Parris, then smiled with honest affection at the old man. "He may not wake up for hours."

The Ute policeman put his hat on. "Tell your grandfather . . . if he remembers anything . . ."

Myra nodded, and brushed a wisp of dark hair from her forehead. "I doubt he's ever forgotten anything that happened in his whole life." She looked wide-eyed at Scott Parris. "Will you want to hear what Grandfather has to say?" Her tone was openly hopeful.

Parris blushed and nodded. "Oh . . . yes, ma'am. I'll sure be there if Charlie tells me that you're going to . . . I mean your granddad needs to see me . . . uh, I mean us."

She licked at her upper lip. "I live here all alone except for Grandfather. And my baby." She smiled lovingly at the child, whose freshly scrubbed skin was quite red. As if all the blood flowed at the surface of his chubby little body. "This is my little Chigger Bug. Grandfather," she explained with a quick glance at the old man, "calls him CB for short."

It was as if Moon had vanished; all her attention was directed at Scott Parris. "You could drop by anytime you want to." Her eyes sparkled with a mysterious fire; there was a hint of a smile on her freshly painted lips. "To see Grandfather, I mean."

Chigger Bug grinned at the *matukach* policeman. He flung the rubber duck away and raised a chubby red hand at Parris; he waved the milk bottle with the other paw. "Gabba . . . dababba . . . dadda!"

Moon grinned at his "pardner"; Parris was tugging at his collar and his ears were turning a dull red.

"Well," Parris mumbled, "I guess Charlie . . . he'll call me if . . . I mean I don't come down here all that often and . . ."

Myra's eyes went flat with disappointment. She shifted her weight to better balance the baby. "Well." She glanced at Moon. "When Grandfather's ready to talk some more, I guess I could bring him to the police station to see you." With a flip of her head and a flourish of her long hair, she turned her back on Parris and left the old man's room.

Moon clamped a huge hand on Parris' shoulder. "Well, pardner, I don't know what it is. But you've sure got a way with the ladies."

Scott Parris tried to think of something to say. It was always like this around women. They just didn't seem to take to him. But what'd he done, for cryin' out loud?

❖

Even for an elder, Walks Sleeping is filled with many years. A hundred and one Moons of Grass Is Tender, as many Moons of Dead Leaves Falling. He is wearied from much living. A Cheyenne arrow in the throat had killed his father, a fall from a white mule broke his mother's neck. Such misfortunes as these will snuff out a life quickly. But a hundred winters cool the flame slowly, until the last flicker finally goes out in the belly, leaving barely an ember to warm the receptacle of the soul.

THE SHAMAN'S BONES

The ember eventually turns to ash, the ash grows cold. Only then will the spirit depart.

Even here, in this precious land of his youth, among the stark blue mesas, under the soft shadows of the San Juans, in these fertile valleys that cradle the sweet waters of the Piños and the Piedra—even here, life must carry with it the seed of death. It is necessary. Even good.

On this mild autumn night, he lies on his sagging iron bedstead, shivering under a new cotton quilt. His sightless eyes dart rapidly under his lids. As the dreamtime comes, the blind man sees distinct forms and vivid colors.

The old man dreams his dream.

In his vision, Walks Sleeping is standing in a small pasture, bordered on all sides by thick stands of lodgepole pine. He feels the welcome warmth of sunlight on his back. Before him is a house such as those built by the *matukach*. The white men love squares and rectangles. Ahhh . . . these Europeans have never understood the value of the circle, where there is no beginning or end. And no dark corners where ghosts may hide.

This is a small house with an open door. He feels his feet floating over the surface of the grass, toward this building made of red bricks. He passes through the doorway. The sunlight is gone; it is cold in this place. Like the bottom of a deep pit.

Inside the structure, there is only one room—which appears to be much larger than the house. Dreamers are not bothered by such contradictions. There is deep purple paper on the walls. The ceiling is painted white, and from the center of it a chandelier of tallow candles hangs on a tarnished brass chain. A brown carpet covers the entire floor; it is faded in arcs where sunlight filters through the mullioned windows.

In his dream the blind man does not look through his eyes; therefore he can see every detail of the worn carpet, the hideous purple wallpaper, the white plaster ceiling, the flickering candles on the wrought-iron chandelier. The room is almost empty of furnishings. There is no table, no lamp, no bed. There are only three straight-backed wooden chairs. One of these chairs is empty, as if waiting for someone who will come and sit. The other two chairs are placed facing one another; they support a varnished wooden coffin.

At this moment the old man realizes that he is walking through a dream. And perhaps, just perhaps, seeing that which is not yet. But is to come.

"Ah," the dreamer whispers to himself, "that box must be for me. I hope it is soft inside . . . and warm." He taps his knuckles on the box and is pleased to find that it is sturdy. He uses both hands to raise the heavy lid.

Walks Sleeping leans forward to examine the inside of the coffin. He peers into the cold mist that drifts upward from the enclosure, and is mildly disappointed by his discovery. A body already occupies the wooden box. The swirling haze conceals the face of the occupant of the coffin, but the old Ute is absolutely certain about two matters.

First, this is not his body.

And the second is this: he will surely return to this place . . . and see the face of the corpse.

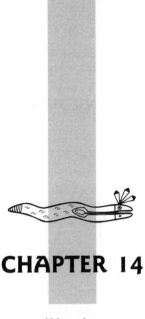

CHAPTER 14

Wyoming
The Pynk Garter Saloon

Fat Sam's lower lip trembled. "How long you gonna be gone, Lizzie?"

The woman in black stood near the saloon door, searching a small purse for the keys to her sleek automobile. "As long as it takes."

"It sure gets quiet around here . . . when you're gone."

She pulled on a pair of black suede gloves. "Business is business." She blew him a kiss and laughed.

He stood at the door and watched glumly until the shining black Mercedes turned east onto the four-lane. Until it receded into the midnight. Sam closed the door and retreated into the dusty half-light of the Pynk Garter Saloon.

Aggie Stymes stood by a dirty window in Unit 1, which was situated at the western end of the City Limits Motel. The motel manager watched the Mercedes pull away from the Pynk Garter Saloon. The woman who wore a pink garter on one thigh (so they said) . . . she was driving the expensive car.

"Bitch," Aggie muttered. "Slut." The hard-eyed woman lit a cigarette and blew the smoke against the windowpane. "Someday, Lizzie . . . someday I'll fix you . . . fix you good."

JAMES D. DOSS

✪ Shoshone Country ✪

The great man's name was Washakie, which in the Uto-Aztecan language of his adopted tribe means "Gourd Rattle." There are many wonderful legends about the Shoshone's greatest chief. The most remarkable aspect of these romantic stories is that most of them are true. One of the best-known tales is about an event that occurred in 1866, when the fierce people who called themselves Crow came to hunt buffalo along the Wind River. They brazenly camped in Shoshone territory near a large flat-topped mountain. Now Washakie, chief of the Shoshone, was a wise leader who hated to expose his people to the terrors and waste of war. But this was a serious problem. The Shoshone were a small tribe and there were many Crow camped on the riverbank. It was also well known that these Crow were a people who feared nothing. But to ignore this intrusion would be a clear signal that the Shoshone could not defend their lands.

Washakie took council with the elders, and also listened to intemperate words from the brash young men who wanted to attack the Crow encampment immediately. They were, they insisted, not afraid to die. All night the chief pondered about what to do. And upon the morning, what he did was this. He sent a scout bearing his solemn demand that the Crow depart immediately from Shoshone lands. In a conciliatory gesture, the Shoshone chief suggested that they could do some profitable hunting near the Owl Creek Mountains, where there were many elk. The scout who carried this message was accompanied by his young wife; this would be proof to the Crow that his mission was not warlike.

The haughty Crow were not impressed by this message from Washakie. They promptly put the Shoshone scout to death. Moreover, they sent his terrified young wife back with this message: We Crow are a powerful people; we will hunt wherever we please. And if Washakie objects to our presence, we will be pleased to kill every Shoshone that may be found in the shadow of the Wind River Mountains.

Washakie was greatly displeased.

The Shoshone chief immediately sent an urgent message to his Bannock allies, who were camped not far away on the banks of a narrow stream called the Popo Agie. The Shoshone were soon joined by an enthusiastic party of Bannock warriors, under the able leadership of Chief Tigee. The combined forces of the Shoshone and Bannock lost no time in mounting a fierce attack on the Crow encampment. The battle was bloody, and it raged for several days. When it became clear that many warriors were being lost with neither side gaining any advantage, Chief Washakie again spent a troubled night considering his dilemma. To continue the fight would sacrifice many lives for nothing. To give up the battle would mean giving up the land. Either way, the tribe would surely perish. He prayed for wisdom.

Upon the morning, he made this bold proposal: He and the Crow chief, Big Robber, would fight to the death. The victor's tribe would control the Wind River Valley forever. It was a huge gamble for the Shoshone. Big Robber was eager to accept the challenge, and the Crow warriors shouted words of encouragement as their proud chief rode off toward the big mountain with the flat top, where the epic contest would take place.

The sun was high when the chiefs met. They were mounted on fine horses; each man held an iron-tipped lance in one hand, a heavy buffalo-hide shield in the other. Prayers were sung, then taunts and threats were shouted. These necessary preliminaries completed, the chiefs raised their lances and made the first brutal charge. There were loud grunts and curses. Horses snorted and collided and broke wind. As a few selected members of each tribe watched, the combat continued for minutes that seemed to stretch into hours. The witnesses heard many hoarse cries and victorious shouts . . . the strong horses pawed the earth; they reared and fell and got up to fight again. The auburn sand was splattered with fresh blood from animal and man. It was a terrible fight and it was difficult to tell who might have the edge—a fine yellow dust clouded the shouting men and their struggling mounts.

Finally all was quiet in the shadow of the flat-topped mountain. One man emerged from the bloodied ground.

The man was, of course, Chief Washakie.

The victorious Shoshone held Big Robber's bloody heart high on the tip of his lance. From that day, the mountain was called Crowheart Butte.

The Crow mourned the death of their chief—they sang the traditional death songs until the sun was lost under the far horizon. But true to their word, the people who called themselves Crow left the land of the Wind River to the Shoshone. A few survivors would return more than three decades later to mourn the death of the great man who had killed their chief.

The Shoshone and Bannock warriors held a victory dance that did not end until dawn of the following day. It was widely reported that Washakie ate the heart of his adversary. Some old men still insist that this is what happened; others smile knowingly and dismiss this lurid element as a legendary embellishment upon the history of how Washakie saved the Wind River country for his tribe.

Many years later, when Washakie was nearing his hundredth autumn in the ancestral lands nourished by the waters of the Wind River, he was asked by a white rancher if the stories were true . . . had he actually eaten the heart of Big Robber, the chief of the Crow nation?

"Ahhh," the aged Shoshone replied in a croaking whisper, "youth does foolish things."

Washakie was a youth of sixty-eight years when he killed Big Robber with an iron-tipped lance. The Shoshone chief was one hundred and two years old when he died on the twenty-third day of February, in the year of 1900.

✧

Nearly a century after Washakie's death, another Shoshone youth dreams his dreams of glory. He imagines that he has inherited a touch of Washakie's wisdom. Young men's imaginations conjure up a host of vain illusions.

This unfortunate young man has not heard a sound since the Fourth of July, four years earlier. That was the day in Casper when the drunken prostitute had, with merry enthusiasm, smacked a beer bottle against Noah's skull three times before the thick brown glass shattered. His father, who has many strong opinions that are dead wrong, believes that Noah's injuries have addled his brain.

But this is not true—Noah is as clever as he ever was.

This young man has given up the name of his father. Now he wishes to be called Noah Dancing Crow. This is not actually a proper name for a Shoshone, but Noah, who had deprived himself of all food and drink for three scorching days during a Paiute Sun Dance, was inspired by a strange vision involving a crow. The shining black bird had appeared in the center of the Sun Dance corral, near the sacred tree. The crow had, it seemed to Noah, danced . . . after a fashion. Actually, the enigmatic bird had hopped about on its left leg, with the right leg folded under a ruffled wing. A more literal visionary might have adopted the name Crippled Bird. But Noah, as his father had always complained, was apt to miss the point. The young man was, indeed, prone to jump to conclusions without a careful consideration of all the facts before him.

The impetuous young Shoshone had made the dramatic announcement about his new name at the dinner table. Now, Noah's father was a very traditional Shoshone; he was not pleased by this development. The old man had pointed his coffee spoon at his son and voiced his frank disapproval of this name change. Noah's mother had gently agreed with her husband's assessment, and suggested that her son sleep on it.

His young sister had giggled at him, flapped her chubby arms like wings, and made harsh cawing noises. The deaf man could not hear the crowlike noises, but he got the picture.

His father, taking note of the stubborn expression on Noah's face, threatened to whack him on the butt with a cane if he did not give up this foolishness.

Noah read their lips, and clearly understood his parents' position. But their protests did not matter in the least. When an impressionable young man has had his vision, he is not to be reasoned with, and such threats fall on deaf ears. Particularly in this instance.

Moreover, Noah had not told his parents the most important aspect of his vision. The dancing crow had spoken to him, told him about what was to come. Noah's path would cross the path of a powerful Ute . . . a Ute who would restore his hearing! There was no Ute within a hundred miles except the peculiar man who had a cabin in the multicolored canyon called Cradle of Rainbow Lizard—and no Ute had as much of the Power as Blue Cup. The old man was, in the Shoshone tongue, a *bugahant*. So Noah had left his father's house—and apprenticed himself to the shaman.

✧

This was surely the sign the old shaman had been waiting for. The *Bitter Springs News* was three days old now, but the headlines were startling:

UTE SOUGHT IN BRUTAL HOMICIDE
WIFE'S BODY NAILED TO TREE

Blue Cup read and reread the two columns. Now the thief was wanted for murder! The old man's thin lips moved as he read, for the fourth time, the most intriguing sidebar:

AP/Ak Chin, AZ—The Papago (Tohono O'otam) tribal council has authorized a payment of five thousand dollars for information leading to the location of Provo Frank, who is wanted for questioning by Wyoming authorities. An additional reward of ten thousand dollars will be paid for information leading to the arrest, indictment, and conviction of any person for the murder of slain tribal member Mary Frank. Those who provide such information may remain anonymous by calling the following number . . .

Another brief article reported that the Southern Ute tribe, obviously embarrassed by this scandal in which one of their members was suspected of murdering a member of the Papago tribe, would match the reward offered by the tribal council of the Tohono O'otam. Blue Cup thought about this. Any man who helped the police find Provo Frank would be paid quite handsomely. And such a man would gain the gratitude of the People.

It was time for action. And though he was annoyed with the unreliable Shoshone, he would need the young man's help.

☼ Wyoming, Valley of Stinking Waters ☼

It had been a very long journey over vast drought-stung grasslands, through dusty draws where no water had flowed since the snowmelt, over the rim of a crumbling mesa. The sun was now past its zenith and the two men had been walking since the first glimmer of dawn.

The Shoshone was dressed in faded jeans, white Nike running shoes, a tattered blue work shirt, and a Cubs baseball cap. Noah Dancing Crow carried a heavy canvas pack on his back, and his legs ached as he followed the old Ute *bugahant* along the sandy plain between two great yellow-orange buttes. Noah did not know it, but this willingness to work hard was the primary reason that the Ute shaman tolerated the Shoshone's company. Noah was relieved that the old man had said nothing more about his recent dereliction of duty. He realized that he was to blame for the theft of the powerful object from the sacred place. But he had done his best. Everyone has shortcomings and makes mistakes. Now and then.

The old man padding tirelessly along in front of him wore moccasins that he had stitched from soft deerskin two winters ago. Brand-new khaki pants were held around his thin waist with a braided rawhide cord. The shaman—and this was amazing to his young Shoshone apprentice—wore no shirt in the blazing sun. Long gray-black braids swung along the old man's bare back as he walked.

Abruptly, Blue Cup paused. He lifted his face and sniffed at the air like an old hound. Yes . . . this was very near the place. Now he picked up his pace; the Shoshone, somewhat energized by the old man's excitement, followed at a slow trot.

At first it seemed to Noah that the land was unchanged. But within minutes, they were on the rim of a shallow, elongated depression that was twice the size of a football field. The Shoshone thought this must be a "blow" where the winds had carried away the sands. Noah was half-right; he followed the old Ute into the basin.

Blue Cup slowed; he walked deliberately, almost cautiously, toward the center of the depression. The old man stopped before a glistening boulder. Noah, who stayed a few paces behind his teacher, thought the black rock was shaped oddly . . . like a great lumpy potato. The visible portion of black monolith was the size of a large automobile. But the lump of stone that could be seen was a mere wart on a hog's back. Like an iceberg floating in this sea of sands, much more was concealed beneath the shifting surface.

The old shaman reached out with the tips of his fingers as if to caress the sacred object, then withdrew his hand like a timid lover.

Noah squinted at the stone and made mental notes: There were splotchy pockmarks, where it appeared that cannonballs had been fired at the black stone. There were also regions where the stone was rough, like coarse-grained sandpaper. And there were flat, smooth surfaces that glistened like ebony mirrors. On these shiny portions there were sketches that had been made for centuries by many tribes. There were crude figures of Coyote and Wolf. Of Horned Toad and Sky Lizard and Tree Frog. Eagle and Dragonfly were also there. There were stick drawings of human beings. And horned figures. These represented *bugahant*, the shaman. *Kokopelli*, the flute player with the humped back, was on the shining stone. There was one humanlike figure that was upside down and headless . . . This represented Who-Is-It. This was Death.

And there were many other symbols. The zigzag of lightning, the cross symbol for stars. And Cloud-Spirit was there on the stone. This was a humanlike form: a square head, a rectangle trunk; arms and legs were symbols of lightning stretching from the corners of the trunk.

Noah eased the pack from his back and groaned from the ache in his shoulders; he pointed at the black boulder. "Is this the sacred stone that was spat from the mouth of the moon? The living stone that came from the sky with a long tail of fire?"

The shaman nodded. Blue Cup stood a yard away from the boulder, and raised his hand to indicate that the Shoshone should not approach. The shaman's apprentice understood, and obeyed. This was surely the mysterious stone that he had heard whispers about. Some of the old Shoshone men said that long ago, even before Coyote had created human beings, this great black boulder had fallen from the heavens. But the Bannock grandfathers argued that the stone had arrived more recently, and that seven sleeps before it came, there had been a flash of fire on the face of the moon. When the stone fell, there was a long finger of fire in the sky. It was as if the sun had risen at midnight. The Bannock swore that one of their women saw it fall to earth during the Moon of Dead Leaves Falling, and called others to watch. A great fire had spread out from the stone and burned until the snows came. Even after the flames had died, water from melted snow boiled around the stone. Not long after the stone had cooled—it was during the Moon of Grass Is Tender—the fierce men with bronzed faces and black beards had come and brought horses and gifts of glass beads and iron knives. These same men had also brought the sickness of pox and coughing blood. The stone had surely been an omen of these terrible things to come. But Noah was cautious about believing such tales; old Bannock men said many things. And their women saw many things.

But Shoshone and Bannock and Arapaho agreed on one point: this was a place with very strong magic, where the *bugahant* came to do wonderful, secret things.

Blue Cup turned toward the Shoshone, so the deaf man could see his lips.

"This is a sacred place."

The Shoshone nodded submissively. Ordinary men must not approach.

Blue Cup waved his hand to indicate the boulder and the ground nearby. "It is a dangerous thing for you to be here."

Noah Dancing Crow frowned. What bad thing might happen to him in this place? But he did not dare ask; such a question might be seen in Lower World as an invitation. Once summoned, the curse would come to him like an owl, and sit on his head.

The old man pointed to two petroglyphs that stood alone on the largest of the shining black surfaces. The figures were simple. On the top were three nested circles. On the bottom, five. "This," the teacher said as he pointed to the top petroglyph. "Do you understand the meaning of this symbol?"

"Yes," the student answered. Noah used the Shoshone word: "This is *Apo*. This is the Sun."

"Yes," Blue Cup said. He deliberately used the Ute word. "*Tava-ci*. The Sun. Tell me, Noah Dancing Crow, what is the meaning of each of the three circles?"

"The outer circle is the halo around the sun," Noah said slowly; then he hesitated. "I think the second circle is . . . is the body of the sun."

"And the inner circle?"

His grandmother had told him about this long ago. Noah thought hard, and it made his head hurt. But it was no use; he could not remember.

"The inner circle," Blue Cup finally said, "is the umbilicus of the sun."

Noah watched the old man's lips say the strange word; he frowned in puzzlement.

"The umbilicus," Blue Cup added, "is where the Power for the earth is made. It is where the warmth comes from. And all the animals. And the plants . . . everything that lives. That is where we get our food."

Noah barely nodded; the Shoshone's face revealed his embarrassment at his ignorance.

Now Blue Cup pointed to the lower figure. It was larger. Here were five concentric circles, laboriously pecked into the hard surface.

"Do you understand this?"

"Ahhh . . ." the Shoshone answered hopefully, "is this the footprint of Death?"

"No," Blue Cup said with a disdainful curl of his lip. "The footprint of Who-Is-It, the one the Hopi call *Maasaw*, that is *four* circles, not five."

"What do the four circles mean, Blue Cup?" Noah leaned forward expectantly. "How do they represent the footprint of Death?"

Blue Cup, who did not know the answer to this question, opened his mouth, then clamped it shut. Finally he spoke: "We are talking about *five* circles, not four."

The Shoshone accepted this rebuke without responding.

"Noah Dancing Crow," the old Ute barked, "do you know what these five circles represent?" He watched the Shoshone's face, which was contorted as if in pain.

Now very ashamed, Noah shook his head to admit that he did not.

"The five circles," Blue Cup said solemnly, "is the Tunnel Between Worlds." He moved his finger close to the boulder, as if to touch the petroglyph, but did not. "From such sacred places, spirits come into Middle World, where human beings live. Through this Tunnel, the spirits can also leave Middle World." The old man's face had a smug expression as he stared down his nose at the Shoshone. "For those human beings who have the Power, this is the entry into Lower World." Some human beings, it was rumored, could even approach the bright edge of Upper World.

"Ahhhh," Noah said, "then this is the five circles . . . where the *bugahant* can . . ."

"Yes," the shaman said. "This is the place where those who have the Power can leave this Middle World and go on great journeys. And have powerful visions. I will go on such a journey . . . and learn where Provo Frank is hiding." Now Blue Cup pointed to a large juniper, which stood a few paces from the black stone. "Go over there. Sit under the tree."

The Shoshone took the canvas backpack with him and leaned it against the trunk of the tree. He sat under the juniper with his shoulders hunched forward, hugging his knees. He had heard wonderful stories from his grandfather about this stone and what was possible here. Now he watched the old Ute with considerable expectation.

Blue Cup saluted the sky, *tukwu-pi*, then the earth below, *tuwi-pa-tukwa-yi*. Now he would face each of the cardinal directions and offer a prayer.

First he turned his face toward the north, where the Ice People make winter in the frozen clouds. *"Nitukwu."* Put fire in my hand.

He turned toward where the moon goes to bathe in the great waters. *"Nitukwa tapai-yakwi-nu-ti."* Keep me from thirst.

133

The *bugahant* turned his face to the place where the summer comes from. *"Nitukwa tua."* Keep my belly from suffering hunger.

Finally he turned his face toward that horizon where the sun rises. *"Tapai mawisikwa."* Burn the flesh of my enemy.

The shaman picked up a handful of orange sand and let it spill slowly through his fingers. He muttered another long incantation, then placed his right hand upon the boulder, directly over the five concentric circles. The Tunnel Between Worlds. The shaman leaned forward slightly and closed his eyes. He began to sing.

Noah could not hear the words, but the faithful Shoshone sat immobile and watched the *bugahant*.

After a while, the shaman ceased his singing. But still he leaned on the great black stone that had fallen from the sky, his palm pressed hard against the five circles. The veins on the back of his hand stood out like blue cords.

And Noah sat. And scratched at sand fleas. And watched. And licked his dry lips. He wanted to drink from the aluminum canteen, but his teacher took no water, so it would not be a good thing to show weakness.

Great beads of perspiration formed on Blue Cup's skin; a swarm of gnats danced around his head. But the old shaman showed no sign of discomfort. Nor did he move.

The sun gradually fell toward its nightly rest in the endless waters. The shadow of the juniper reached out to touch the black stone.

A dusty blue twilight drifted across the high valley, and the Ute *bugahant* did not stir. Still he leaned with one hand upon the stone.

The first portion of true darkness came to the land. Owls called to their kind. Fox and coyote darted through the dry sage like gray ghosts. Bats scuttered from a small cave in the mesa wall; they darted about, probing the darkness with sonar, gorging themselves on tiny sage moths and fat green flies.

Still the old shaman leaned on the stone. His belly did not move with shallow breaths. He did not sweat. Blue Cup seemed to have become a statue . . . a figure chiseled from stone—the Shoshone imagined that the old man had become one with the black boulder. Maybe the old *bugahant* had lost consciousness. Or maybe . . . maybe he was dead.

Noah had almost ceased to care. His buttocks were sore; he was also terribly thirsty and his eyes had begun to burn from so much watching. All afternoon he had half expected to see the old man fall through the stone. That was, after all, what a *bugahant* reportedly did when he leaned against the Tunnel Between Worlds. Surely this was why Blue Cup had come to this sacred place. To fall through the stone into another world. For a vision quest—to locate that thief who stole the sacred object. But now it appeared that this must be a very solid boulder; even Blue Cup could not pierce it with his right hand.

Ten thousand stars sparkled over their heads, and still the old Ute did not move from his position by the dark stone.

The Shoshone sighed. Another disappointment. And then he remembered his mother's stern warning about Blue Cup:

> *"You should stay away from that skinny old man. He is a crafty Ute and you are a simple boy. Blue Cup will find some way to trick you."*
>
> *"But, mother,"* he had said earnestly, *"I am a man. I must learn how to gain the Power. And,"* he had reminded her, *"no Shoshone has the Power like the Ute. And Blue Cup is a Ute who has great Power."*
>
> *"If you want to learn about the Power from one of them Utes,"* she had snapped, *"then go down to Ignacio and learn from Daisy Perika. That old woman is not a trickster, and they say that she gets her Power from that Ute dwarf who lives under the ground in a badger hole. The one they call p-too-koop."*

But his mother had not understood. Noah Dancing Crow had not told her about his vision . . . where the crow that danced had told him that a powerful Ute would give him back his hearing. There were only two Utes who had a share of the Power. One was Daisy Perika. But how could a man get his power from an old woman who claimed to talk to dwarfs? It was embarrassing. No. It was necessary that Noah stay close to Blue Cup; this old Ute had a very great share of the Power. And if Noah was patient, and did what he was told to do . . . someday he would be able to hear the harsh *keee-eee* of the red-tailed hawk . . . the wind talking in the aspens . . . and the fine voice of Willie Nelson. Noah liked the one about blue eyes crying in the rain. The song made him want to cry also . . . but he had not heard it since the woman broke the bottle on his head.

As the stars moved across the sky, the Shoshone tried hard to stay awake. By midnight, he was asleep, snoring loudly.

Blue Cup did not move.

The old shaman leaned against the stone, the morning sun hot on his forehead. His arm seemed to be paralyzed. His tongue was swollen from a terrible thirst and his lungs burned with each breath. But he was determined to find Provo Frank.

The young Shoshone watched his mentor in awestruck admiration. Surely there was no one with such iron will as this old Ute! Now he saw the old man's lips move. Noah leaned forward and squinted, straining without success to understand the *bugahant's* words.

The Ute shaman whispered hoarsely: "I, Blue Cup, say . . . the thief shall not hide from me . . . I shall find the place where he is . . . ahhh . . . Let it be so!"

The Shoshone's mouth was now dry as cotton. And Blue Cup's eyes were closed. Noah sneaked a quick drink of water. As he drank from the canteen, the Shoshone closed his eyes for maybe one second. Or two. When he opened his eyes, Noah caught his breath. Only the blink of an eye before, the old Ute had been there, with his right hand pressed hard against the shining black stone. Leaning against the five concentric circles . . . the Tunnel Between Worlds.

Now the *bugahant* was gone.

The unsettled Shoshone struggled to his feet. He put his hand by his mouth and shouted: "Blue Cup . . . where are you?"

Even though Noah was stone-deaf, he heard the shaman's answer echoing back from all around him, from nowhere. It was much like the sounds he heard in his dreams. The pair of blue-black ravens that sat on a nearby piñon snag also heard; they cocked their heads at the Ute words from the old shaman.

"Páa-nukwi-ti. Páa-nukwi-ti."

Noah recognized the Ute words. But why had Blue Cup gone to the river? Maybe—the Shoshone licked at his parched lips—the old man had also needed a drink.

But the old man had found a specific river. The river called Piedra, that flowed through the land of the Southern Utes . . . and not far from the home of Daisy Perika. Surely Provo Frank was near this place.

Noah was sleeping soundly when the old man kicked him on the sole of his foot. The deaf man was on his feet in a moment, grinning sheepishly at the powerful *bugahant*. He wanted to ask where Blue Cup had gone, but he held his tongue.

"Let's go," the aged Ute said as if nothing unusual had occurred. "We have a long walk."

❖

Blue Cup leaned on the cold metal of the surplus U.S. Army Jeep; he used his horny thumbnail to scratch at the mummified remains of a yellow moth on the flat, sandblasted windshield. The old man gazed thoughtfully across the broad hood toward the deaf Shoshone, who was watching the shaman's lips with considerable expectation.

"The white man's law," the Ute said, "won't get back what was stolen from me. Those policemen, they'll never find it."

The Shoshone nodded. "Well, I don't know . . . that Harry MacFie—

he has eyes like the eagle. My uncle says that MacFie can see a black cat in the dark at two hundred yards." He frowned at the old *bugahant*. "Tell me . . . this power that makes the eyes see—is it different from power that makes the ears hear?"

"All Power is the same," the shaman said curtly. "If a man has enough of the Power, he can see the dark side of the moon . . . and hear the whisper of great stones that pass near the earth."

"It is good to know such things," Noah said, and nodded as if he had increased in wisdom. As he thought about the implications of what he had learned, his eyes took on a peculiar, vacant look that annoyed his teacher.

Blue Cup waved his hand impatiently. "When we get down to the reservation where the Southern Utes live, where Provo Frank is hiding, there will be many things that we must accomplish. We will prepare ourselves as if we were to do battle." He glared at the Shoshone to make sure the young man understood the gravity of his pronouncement. "We will need supplies." He kicked gently at a tire on the old Jeep. "And we will need reliable transportation." Blue Cup patted the steel engine hood as if it were an old hound's head. An expression of affection visited his features, then departed quickly, like an unwelcome visitor.

Transportation . . . Yes . . . this made sense. Noah Dancing Crow nodded enthusiastically. "Horses." The Shoshone clapped his hands and shouted, "We will steal many horses."

The shaman closed his eyes and groaned. "It is much too far for horses. You will drive me down to Bitter Springs tonight. I will leave first, because there is no time to waste. You stay on an extra day and load the Jeep with supplies. You'll buy a small tent for me to sleep in. And plenty of food. Once you have the provisions—" he turned and pointed in the direction where the geese would soon fly "—you will follow me to the south. To the place where that old woman lives . . . the woman who gives shelter to my enemy." Blue Cup hesitated to say Daisy Perika's name aloud; there was Power in a shaman's name that could injure the one who voiced it carelessly. Blue Cup took the old woman far more seriously than he would dare reveal to this superstitious Shoshone. He removed a piece of yellow ruled paper from his shirt pocket and unfolded it on the hood of the Jeep. "I have made a map to show you how to find the place where I will camp."

Noah's eyes blinked nervously back and forth between the paper and his master's lips.

Blue Cup spoke slowly, so the deaf man would understand. "The old woman has a trailer home at the mouth of *Cañón del Espíritu*." He tapped the carefully crafted chart with his fingernail. "This is the place where that long mesa of the Three Sisters is a great barrier between the Canyon of the Spirits and the Canyon of the Serpent." Blue Cup ran his fingertip along the wrinkled yellow paper. "Here is where you will leave the gravel road and drive to an arroyo near the mouth of the *Cañón del Serpiente*. In this arroyo there is good shelter from the west and the north winds; that is where I will set up camp." It was a place where Blue Cup had spent many nights under the night sky. But that was a lifetime ago . . . another world.

Noah, who loved to travel, grinned and rubbed his grubby hands together. "It would be good if we traveled *together*. We could sleep in the mountains. Stop at truck stops and eat hamburgers and drink strong coffee." Noah Dancing Crow's youthful ambition had been to drive one of the big trucks and haul heavy loads from Maine to California. And sit in fine truck stops and eat juicy hamburgers with slices of tomato and onion. And drink bitter coffee and discuss terrible road conditions and speed traps and the high price of diesel fuel with other truck drivers. And have plenty of greenbacks to buy the delectable favors of truck-stop whores. Sometimes, on dark rainy nights, he still rolled this ambition around in his mind and felt some regret that he did not drive a big diesel truck. But now the Shoshone had a more noble calling. The Power.

Blue Cup had painful memories of the last time he had driven the stiff-springed Jeep on a long journey to the state of Sonora. For four days he had camped in the rugged badlands east of *Nacozari de Garcia* and suffered the bite of flea and sting of centipede. For all his suffering, the shaman had gathered less than a pound of tiny hallucinogenic mushrooms called *visionario grande* by the locals who had tasted its flesh. It was a treasure worth all the shaman's suffering in the Sonoran wilderness. He loved the old Detroit rattler, but the tailbone at the base of his spine had ached all winter from that bone-jarring journey to Mexico and back. He had no desire to drive the Jeep on a long trip.

"Yes," Noah repeated for emphasis, "it would be good. The two of us men, traveling together."

"I will leave first and set up the camp," Blue Cup said firmly. "You—" the old Ute pointed two fingers at the Shoshone, then at the old automobile "will bring the Jeep and the supplies." And that was that.

Noah's face was a bleak reflection of his disappointment; his mouth fell open to reveal pitiful rows of uneven, yellowed teeth. "But . . . how will you . . ."

The shaman raised his left arm in a dramatic gesture toward the pale morning sky, where a lone osprey soared over the valley near the rusty face of Iron Mesa. "I," Blue Cup said, "have the Power. I also have a far better way to travel."

It was true.

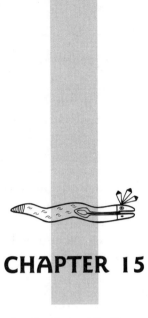

CHAPTER 15

Colorado, Southern Ute Reservation

The child was sitting cross-legged on the linoleum that covered the kitchen floor. She was turning the pages of an old magazine, looking at the pretty pictures. The kitten was curled up beside Sarah, asleep. Dreaming.

Daisy Perika, her hands wrist-deep in warm dishwater, was scouring a greasy iron skillet with a red plastic pad. The old woman's mind had wandered to the past. When she had a man in the house. When she was young . . . when her back didn't ache and she could work all day and not get tired. Her thoughts drifted back to the child near her feet. The little girl's presence was a comfort. More than that. A blessing. Daisy was in no hurry for Provo Frank's return. Especially now that the police had found his Papago wife's body on that tree. It didn't sound like something a Ute would do. A 'Pache maybe, but not a Ute. But there were so many evil spirits at work in the hearts of men . . . who could say what even one of the People might do? The old woman shivered, as if some invisible blade of ice had touched her heart.

The child closed her eyes tightly, and waited. The little window was there. She watched the curtains part. Ever so slightly. Then a little more. She could see him. Aunt Daisy would want to know. "The old man is coming."

Daisy wrung out a soapy dishrag and looked down at the little girl. The kitten was awake now, licking at its paws. "What old man?"

139

Sarah nodded toward the door. "The old man Daddy went to visit."

Daisy Perika's hands, though warmed in the dishwater, suddenly felt chilled. "How do you know he's coming?"

Sarah shrugged. "I see him through the window." She closed her eyes again and, through the little window, watched his approach. He seemed so tired as he climbed the porch steps. The child felt sorry for this old man.

The old woman thought Sarah meant the small kitchen window; but Sarah was sitting on the floor, and the windowsill was a good three feet high. Daisy left the sink; she looked out the window toward the lane. There was no automobile coming, or she would have heard it. And no old man to see. No man of any age. She turned to scowl at the child, and was about to say something about "foolishness" when the heavy knock fell on the door behind her.

"Ahhh," Daisy cried, stumbling away from the door.

The child giggled.

"Who's there?" Daisy called hoarsely.

No answer.

The old woman hesitated, then opened the door. She caught her breath at the sight of the skinny old fellow who stood on her porch. He leaned uncertainly on a knobby mulberry staff. She might not have recognized his wrinkled face, except for the curved scar above his left eye. An old scar that another one of the People had put there with a knife. A long time ago.

He blinked in disbelief. "Daisy?" She had been a young woman when he'd last laid eyes on her. A pretty woman. Now she was old. And homely, he thought sadly.

Daisy looked him up and down. Starting at his wrinkled, weather-beaten face. Then at a brand-new black-and-white checkered shirt. Faded jeans. Dusty rawhide boots. Her eyes went back to his face. To the pink scar over his eye. "Blue Cup?"

He nodded.

"Where'd you come from?"

He gestured with the staff to indicate the direction. "Got a camp a ways off."

Her eyes narrowed in suspicion. "What're you doin' here?"

He seemed disappointed at the curt reception. "Well . . . I came to see you."

"What about?" she snapped.

The old man looked past Daisy, at the child standing behind the old woman. "I've come down from Wyoming. Looking for Provo Frank."

Daisy stepped outside onto the porch, closing the door behind her. "Be careful what you say in front of the child."

He looked hopefully at the door. "That's Provo's little girl, then?"

Daisy glanced over her shoulder, to make sure the door was tightly shut. "She don't know . . . about what happened to her momma."

He leaned his lean butt on the porch railing. "Well, from what I read in the newspapers, it's not something a child should hear about."

"It was an awful thing," Daisy agreed. "Why're you looking for her daddy?"

"He took something that was mine." The old man's lips went thin. "And I intend to get it back."

Daisy sighed. Since he was a little boy, Provo had been taking things that weren't his. "What'd he take from you?"

The old man hesitated. It was an impertinent question. "A sacred object," he whispered.

Daisy understood. It wouldn't be right to ask any more questions. She looked over the old man's shoulder. Toward the yawning mouth of *Cañon del Espíritu.* "Provo always was . . . a problem to his parents."

"He's a thief," Blue Cup said matter-of-factly. "And also a murderer."

"I don't want the girl to hear that the police are looking for her daddy."

"Well, she won't hear it from me," he said. "But I'd like to talk with her. Maybe she knows—"

"Sarah don't know where her daddy went," Daisy interrupted. "He just dumped her and that ugly little cat here on me, and then took off. I expect I'll have to feed the both of 'em till kingdom come."

Blue Cup turned and looked toward the mouth of Spirit Canyon. He'd once killed deer in that canyon. And fished for trout. It seemed like a thousand years ago. "Just the same, I'd like to talk with her." He smiled. "I'd consider it a favor."

Daisy recognized the streak of stubbornness behind the smile, and she felt a growing sense of respect for this skinny old man. He had a thing to do and he was going to get it done. And, more than that, he was one of the People. "You'll have to watch what you say."

The old man was suddenly very still. Very silent. Listening. Looking.

Daisy Perika felt it too. She was being watched. She turned away quickly and opened the door. "Come on in, then."

The old Ute shaman barely heard Daisy's invitation. The *bugahant* had felt a sudden sense that he was very close to the man he was seeking. Blue Cup's slitted eyes were scanning the rim of Three Sisters Mesa. If a man as much as batted an eyelash up there, he'd damn well see it. But he saw nothing. No one. Only the stark sandstone outline of the Three Sisters . . . squatting on the flat ridge for all eternity.

The slender form of a young man stood on the crest of Three Sisters Mesa. With the terrible intensity of a hawk stalking its prey, he watched

Blue Cup enter the home of the shaman. Where the child was. He was very still, as immobile as the eternally silent trio of sandstone women.

He didn't bat an eyelash.

Blue Cup sat at the table, a mug of sweetened coffee in his hand. He and Daisy talked about the old days. Before the electric wires were strung on the wooden poles, before the road through Ignacio was paved. They talked about the boarding school for Ute children, where they were given *matukach* names. And taught to speak English. And forget the sacred language of the People, the sacred ways of the People. The child came close to Daisy, to listen. He sipped at the coffee and blinked at the child. Sarah leaned comfortably on the elderly woman's hip.

The old man, who did not know how to talk to one of such tender years, cocked his head to one side. "So," he said.

Sarah had the little kitten tucked under one arm; it tried without success to escape her clutches. She looked at the cracked linoleum floor, and sucked at her thumb.

Blue Cup cleared his throat and pulled at a leathery earlobe as he stared at the little girl. "Well then . . . so . . ."

Daisy stirred a spoonful of sugar into her coffee; she felt sorry for this pitiful old man. He'd kept himself away from people too long. And away from the People.

Unexpectedly, Sarah looked up. Square in the shaman's eyes.

Inwardly he flinched. It was as if this child had looked directly into his soul, and he felt naked. "So . . ." he began uncertainly.

Sarah took her thumb out of her mouth. "So what?"

Daisy chuckled and her old body shook. "It sure is a fine entertainment—listenin' to you two have a conversation."

Blue Cup smiled crookedly at Sarah. "You . . . and your folks . . . you came from Utah up to Wyoming?"

Sarah nodded.

"And after you left Wyoming, your daddy . . . he brought you down here?"

She nodded again.

Blue Cup leaned forward in his chair, sloshing coffee onto the linoleum. "So . . . where is your daddy at now?"

"With Mommy, I guess."

Blue Cup caught a hard look from Daisy. "When's he coming back? To get you . . . ?"

"Daddy'll come back on my birthday."

He smiled. "Ahhh . . . and how old will you be?"

Sarah held up four fingers. And a thumb.

"And when is your birthday?"

"Five of October."

"Well now," he said, "that won't be long in coming."

"And," Sarah said brightly, "Daddy will bring me a birthday present. A little horse."

Daisy rolled her eyes at the notion of Provo Frank bringing his daughter a horse. That young man was such a bag of wind.

"Well," Blue Cup said softly, "a birthday is a fine thing." He couldn't remember when anyone had celebrated his own birthday. Or given him a present. Not even when he was a little boy. "I think maybe I'll bring you a present too."

Sarah smiled and it warmed his heart. "What kind of present?"

Daisy felt a pang of jealousy. "I'll make you a cake, Sarah. With little candles. And lemon icing."

"Chocolate icing," the girl said.

"Chocolate," Blue Cup said thoughtfully. "Now, that's my favorite too."

Daisy glared at the old man. "You'd best be going now. Me and Sarah, we got lots of things to do. Don't need no old man underfoot."

Blue Cup gripped his knobby staff and pushed himself erect.

Sarah followed him to the door, tugging at his trouser leg. "What *kind* of present?"

He looked down at the dark eyes and frowned thoughtfully. "Something you'll like, I expect." Something special . . . something to set the crabby old woman's teeth on edge.

Daisy ushered him outside and closed the door in the child's hopeful face. "Her big-mouthed daddy ain't gonna show up on her birthday. And she ain't gonna get no horse for a present. So don't *you* go making promises you don't intend to keep."

Blue Cup stood on the porch and looked at the tarnished brass knob on the closed door. He scratched at his chin. "Maybe I'll bring that little girl a big three-layer cake for her birthday. Chocolate icing an inch thick. And," he added slyly, "it won't be something made from powder in a cardboard box. I'll get *my* cake from a fancy bakery up in Durango." He grinned merrily at the old woman. "But I got to get back to my camp. I'm expecting a Shoshone friend to show up with some provisions."

She hustled him off the porch. "Then get on your way now," she said gruffly. But Daisy smiled at the old man, jauntily swinging his mulberry staff as he walked away. He was ugly as a horned toad, but she liked a man who had a sense of humor. And even with the child in her home, this was still a lonesome place for an old woman to live.

*   *   *

Sarah hugged the kitten to her neck; she stood on tiptoes at the trailer window to watch the funny old man leave. "On my birthday," she whispered to Mr. Zigzag, "I want to go on a picnic. And have chocolate ice cream . . . and chocolate cake. With lots of icing." The kitten licked its lips and purred.

✵ Wyoming ✵

The highway patrolman pulled on his thin leather gloves and reached behind the pickup seat. His fingers found the heavy instrument wrapped in a burlap bag. Harry MacFie paused, squinting his blue eyes to see in the dim starlight. It was nearly midnight and the moon wouldn't rise over the eastern horizon for almost three hours. There should be enough time, but none to piss away. He didn't actually *think* about what he had in mind, because the time for thinking was past. He'd already crossed that bridge.

He left his pickup parked in the dark shadow of a gas station. His boots crunched in the white gravel as he approached the rear of the rectangular structure. The heavy-duty bolt cutters he carried at his side were massive, stretching the muscles in his right arm. He rehearsed his plan, and the possible pitfalls. In the unlikely event that anyone saw him outside, well, that was no problem. He was a sworn officer of the law, and he was just driving by. He'd seen the bolt cutters lying in the parking lot and stopped to investigate. If he was discovered inside, well, that was kinda dicey, but he'd talk his way out of that too. He'd discovered a broken lock, and had gone inside to investigate. To confront the burglar. Or burglars. This brought an uneasy smile to the Scotsman's face. *He* was the damn burglar. They got wind of this over in Cheyenne headquarters, he was dead meat. And forget about retirement benefits. He sighed at the injustice of it all; enforcing the law sure wasn't a job for sissies.

When he was within two paces of the rear door, MacFie stopped and turned his back to the building. His sharp blue eyes probed the near-darkness, and his ears absorbed the few sounds. There was nothing to see but the starlit plains and less than a half dozen buildings. To the east, the streetlights of Bitter Springs twinkled halfheartedly. There was nothing to hear but the distant hum of a westbound diesel passing in the night. And a low wind moaning in the eaves of the deserted building. A cold wind.

The policeman went to work with the bolt cutters. In less than fifteen seconds, he'd nipped off the padlock. Before he left, he would put the damaged lock in his pocket and replace it with an identical unit. It was helpful, having an old buddy down in Denver who was a locksmith. The duplicate padlock had the same number, same core, as the one he'd just destroyed. When someone put a key in it, it'd work just fine. He was well pleased with himself. Once he was gone, there'd be no sign anyone had been in the place. He closed the door and leaned the bolt cutters against the imitation maple wall paneling. Fortunately, there were no windows in this storage room; he flicked the switch by the door and squinted as two rows of fluorescent lights flashed on with a buzzing crackle.

The lawman looked around. There was a metal desk in one corner, stacks of cardboard boxes everywhere else. Much of it was expensive stuff. Merchandise that could be sold just about anywhere except in Mormon country. Untraceable merchandise. Well, this had been dead easy. A man could make a living, breaking and entering. No wonder there were so damn many thieves at work in the good old U.S. of A.!

Without taking his driving gloves off, he got to work.

It was almost two hours before the policeman found what he was looking for in a small utility closet. It was in a space behind a large circuit-breaker panel. Weary as he was, MacFie could have danced a jig! Now, when he got the search warrant, he'd know exactly where to look. He wouldn't find it right away, of course. He'd stand back, let the Feds have their chance. Maybe they'd find it with the sniffer dogs. If not, well then, he'd have to give them a bit of help. After this bust, he'd make lieutenant in no time flat.

The highway patrolman placed the stash carefully back in its hiding place, and took great care to remount the electrical panel. It must not look like it'd been removed. Then the stash would be moved out of the building and he'd be right back to square one.

A pair of eyes scanned the lawman's truck. Of course. Sergeant MacFie was up to no good. Yes . . . the snoopy highway patrolman was getting to be a problem.

But problems have solutions.

MacFie closed the door carefully behind him. He hung the new padlock on the hasp and snapped it shut. The moon would be up before long, so it was time to make tracks. He trudged wearily back to his pickup, the sound of his footsteps a harsh intrusion into the comfortable silence of night. Even the voice of the wind had fallen off to an occasional whisper.

MacFie pulled his right-hand glove off with his teeth and fished in his pocket until he found his keys. He unlocked the door, pitched the glove into the pickup cab, and jammed the key into the ignition switch. The lawman was reaching behind the seat to deposit the bolt cutter when he sensed, rather than heard, the presence behind him. The skin prickled on his neck. He turned slowly and saw the silhouette outlined against the starlight reflected off the white cinder-block wall of the Texaco station. Instinctively, like he'd hit his thumb with a hammer, MacFie's mouth attempted two words—one an expletive.

"Oh sh—" was all he managed.

✧

For Noah Dancing Crow, this urgent motor trip to the land of the Southern Utes had been the finest time of his entire life. He had visited several truck stops and eaten greasy hamburgers and drunk quarts of bitter black coffee. As he traveled, the Shoshone had overcome his customary shyness. He had chatted amiably with the drivers of the rusty Reos, shining new Fords, old pug-nosed Macks, and lusty chrome-plated Peterbilts with luxurious sleeping quarters fitted snugly behind the driver's seat. These modern-day folk heroes pulled great shining semis, grease-caked flatbeds and lowboys, dusty belly dumps and end dumps. These chain-smoking, heavy-footed men in shiny Tony Lama boots and fancy Stetson hats, these hardworking women in tight-fitting jeans and plaid shirts, they moved all those essential commodities that must be moved. Tons of hybrid corn from flat Iowa fields to feed fat Nebraska beef that were eaten by hard-muscled Montana miners who dug low-sulfur coal to fuel a great Chicago mill that produced steel for a plant in Gary that manufactured fine red tractors for those hardworking corn farmers on the flat fields in Iowa. Noah marveled at this. It was as the old ones had always said: all life in this world—everything that happens—is a great circle.

Noah had inquired about the road conditions along Route 24 between Leadville and Buena Vista and on southward to Poncha Pass. He had also watched their lips tell wonderful stores about other places like Creede, where the infant Rio Grande was choked with swarming schools of rainbow trout that would strike at any kind of bait, even bubble gum. And Telluride and Snowmass and Aspen where the tourists were rich and beautiful and clever. Noah, who was neither rich nor beautiful, nor very clever, decided that he would like to mingle with such people.

In a Salida truck stop, Noah was downing the last swallow of his third cup of black coffee. He was thinking about the only way out of the Circle of this world. As he mused, a thin black woman sat down on the stool beside him and ordered a glass of buttermilk. The Shoshone asked where she was headed.

She was, her sensuous lips replied, pulling a lowboy to Salt Lake.

He turned and saw the trailer. The merchandise was covered with green tarps. What was her load?

Her lips smiled. Four dozen pine coffins, they said.

The end of the Circle.

Noah Dancing Crow put his money on the counter and hurried away. He was running well behind schedule.

It was dawn when he arrived in the land of the Southern tribe of the once fierce Utes. The Shoshone was relieved to discover that Blue Cup's handmade map was accurate and easy to follow. Noah found the old man's campsite nestled in a shallow arroyo near the mouth of *Cañón del Serpiente*. Blue Cup was not there, but his small campfire was still warm and his sleeping bag was rolled up and stashed in the fork of a piñon.

Noah unloaded the Jeep, set up the shaman's new canvas tent, and placed the cardboard boxes with canned food, beer, bottled soft drinks, and toilet paper inside this shelter.

For the rest of the day, the Shoshone scouted the countryside between *Cañón del Espíritu* and the great manmade lake to the south that was named after the Navajos. He soon knew the location of every secluded cabin, the layout of every ranch and farm. And, more important, he knew where to find every horse in every corral.

He also knew where Daisy Perika lived. He was careful not to be seen near her home, because she had strong powers—much like Blue Cup. She also had a nephew named Moon, who was a policeman for the Southern Utes. Neither Moon nor Mrs. Perika were people to be trifled with; Blue Cup had told him this.

That evening, as the Shoshone sat alone by the campfire, he began to brood. Noah Dancing Crow desperately wanted his hearing restored. He was also homesick for his Wyoming camp, in the shadow of Crowheart Butte—where Chief Washakie had made a big name for himself. It was said that on the night before the battle with Big Robber, the Shoshone leader had been given a sign from the heavens. An arrow of fire had streaked across the sky and struck the face of the moon—an omen that he would be victorious against the Crow chief. Noah Dancing Crow wanted a sign that his dead ears would be healed. He asked Coyote for a sign from the heavens where the spirits lived. Or from the night, where the ghosts lived. From anywhere. It wasn't much to ask.

He watched patiently. For at least three minutes.

There was no sign.

Noah yawned. Too exhausted to put up his makeshift tent, the Shoshone crawled under the Jeep and rolled up into his wool blanket. Within moments, he was snoring.

He was not aware of the sleek gray figure that slipped silently into the camp. The coyote padded about for a moment, sniffing. It settled by the Jeep, its long muzzle resting on overlapping paws. The coyote watched the deaf man while he slept. Though hungry, it ignored the delectable black mice that scurried about, often within inches of its sharp teeth. The animal did not stir until the hint of a new dawn tinged the horizon.

The Shoshone's dreams had become mingled with the dreadful tales he'd heard from the Ute *bugahant*—terrible encounters with the ancient ghosts who inhabited *Cañón del Espíritu* and the awful reptile demons who lurked in the dark corners of *Cañón del Serpiente*. Noah was lost in these morbid visions when he felt the cold hands on his ankles, pulling him from under the Jeep. The terrified man screamed and choked on his spittle; he tried to get up but tripped over his feet, fell onto the campfire, and singed the few hairs on his bare chest. He rolled to one side and saw the familiar figure of Blue Cup towering over him in the light of the rising sun. The old man was smiling.

Noah got to his feet and rubbed at the plump blisters bubbling up on his chest. It would not have occurred to the good-natured Shoshone to be angry with the powerful shaman. The deaf man watched the lips of the aged Ute.

"It is good to see your face, Noah Dancing Crow."

Noah smiled amiably through his pain. "It is good to see you, Blue Cup." He had been lonesome for the old man's company.

"When did you get here?"

Noah attempted to appear nonchalant. "Yesterday."

Blue Cup scowled at his apprentice. "You should have been here two days ago."

Noah grinned self-consciously. "It took me a while to get everything done in Bitter Springs. Lots of stuff to buy."

The old Ute sighed and shrugged. Good help was hard to find.

Noah looked at a hawk gliding toward them. He hesitated to ask. "How did you . . . ahhh . . . bring yourself to this place?"

Blue Cup watched the hawk spread its wings and light gracefully on the tip of a dead ponderosa. The shaman gestured toward the majestic bird of prey. "I have my own ways to travel." He waited for Noah's curiosity to grow. "On this trip I rode in the soft belly of a great beast that had no soul. This beast roared and shook and I did not know whether, at journey's end, my spirit would still be inside my body. Moreover," he added with an air of deep mystery, "many other souls rode with me. Some of these were mad, some shrieked without ceasing, others . . ." He wrinkled his nose at the memory. "Others smelled most foul." But it was a very reliable form of transportation.

The Shoshone shuddered and, not for the first time, felt a spasm of doubt about his chosen vocation. To gain a measure of that Power, would he be compelled to do such awful things as Blue Cup did? Would he have the courage to ride in the belly of a great beast, in the company of a multitude of shrieking, foul-smelling demons?

Blue Cup slipped his hand in his jacket pocket to touch the proof of his unlikely tale; the shaman rubbed the worn talisman between his finger and thumb. On the object was the symbol of the beast. Also on the object, made indelible into the soft flesh of processed pine pulp, was inscribed the very name of the beast.

Greyhound.

☼ Wyoming ☼
North twenty sections
The Colter Hereford Ranch

The old cowboy wore a tattered sheep-lined coat that hung just past his knees, and a hat he'd won in a poker game up in Billings thirty years ago. The brown felt hat was pulled hard over his half-frozen ears.

Pinky Coleman rode Spooky Gus, a worn-out chestnut horse who would've been packed in two hundred cans of dog food if Pinky hadn't liked him so much. They went forward unflinching, the frigid west wind whipping hard at them. Toward the St. Peters line shack where he'd bunk for the night. The man didn't gave a damn about the weather. The horse, who was more sensible, did.

Pinky would live this way until the day he died, because he was stubborn as an Arkansas mule. And also because he was a romantic. He had six more miles of barbed-wire fence to check before the shadows got long. He congratulated himself for this: He didn't have to repair the damned "bob-wire" fence. He'd merely make note of any breaks; them young bucks in their baseball hats would come out in their four-wheel drive pickups and do the manual labor. He'd ride for another hour, then stop and eat one of the baloney and mayonnaised cheese sandwiches in his saddlebag. And drink a quart of buttermilk. And they paid him eight dollars an hour and he slept (rent-free!) in a hundred-year-old log cabin with a fireplace.

What a life.

His eyes weren't so good as they had once been, so Pinky was within thirty yards of the thing and still didn't see it. His horse shied and whinnied. The wary cowboy leaned forward in the saddle; he found a pair of spectacles in his shirt pocket and hung these on the bridge of his nose. He gently nudged his bootheels into the animal's flanks. "C'mon, Spooky. Easy." The horse moved forward with some hesitation; the rider saw something like a dark shadow . . . up ahead off to the right. Just a little ways outside the fence. He urged the animal forward and squinted until the picture was focused more clearly on the retinas of his gray eyes. It was a blackened splotch on the ground, in a shallow arroyo. Near the gravel road that headed south from the interstate.

The horse stopped, bracing its front legs. This, Spooky Gus was saying, was damn well far enough. Nope. This old fella wasn't going any farther. Pinky dismounted and hung the bridle over the "bob-wire." For no particular reason except habit, the cowboy removed a long-barreled Colt .44 from his saddlebag and jammed it firmly under his belt buckle. It occurred to him that a misfire would sure prevent him from fathering any more children. Well, that didn't matter a hell of a lot. The ones he'd already fathered was all lawyers and politicians and such. Not worth the powder it'd take to blow 'em to hell. And he was seventy-eight years old last March, so it was a little late to be raisin' young-uns anyhow.

The old cowboy groaned as he forced his stiff limbs to climb over the three strands of barbed wire, to the road side of the fence. He maneuvered gingerly down the bank of the rocky arroyo. Wouldn't be a good place to sprain an ankle. No sir. Not with Spooky Gus over there on the other side of the fence. Now he could see it pretty well. Maybe some kind of campfire. Town folks from Bitter Springs, most likely. Out havin' themselves a picnic. Or stoned kids havin' a blanket party. Damned good thing there wasn't nothin' but rocks in the arroyo or the fire would of spread to the rangeland.

Pinky was within two paces of the blackened patch of earth when he paused to sniff. No doubt about it. Gasoline. This hadn't been no regular campfire . . . there was lots of bones in the ashes. Looked like somebody had burned some kinda carcass. Prob'ly a dead dog . . . or a calf. Locals was always using the ranch road for a damn dumpin' ground. Pinky noticed something odd in the ashes . . . something that gave his guts that queasy upchuck feeling. He leaned over, squinting hard to make sure of what he thought he'd spotted. Yessir. No doubt about it. Great big chunk of head-bone.

Human head-bone.

This, he thought, sure hadn't been no picnic.

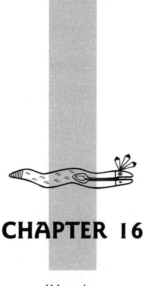

CHAPTER 16

Wyoming
City Limits Motel

Billy Stymes was in his customary position. In the large recliner. In front of the color TV. Watching a rerun of *Gilligan's Island*. That little black-haired girl was sure cute as a bug.

The telephone rang; he waited for Aggie to answer the infernal thing, then remembered that his short-tempered wife was out cleaning rooms. There were only five lodgers at the moment. The two big cops from Colorado (dumb jerks who couldn't find their asses with both hands!), a young couple from New Jersey, and a liquor salesman from Jasper. He'd just sit and wait until the caller gave up.

The telephone continued its ringing.

It was annoying. Billy drained the last swallow of warm beer, then slammed the empty can down on a lamp table near his right hand. He cranked the chair to a position that put his feet on the floor, and lumbered into the front office. He snatched the receiver off the cradle.

"Whatcha want?" he snapped.

It was a soft, creamy female voice. "Is . . . is this the City Limits Motel?"

"Uhhh . . . yeah." He scratched at his belly.

"May I speak to—"

"Just a minute." He found a pen and a scrap of paper. "Okay. Shoot."

"May I speak to Mr. Scott Parris?"

He scribbled the familiar name on the paper. "He ain't here."

"You mean he's checked out?" The disappointment was almost palpable. This was the cop's chick. And if she looked half as good as she sounded . . .

"He ain't checked out yet. He's just not in right now."

"Oh." There was a pause. "May I leave a message?"

"Sure. Shoot."

"Please tell him . . . tell him that Anne called."

"Anne who?"

"Anne Foster."

"You got a phone number?" He was grinning into the mouthpiece.

"He has my number."

"Okay." And I bet he does, chickee. "I got it all wrote down." He dropped the pen onto the Formica counter, and crumpled the paper in his moist palm.

"Thank you." She hung up.

Billy Stymes dropped the unfinished message into a wastebasket. Boy, that sounded like some cute chick. Maybe as cute as that little black-haired fox on *Gilligan's Island*. He waddled back to his chair. Too bad the smart-assed cop wouldn't know he'd got the call. That made Billy chuckle. The half-wit reached for an unopened can of Mexican beer.

The raven swung on its perch and croaked.

"You want a drink, Petey?"

The sleek dark bird tilted its head sideways and spoke: "Peel me a grape."

Billy chuckled. "Peel your own grape, Petey."

✪ Bitter Springs, Wyoming ✪

The medical examiner's office was a fifteen-foot square with yellow paint on the plastered walls and worn green carpet on the hardwood floor. There was a gray metal desk backed up to the street window; on the desk was a yellow legal pad, a painted can with assorted writing instruments, and a potted Christmas plant that wanted water. There were two visitor's chairs; the three lawmen were standing. Waiting.

Tommy Schultz, nine years a lieutenant in the Wyoming Highway Patrol, had sad hound-dog eyes that blinked and watered like he was trying out a new pair of contact lenses. "Harry MacFie is dead," he muttered for the third time in as many minutes, and shook his head. It just didn't seem possible . . . like the world was turned upside down.

THE SHAMAN'S BONES

Moon and Parris glanced at each other. The Ute asked the question. "You certain it's Harry's bones?"

"We found his belt buckle in the ashes."

"Any notion where he might've been when it happened?"

"Not yet. We found his wheels out in the boonies. Half a mile south of the four-lane. 'Bout a mile from where he . . . the remains was found. No prints. Door handles, steering wheel'd been wiped clean. Funny thing . . . we found Harry's right-hand glove in the truck, but not the other one." Tommy Schultz popped the tab on a 7-Up and drank half the can in a long swallow. The tall man with the large eyes and the sallow complexion blinked at the Colorado lawmen like he couldn't quite place them in his memory. "Harry, he was kinda unconventional . . . but he was my best man." He killed the last of the soft drink, crushed the flimsy can in his hands, and tossed it into a plastic waste can. A pair of tears made traces down the gaunt man's leathery face; he wiped at them with the back of a hairy hand. "First we got a woman with her skull busted, nailed to a tree, eyes pecked out by birds. Now I lost my best officer . . . and he's barbecued like a . . . " Lieutenant Schultz closed his eyes and tilted his big head backwards, as if looking heavenward. He whispered a prayer: "God Almighty, please help me find who did it."

Scott Parris paced back and forth in the medical examiner's antechamber. His Ute friend got tired of standing; Moon straddled a straight-backed chair.

The heavy oak door at the far end of the room opened and the medical examiner appeared. She was removing a pair of rubber gloves; all three lawmen looked for signs of blood, but the gloves were clean. The little woman wiped away a wisp of gray hair and peered at them through a delicate pair of gold-rimmed spectacles. "Well, the dental evidence is conclusive. It's definitely Harry MacFie."

Lieutenant Schultz paled even further. "He . . . he was burned to death?"

"Can't be certain, Tommy. There was some evidence of damage to the skull. I'd say he was struck on the forehead. Hard enough to cause death. Then his body was burned." She pitched the rubber gloves into a plastic wastebasket.

Tommy paled one more shade, just shy of a dead man's gray pallor. "That Papago woman died from a blow to the head." He blinked his eyes at Moon. "And the arroyo where MacFie's remains was found . . . it's not two miles from the ridge where that poor woman was nailed to the tree."

Scott Parris stared out the window at the busy highway. It was all so normal. A semi truck slowing for a traffic light. A station wagon packed with Cub Scouts. A U-Haul with Montana plates. A young woman on a bicycle. Everyone eventually died, but life went on. Individuals died. But the species preserved itself. "What about . . . his eyes?"

The ME shoved her hands into the ample pockets on her crisply starched white smock. She knew what he meant. She still had bad dreams about the eyeless corpse of the Frank woman. "There was no soft tissue left to be examined."

Parris closed his eyes. Tightly. "Then his eyes could have been removed from the sockets before the body was burned."

"Could've been," she said with an odd expression, "but there's no evidence they were. Of course . . . I guess there wouldn't be." The medical examiner turned away quickly and left the lawmen standing in her cold, barren office.

Tommy Schultz turned his back and stared out a rear window onto a lawn that was barely kept alive by the city water system. He tried to focus his eyes on the immobile limbs of a dead elm. "Harry," he said, "you should've been more careful."

☼ Bitter Springs Pioneer Cemetery ☼

The pallbearers were seven men and one slender woman. Four were members of the U.S. Marine Corps; the balance were senior officers in the Wyoming Highway Patrol. This included Lieutenant Tommy Schultz, a captain from Rock Springs, and a major from Cheyenne. The major had made special arrangements for the Scotsman's funeral; a piper would play for Harry MacFie.

Charlie Moon and Scott Parris watched the pallbearers strain under the weight of MacFie's coffin. They moved it only a few yards, from the black Cadillac hearse to the stainless steel rack at the slit mouth of the grave. Aside from the visiting Colorado policemen and the uniformed pallbearers, there were about two dozen mourners.

Mrs. MacFie, who leaned on Tommy Schultz's arm, was a small woman with prematurely gray hair and a dazed expression. She stood by the coffin and watched with mild apprehension. As if that rascal Harry might lift the lid and wink a fine blue eye at her. Maybe this was one of his awful, tasteless jokes.

Charlie Moon fixed his gaze over the widow's head. On a distant gray peak nestled in the Wind River Mountains, wrapped in a shroud of snow-white mist. In this country, winter was never far away. Moon heard the sound of the Miata first, then Scott Parris heard the automobile. The chief of police looked over his shoulder; he squinted at the car and its occupant. He recognized the strawberry hair. What was *she* doing here? Then he knew. Of course.

Moon leaned close and whispered, "Well, pardner, looks like Sweet Thing drove all the way up here to see you."

Parris turned his back, hoping Anne wouldn't realize that he'd taken any notice of her arrival. His jaw was set like a vise, and he fairly spat the words out. "She's working on the same damn thing we are, Charlie. For us, it's a couple of homicides. For Anne, it's a story." Sure. The strange and untimely death of Mary Frank. How it ties in to the death of Harry MacFie.

Moon walked easily up a grassy knoll to the spot under a poplar where Anne had parked the little blue car. He touched the brim of his Stetson and nodded.

Anne pushed herself up from the seat, and was careful to make no noise as she pushed the door shut. "Hi, Charlie. Sorry to be late, but I had a hard time finding this place. You could've called me earlier. I've been breaking the speed limit for the past two hundred miles."

"Well," Moon said amiably, "I'm glad to see you too."

A faint smile visited her face and then was gone. She nodded toward the distant back of Scott Parris. "How about him?"

Moon frowned and glanced at the cluster of people near the grave site. "Him? Oh, he's . . . well, you know Scott. He was kind of surprised to see you."

He followed Anne halfway down the knoll toward the gathering. She stopped at a respectful distance and took a small spiral notebook from her purse. "Well, I've come a long way, Charlie, and I've got to make a living." She held a ballpoint over the page. "Tell me what's happening."

"Me and Scott," he began, "we came up here to learn what we could about Provo Frank, maybe get some notion of where he might be. We found out he'd stole something that belonged to an old Ute who lives in a shack out in the boonies. Scott, he found the remains of . . . Provo's wife. We went back to Colorado and followed a couple of leads that didn't go anywhere. Then Harry MacFie, he ups and gets himself killed. So we came back for the funeral. That's about it."

The Ute was standing slightly behind the pretty redheaded woman; the journalist hadn't asked him for names or dates. Or what the leads were. He knew she hadn't heard a word he'd said.

"Then Scott's Volvo got stole by a troop of Girl Scouts armed with switchblades who also took our wallets. So me and Scott, bein' without transportation and flat broke, we robbed a Texaco gas station and used the loot to buy us a pair of hang gliders. We're gonna fly back to Ignacio tomorrow morning. If the wind's right."

Anne nodded absently.

She had filled the page with her scribbles. The Ute leaned over and read what she had written. It might be true, he thought. But it was hardly an accurate record of the account of events he'd told her about. It said:

> Scotty is a big dumb jerk.
> Scotty is a big dumb jerk.
> Scotty is a big dumb jerk.
> and so on

"You know," Moon said, "he won't appreciate that."

She looked up, blue fire flashing in her eyes. "Well, I don't really care what he appreciates." A tear found its way down her cheek; she wiped it away quickly. "Anyway, Charlie, he *is* a big dumb jerk."

"Well, sure. But that's not what I meant."

She blinked a pair of enormous blue eyes at him. "No?"

"No." Moon put on his best poker face. "He hates to be called 'Scotty.' "

Anne barely smiled, and the effect was bitter. She turned to a fresh page and began to write again, in large block letters:

SCOTTY SCOTTY SCOTTY
SCOTTY IS A BIG DUMB JERK

✪ On a knoll above the cemetery ✪

Now, Colin MacFie was of the Celtic clan *Dubhsithe*, as the Oronsay MacFies were called in the rolling Gaelic tongue. A wee bit vain, he was a proud figure of a man, resplendent in the red and green tartan kilt and wool jacket of deep maple green. And Colin's face was very pale, like polished marble. Like all of the *Dubhsithe* clan before him, this Colin had a reputation for being an impatient man. But he had his duty to perform, so he stood under the tall pines and waited.

Ahhh . . . he sighed. It was a most terrible lonesome work, this. And the mourners, they shall not see me as I stand afar from them in this wooded place. But patience now, my soul, for duty to kin in need is fair work indeed. And surely, is this Harry MacFie not a direct descendant of

Archibald MacFie, bonny Scottish king of the sweet velvet island of Oronsay? Why, the saints know that he is! And when such a man as this passes on to his reward, there is a clan tradition to be upheld. Yes. Tradition. But by the precious blood of the martyred saints, this was surely a terrible lonesome duty. But never mind; the cold corpse of a MacFie would hear the sweet sound of the pipes and the brave lad would surely smile. Moreover, on some occasions, one or two of the mourners might truly hear the sweet message of the pipes. And upon hearing, be greatly blessed. This thought brought a tear to the eye of the piper; he wiped it away with his sleeve.

Colin mused about his own adventures in this life that God had given. So many yesterdays. So many strange journeys.

The pale man made the pipes ready.

Scott Parris stood with his back to the wonderful, exasperating woman with strawberry hair. And felt her lovely blue eyes boring, twisting into his back. He imagined he caught a scent of honeysuckle. What did Anne want him to say? That he would survive without her, but that his life would be little more than waiting for his own grave? What did she want?

His confused string of thoughts was interrupted by a long, strained lament from a nearby hillside. The first bleat was not unlike a muffled diesel horn, then the call was transformed into a bittersweet song. Filled with a deep, mournful longing. This melody was vaguely familiar . . . yes. "Flowers in the Forest." Parris turned his head to see where this lone piper stood. He squinted and scanned a steep, rocky hillside where a patchy grove of ponderosa leaned stubbornly against the Westerlies.

Parris turned to Daphne, who wore a wrinkled black dress. The tall woman stood unsteadily, wiping at puffy eyes. "This piper," he said, "it's a fine touch for a Scotsman's funeral."

The waitress turned, having barely heard what he had said. "Piper? Oh yeah, it's too bad."

He leaned close, to hear her words over the wind that tugged at the brim of her little black hat. "Too bad?"

"Yeah, that boy who was gonna play the pipes for Harry . . . he was some college kid from over at Casper. Last night he got throwed off his motorcycle and got some ribs broken. And busted his lip." Her sour expression said that if the kid had any kind of grit, he would have showed up anyway, and played the pipes for Harry.

Parris turned to stare at the hillside. So. There is no one there. The power of suggestion pulls at me. The wind moans in the pines. And my imagination hums a tune in my ear.

But the mind is an infinite world unto itself. As he thought about the pipes, the barely audible strains of "Amazing Grace" seemed to drift over the cemetery. From some other place. Some sweet land, impossibly far away. But this was foolishness! Scott Parris decided to ignore these disturbing sounds. To accomplish this, he concentrated on the words of the Presbyterian minister, whose deep, expressive voice was strangely comforting, as if the Savior were speaking through him:

> ". . . he who enters by the door is the shepherd of the sheep
> . . . and the sheep will follow him, for they know his voice
> . . . I have come that they may have life
> . . . and may have it more abundantly."

And the melancholy call of the piper's song gradually melded with the wind in the pines. The minister's resonant voice continued and was heard over the sound of the winds.

"In My Father's house are many mansions . . ."

❖

The piper paused and wiped the mouthpiece with a yellowed silk handkerchief. "Amazing Grace" was one of these modern pieces, but it was popular with mourners. Ahhh, Lord . . . soon this thing would be finished. The next would be the final song on this solemn occasion.

Colin MacFie had no doubt that the corpse himself would hear the dirge . . . and so he drew a deep breath and began . . . "My Lodging's on the Cold Ground."

❖

Billy Stymes waited until he saw Fat Sam's dust-streaked old Buick leaving the parking lot of the Pynk Garter Saloon. It was no mystery where Sam was going. The bartender was heading into town—to the Main Street Barber Shop. Old Sam got his thinning hair trimmed on the last Saturday of every month. Like clockwork. Billy whispered to the raven, who sat on his shoulder, "Now, watch what you say around Lizzie . . . she's a real lady." This particular lady was, in fact, the object of Billy Stymes' lust.

Lizzie Pynk was sitting at her customary table in the corner of the Pynk Garter Saloon; she had been gazing out the window at a blue jay that was perched on the swaying branch of a Russian olive. The jay was fussing at its reflection in the windowpane. "Stupid bird," she said, and lit a filtered cigarette.

Lizzie turned away from the window when she heard the creak of the door hinges. She knew who it would be. Every time Sam went for a haircut, Billy Stymes showed up with that smart-assed raven perched on his shoulder. Just like clockwork. The man was, appropriately, grinning like an idiot.

He approached the table like a supplicant to the dark queen, nodding and grinning.

"H'lo, Miz Pynk."

"Hello yourself, Billy." She didn't have to pretend to look bored.

He looked around and blinked as his pupils adjusted to the near-darkness in the saloon. There were no other customers, and this was a relief. Billy Stymes was a shy man.

"How's things?"

"Things," Lizzie said, "are dandy. You want a drink?" She knew exactly what he wanted. Billy Stymes was, though not a particularly fine specimen, a man nevertheless.

"Later, maybe." He was staring at her knees.

She laughed, and the sound was like little bells tinkling. "Have a seat."

He pulled a chair from under the table and sat down. The raven lurched to keep its balance on his shoulder. Billy licked his lips. "I hear . . ." He reddened.

"What do you hear, Billy?" She blew smoke into his face. He was so incredibly stupid and transparent, the combined qualities were almost like charm.

"I hear . . ." He put a chubby finger under his collar and pulled. "I hear you sometimes take a bet." He was staring so hard at her thighs that she could feel his gaze touching her.

Lizzie crossed her legs; the black skirt climbed just above her knees. "I don't know what you mean about bets . . . gambling is illegal hereabouts."

His expression of little-boy alarm pleased her. "But," she said, "sometimes I do make a friendly wager. With customers I *like*."

Billy was sweating. He squirmed in his chair. "You mean about the . . . the . . ." He couldn't say it.

Lizzie leaned forward. "You want to guess which leg the pink garter's on, don't you, Billy?"

He bobbled his big head in a series of emphatic nods.

"You got the price, big boy?"

His hand shook as he laid a ten, a five, and some ones on the table.

"That's only twenty dollars, Billy." It would be fun to tease him. "The price has gone up."

Disappointment swept across his face like a cloud across the moon. "But I thought . . ."

"Inflation," she said with a wave of her slender hand. "New price is forty dollars. Now, you slap forty on the table, pick the leg you want a gander at. I'll show you the garter on that leg, Billy-boy. If it's pink, you get to keep your cash. If not . . . well, your money's mine." It was fascinating how many men never asked to see the other leg. To make sure the pink garter was really there. But it was well known that Lizzie had her ethical standards. She would not cheat a paying customer.

Billy was wiping the table with the greenbacks. "But I don't got no forty—"

She shrugged dismissively. "Too bad."

The man's face was beaded with salty sweat. "Waitaminute. I got somethin' else." He dug into his pockets and came up with a shiny ring. It had a turquoise-blue stone the size of a dime. Triumphantly Billy placed this on the table with the bills.

Lizzie lifted the shiny ornament between two delicate fingers and frowned. "Junk," she said. She tossed it toward the man, whose reddening face showed the extent of his pain.

"N-n-no," he stuttered, ". . . it ain't . . . it's worth at least twenty dollars. I found it with these. . ." He reached into his jacket pocket, then dumped a handful of jewelry on the table. A dozen rings. A half dozen bracelets. A scattering of earrings.

"You *found* this stuff?" It sounded like an accusation.

He clamped his mouth shut, almost biting his tongue.

A pretty eyebrow arched over a dark eye. "Where'd you find all this costume jewelry?" Lizzie Pynk had tried hard to sound like it didn't really matter. But a woman in her line of work could never know too much . . .

Billy hung his head and stuck out his lower lip. He picked up the largest bracelet and polished the false pink coral setting against his shirtsleeve.

"You tell me where you found the pretty trinkets," Lizzie said sweetly, "tell me all about it . . . and maybe I'll let you find the pink garter all by yourself. No charge, Billy-boy."

He looked up doubtfully. Surely she wouldn't . . . not really . . .

She kicked off both her black high-heels and, very deliberately, one at a time, placed her small, stockinged feet in Billy's lap.

The man was struck dumb.

"And after you find the pink garter," she whispered, "you can take my stocking off, Billy. And then you can put a pretty ring on my toe." She wiggled all her little toes. Prettily.

Billy Stymes felt his heartbeat pulsating in his ears. He placed his trembling hands on her feet. He caressed them gently, as if they were little kittens, curling up in his lap. He licked his lips and muttered, "Oh my, oh my . . ."

He'd completely forgotten about the gawking raven on his shoulder, when the feathered creature squawked these words:

"Way to go, cowboy! Where is it . . . where is it?"

CHAPTER 17

It is dawn; Noah Dancing Crow sleeps in the long shadow of Three Sisters Mesa. And he dreams. He rolls and groans under his army-surplus blanket.

He is awakening from the reality of dreams . . . returning to the false land, where the sun is scorching hot, the nights unbearably cold, the wind never ceasing to whip the loose edges of the tattered canvas of his makeshift tent. And where a man is always hungry, or thirsty, or itches, or his teeth hurt. And where, unlike the sweet maidens in his dreams, women take not the least interest in him. Noah is leaving the true land of those who sleep, that world of heroic visions. Where pretty women talk to him, caress him, even share his bed. The Shoshone man sits up, pushes the blanket away, and rubs at his eyes. The dream had been very real, more real than what he sees around him. In his dreams Noah can hear the least sound, even the passing whisper of a swallow's wings.

When he is awake, the Shoshone does not hear the sound of the wind in the piñons, nor does he hear the hopeful call of the mountain bluebird from the scrub oak. But Noah remembers his dream.

In his dreams he is always in the Wind River country. In this dream he was a great bird, with wings that lifted him far above the earth, far above his troubles. He had winged his way over the broad canyons, he had circled seven times over the shimmering ribbon of the Wind River, he had soared with the red-tailed hawks over the distant peaks of the Owl Creek Range. But the omen had been presented to the dreamer as he soared low over the Antelope Hills. The deaf Shoshone had seen a lean old jackrabbit, sitting under a green sumac. A jackrabbit with enormous ears. Though he had hardly made a sound, the crafty rabbit had heard him coming. And then the animal spoke to him.

Now he sits on his olive-green blanket and considers this strange dream-vision. Noah knows what he must do. He unrolls a dusty yellow blanket and removes an old but well-oiled Winchester pump rifle. The Shoshone loads six .22-caliber cartridges into the cylindrical magazine under the barrel.

The promise of the jackrabbit echoes in his mind.

Noah was tending the small campfire when he sensed that Blue Cup was nearby. Because of his disability, he did not hear the old man approach. Neither did Noah see the Ute shaman, nor did his nostrils catch any scent that might have hinted at Blue Cup's presence. Noah Dancing Crow *felt* his teacher's presence. And what Noah felt was a tingling of fear. But it was a delicious fear, like the dread little Shoshone boys delight in when they are told awful nighttime stories. Tales of red-haired cannibals who live in the Humboldt Mountains—in dark caves littered with the bones of bad little boys. Legends of the terrible *NunumBi*—the ugly little people who shoot invisible arrows at naughty children.

He would pretend not to notice the presence of the *bugahant*; it pleased Blue Cup to believe that he could approach without being detected. The Shoshone took a pinch of red pepper from a plastic bag; he used his fingertip to spread this pungent powder over the pale skin. Jackrabbit flesh was not particularly good to eat, and the ears were mostly gristle. The Shoshone carefully placed each ear onto a pointed piñon stick; he mounted this assembly above the smoking embers of his campfire. As he watched the hair singe on the rabbit ears, Blue Cup's presence became stronger. The Shoshone imagined that he could almost feel the old man's warm breath on the back of his neck. But it would be cowardly to turn and look; Blue Cup would be scornful of this sign of weakness. And Blue Cup held the keys to the Power. Noah waited until the jackrabbit ears were shrunken and crispy, then decided to get the unpleasant task over with. He was gnawing at the stringy flesh when the shadow of Blue Cup fell across his shoulder. Noah pretended not to notice.

Blue Cup had observed that, since Noah had departed from the stabilizing influence of his parents, the young man had developed some unseemly habits. He did not comb his hair. He often neglected to bathe, or clean his teeth. And having neither mother to cook his meals nor hard cash to buy food, the Shoshone ate whatever he could kill with his little .22-caliber rifle. Gray squirrel, cottontail, quail. When these were unavailable, he would make a supper of the occasional porcupine or tortoise. This diet, Blue Cup could understand, even accept. But now Noah Dancing Crow was consuming the stringy ears of a jackrabbit! The old Ute stood, sniffed the aroma of Noah's meal, and wrinkled his nose. The stink of the singed rabbit hair was unpleasant—it was necessary to get upwind from this odor. The gaunt shaman stepped in front of the deaf Shoshone and waited until Noah looked up at his face.

"Good morning, Noah Dancing Crow."

Noah read the old man's lips. "Hello, Blue Cup." Now he used the Shoshone word for "medicine man" to flatter his guest. "Is the great *bugahant* well?" It would be very bad luck if the old man died before he kept his promises.

Blue Cup scowled at the tatter of ear between Noah's yellowed teeth. "Not so well, my Shoshone friend."

Noah stopped chewing on the rabbit's leatherlike ear. He thought of offering to cook the rabbit's carcass for the powerful Ute *bugahant*, then thought better of it. "Not well?"

Blue Cup looked toward *Cañón del Espíritu*. And the trailer home of Daisy Perika. "I have found no trace of that thief . . . Provo Frank."

Noah spat an indigestible shred of gristle into the campfire, which licked a hungry tongue of flame at the morsel. "Maybe," he said, picking singed rabbit hair from between his teeth, "he's gone down to Mexico." Noah had always thought, if he got in big trouble, he'd go to Mexico and live on a beach somewhere. Fishing and sleeping.

Blue Cup nodded solemnly. "The thief's daughter is with the old woman." He squatted across the fire from the Shoshone. "So I expect he'll be back. Even though the newspapers say he murdered his wife."

Noah nodded. These days, men were doing many bad things. But sometimes a man had to do hard things. The Shoshone gnawed on the jackrabbit ear, then licked his lips. "I will help you look for him."

The old Ute sniffed and squinted at the paltry meal. "What is it that you eat?"

The Shoshone hesitated. "I eat the ears of the jackrabbit."

The shaman sighed. "And why do you do this?" He thought he knew, but it would be entertaining to hear the Shoshone explain his actions.

The young man hesitated; Noah wiped the back of his hand across his lips and spoke with all the confidence he could muster. "I eat the ears of the jackrabbit so that my ears will regain the power to hear."

This Shoshone was a very superstitious man. But he was also young and strong, and therefore useful to a man whose bones were brittle with age. Properly directed, Noah was also entertaining. Blue Cup pushed himself to his feet so that he might tower over his gullible student. "No,

Noah Dancing Crow." The crafty old shaman assumed a sad expression. "Doing this . . . it will not give your ears the power to hear."

Noah was suddenly a defeated man; he stopped chewing and stared dumbly at the remains of the rabbit's ear. He had gone to much trouble . . . done some hard things . . . and all for nothing? "What have I done that is wrong?"

Blue Cup stared down his nose at the deaf Shoshone, who waited to read his teacher's lips. The canny old Ute spoke slowly. "You have done nothing wrong . . . but you have not done *enough*."

Noah's brow wrinkled in puzzlement. "I have not done . . . enough?"

Blue Cup nodded vigorously. "I thought I had taught you better than this." The old man gazed over Noah's head, as if he could see dark mysteries in the distance. He raised his right arm and gestured dramatically, as if his wrinkled hand were a wing in flight. "The power of hearing is not in the rabbit's ears alone." He pointed at the carcasses by the campfire. "The power of any creature is in every part of its body." He waited.

The implication of this pronouncement dawned gradually on the Shoshone, and he did not like it. Noah's mouth was dry as he spoke. "Do you mean . . ."

"It is so, Noah Dancing Crow," the Ute shaman thundered, for he had learned that when he spoke loudly, men listened. Even deaf men. He paused for dramatic effect . . . then: "You must consume the entire jackrabbit if you wish to gain the power for your ears to hear. Even then," he added, "there is no guarantee."

Noah rubbed his hand across his belly. "Ooooh . . . I must eat every part?"

"Every part." The shaman glared at the Shoshone and pointed at the rabbit's sinewy carcass. "Eyes. Tongue. Brain. Entrails. Feet. And you must chew up the bones. The strongest Power is in the marrow of the bones. But," Blue Cup added with a note of fatherly caution, "you should not eat the hair. Rabbit hair will cause constipation. Of course, if you do not have the stomach for it . . . perhaps you were not meant to have the Power." The Ute turned his back so the Shoshone could not see his thin smile.

"The feet, and the guts, they will be hard to eat. And the bones . . ." A surge of nausea tugged at Noah's stomach. "I may," he muttered, "vomit it up." The Shoshone stared at the scrawny carcass of the jackrabbit; his stomach rumbled in protest. It must be done. But this unpleasant task was going to take a long time.

And a lot of red pepper.

James D. Doss

✪ Near the mouth of *Cañón del Espíritu* ✪

Daisy dropped a dollop of lard in the hot iron skillet; she watched the fat sizzle and pop. When she could get to town, there would be some shopping to do. Some flour and bacon and eggs. And clothes for Sarah. Her scoundrel of a father had dropped the child here with next to nothing. Men were such dunces without a woman's hand to guide them.

Then there was the kitten that purred incessantly and rubbed against her ankles, its touch light as a butterfly wing. And climbing on everything and chasing the flying grasshoppers and fluttering moths. Daisy Perika was certain that her eyes had watered since the animal had arrived, and she had begun to sneeze. It must be, she concluded, an allergy to cat fur.

But her thoughts drifted back to the child. Ahhh . . . the child. A tiny girl who stood on tiptoe for hours, staring out the trailer window. Then Sarah would flit around the kitchen like a hummingbird, asking all sorts of childish questions. This morning's conversation was still ringing in her ears.

"Aunt Daisy, where does the cold wind come from?"

"From a place at the top of the world, in the great land of blue ice where the sun can't shine."

"Where do the clouds go when they go away?"

"The clouds go to any place where God's people perform the sacred dance and call upon the thunder and rain." Had this child's parents taught her nothing?

"Where does the moon get its light?"

"From the sun, child. It's a reflection—like off of a mirror."

"Then where does the sun get its light?"

"Before the earth was made, God lit a great fire in the belly of the sun."

"Did God make the rattlesnakes and lizards and hairy centipedes, Aunt Daisy?"

"Of course." The Great Mysterious One, for deep reasons that He alone understands, made mouthy little girls who annoyed old women with endless questions. Why not create other pests as well?

After this, the child had sat for a long time in silence, staring at a tiny black beetle resting legs-up on the linoleum floor. "Tell me, Aunt Daisy." Sarah had whispered that final question, ". . . where do we go when we die?"

"Naughty little girls," the old woman replied gruffly, "who bother their elders with many foolish questions, they go to the high snow peaks of the Never Summer mountains. They live in little square houses made from blocks of ice. With only hairy-faced mountain goats and hungry bears for company. But," Daisy had added as a tender afterthought, "sweet little girls, they go to the soft green valleys of the Always Summer mountains. There are lots of flowers there, and streams, and pretty yellow birds."

"The Always Summer mountains," Sarah sighed, "is where I'll go. To have a picnic with the angels."

Aunt Daisy this, Aunt Daisy that. It would be a welcome day when this annoying chatterbox went back to Utah. Or even to her Papago grandparents down in the Arizona desert. Where she could learn to lie on a flat rock in the sun, like a brown desert lizard. Then there would be much peace. And endless quiet. But inexplicably, the old woman's eyes were moist again.

It must be that damn cat.

After the breakfast dishes were soaking in the sink, Daisy Perika found her old raincoat and pushed her stiff arms into the sleeves. The child looked up hopefully. "No, you can't come. I got work to do."

If she had not gone to dig some roots, she would never have seen him. Daisy Perika was walking toward the mouth of *Cañón del Espíritu* when she saw the lone figure. He was standing on the bluff of Three Sisters Mesa, his slender form a stark profile against the pale blue of the morning sky. There was something *odd* about him. Part of this strangeness was the way he stood . . . so very still. But it was less what the shaman saw than what she *felt*. She could feel his eyes. She could sense his need to communicate. The old woman started to call out, then hesitated. Daisy did not wish to acknowledge that she had seen him. There was a tinge of doubt in the shaman's mind about who it was that she saw standing like a watchman on the edge of the mesa. It looked like Provo Frank. But somehow . . . different.

Something bright flashed in the old woman's eyes for an instant. The reflection of the rising sun off a stone, perhaps. She blinked.

He was gone.

Daisy turned away. It was time to walk up to the road and check the mailbox.

❖

Daisy Perika sat on her porch steps, squinting at the weekly tribal newspaper. According to the *Southern Ute Drum*, the police in four states were looking hard for Provo Frank . . . there was no doubt at all that he'd killed his Papago wife. The Ute woman could hardly believe that he'd have done such a terrible thing—but there it was in the *Drum*, in black and white. So everyone would think it must be true. And maybe . . . but she pushed the dreadful possibility from her mind.

Not a half hour earlier, Daisy had seen Provo plain as day—standing up there on the edge of Three Sisters Mesa. She'd thought long and hard about what to do. It would be best if Charlie Moon arrested Provo. If somebody else found him first, they might not take the boy alive. He was a stubborn one—and not afraid of a fight. But Provo liked Charlie.

But how was she to get word to her nephew, her with no telephone and precious few visitors? It seemed hopeless. But Father Raes always said that when you didn't know which way to turn, you should pray. Ask for help. God, the Catholic priest had assured her more than once, already knows exactly what we need. But we should ask just the same. This seemed odd, but when the Ute woman needed help, it was not her habit to ruminate over philosophical issues.

Daisy bowed her head. "God," she muttered, "you know that I don't have no telephone, and I need to get word to Charlie. The lady that brings the mail to my letter box has already come and gone, and I don't expect Gorman Sweetwater for at least a week. If you could send someone out here . . . and by the way," the shaman added pointedly, "this is kind of important, so it wouldn't be a good idea to take all day."

She lifted her face to heaven and waited expectantly. Knowing that the Great Mysterious One always responds to those who have even a tiny little mustard seed of faith. She figured she had a pound of mustard seed. At least.

Now some say that God works in mysterious ways . . . and others claim that the Creator of Universes has a divine sense of humor.

Within seconds she heard the sound of an automobile. It was still far away. The old woman closed her eyes and listened. This was not Charlie Moon's big Blazer. Nor was it Gorman Sweetwater's old Dodge pickup truck with the loose tailpipe. No. This was not a familiar sound.

"Sarah," Daisy shouted through the screened door, "you stay inside."

The automobile appeared over a juniper-dotted ridge. It was a large black sedan. An old one, too, with rusty fenders. Trailing a cloud of blue exhaust. The front bumper rattled as if it were supported by baling wire. There was a billow of steam puffing from under the hood—it made a screeching whine . . . more like a demon's car than something made in Detroit. As soon as this thought entered her mind, Daisy was able to see the automobile more clearly.

There was no driver!

The old woman wanted to run, but she was almost frozen by fear. It would run her down, smash her flat as a wet tortilla! Daisy turned toward her porch and made a valiant attempt to escape. She could feel the hot breath of the demon machine upon her neck, the screeching whine reverberating in her skull. When she was almost to the porch steps, the engine coughed and shuddered and was silent.

She stopped and glanced over her shoulder. Daisy caught her breath when the hot engine dieseled—it sputtered back to life, hiccuped twice, and died. The old woman turned slowly to squint at the automobile. It was old. And also ugly.

Someone called her name. "Daisy . . . Daisy dear." The shaman did not answer—it could be a demon. Or the White Owl from the land of the dead.

A wisp of steam drifted from under the hood. But there was still no one to be seen in the black sedan. The voice called out again:

"Oh, fiddle-faddle."

Now the Ute woman recognized the voice. She hesitated, then frowned at the foul-smelling heap of rusted steel and worn rubber tires. "Louise Marie?" There was no answer. The Ute woman exhaled a long breath and tried to ignore her thumping heart. She hobbled stiff-legged toward the car, braving the aromas of raw gasoline and smoldering rubber.

The old woman's gray head was not visible until Daisy Perika stood beside the aged Oldsmobile. Louise Marie LaForte sat uncertainly under the steering wheel, like a plump frog in the shade of a poisonous mushroom. "Oh, double fiddle-faddle. And consarn and blast this trouble-some buckle."

Daisy reached out to touch the tips of her fingers to the heavy door. "When did you start driving a car?"

The elderly French-Canadian woman fumbled with the heavy chrome buckle on the seat belt. "Why, just last Tuesday, that was when I bought this car off a hog farmer up by Oxford." She smiled a sweet smile that featured a glistening gold tooth. "Now I can come out and visit with you whenever I take the notion."

Daisy's expression was blank. "I wouldn't want you to go to so much trouble on my account."

"It's no trouble." Louise Marie fumbled with the buckle. "I'd of come out to visit earlier, but I've been feeling poorly. Think I had a touch of the mulliegrubs in my lower colon."

"Uh-huh. I hear there's a lot of that goin' around." Daisy's eyes measured the top of the short woman's head against the bottom of the cracked, dusty windshield. "How in the world do you see to drive this thing?"

"Not so well, Daisy. I have to peep out through the steering wheel." Finally she had managed to unsnap the buckle. "I got to get me a couple of cushions to sit on so's I can see better."

Daisy helped her open the heavy automobile door; Louise Marie slipped to the ground with a great sigh. She was a head shorter than Daisy.

Louise Marie opened the rear door and found a large pink plastic satchel; she leaned forward to give Daisy a nearsighted gaze and raised a hand to wave with her fingers. "Well, ding-a-ling."

The Ute woman looked suspiciously down her nose at the peculiar French-Canadian woman. "Ding a *what?*"

"I," Louise Marie announced with an air of importance, "am your new Avon lady."

Daisy took a step backwards. "You're my *what?*"

This old Indian woman was slow to catch on, but Louise Marie considered herself to be a patient soul. "I'm your Avon lady . . . you know . . ." She raised her hand again and shook an imaginary bell in Daisy's face. "I'm your local *ding-a-ling.*"

"Ah yes—I've heard some talk about it," the Ute woman muttered with a wicked grin, "but come on in anyway. I'll fix you some coffee." Almost too late, Daisy remembered the child. "But first give me a minute to straighten the place up. You wait by the porch, and I'll come get you when I'm ready."

Louise Marie frowned impatiently and glanced at the gold-plated Lady Elgin watch strapped onto her liver-spotted wrist. The watch had not run since her long-departed husband had pried off the cover and dripped a drop of 3-In-One lubricating oil into its complex works. "Well . . . all right," she muttered to herself. "But don't take too long. I got a big territory and lots of other calls to make."

Daisy leaned close to the child and whispered, "The Avon lady is here. You can hide under the sink with your cat." If Louise Marie LaForte learned that the child was here, all of Ignacio would know before the sun came up again. And people would start talking about why Provo's daughter was with Daisy Perika. Why was the child not in Arizona, with her mother's people? That's what they would say.

"I don't want to hide under the sink," Sarah said. "I saw some great big bugs under there."

"Then go and hide in the bedroom. You be real quiet, and I'll get rid of her as soon as I can." Sarah snatched up her cat and tiptoed through the bedroom door.

The Ute woman turned the propane flame on under a half pot of stale coffee.

She opened the door for Louise Marie, who was laboriously making her way up the steps. "Come on in," Daisy said with the resignation of a victim who has no means of escape, "and let's see what you got to sell."

Her visitor looked around anxiously. "Now, where did I put my sample case?"

The Ute woman pointed at the pink case. "It's right there in your hand."

Louise Marie chuckled amiably. "Well, so it is. I just keep forgetting to remember what I do with things."

Daisy nodded sympathetically. "They say that happens when you get old."

"My memory is gettin' so bad, I could hide my own Easter eggs." Louise Marie sat down at the kitchen table and removed a handful of samples from her big plastic satchel. "Let's see now . . . I got cologne. And bath oil."

"I don't want no slickery oil in my bathtub. I might slip and fall down."

"What about lipstick?"

"I don't never use it."

Louise Marie hesitated. But she was a professional and this woman needed professional advice. "You know, Daisy." She smiled sweetly. "If you . . . well, prettied yourself up a bit, you . . . you might find yourself a man."

Daisy leaned back and cackled. And wheezed. Finally she was able to speak. "I had myself some men, and let me tell you something. In the long haul, they ain't nothing but trouble." She wiped merry tears from her eyes and blinked at the little woman. "Believe me, Louise Marie, a woman is better off without having a man around to worry her."

Now the old French-Canadian woman's eyes went moist. Too late, Daisy remembered that Louise Marie's man had walked away years ago. And never came home. The Ute woman immediately felt sorry for her remarks. It was one thing if you had a man and he died; you couldn't blame him much for that. But when he just upped and walked away, well, that was a different matter altogether. Even if you was better off without him, it was still a mean thing for a man to do. The Ute woman leaned close to Louise Marie and patted her hand. "Yes . . . that fellow who brought you down here from Canada . . . ummm . . . I still remember his name . . . Bruce Two Ponies."

"Henry Gray Dog," Louise Marie sniffed.

"Yes . . . that little Micmac."

"He was of the Iroquois, the Five Nations," Louise Marie snapped. "And he stood six foot two in his bare feet."

"Yes," the Ute woman said with a solemn nod, "I remember him like it was yesterday."

"And I never heard a word from him after he left." Her lower lip trembled. "Don't even know if my man is alive or dead."

"Well, don't worry," Daisy said in a comforting tone, "more'n likely he's dead as last summer's grasshopper." She'd heard someone say that most Micmacs didn't live long enough to see their grandchildren.

Unaware of the horrified expression on Louise Marie's face, Daisy nudged the satchel with her toe. "Well, I expect you must have something in there that I need." She peered inside. It was a strange collection; not all of it bore the Avon trademark. There were odd bits of costume jewelry. Dozens of lipsticks. Bottles of aftershave in strange shapes. Old-fashioned pistols and antique cars. Even a fat glass rhinoceros. And there was mascara. "Do you have a catalog?"

Louise Marie waved the question away with a nervous flutter of tiny hands. "Catalogs, I don't have today . . . but baby oil, I got some."

"What," Daisy asked sharply, "would I want with baby oil?"

The saleslady had recovered. "Our baby oil," Louise Marie chirped, "is good for repelling insects. Like them big black bloodsucking mosquitoes that come up from the riverbank in June."

Daisy picked up a dusty bottle of aftershave in the shape of a flintlock pistol. "I didn't know they made these anymore."

"Well, they don't, dearie." A hint of anxiety was in her voice. "Thing is . . . I don't sell that two-for-a-nickel *new* stuff, just the . . . the fine old classic products."

Daisy squinted one eye at the peculiar little woman. "Louise Marie, are you tryin' to sell me *used* cosmetics?"

"They ain't used." The short woman hesitated. "All of my merchandise is . . . is what we in the trade call . . . umm . . . previously owned."

"Well, that makes all the difference." Daisy glared at the lipsticks. "But where do you . . ."

"At flea markets. Garage sales." Louis Marie set her little mouth defiantly. "I only deal in the *classic* products."

The Ute woman grinned. "You ain't no authorized Avon saleslady, are you, Louise?" That was why the French-Canadian woman had no catalogs.

"Well, if you want to put it that way . . . *non*. But some real nice collectibles, I got."

Daisy sighed. For the past week, nothing had been quite what it seemed. She got up and removed the bubbling coffeepot from the propane burner.

Louise Marie was swiping at her lips with a previously owned lipstick; a bit of the crimson smear was on her chin. "See? Paris Holiday. It does something for me, *oui*?"

" 'Wee,' " Daisy agreed. "It sure does do something for you." Something best not mentioned. But Daisy suddenly felt wicked and guilty. Louise Marie LaForte might be foolish, but she had a good heart and deserved better treatment. "You can put me down for a bottle of that insect-repellent baby oil. But I can't pay you till my Social Security comes next month."

Louise Marie clasped her little hands in delight. "That's okay, dearie. You're my first sale, so I'll let you have it for a bargain price."

It occurred to Daisy that this peculiar old woman could be of some help. Provo Frank was out there somewhere. It would be good if Charlie Moon knew this. She poured hot coffee into a plastic mug and pushed it across the red checkered oilcloth toward the counterfeit Avon lady. "There is something you can do for me."

Louise Marie was always happy to do a favor. "*Oui* . . . tell me what it is." She sipped at the coffee and made an ugly face. She mumbled something in French that the Ute woman did not understand. It was just as well.

Daisy frowned at the scarlet lipstick stain on Louise Marie's coffee cup. "I need a favor. I don't have no telephone out here, so it's hard for me to get in touch with people."

"Well," her visitor said, "you ought to get one installed right away. I got Call Waiting on my telephone and don't know what I'd do without it." Louise Marie waited; no one called. Except robotic voices reading long spiels about good causes, which were always followed by requests for money from the poverty-stricken widow. Louise Marie was so grateful for these infrequent calls that she always sent a dollar or two after her pension check came in the mail. Now her name and telephone number were eternally inscribed on that universal List.

"Sure, I'll get me a phone installed," Daisy said. She glanced at a red coffee can on a shelf above her stove. Inside the can, under a half pound of coffee, was fifteen dollars and some change. "They'd only have to string up about six miles of new line to get me hooked up. I guess," she added sarcastically, "I could pay the phone company with a bag full of pretty rocks."

"Oh no, Daisy," her guest said sweetly, as one might speak to a slow-witted child, "I'm sure they'd want cash." Louise Marie looked around the kitchen, where nothing was new. "Yes . . . cash on the barrel head."

The Ute woman sighed with exasperation. One thing worse than being lonely was suffering some of the peculiar company that drops in unexpected. Daisy put her face in her hands and closed her eyes. "Louise." She said it slowly. "When you get back to town, I need you to go over to the police station. And see Charlie for me."

Louise Marie was pleased at this excuse to go see Charlie Moon; she was quite fond of the big Ute policeman. He never failed to answer her calls, even though she was in the jurisdiction of the Ignacio town police.

But the old woman was envious that Daisy Perika had such a fine nephew to look after her—she had no one. "What'll I tell him?"

"Tell that big buffalo," Daisy snapped, "I want him to come out here and see me. Right away."

Doubt flashed over Louise Marie's face. "I heard he was gone somewheres . . . maybe up north . . . to Wyoming."

"Soon as he's back," Daisy said firmly, "tell him I said to come out here."

"Is it something important?"

"No."

Louise Marie sat for most of an hour, bringing the Ute woman up-to-date on the "happenings" in town.

Finally, when she was talked out, Louise Marie pushed herself up from the table with a grunt. She glared suspiciously at the coffee cup like Snow White should have looked at the pretty apple. "Well," she said through her half-painted lips, "I must get along now. Got other calls to make." She waved her fingers and hobbled toward the door.

Daisy followed her down the porch steps and to the car, feeling oddly sorry that the balmy woman was leaving. The Ute woman walked a wide circle around the black automobile; she squinted at the rear bumper. "Louise Marie, that license plate is five years old."

The little woman was fixing herself under the steering wheel; she puffed and groaned. "Well," she said by way of explanation, "the car is a lot older than that."

"If the police see that old license plate," Daisy warned sternly, "they'll take your driver's license away."

"Hah," Louise Marie shot back as she turned the ignition key, "the joke's on them, dearie."

The Ute woman leaned against the door and frowned at the driver. "The joke's on them? The police?"

"Sure." Louise Marie chuckled. "I don't *have* no driver's license." With that, she threw the gear into reverse and backed away with rear wheels spinning.

Daisy watched the automobile lurch over the hill, apparently minus a driver. The old shaman crossed herself. "May God and His angels watch over you, Louise Marie. And," the shaman added as a solemn afterthought, "may the Great Mysterious One protect other folks who're out there on the highway with you."

Sarah sat near the foot of Daisy's small bed; she whispered into the kitten's ear, "Mr. Zigzag . . . I thought of something. D'you want to hear what it is?"

The kitten purred, and she took this to be a definite yes.

"Daddy will be coming back to get us," the child said, "and I'd like to go on a picnic. Would you like to go too?"

He put his mouth to her face. The kitten purred, and licked at her earlobe.

"Oh," she said, "I knew you would."

But where she would go, the kitten could not come.

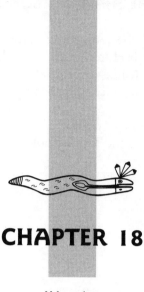

CHAPTER 18

Wyoming
The Pynk Garter Saloon

Fat Sam was clearing a table of beer glasses when he heard the throaty growl; he glanced at the window and saw the black Harley. The bearded, heavyset man who dismounted was dressed in black leather jacket and fringed leather chaps. His black T-shirt was emblazoned with the words MISSING IN ACTION. He wore a dirty red scarf on his head; sky-blue sunglasses with circular lenses were perched on his red nose. The beginning of a beer belly bounced as he made his way to the door of the Pynk Garter Saloon. "Hey, Lizzie," Sam chuckled, "we got us a customer."

She'd been watching the television set mounted over the bar. "What kind?"

"Some redneck trash."

The door opened and the man swaggered in. He threw one thigh over a stool and rested his elbows on the bar. Unconsciously he fondled the waxed tips of his handlebar mustache.

Lizzie smoothed her dress over her thin hips and went behind the bar. "What'll you have?"

The motorcyclist cleared his throat and scratched at his sunburned neck. "What I'll have, missy—" he looked her up and down with an appraising eye "—is the best stuff you got. Somethin'," he added slowly, "that'll put some starch . . . in my collar."

176

Lizzie leaned on the scarred oak surface of the bar, her face inches from his. "I doubt you could handle the best stuff I got, sonny. Or—" now she smiled sweetly and licked her lips "—that you could afford it."

The man jammed a grimy paw into his hip pocket. He opened a canvas wallet and displayed a wad of greenbacks half an inch thick. He peeled off a hundred-dollar bill and laid it on the bar. Under Lizzie's chin. She tried not to stare at the crisp new bill. Lizzie tried so hard. But she couldn't help herself.

Now the customer grinned, exposing a row of fine teeth between his chapped lips. "Anything you got for me, sweetmeat, I can pay the freight."

✪ Bishop Boulevard, Cheyenne ✪
Headquarters—Wyoming Highway Patrol

The bearded man in the three-piece suit offered his hand. "I'm Lloyd Cuffman." He said it like the Colorado cops should have heard of him. "Six years with Central Intelligence, four with DIA. Nine years with the Drug Enforcement Administration. Last four in Undercover Ops." He jutted his chin forward. "When I bust drug pushers, they do time. Big time."

"I'm Charlie Moon," the big Ute said. "I mostly ticket jaywalkers. If they get smart with me, I call their moms."

"I'm Scott Parris," the other man said. "I'm in charge of parking meters."

Cuffman, who detested wise-ass, small-town cops, managed to smile wearily. The effort hurt his face.

"Sit down, boys." Lieutenant Tommy Schultz waved his hand to indicate a soft leather couch against the north wall of his office.

Charlie Moon sat down first; the springs creaked. Parris sat beside his friend. Neither man had a notion why the Wyoming Highway Patrol officer had called them to his office to meet a DEA undercover cop.

Cuffman's fingers went to play with the tip of his waxed mustache. "Officer Schultz called our people in when he found some notes made by the late Officer Harold MacFie."

Tommy Schultz nodded politely to the Fed and took the cue. "Harry MacFie had some suspicions that Lizzie Pynk was pushin' drugs over at her saloon. He'd never mentioned it to me. I expect he wanted to set it all up himself." And take all the credit, of course.

The DEA cop was pacing, his hands folded behind his back. "It was easier than we'd figured. I checked out a Harley and some leather duds and paid a visit to the Pynk Garter Saloon." He paused to grin at the Colorado policemen. "In twenty minutes flat, I made a buy. Cocaine. Sweet and pure." He waited for an awed response from the hick cops, and got none.

"We arrested Lizzie and Fat Sam soon as DEA forensics authenticated the substance," Schultz said.

Cuffman puffed his chest out. "On the basis of the dope I bought off of 'em, we got a search warrant. Brought in Storm Trooper, our primo sniffer dog. Found the stash in ten minutes." The bearded man laughed and stroked his mustache. "It was behind a circuit-breaker panel. All these dope pushers think they're so damned clever. Hell, we'd have found it in an hour *without* the dog."

Moon got up from the couch. The Ute could see where this was going. "Provo might have got himself soaked with alcohol. But I don't think he'd have bought any drugs."

The DEA cop shrugged. "You may be right. But . . ." He glanced at Tommy Schultz. "That Pynk lady may have spiked his drink."

Parris frowned. "Why would she have done that?"

Cuffman shrugged again. "Hell, how should I know? Maybe she wanted him zonked out so she could go through his pockets. Maybe she did it just for the hell of it. These kind of people . . . they ain't like you and me." He meant the association as a compliment.

Moon figured it was time to head south. To his little home on the Piños. "Even with all the evidence, I've never been able to believe that Provo would . . . would do what was done to his wife."

"Lissen," the DEA cop said in exasperation, "that Lizzie broad had a whole pharmacopoeia of drugs stashed. Some common stuff. Cocaine. Crack cocaine. Heroin. LSD. Even some designer drugs . . . some of which our chemists haven't even identified yet. She could have dropped something in his drink and maybe he went wild. Hell," he added, "he may *still* be wild. Or it may come and go. This Provo Frank may be a damn Jekyll and Hyde."

"That," Parris offered, "would explain his vicious attack on my officer." The picture of Alicia Martin's broken face flashed before him; it was as if a demon had dropped a lump of ice in his belly. He turned his back on the DEA cop and stared out the window at an ash tree that was bent with the wind. The damn wind.

"There's more, boys." Tommy Schultz lowered his voice to enhance the drama. "Remember that glove of Harry's we found in his pickup? The forensics techs found traces of cocaine on the tips of the fingers. It's a perfect chemical match for the coke we found in the Pynk Garter. So

Harry must've found her stash. Probably on the night he died. It's a good bet that Lizzie is responsible for Harry MacFie's murder."

Scott Parris turned away from the window. "You'll need a lot more than some cocaine on his glove to prove that she killed him."

Schultz nodded. "And we got it. You remember Aggie Stymes, the lady who runs the City Limits Motel? Well, she told us that she saw Harry's pickup parked over by the Texaco station after midnight. Not two hundred yards from the Pynk Garter. Same night he disappeared. Now, Harry was off duty that night, and he wasn't using his state-issue black-and-white. I figure Harry was snoopin' around the Pynk Garter after closin' time. He found the cocaine and they surprised him. Either Lizzie or Fat Sam could've killed Harry. Then they hauled his body out there, poured some gasoline on it . . . and lit the match. If it hadn't of been for that old cowboy, we might not of found any remains for years. Maybe never."

Schultz was pleased to see that he had their full attention. "When I got a warrant to search Lizzie's saloon for the drugs, I also got one for her house, and Sam's apartment in town. And got the judge's permission to look for any connection to Harry's murder. See—we'd found a little hank of black thread on a thorn bush at the place where the killer had set fire to poor Harry's body. Turns out the fiber's a good match to one of Lizzie Pynk's black dresses. And we found a print by the gravel road that's a dead ringer for one of Fat Sam's boots. Right down to a thumbtack stickin' in the heel."

Parris watched the highway patrolman's face. The man's eyes betrayed his uncertainty. "Have you questioned them about it?"

Schultz nodded. "So far, neither Lizzie nor Sam admits to having anything to do with MacFie's murder. But we've got 'em cold on the drug charge, so they ain't leavin' town. Sooner or later, one of 'em will want to make a deal . . . and blame the homicide on the other one."

The Ute policeman offered his hand to Tommy Schultz, then to the DEA cop. "Thanks for keeping us on top of this, fellas." If Provo Frank was still suffering the late effects from some mind-warping drug, he had to be found. Before he nailed somebody else to a tree. Provo wouldn't be far from his daughter. And Aunt Daisy. Moon turned to Parris. "Pardner, you about ready to go home?"

For the first time since the morning when he'd led Charlie Moon to the dreadful tree on the windswept ridge, Scott Parris was feeling alive again. Like a man who had things to do in this world. He jammed his felt hat down to his ears. "I'm more'n ready."

James D. Doss

☼ Colorado ☼
Southern Ute Reservation

Walks Sleeping waited patiently while his granddaughter tucked the quilt under his feet. The old man's feet and hands were always cold, even when the air wafting through his window was gentle and warm. Despite his near-blindness, he knew that it was night. There was no light from the window that looked toward the sunset.

The slim girl leaned over and kissed him lightly on the forehead. "Good night, Grandfather." As she paused in the bedroom door, he could barely make out her shadowy outline in the yellow glow of light from the hall. He waited for those two words that she always said.

Myra smiled and waved, as if he were departing. "Sweet dreams."

His granddaughter closed the door and he was covered in his customary darkness. The old Ute closed his eyes and thought about Charlie Moon and the *matukach* policeman. Why must these young men bring the past back to haunt him? Such memories were best left to the shadows of forgetfulness, where they wandered aimlessly in the wasteland—like the homeless ghosts. He realized that it was important for the policemen to understand why Provo Frank had stolen something valuable from Blue Cup. But the police could do nothing that would help, even if they knew everything that he knew. This sort of problem needed another type of solution altogether. It might take a long time, of course. But the Great Mysterious One had created the minutes and days and years, and had plenty of 'em.

While he was thinking about these things, the old man gradually drifted into that peculiar gray world of half sleep. It was pleasant. In this world he was no longer a blind man. He stood on a gravel road by the river and saw many things:

Stars twinkling over the San Juan Range.

A wild turkey ran into some willow brush on the bank of the Piños.

An old black Packard roared by. The Sioux, Pierced Nose, was gripping the wheel and grinding the gears as he shifted.

On a pine stump . . . he saw a small cedar box with a wonderful treasure hidden inside.

Now he was at a picnic on the banks of the Piños. There were strange trees along the bank of the river . . . not the usual cottonwoods and willows . . . trees with pink and white flowers . . . fat yellow bees buzzed around the plump blossoms. Someone gave him a fresh slice of watermelon . . . he took a bite and tasted the incomparable sweetness of it. He spat a slippery yellow seed into the river. It floated away on the currents.

Something warm brushed at his ankle.

THE SHAMAN'S BONES

At his feet, the dreamer saw a small kitten. The kitten mewed pitifully; he was pleased to follow the animal down a narrow path that wound, seemingly without purpose, through the flowered grove. The kitten was following someone. Far ahead on the path, Walks Sleeping could see. A man—leading a small horse. On the back of the horse was a child. Walks Sleeping and the kitten trotted along behind them, but the man, the horse, the child . . . they disappeared into the heavy mists of unknowing.

Walks Sleeping felt himself moving relentlessly forward.

At the end of the path, almost hidden in the trees, was a small house with a carefully kept lawn. It was constructed of old red bricks and it had a fine, straight chimney, also of red bricks. The pitched roof was an intricate array of gray slate shingles. There were no houses in Ignacio like this . . . but it looked very familiar. Yes, he had certainly been here before. In another dream, perhaps.

The kitten stepped lightly over the threshold into the open door; Walks Sleeping followed the animal. Inside the brick structure (it was not a dwelling), there was a single room, with deep purple paper on the walls. The ceiling was painted white, and a wrought-iron chandelier of tallow candles was suspended by a chain. The room appeared to be much larger than the house, but the strange shift of dimensions did not bother the old man. A dreamer will accept the most absurd contradiction. In the room were only three pieces of furniture . . . a matched trio of straight-backed wooden chairs, like the ones the *matukach* make in New England.

In one of these varnished chairs sat a young man, whose face was like stone. It was Provo Frank. Behind the man stood his wife. It was the woman of the Tohono O'otam; she wiped streams of tears from her face.

Two other chairs were positioned before them; the chairs faced each other. They supported a small wooden coffin.

This was not good.

Walks Sleeping did not wish to approach the coffin, but his dreamer's feet carried him forward without touching the floor of the room. As he glided like a swan on a glass pond, the lid on the coffin opened. Inside was the body of a child. Her dark hair was fixed in two braids; in her hands she held a small bouquet of yellow roses. It was a bad thing to look upon the face of the dead . . . the dreamer shuddered and tried to back away. Gradually the grim vision faded.

The old man flailed his arms at the impenetrable darkness that sat upon his face. When he could find his breath, Walks Sleeping called for his granddaughter to come to him.

✿

The baby was asleep at her feet, cuddled in a cardboard box lined with a cotton blanket. Chigger Bug sucked rhythmically on his thumb and dreamed soft dreams of his mother's breast.

Walks Sleeping was seated on a cushioned chair, directly across the kitchen table from his granddaughter. He gazed toward her with opaque eyes, and saw only shadows of shadows. He drummed his fingers on the blue oilcloth. He had told her about the dream. Myra was young, but she was attuned to the old ways. One of the reasons that Walks Sleeping loved this particular granddaughter so dearly was that she never dismissed his visions as foolishness.

She thought about it for a few minutes, then spoke. "You know," she said, "you'll have to talk to . . . the police."

He noted that she did not say, "You'll have to talk to Charlie Moon." She was thinking about that *matukach*. Furthermore, her voice had that special tone. He felt for his mug, and took a long drink of lukewarm tea. He would yield to her will, just as he usually did. But it would not be a good thing to let this headstrong girl believe that she was the head of this house. She would be giving him orders all day long, like he was a child.

The old man cleared his throat.

Myra stiffened her back in anticipation.

"I have decided," he said with the air of one about to make a great announcement, "that I should talk to Charlie Moon." He paused and shook his head as if annoyed. "If his *matukach* friend is underfoot, maybe you could get him out of the way. So I can talk to Charlie about tribal business."

Myra hid a smile. She was never really sure how much the old man could see. Or sense. "If you think that's best, Grandfather."

He tilted his head. "Then you'll call Charlie today . . . ask him to stop by?"

She ran a small hand along her slender thigh, frowning at the faded dress. "First I need to go to Durango . . . to do some shopping." For a brand-new dress. And new shoes. She flicked a piece of lint off her threadbare skirt. "I expect Charlie Moon has lots of police work to do. He can't keep coming out here to see you every time you got something to tell him." Her face wore the satisfied expression of a clever conspirator. "I'll call the police station later to see . . . to see if Charlie's there." She'd talk to the SUPD dispatcher and ask whether the handsome *matukach* policeman was still working with Charlie. Maybe he'd already gone back to Granite Creek. Myra glanced at the baby. "Before I can take you to the station, I'll need to get someone to take care of Chigger Bug." Sometimes a baby scared a man off. Men were so easily frightened, like big, dumb sheep. They needed time to adjust to a new situation. And a good woman to shepherd them.

The old man sipped at his tea, and enjoyed the soothing warmth on his toothless gums. Walks Sleeping was quite satisfied with his life. And with Myra. This was a very clever girl.

But not quite clever enough to deceive her grandfather.

✸ Ignacio ✸
Southern Ute Police Department

Except for brief stops to fill the Volvo's tank and the Ute's belly, Charlie Moon and Scott Parris had made a nonstop drive from Wyoming to southern Colorado. The Ute policeman was frustrated. He'd called SUPD Police Chief Roy Severo from Bitter Springs and insisted that an officer be sent to Daisy Perika's home to guard her and the child. Severo didn't put much stock in the "hypothetical" aftereffects of drugs, and was certain that Provo Frank would never harm his own child. And everyone knew how the young man loved Daisy Perika, who'd befriended him when he was a boy. Not only that, Severo was short on staff. One officer was out with the flu, another had taken a better-paying job at the Sky Ute Casino, and three more were in the mountains with a search party looking for a couple of lost deer hunters. So unless there was strong indication of a threat, it just couldn't be done.

The two lawmen, on their way to Daisy Perika's home, stopped at SUPD. Moon dispensed a cup of coffee from the aluminum pot and glanced at his mail. He found a neat typewritten note from the dispatcher and waved it to his friend. "You remember Louise Marie LaForte?"

Parris was gnawing hungrily at a stale cinnamon bun. "The old French lady who calls you out to her house every week? The one who's always hearing prowlers?"

Moon grinned. "She stopped by the station while we were in Wyoming. Told Nancy Beyal that Aunt Daisy wants me to come out and see her. Maybe," Moon said hopefully, "she's got some notion about where Provo is hiding. Maybe the little girl said something . . ."

"Five'll get you ten, our Mr. Frank is camped within three miles of Daisy's trailer," Parris said. "If I'd left my daughter with someone, I'd want to stay close by. Keep an eye on things." Of course, he didn't have a daughter. Or a wife.

Moon tasted the coffee, then added an additional spoon of sugar.

"If the guy's suffering from late drug reactions," Parris said, "he could be pretty damn dangerous."

Moon stared at the contents of the cup. "Chief Severo don't see it that way."

"It does seem pretty unbelievable," Parris said, "that he'd harm his own daughter." It was unthinkable. But the bastard *had* nailed his wife to a tree. And broken Officer Alicia Martin's fragile little face with a beer bottle. This hardcase needed to be taught a serious lesson.

"I doubt he's ever even spanked the little girl," the Ute said. "But if Provo's been drugged up on something . . . Anyway, I intend to go out there and watch after Aunt Daisy and the little girl."

"Well, I'll tag along myself. Might just be a chance to nail him." Parris immediately regretted the unfortunate phrase.

Moon was about to reply when the slender young woman pushed her way through the heavy door; she was leading an old man. During his frequent visits to the reservation, Scott Parris had seen most of the pretty girls within a dozen miles of Ignacio. But who was this young lady? The old man whose sleeve she tugged at was Walks Sleeping. So this was the skinny granddaughter. Who had carried a fat boy child. Well now . . . she didn't look like the same person.

Myra Cornstone was wearing a flimsy white summer dress with a pleated skirt. A red leather belt circled her tiny waist. The filmy skirt whipped about her knees like tissue paper in the breeze that drafted through the open door. The pretty girl also wore shiny red high heels that looked fresh out of the box. The crimson hue of the shoes matched the glistening color of her lips. Little Myra didn't have the baby on her hip this time. This part of her anatomy was, in fact, quite free . . . unencumbered by the least burden. Parris watched her narrow hips oscillate under the white frock as she walked toward him. For all her poise, the young woman was balanced somewhat uncertainly on the stiletto heels; this only added to her girlish charm. Being a trained observer, Parris felt obliged to take note of this relevant fact: she wore silk stockings. Moreover, the stockings were stretched over the gently curved surface of rather shapely legs. The material had a lacy design that was barely noticeable unless you looked closely.

Parris realized that he was looking closely. Very closely. He forced himself to look elsewhere. At the wrinkled old man. What a contrast. He returned his attention to the young lady. Myra Cornstone was maybe half his age. If that. But he'd noticed that this young woman did not wear a wedding band. For whatever that might mean.

Delivering the aged man had been a hard task for the patient grand-daughter of Walks Sleeping. The old Ute's head was tilted slightly backward, as if his blind eyes watched the heavens. He walked stiffly with a shining black cane in each withered hand; the young woman steered him toward a chair. Once the blind man was taken into protective custody by Charlie Moon, she moved, ever so gradually, closer to Scott Parris.

Parris responded by doing what he does best. He grinned and blushed. And stumbled over his feet.

Myra declined the chair he offered. Instead, she stood very close to Scott Parris. Briefly smiling up at his beet-red face. These big, awkward men were so laughably, hopelessly, dopey. And—Myra sighed inwardly— so wonderfully appealing.

Walks Sleeping sat down with a grimace, as if he expected the chair to be uncomfortable. The old man looked around the room—through the perpetual fog—until he sensed a shadowy figure that was large enough to be Charlie Moon.

The Ute put his hand on the old man's shoulder. "It is good to see you, Grandfather."

"Ahhh . . . it would be good to see you, Charlie Moon." He grinned at his small joke. "Don't you wonder why I have come to visit you?"

"No," the big Ute policeman said softly. "I've been expecting you."

The old man continued as if he had not heard Moon's comment. "I got some stuff to tell you."

Moon pulled up a chair and seated himself in front of the aged Ute.

"When you came out to see me, you wanted to hear about what it was like in Ignacio . . . in nineteen and thirty-eight . . . that year when I was tribal chairman. The old days."

Moon glanced at Parris, who forgot about the girl and moved closer to the old man. "I'd like to hear whatever you have to say," the Ute policeman said.

The granddaughter, having lost Parris' attention, bit her lip. She turned away with a swirl of her pleated white skirt and left the echo of clicking high heels in her wake. She found a vending machine in the hall, pushed two quarters and a dime into the slot, and pressed the lighted button that said Diet Pepsi. Myra sighed and told herself that the *matukach* policeman was probably not interested in a woman who already had a baby to raise. Men were such hopeless children. Not one in a hundred knew what was good for him. Or *who* was good for him. Men . . . the big, dumb bastards. She hated every one of them! Well, except maybe one . . . or two.

But this girl, the product of countless ancestors who had conquered far greater obstacles, was not finished. No. This daughter of tribes whose names were lost in prehistory—she had not yet begun to fight. Myra glared at the dispenser of chilled cans. She thought her thoughts. And plotted her plots. She discarded one plan, then another. Finally the Ute girl whispered under her breath—as if sharing a sweet secret with herself. She removed a pretty red shoe from her tiny foot. Very deliberately, balancing herself on the shod foot, she pressed the long heel into the coin-return slot on the vending machine. She twisted the new shoe until the long heel separated itself from the thin sole.

Thus prepared, Myra smiled.

Walks Sleeping turned his gaze toward the cloudy figure of Scott Parris. He sniffed. "You are the white man . . . the *matukach* policeman from Granite Creek?"

Parris nodded. "Yes."

Walks Sleeping wrinkled his nose. "I thought so. I can always tell a white man by his smell."

Moon's scowl was wasted on the blind man. "Grandfather, this man is my friend."

Walks Sleeping chuckled. "Then maybe *you* should ask him to leave. So I can talk about Ute business."

"Listen," Moon said firmly, "Scott Parris is my pardner. Anything you want to say to me, he can—"

Parris interrupted. "Charlie, I think it'd be better if I left you alone with this charming old gentleman."

"Yes," Walks Sleeping said with a dismissive wave, "why don't you go check on my granddaughter? See if she's all right."

Scott Parris was happy to leave the presence of this old man who insulted him. And clearly enjoyed doing so. Furthermore, he told himself, he much preferred the company of a human being who was not wrinkled like a desiccated prune and who had not been a grown man when the Wright brothers flew their contraption on the beach at Kitty Hawk. One thought leads to another. He went to find the young woman who knew how to wear a filmy white dress. And silk stockings.

Myra was sitting under an elm in the parking lot. She had a broken red shoe in one hand, a heel from the shoe in the other. By the time he was within six paces, a fresh tear had traced its moist path along her pretty face.

The gruff policeman was overwhelmed by a great wave of tenderness. And uncertainty.

"Well now, Myra . . . uh . . . Miss Cornstone . . . what seems to be the problem?"

Myra sighed and shrugged, as if her life were empty and hopeless beyond repair. She wiped the tear away with the back of a tiny hand.

Walks Sleeping rubbed at a swollen knee and wondered how long it would be before he crossed that deep river.

Charlie Moon pulled his chair close to the old man; there was a mild reproach in his voice. "You have insulted my friend, Grandfather."

"Yes." Walks Sleeping uttered a raspy chuckle. "And I did it on purpose." Old men had certain rights. And responsibilities. To the People. And to family. Especially to an unmarried granddaughter who had herself a son to raise. By now the unwary *matukach* would have found what he was looking for. Or what was looking for him. Walks Sleeping grinned a toothless grin. He hoped the white man had a pot of money in the bank. Or at least owned some land.

Charlie Moon towered over the old man. "Grandfather, it would help me if I knew what Provo stole from Blue Cup. It may have had something to do with the year you were tribal chairman."

The blind man cocked his head and nodded. "Nineteen and thirty-eight. I do not know for sure what Provo may have taken from Blue Cup. But there was something . . ."

Moon leaned over. "Yes?"

"It was a thing that had much power," the old man said dreamily. "A whistle. Made from the bone of an eagle's wing."

"Bone whistles are not all that uncommon," the Ute policeman said. "It might be hard to identify the stolen property."

Walks Sleeping's belly shook with laughter. "Oh, you'd have no trouble knowing if you saw *this* whistle. He held his finger about two inches from his thumb. "It's about this long. And it has a silver ring fitted around it."

Moon squatted beside the old man. "What else can you tell me about this whistle, Grandfather?"

Walks Sleeping closed his eyes; his face was suddenly hard. "Nothing."

Parris attempted, without success, to press the heel back onto the little steel nails protruding from the naked heel of the red shoe. "How'd it come off?"

She shrugged. "I was getting a soft drink at the machine—and pop. Off it came." Myra was standing now, balanced on one foot. She leaned lightly against him. For support.

He mumbled an apology for not being a "very good handyman with broken things that need fixing." Myra offered the opinion that he had very good hands and not to worry about the shoe. She would save some money and buy another pair. She gazed up with doelike eyes. Maybe he could come along and help her pick out some new shoes? She also needed to buy some other clothing. "Just some little things," she said. Myra looked away shyly to indicate that these were such "little things" as could not properly be mentioned in front of a gentleman.

The big cop blushed like a crushed beet and mumbled incoherently about how they sure didn't make shoes like they used to. Gradually she had him backed up against a sturdy elm trunk. He tried to speak; nothing more than little choking sounds came from his mouth.

She stared at him, a faint smile playing on her lips.

The policeman ran a finger under his collar. At first he merely perspired. Soon he sweated. Like a coal-mine mule.

The girl well knew the solution to his problem. But she told him that she thought his collar was a size too small. And maybe his string tie wasn't on just right. Myra took her good shoe off and pitched it aside. The girl stood very close, on the tips of her toes. She reached up and unbuttoned his collar.

His relief was plain to see.

Myra Cornstone then proceeded to adjust his string tie until it was . . . well, perfect. Because she was meticulous by nature, it took her a long time to do this.

Parris' blood pressure climbed to a level that made little squirt-popping sounds under his ears with every heartbeat. But he didn't mind. Not at all.

Myra Cornstone. He said it over and over to himself. Yes, it was a pretty name. Very pretty. At this moment the slender girl could have been burdened with such a moniker as Maggotty Mudpuppy and he would have thought it a lovely, romantic name.

Walks Sleeping closed his eyes and thought about it. There was nothing that Charlie Moon or all the police in Colorado could do to prevent what he had seen in his terrible dream. It flashed before his blind eyes once more . . . the lone horseman leading the child away . . . the mourning parents . . . the tiny girl in the casket . . . like a frozen doll whose eyes were forever closed. Walks Sleeping had lived for summers beyond memory, and he knew many things.

He knew this: There are dreams, and there are *visions*.

Dreams are sometimes true, and dreams can also tell a man things that are not true.

But visions do not lie. Never.

The child was either already dead . . . or was soon to die.

No, he assured himself. Even if he told Moon, the big policeman would think it was nothing more than a foolish old man's dream. But it wasn't a wasted trip. He'd told Moon about the sacred eagle-bone whistle. And on the way home, Myra would stop at the drive-in restaurant and buy him a hamburger and onion rings. The blind man licked his thin lips in anticipation.

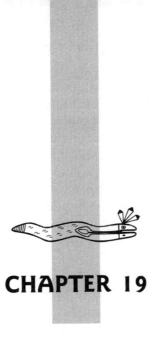

CHAPTER 19

The policemen stood in the south doorway of the Southern Ute police station, watching Myra Cornstone lead the old man to her red Toyota pickup. The blind man's canes clicked on the graveled parking lot.

Moon grinned at his "pardner." "Well, I'm sorry the old man was cantankerous this morning. You find anything useful to do while I was talkin' with him?"

Scott Parris felt his neck growing warm. He attempted to look away from the slim figure in the white dress . . . the red high heels . . . but it was not possible. "Well, I . . . uh . . . I interviewed Myra . . . Miss Cornstone."

"Good," Moon said. "You learn anything?"

"Yeah," Parris muttered. "Learned that I wish I was twenty years younger."

Moon laughed so loud that Myra looked back over her shoulder. She waved her fingers and smiled. Parris waved back, grinning like an idiot.

"Well," the big Ute said, "I've said it a hundred times before. You sure got a way with the women, my friend."

Parris watched the young woman drive the red pickup out of the parking lot, onto the pavement. She rolled the window down—and blew him a kiss! Parris' knees went weak . . . the policeman blushed to his socks and hung his head.

Moon shook his head in wonder. "Well now, if that don't just beat everything . . ."

"Oh, stow it, Charlie . . . I'm just a father figure to that little girl . . . that's all."

The big Ute sighed. "Sugar-Daddy is more like it."

Parris was straining to see the red pickup as Myra turned right at the Sky Ute Lodge parking lot. "So what'd the old geezer have to tell you?"

Moon shrugged. "He thinks maybe the sacred object Provo Frank stole from Blue Cup was a bone whistle."

"Whistle? That's all—?"

Moon smiled at his *matukach* friend. "This wasn't an ordinary whistle. It was made from the wing bone of an eagle. And has a silver ring around it."

"Did he explain why Provo Frank would have stolen it from Blue Cup—or why it's so important?"

"He did not," the Ute muttered. "And the old fox knows a lot he isn't telling me."

"He's sure a hard-nosed old galoot." But he has a nice granddaughter.

"Why don't we go out and see Aunt Daisy." The hint of a sly grin touched his face. "She likes you. Maybe you could explain why we've got to take the little girl away from her . . . all about the need for protective custody."

Parris snorted. "What's this 'we' stuff? I don't intend to take that little girl anywhere." He was intending to enlarge on the issue of jurisdiction when he was interrupted by Nancy Beyal. "It's your office in Granite Creek, Scott. Sounds urgent." The dark-eyed dispatcher offered him a cordless telephone.

He pressed the plastic instrument to his ear. "Yeah?"

Moon waited; Nancy took a final look at the men and wandered off to continue her watch at the radio console.

Parris listened to a hurried report from Clara Tavishuts. "Uh-huh. Understand. Okay. I'll be there—" he glanced at his watch, "—before dark." He pressed the Off button on the telephone.

"So," Moon said, "sounds like you'll be heading north?"

All the color had drained from the white man's face. "I expect you'll want to go along."

"Much as I enjoy your company, I need to go out and check on Aunt Daisy . . . and Provo's kid."

"That can wait."

"Why?"

He told the Ute why.

Within three minutes, Scott Parris' Volvo and the big SUPD Blazer were roaring north along Route 151. Exceeding the posted speed limit.

Scott Parris experienced a sinking feeling as he braked the Volvo to a skidding stop on the gravel road; Moon's big Blazer stopped a yard behind him. The flashing red lights on Leggett's black-and-white were almost synchronous with those on an ambulance. It would depart without a client. Transport would be provided by the county coroner's gray van, which almost blocked the narrow lane. This conveyance had no need for screaming sirens and emergency lights to clear a path through the busy traffic of the living. The van's occasional passengers had infinite patience. For them, time did not exist.

The sun attempted vainly to penetrate a layer of gray mist, then retreated. A gloomy darkness had already settled in the rocky ravine beneath them.

Leggett muttered something about being pleased that Officer Moon was able to come on such short notice. The efficient policeman was wielding a five-cell flashlight like a baton as he gave Chief Parris and the big Ute a terse briefing on what he had found. The condition of the vehicle. Broken windshield. Broken axle. And of the body. Broken neck.

"This accident," Moon whispered, because this seemed to be a graveyard. "Any notion about when it happened?"

Leggett gestured toward the mine guard's shack in the distance. "We know precisely when it happened. The caretaker who works for the mining company heard the crash almost two weeks ago. On the same day Mr. Frank stole Eddie Knox's pickup. It was a few minutes after seven P.M."

Parris squinted toward the animated guard, who was retelling his story to a bored Colorado state policeman. "This guy's certain about the day?"

Leggett nodded, then referred to the neatly penned entries in his notebook. "Caretaker remembers the movie he was watching on his television set when he heard the noise, and we've checked it out. It was *She Wore a Yellow Ribbon*. He came out and had a look around, but didn't find anything. Said he thought maybe it was a boulder that'd rolled off the mountain. But he'd been having some troubles with teenagers parking on mine property, so he closed the gate across the entrance road and locked it. After that, he went back inside to watch the rest of the old Duke flick. And," Leggett added, "the gate's been closed and locked ever since." There was no way the accident could have happened any later.

Moon pushed his hands into his jacket pockets. "So how come he found it now?"

"About noon today," Leggett said, "the caretaker was making his rounds. Heard something—maybe a cougar—moving around down in the brush. Went back to his shack and got a deer rifle with a telescopic sight. When he got back, he didn't see anything move, but he caught a glint of sunlight off the windshield. That's when he called Granite Creek PD. You want a closer look?"

Charlie Moon and Scott Parris followed Leggett down the steep embankment. They had descended forty feet before Moon could see the rocky creek bottom illuminated by Leggett's big flashlight. The pickup truck was sitting almost upright, but the deep dents in the steel body were grim evidence that it had rolled all the way to the bottom.

Parris stumbled over a chunk of granite, then grabbed at the rope that had been rigged from a string of aspen saplings on the slope above them.

Leggett directed the flashlight beam into a broken window.

Parris grunted; he was a bit out of shape for this sort of activity. He braced himself with one hand against the crushed steel door. The face was like candle tallow. But it did resemble the man he'd seen in photographs. "You sure about the identity?"

Leggett looked up the slope; the paramedics were rigging a stretcher. "Won't be official until we match fingerprints. Perhaps Officer Moon would like to take a look."

The Ute grunted his displeasure. Perhaps Officer Moon would rather be in Philadelphia. But he had a look. For a long moment, Moon didn't breathe.

"This time of year," Leggett said, "sun doesn't shine down here. Stays real cold."

The big Ute shivered in the half-light. If Provo Frank's body had not been discovered, it would have been preserved all winter without decay. Unless the coyotes got to it. Moon turned away from what he had seen. He blinked into the darkness, then rubbed his eyes. Somebody would eventually have to tell the little girl that her momma was gone . . . and now her daddy . . . maybe the lady at Social Services was trained for stuff like that. He'd drop by and see her tomorrow. Or maybe the day after.

Or next week.

"You know, Charlie," Scott Parris said softly, "sometimes I think about gettin' myself a new line of work." And maybe a new life.

Moon sighed. He began the climb up the side of the dark ravine. Toward the light.

It was a long way up.

✧

Daisy was awakened by the uneasy knowledge that someone was watching her. When she opened her eyes, the tiny girl was standing patiently by the side of her bed, clutching the kitten close to her neck. Both were staring at Daisy.

The old woman groaned and rolled over to face the wall. "It's bad luck to look at a person who's asleep."

"Is it? Really?" Sarah rubbed the fur on Mr. Zigzag's neck and was rewarded with a motorboat purr. "Why is it bad luck, Aunt Daisy?"

"Because," the grumpy old woman muttered, "the person who is sleeping might wake up and give your nose a good twist."

Sarah laughed. "Do you know what day it is tomorrow?"

Daisy turned on her back and looked at the bowl-shaped plastic light fixture on the ceiling. There were a dozen dead flies in the thing. The place needed a good cleaning. "Tomorrow . . ." she said absently. What was tomorrow? "I think tomorrow must be Friday, because today is Thursday."

"Tomorrow is Friday." Sarah leaned over and whispered urgently, "But it's also something else." The kitten yawned and licked its paw.

The old woman put her feet on the floor and began the search for her slippers. "Something else?"

"Tomorrow," Sarah announced proudly, "is my birthday."

Daisy raised an eyebrow. "Your birthday? How old will you be, fifteen? Twenty-six?"

The child proudly displayed all of the tiny fingers on her left hand. And the thumb.

The sleepy woman leaned forward; she squinted at the hand and pretended to count. "Let me see . . . how many is that? Three? Eleven?"

"Five," the child said solemnly. It was sad that this old woman could not count.

Daisy pushed herself up from the narrow bed; she pulled a cotton robe over her nightdress. "Five, huh?" She stretched and yawned while the child watched. "Well now. By the time I was five, I had already killed a middle-sized bear, skinned it, and used the hide to make a fine winter coat for my daddy." She frowned at the child. "You killed yourself a bear yet?"

Horrified at the thought, Sarah shook her head quickly. She loved all of God's furry creatures.

Daisy sighed. "No matter. Anyway, I guess if you're going to have a birthday, that'll call for some kind of celebration." There was a package of yellow cake mix in the cupboard. And somewhere, there was a little box of birthday cake candles. Pink ones. Just right for a little girl.

✸ Blue Cup's camp ✸

Since he'd turned his ankle stepping off a curb in front of the Durango Bakery, the old man had spent many hours sitting quietly in the camp. Thinking his thoughts. Blue Cup mused about many things, but mostly he devised plans for finding Provo Frank—that thieving bastard! The shaman went into a light trance, attempting to discern some subtle clue that would lead him to the criminal who had stolen his most treasured property. The vision was intermittent and weak. But he had certain impressions . . . a dark, cold place. Where the sun did not shine. Oddly, there was one sensation that was remarkable in its strength and consistency—the fragrant aroma of tobacco! But Blue Cup could not fathom what this might mean.

He also spent much time listening to KSUT on his portable radio. There was music and "Prairie Home Companion" and Click and Clack laughing their way through "Car Talk." And local news. But no word about the search for Provo Frank.

Noah, following the *bugahant's* instructions, had made a pasty concoction of yucca root, river clay, black pepper, and water. As he rubbed the ointment onto the old man's swollen ankle, the young Shoshone was in a jubilant mood. He'd been doing some scouting. "Over by Arboles, there is some good ranchland."

The old man grunted. He didn't care a nickel about ranchland.

"There is a rich Navajo who has a big place there, with a little creek and lots of good grass."

"Don't rub so hard."

The deaf Shoshone, whose attention was fixed on the swollen ankle, did not see Blue Cup's lips move. "And this rich Navajo, he has a bunch of horses." Now he looked up at his mentor's face. "Many fine horses."

"I am happy for him," the old man grumped. "I hope he lives for a thousand years. And has many strong sons and all his daughters marry rich men. That's enough." He waved the Shoshone away and rubbed at his sore ankle. It wasn't throbbing quite so painfully.

Noah stood up and smiled benignly at the old man. "Is it better?"

"It feels worse than ever," Blue Cup snapped.

Noah Dancing Crow looked toward the south. Toward the place where the rich Navajo lived. "It would not be hard to steal one of those horses," he said with a sense of bittersweet longing. "I could take it back to the Wind River reservation." And give it to my father. Maybe he would let me come home again. And my mother would make biscuits and buttered corn . . . and mutton stew.

Blue Cup was incredulous. "You want to steal a horse?"

Noah Dancing Crow slapped his chest with his palm. "It has been many years," he said, "since a Shoshone has stolen a horse from a Navajo." It was a very good thing for a warrior to steal a horse from any man. But to steal a horse from a Navajo . . . well, that would be a glorious story that would be told and retold among the Wind River Shoshone. Even, he imagined, among the People at Fort Hall and Duck Valley. Yes—the tale would be told for years beyond counting! The name of Noah Dancing

Crow would be remembered along with other great men . . . like Washakie the great Shoshone warrior chief. And Wovoka, the Paiute prophet, that dreamer of dreams. Noah had an extravagant view of the importance of stealing a single Navajo horse.

"Well," Blue Cup said with biting sarcasm, "that is a very clever idea. I'm sure the Navajo would not miss one horse from his herd. And even if he did, he would not bother to tell the police, because he is so rich— what is the loss of one horse among so many? And even if he told the police, how would they ever discover that you had stolen the animal? Surely there are no Utes who could track a horse to our camp."

Noah read the words on his teacher's lips, but did not comprehend the sarcasm. The old man was right, of course. The Navajo would never miss one horse, and even if he did, he'd just think it had jumped the fence. And those Ute policemen drove around in fancy automobiles and talked on radios. Surely there was not one who could track a clever Shoshone warrior. He could tie cloth on the horse's hooves so that it would hardly leave any tracks at all . . .

"The one thing you haven't figured out," Blue Cup continued with a twinkle in his eye, "is how to get a horse back to Wyoming." For a moment the old man pretended to consider this problem. "Maybe we could tie it behind the Jeep and it could trot along the highway behind us." He paused and shook his head. "No. That would not work. The horse would slow us down. We'd be weeks getting home." Blue Cup snapped his fingers. "I know. I can sit in the back seat, and the horse could sit up front with you."

Noah, who was not gifted with a generous appreciation for dry wit, was frowning at the old man. A horse could not sit in the seat of a Jeep. Had the old Ute *bugahant* lost his wits?

"Yes," Blue Cup continued with increasing enthusiasm, "the stolen horse could sit up front in the passenger seat. And read the road map for you, and watch the route signs, so you would not make any wrong turns." The old man laughed. Until tears ran down his cheeks.

The Shoshone, who had rarely seen Blue Cup laugh, was astonished. And now he realized that the old man was making sport of him. Deeply hurt, Noah turned away.

Blue Cup picked up his mulberry staff and tapped at the young man's heel. The Shoshone turned to look at the old Ute's face.

"Don't sulk, now. I'm an old man and I don't have much to laugh about. Besides, I have something important for you to do."

With some reluctance, Noah squatted in front of the old man. In spite of his bad treatment, the Shoshone was eager to please the old *bugahant*. Someday Blue Cup would work his magic and restore Noah's ability to hear the moaning of the wind . . . the sweet songs of birds. And someday perhaps the *bugahant* would share some of the Power with his loyal Shoshone friend.

"While you've been running around doing nothing useful, except maybe coveting the rich Navajo's horses, I've been watching Daisy Perika's home. Every day. From sunrise to sunset. Just in case Provo Frank should come back. Sometimes . . . sometimes I can feel him . . . very near."

Noah nodded. It was true that the old man had been doing all the watching.

"But since I tripped over that curb last night—" Blue Cup pointed at his swollen ankle "—I can't walk three steps. So you've got to do the watching for me."

The Shoshone, still somewhat sullen, nodded.

"Tomorrow is the little girl's birthday. She believes her father is coming back . . . to bring her a pony." Blue Cup paused and looked toward the blue outline of Three Sisters Mesa. "I don't think he's coming back, but I want you to keep watch just in case. If he shows himself—" he glared at the Shoshone "—you keep out of his sight. But follow him to where he's camped. Then come back and tell me where he is." He tapped Noah's knee sharply with the mulberry staff. "You understand?"

The Shoshone nodded. It was a simple enough job. Even a fool could do such a simple thing.

"Good." The old man laid his staff aside and stretched out on his woolen blanket. "There's a little knoll where you can watch from—just east of the old woman's trailer. It has a grove of piñon that make good cover. Tomorrow morning I want you there before first light. Take some food and water too. I don't want you to leave until dark. If the thief hasn't shown up by good dark, then you can take this down to the child." He pointed to a large white box in the rear seat of the Jeep. It was tied with a pink ribbon. "It's a chocolate cake. I bought it yesterday in Durango for sixteen dollars. You can tell the little girl it's from me." Daisy Perika would be very jealous of the fine cake. The old man smiled with genuine satisfaction. "Tell the child I'll come by to see her when my ankle's better."

The old man settled his head on a fold of blanket and began to whisper to himself: "I expect that child knows a lot more about where her father is than she's letting on. If only I could talk with her privately . . . without that troublesome old woman hovering about . . . I might learn where her thieving father is hiding . . . maybe the child even knows where he hid the sacred object . . ." Blue Cup drifted off toward a restless sleep, still muttering to himself.

The Shoshone had been reading his master's lips.

*   *   *

Two hours later, when the moon was just rising over the rounded peaks of the San Juans, Blue Cup was snoring loudly. But the Shoshone was wide-awake. Noah Dancing Crow was tingling with excitement—he would not sleep at all on this night.

The notion had illuminated his mind like a sudden flash of lightning at midnight. It was a marvelous idea. A grand idea, he was certain, that would convince Blue Cup that he was not an imbecile. He would be seen as a man worthy to have his hearing restored. A man worthy to receive his rightful share of the Power.

The Shoshone's plan was, in fact, innovative. It was also, from a certain skewed view, a marvelous idea.

It was a marvelously bad idea.

The Shoshone got to his feet, took a long look at the sleeping *bugahant*, then trotted off into the night. Toward the Navajo's fine ranch.

❖

Daisy Perika ignited her plastic cigarette lighter; she touched a spear of yellow flame to each of the five pink candles on the two-layer chocolate-iced cake. "Now," she said to the child, "blow 'em all out and make a wish." The old woman made her own wishes. That she would never be lonely again. That Provo Frank would leave this child with her, to be a sweet companion to an old woman who was approaching the banks of that deep river. Those terribly swift waters.

It was blatantly selfish, she knew. But in this hard world, a person had to look out for herself. And the presence of the child would be such a great comfort.

The little girl stared thoughtfully at the candles. When the little flames went "out," where would they really go? When someone left you, where did they go? "Aunt Daisy," the child said, "where's my mommy gone . . . and my daddy?"

The old woman tried to swallow the lump in her throat. "I'm just somebody who lives by herself out here in the wilderness. Nobody ever tells me where they're going."

The child rolled her large brown eyes upward to see the old woman's face. "Daddy always said that you know just about everything."

Daisy started to offer her opinion of Provo Frank, then clamped her mouth shut.

The child reached over to tug at the old woman's sleeve. "Is something wrong . . . something I'm not supposed to know about?" Grown-ups were always keeping secrets.

"Someday . . . when you're all grown-up . . . then we'll talk about such things."

"But you're awfully old," the child pointed out, "so when I'm all growed-up, you'll be dead. Will you talk to me after you're dead? Like a ghost?"

"Hush such foolish talk," the old woman said sharply. It was bad enough luck to talk about dying. But to speak of ghosts—had this child's parents taught her nothing? "Now, blow out the candles on your birthday cake. But first, make a wish."

Daisy watched the girl sit and stare at the candle flames; the tiny flickers of fire reflected in her eyes.

Sarah closed her eyes tightly. At first there was only darkness. Then a point of light, darting about like a firefly. Coming closer. Blooming like a white blossom. Taking shape. Now she recognized the small window. Only a little light filtered in through the curtain that covered the window.

Sarah made a most solemn wish. And said a simple prayer to the angels. She blew hard until all the candles were extinguished.

The child waited. Now the little window grew . . . taller . . . wider . . . It was a large window now, with a heavy wooden frame. As she watched through closed eyes, the heavy curtain was pulled aside by an unseen hand. Sarah looked through the window—and what she saw was very strange . . . and confusing. Tiny wrinkles furrowed the child's brow. Sarah understood this: She would soon be leaving this old woman's home. She would go away. But *where* was she going?

Noah Dancing Crow, in normal circumstances, was a patient man. But on this morning he was approaching a turning point in his life. A crisis. And he wanted to get the thing done.

Since long before the sun had risen, the Shoshone had fidgeted nervously while he waited. And watched the trailer home in the broad valley at the mouth of the Canyon of the Spirits. He had set himself on a daring course that carried with it a great risk. During the night he had lain sleepless by the stolen horse, staring at stars and wisps of drifting clouds. He tried hard to dismiss the task that lay before him from his troubled thoughts. He tried even harder not to think of his mother, but her worried face was ever before him. In the thin clouds. In the moonless sky. Even when he closed his eyes, he could see her. There was a great sadness in her eyes. As if she knew what her son had decided to do—and was ashamed of what he had become. And was becoming. But, he rationalized, a man must do hard things if he is to amount to something in a difficult world. Noah set his jaw and ground his teeth. It would be very hard to do, of course, but it must be done. If a man wanted his share of the Power, there was a price to be paid.

He forced his thoughts to other matters. The Shoshone was pleased that he had stolen such a fine horse. Though it was not a big horse, it was well proportioned and had good markings. He rubbed his hand on its neck and the animal bobbed its head up and down in appreciation.

Noah dismounted and leaned on the horse; he set the boxed cake on the ground and lit a cigarette.

The sun was high when the Shoshone saw Daisy Perika emerge from her trailer home. Yes. It was just as Blue Cup had said. The old woman was trudging up the dirt lane toward her mailbox. She was feeble and walked very slowly. It would take her maybe twelve or fifteen minutes to make the round trip. It should be time enough. Noah Dancing Crow mounted his stolen horse and gently nudged his heels against the animal's flanks. As he ducked his head to miss the branch of an old juniper, he imagined he saw his mother's face on the ground. She was weeping at the shameful thing he was about to do. For a moment, a pang of guilt rippled through his gut. Noah Dancing Crow hesitated. Then he remembered what he wanted most of all.

The Power.

Ceremonially the young man spat his guilt upon the dusty ground and said farewell to it. He felt a wonderful surge of confidence; Noah knew he would get it exactly right. And Blue Cup, when he saw the child, would be surprised, and very pleased with him. The old man would talk to the little girl, and maybe she would tell the Ute *bugahant* something that would lead Blue Cup to her thieving father.

Once more he rehearsed the words he would say to the child when she was close enough to see him well. And realize that he was a stranger.

As he rode into the mists that had settled in the valley, the Shoshone decided to practice his memorized speech: "Hello, little girl." Noah smiled and nodded at an imaginary child. He put a friendly expression on his face and waved his hand. "This big chocolate cake and this fine horse—they are your birthday presents. And I have come to take you to see your daddy."

Aunt Daisy had left on the long walk to the mailbox; the trailer was silent except for the throbbing hum of the old refrigerator.

Sarah sat at the small kitchen table, staring at the cake with five pink candles. The child had no appetite for the birthday cake. She had not been really hungry since she woke up this morning. Though she liked being with the funny old woman, Sarah desperately wanted to go home. "Neola, Tabiona," the child whispered to her kitten. "Altonah. Bluebell. Upalco. Altamont." The names of the Utah towns were pretty, like the alternating yellow and purple glass beads strung on her necklace. But when would she go back to see them again?

She knew when, of course. When Daddy came and took her home.

He'd promised to give her a pony for her birthday. But sometimes, late at night, it seemed that she might never see Daddy again. Or Mommy.

Sarah went to the window and watched for the old woman to return with her handful of mail. But something else moved in the mists.

It was a man . . . he led a small horse. He beckoned to the child.

Daisy glanced at a few thin mail-order catalogs. Most of the merchandise was useless junk, and it was all very expensive. But this stuff would make good reading on the long winter nights when the wind pushed against the west wall of her trailer home.

The old woman was within a stone's throw of her trailer home when she saw the man leading the horse away into the mists. And there was someone . . . a small person . . . on the horse. It was Sarah!

For a moment this made no sense at all. Then, the old woman realized . . . of course! Provo Frank had finally come back for his child. But why was he in such a hurry to leave? Was Provo so afraid that Blue Cup would find him?

Daisy Perika shook her walking staff and shouted: "Provo, Provo Frank . . . wait."

The child turned to look; she waved a tiny hand at the old woman. But the man did not look back. With some sense of urgency, he led the horse away.

"Provo Frank," she shouted again, "don't you leave without . . ." But still there was no response from the man.

Daisy glanced at the trailer; the kitten was sitting in the bedroom window. Mewing pitifully, pawing at the thin pane of glass. Sarah had forgotten to take the kitten,

The old woman hurried after the man and the horse and the child, but within a few heartbeats there was no sign of them. Only the lingering mists of morning. And these, like smoke from a great pipe, were slowly being inhaled into the mouth of the canyon. So that was where he was taking his daughter—into the depths of Cañón del Espíritu. Of course. It was Provo Frank's favorite hiding place.

But she would find him; the old woman walked faster. Within minutes of this unaccustomed exercise, her legs ached so terribly that she wanted to weep, but her fury held the tears in check. Daisy was rehearsing what she would say when she caught up to Provo Frank and the small horse he led: "Well now, think of that. I've found me two horse's asses!" This fantasy gave the old woman some comfort.

But not much.

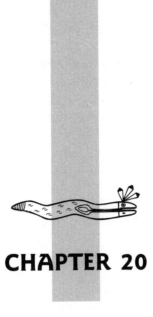

CHAPTER 20

Daisy was less than a hundred yards into the mouth of the canyon when she thought she saw someone . . . or something . . . disappear into a swirl of gray mist. The old woman hurried forward, but her body was not equal to the task her spirit had set for it. Daisy's toe caught on a loop of piñon root—her left leg buckled at the knee. She felt herself pitch forward, the ground came up to slap her face. She lay still for a moment. Her back ached; tingling pains shot up her legs. "Oh God . . . Great Mysterious One," she pleaded, "help me get on my feet. Help me find the child."

She waited.

The silence was heavy. The loneliness unbearable.

Daisy wept.

When her tears were spent, the old woman's breaths became shallow. Her pulse slowed, her hands grew cold. Presently she felt the velvet touch of the cloak of darkness. As the Ute shaman slipped away, she barely heard a fluttering of great wings over her head. But she did not see the magnificent white owl as it settled on an outstretched arm of a juniper snag. The creature cocked its head and blinked enormous amber eyes at the small, still figure of the old woman.

✿

The pain was gone—the body the shaman occupied was strong and tireless. Daisy ran without effort. She followed the white owl as its great wings beat a slow rhythm. Deep into *Cañón del Espíritu* they went. Much farther than she had ever been before. No sunlight fell upon the path, and the canyon had narrowed to a point where the owl's blue-tipped wings nearly brushed the sandstone cliffs. At first the mists that hid the child on the pony had seemed to move rapidly before her, like a shy rainbow that could never be approached by mortals. But now she and the feathered creature were overtaking the smoky cloud. As she felt herself within a stone's throw of the child, the owl vanished into the mists.

The shaman was suddenly alone, isolated in an immense, empty silence. The sharp edge of fear cut away her sense of victory. Daisy paused on the path and considered the perils of the course she had undertaken. A few more steps and she might be lost forever. One never knew what dreadful things might be waiting in those mists.

She was startled when the figure of a man stepped out of the swirling fog. Daisy recognized the wrinkled face of her old friend. It was the shepherd. The shaman took a deep breath. "Nahum Yaciiti," she said.

His face was like chiseled flint, his mouth a thin line. "You are looking for the child."

"I am," Daisy said hopefully, "and you could help me find her."

The apparition did not reply, but raised his arms in an unmistakable gesture. He was blocking the narrow passage . . . and now the mists were moving away rapidly. Perhaps to be forever out of her reach.

This puzzled and annoyed the shaman, who set her jaw. "Why are you doing this?"

He did not budge. "It is dangerous. Angels fear to walk upon this path."

"I've never been mistaken for no angel," the old woman snapped. "Now, stand aside, Nahum."

The old shepherd stood his ground. "No. You must go home."

"Move out of my way, old man, or I'll smack you a good one right between the eyes." She used both hands to raise her walking stick like a club.

For a moment it seemed as if he might oppose her . . . then the form of Nahum Yaciiti receded into the mists.

✡ At the Boundary Between Worlds ✡

The old woman had entered the fog much earlier, but she could not measure the time that had passed. It might have been a few minutes or a few days. Or ten thousand years. Still Daisy moved forward. The shaman was certain that she was no longer in *Cañón del Espíritu*. Indeed, she was not even certain that she was in Middle World. Around her, scurrying among underbrush that she could barely see in the swirling mists, were creatures. And spirits. Some were the spirits of those from Middle World who had died. The shaman was not short on courage, but she was also no fool—she did not look upon their shadowy faces. Instead, she moved forward toward her goal. And wondered how she knew which way was "forward." But she did know.

Now, in the distance, she could barely discern a dim yellow light. She had just noticed this new feature when she broke through the mists . . . into a wide valley that was lush with every kind of tree and flower. Moreover, birds sang in the trees. Butterflies of every color fluttered among the fragrant blossoms.

Before her was a narrow lane, worn deep by the footsteps of many travelers who had come this way before her.

The shaman walked briskly along this path, but she felt a sense of dread. Maybe she had been a fool to ignore Nahum's warning. The old man was a bit peculiar, but he had always given her good advice.

She entered a clearing. It was a rolling meadow, the expanse of grass interrupted only occasionally by a swaying willow. In the center of this clearing was a large tepee. More than a dozen fine horses were tied to a wooden rail outside the dwelling. Many feathered lances were leaned against the rail. Some of the lances had Ute markings, others were identifiable as Navajo, Cheyenne, Shoshone, or Apache. Some had markings that the old shaman did not recognize. But she did recognize the smallest horse. That was the one the child had rode away on.

As she approached the tepee, Daisy saw a man who had been standing behind a massive gray stallion. As the man walked around the horse, the stallion pawed at the ground and snorted. It seemed as if sparks of fire came from the horse's nostrils!

The man was not so impressive as the stallion; he was only a Navajo. But he carried a short, stout lance that was tipped with a smoky, almost transparent obsidian blade.

He stood in the shaman's path and raised the lance to chest level with both hands. "Stop."

"Who're you?"

He did not reply.

"I'm looking for someone," Daisy said, stealing a quick glance at the tepee.

"I'm not expecting you," the Navajo said. To make his meaning clear, he pointed the tip of the spear over her head. "Go back. Now!"

The old shaman struck the ground with her walking stick and squinted at this upstart Navajo. "Don't get pushy with me—I'll go where and when I please."

"If you don't leave," he said with a nervous glance over his shoulder, "I could get in some trouble."

She stared hard at him. This man had thick lips, and beady black eyes set close on each side of the bridge of a large nose. Yes . . . there was something familiar about him. "Aren't you Stonehand Beyal, Nancy Beyal's half brother?"

The man lowered the tip of the spear. He leaned forward to stare at the old woman. "Yes. Are you . . . ?"

"Daisy," she said, "Daisy Perika. I'm one of the People." But this foolish man would believe that the Navajo were the People. "I'm a Ute," she explained. "From the southern bunch. I remember you . . . you died two years ago. Kidney failure, wasn't it?"

"Last year," he said. "It was my liver."

"Oh yes. Your liver. You was the one who couldn't get the bottle away from your mouth long enough to spit. Sure, I remember you well now. And you gambled some, too."

The Navajo muttered something under his breath about mean-mouthed old Ute women, but he did not meet her gaze.

Daisy pretended to be sorry for him. "And now you've got this pitiful excuse for a job just because you drank a bit? And squandered your wages on gamblin' and didn't support your family? That don't sound fair to me." And it didn't. Such a worthless man ought to be strung up and hung out to dry, like so much beef jerky.

The man sighed deeply.

"If you'll do me one little favor—" Daisy patted him on the shoulder "—maybe I could put in a good word for you. But first I got to talk to the child."

The Navajo glanced uncertainly toward the tepee. "I never said there was a child here."

"No, you didn't." Daisy tapped her temple with her finger and winked. "But I know these things."

"You can't talk to nobody in this place," the Navajo said. "It's against the rules."

Daisy sighed. These stuffy Navajos always had their rules. What a bunch of sticks-in-the-mud. No wonder the man had this dumb job. "Well," she said, "I expect *you* can talk to whoever's in the tepee."

He avoided her eyes. "If you don't go back pretty soon . . ."

"You could take the child a message for me."

"Oh, I don't think I should do that."

"Aha," Daisy snapped, "so Sarah *is* here!"

"There's several people here. Maybe she is, maybe she isn't . . ."

"Do you want to move on from this place," Daisy asked, "get yourself a better job?"

The Navajo nodded, but his wary expression betrayed his unease.

"Then," Daisy said, "you got to give up your drinkin' and gamblin'. Ain't that so?"

"There ain't nothin' to drink here but water."

"Good. Then all you got to do is give up your gamblin'. For good."

He frowned suspiciously at the old woman. "How could I do that?"

"Why, it's easy as can be. You make one last bet. With me."

He squinted one beady eye at her. "I don't see how that'd help."

"That's because you was born with a dried-up peach pit between your ears. Now, listen close. If you make one *last* bet, then that'd have to be the end of your gamblin', wouldn't it?"

The Navajo appeared to think about this. Long and hard. Finally he spoke: "Making a bet—it sounds a lot like gambling."

"Well, this wouldn't be *real* gambling." Not the way I'd do it. "It's more like 'gaming.' That's what our tribe calls it at the Sky Ute Casino. Gaming."

"Well . . . maybe if it was just a game . . . but it still don't seem right somehow."

"I figured we'd play the Navajo shoe game," she said quickly.

He smiled for the first time since the day he'd died. "The shoe game. That's one of my favorites."

Daisy smiled benignly. What a chucklehead.

"If I win," the shaman said, "you go and talk to the child for me. Tell her I'm all by myself and lonesome, and she needs to come back to Middle World and keep me company. But win or lose, I leave this place."

An expression of hope illuminated his features. "You'd leave . . . right away?"

"You bet."

"But if I lose the game?" the Guardian asked.

Maybe, she thought, he wasn't as dumb as he looked. "It's plain as the big nose on your face that you *can't* lose, my Navajo friend. Why, you win no matter how the shoe game turns out because—" she pointed a finger at his chest "—you are cured of your gamblin' habit forever."

"I don't know . . ."

"I flat guarantee it. Ask anybody who knows me. I ain't never broke my word to nobody, nor never once told a lie." Behind her back, the shaman crossed her fingers.

The Navajo hesitated only for a moment, then took off his moccasins.

Daisy picked up a shiny black pebble, the size of a half dollar. "Now turn your back and shut your eyes."

He did.

She choked back a laugh. He *was* a chucklehead, for sure. This would be too easy. Daisy considered the right shoe . . . then the left. She was supposed to place the pebble in one of his moccasins. If he guessed correctly where the stone was hidden, he won. The old woman put the black pebble in her pocket. "Now you can turn around."

He did. The Navajo leaned forward. He stared. And pondered. He finally pointed toward the right shoe, and saw an expression of satisfaction spread over the old woman's face. "No." He jabbed his finger toward the left shoe. "That one!"

Daisy picked up the moccasins and gave the left one to the Navajo. He pushed his hand inside; his fingers searched. He turned the shoe upside down and shook it. Empty.

While he was thus occupied, Daisy removed the black pebble from her pocket; she slipped the stone inside his right moccasin. She offered him this shoe; he turned it upside down and watched the stone fall out.

"I lost," he said.

"You can't lose," she said, " 'cause now you're cured of your gamblin' habit."

He stood very still, his gaze fixed on the black stone. "I don't *feel* cured."

"Don't be such a worry-bug. Now you go talk to the child for me."

He glanced toward the tepee. "She may not want to come back to Middle World."

"If she don't," Daisy said sharply, "then you tell her she needs to come back and get that raggedy little cat. Otherwise, I'll have to give it away to whoever comes along. Maybe to some nasty little boy. Or," she added slyly, "tell her I may just make me a pot of cat stew."

"I'll talk to the child," the Navajo said. "But you promised that once we played the shoe game, you'd leave."

"You don't have to hit me with a brick," Daisy said pitifully. "I know when I ain't wanted." The old woman turned away.

☼ Middle World ☼

The shaman lies on her side, her breathing labored . . . the dreamtime slipping away like quicksilver between her fingers. But far off in the distance, she can barely hear Nahum Yaciiti, who is talking with the Navajo.

NAVAJO: "Without the White Owl to guide her, the old woman was frightened. I thought she would give up and go back to Middle World."

NAHUM: "It was necessary that she come to this place alone. She might have turned back, but this woman always does the opposite of what she is told. That is why I told her that she could not pass—that she must go home. Ahhh . . . my friend Daisy, when she gets her mind made up, she is very determined."

NAVAJO: "She is a stubborn and troublesome old woman, who reminds me of my mother-in-law. And, she is a trickster, like Coyote himself."

"Why did you let her cheat you in the shoe game?"

"I was afraid she would never leave if she didn't get her way. I'd have to listen to her complain for the next thousand years. Maybe even a hundred. Did I ever tell you about my mother-in-law—"

"Many times. Anyway, you lost the shoe game. Now you must talk to the child for Daisy."

"Humph. The old woman's gone back to Middle World. There's no way she could hold me to it."

Nahum laughs. "If I were you, I wouldn't bet on that."

✧

Noah Dancing Crow had dropped the boxed cake; he'd been riding hard. When the stolen horse began to tire, the Shoshone had got off and led it by the makeshift rope bridle. Now, his thigh cut by an encounter with a spearlike yucca plant, he sat under the shelter of a sandstone ledge, hunched in a fetal position, hugging his knees. His breath came in short gasps.

The small horse looked uncertainly toward the man, then turned its attention to a tuft of dry grass and began to munch on this poor meal.

He must rid himself of the horse. Noah dared not shout, but he threw a pebble at the animal's flank. The gentle animal, which had taken a liking to this man, looked up inquisitively.

The deaf man mouthed the silent words slowly, so the animal would have no trouble understanding: "Go away, horse. Go away back to your rich Navajo."

The little mare moved closer to the pitiful man, and whinnied to show her affection.

Damn. Maybe this stupid horse only understood Navajo words.

The Shoshone put his face into his hands and sobbed. Luring the child away from the old woman . . . taking her to Blue Cup . . . it had seemed like such a clever idea. But, he assured himself, it was not his fault everything had gone wrong. And he would never speak a word to the old *bugahant* about what he had attempted. No. He would never tell a soul! Indeed, for a few days he would keep his secret well enough.

But before the moon was new, words would pour from his mouth.

☼ Granite Creek ☼
The medical examiner's laboratory

A soft rain pelted the slate roof of the three-story home. A distant rumble of thunder was barely audible in the basement laboratory. Dr. Walter Simpson pulled a pea-soup-green sheet over Provo Frank's body. The medical examiner squinted over his bifocals at the lawman who sat uncomfortably in a metal chair. Scott Parris was rubbing his eyes. The policeman needed a solid twelve hours of sleep.

"Scott, you want to look at the—"

"Hell no, Doc." He groaned. "Why would I?"

"Well, I thought you might want to . . . Oh, forget it." These big tough cops were such sissies. Simpson turned and waddled over to the large stainless steel sink. He removed the rubber gloves, stepped on the foot pedal of a plastic waste container, and dropped the disposable gloves inside. He spoke over his shoulder as he washed his hands. "Death was virtually instantaneous. Caused by severe trauma to the first and second cervical vertebrae. The *ligamentum suspensorium* were completely severed at the apex."

"Which means?"

"Broken neck."

"Any indication of illegal drugs?"

"Like a dirty hypo sticking in his arm?" The medical examiner chuckled. These laymen watched too much television. Expected instant results. "I sent some tissue samples off to a lab in Houston. Should hear something in a few days."

Scott Parris pushed himself up from the chair; he began to pace. Back and forth. Tiger in a cage. From the corner of his eye he noticed an open shoe box on Simpson's battered oak desk. The policeman picked up the box, tilted it back and forth, and mentally sorted the contents. An imitation-leather wallet. A ring of keys. A pack of antacid tablets. Three-blade Case pocketknife. Three quarters, a dime, four pennies. An open pack of Kools. Open . . . but it looked as if no cigarettes had been removed. Odd. And the package was slightly misshapen. Swollen.

Parris used his handkerchief to remove the cigarette package from the shoe box; he squeezed at the slight bulge. Something was stashed inside. Something hard and about the size of a cigarette. Just maybe, a bone whistle that Provo Frank had stolen from the old medicine man.

He tried to sound casual, but Scott Parris could feel his heart thumping. "Doc . . . this junk Mr. Frank had in his pockets . . . You have it cataloged yet?"

"Nope," Simpson said in a tired, flat voice, "I'll get it done tomorrow.

Don't fret, copper, I'll be making a list for you. And checking it twice."
The old physician was drying his hands; he had his back to the chief
of police.

❖

When the shaman regained consciousness, she felt a presence near her.
Daisy barely cracked one eyelid. Then another.

Sarah was sitting near her. The child was picking dandelions and blowing the white fluff into the breeze.

Daisy raised herself on one elbow; it was difficult to see through the
tears. "Are you alright, child?"

Sarah did not answer. She blew more dandelion fragments into the
breeze, and watched them float away . . .

"I was only foolin' about your little cat. I never meant it." The old
woman found a wrinkled handkerchief in her apron pocket and noisily
blew her nose.

But the child did not look at the old woman. Neither did she speak.

❖

The Shoshone waited until twilight before he stumbled into camp. Blue
Cup was sitting by the embers of a small fire, the plastic radio pressed
against his ear. Noah was prepared to answer a barrage of questions: Had
he seen any sign of Provo Frank? Had there been any other visitors? Why
was he so late in returning?

But Blue Cup asked no questions. For this, Noah was grateful. The
Shoshone was, at best, a poor liar. If he tried to evade the truth, the old
Ute *bugahant* would know it immediately.

Finally the aged Ute placed the radio on his blanket. "Well," Blue Cup
said sadly, "we won't have to look for Provo Frank anymore."

Noah squatted on the opposite side of the campfire from the Ute; he
stretched out his hands to the warmth. But the lump of ice in his belly—
this coldness would not be driven away by the spirit of the fire.

"I just heard it on the radio." The old man pitched a piñon knot into
the embers and watched the flames lick hungrily at the dark resin. "They
found that thief's body in a wrecked truck." He pointed. "Way north
of here."

Noah was rocking back and forth. "And the thing he stole from
you . . . ?"

"Ah, yes. The sacred object." The old *bugahant* closed his eyes. "If he
had it on him, the police will have it by now." He wondered if they
would have any idea of what they had in their possession . . . the enormous power . . . but no. The *matukach* would never understand such

209

mysteries. Even if they knew what they had, they would think it foolishness. Superstition. And the magic was impotent if you did not believe. He looked upon the Shoshone with something almost like compassion. "I am sorry that you had to watch the old woman's house all day for nothing."

Noah Dancing Crow watched the flames as the sparks flew upward. Guilt hung about him like a bad smell.

The old man stood up and looked longingly toward the north. "This is a good place, Noah. But it is not my home anymore. Not since many years ago." He looked down at the young man, who seemed unusually subdued. The poor fellow must be tired, hungry.

"Let's get the Jeep packed up, my Shoshone friend. When we get to Durango, I'll buy you all the cheeseburgers you can eat. And a gallon of coffee."

Noah Dancing Crow pushed himself to his feet. He began to break up camp, but he was not hungry for cheeseburgers. Nor was he thirsty for coffee. He repeated these words to himself: *The next time a clever idea comes into my head, I'll just spit it out, like it was a green chokecherry.* But he would not. Before the moon was new, the Shoshone would have a terribly clever idea.

Terribly.

❖

As he drove along Route 160, the ghost of Mary Frank haunted Charlie Moon. On the long stretches of mountain highway, the Ute policeman saw her form walking among the trees . . . dancing a slow waltz with the shadows. West of Pagosa, he stopped on the roadside to stretch his limbs, and heard her whispers in the light breeze that rippled through the branches of young aspens. The policeman was a rational man; he blamed these mild hallucinations on exhaustion. It was a full hour before dark, but Charlie Moon was drained of energy and wanting sleep. Twelve, maybe fourteen hours of unconsciousness. Sleep without dreams.

He pulled the Blazer off the shoulder onto the highway; the asphalt ribbon of Route 160 invited him westward. Homeward. The soft green peak of Haystack Mountain was just visible to the north; the long stem of Chimney Rock was a beckoning finger on the south. Or was it some other type of finger gesture altogether? In spite of his weariness, Moon grinned.

As was his habit when he approached the turn onto Route 151 at Lake Capote, the policeman decided to check in with the station. Moon held the microphone by his chin and pressed the button. Nancy Beyal should be on duty at the radio console in Ignacio. "Moon," he said. "At Capote Lake."

He waited only moments for the response. There was a buzz of static that was hushed by the squelch circuit, then Nancy's voice. "You're kinda fuzzy, Charlie."

More static, then: "Chairman Sweetwater wants to see you ASAP. Go to his home." She was using her "this is official business" voice.

"Give Austin a call. Tell him I don't have time right now."

There was a laugh. "Tell him yourself, Charlie. He's standing right by me."

Moon groaned. "Hi, Austin. I'm pretty bushed . . . could this wait till morning?"

There was some delay while, he supposed, the tribal chairman fumed at the dispatcher. Nancy's voice finally burst through the static. "He says forget it. You be on his front porch in twenty minutes."

"That," Moon said into the microphone, "would require me to greatly exceed the posted speed limit."

Another pause.

"He says that never bothered you before, so put the pedal to the metal."

It was apparent that the dispatcher was enjoying this exchange.

"Ten-four," Moon said. But the chairman was getting a little big for his little britches. He eased off on the accelerator. A policeman could do a lot more policing if he took his time.

The cottonwoods in Austin Sweetwater's front yard were casting long shadows when Moon arrived. The tribal chairman's meticulously restored 1957 powder-blue Cadillac, which was normally parked safely in the driveway, was in the street in front of his two-story brick house. Now, that was odd. And Mrs. Sweetwater's Lincoln wasn't at home. That wasn't odd. The chairman's wife spent most of her waking hours shopping somewhere. Moon nosed the Blazer into the empty driveway. He hadn't had time to shut off the ignition when he saw the chubby man, stomping his way across the manicured lawn—and straight through his wife's geranium bed. Moon smiled; he'd sure catch hell for that.

"Dammit," Austin Sweetwater yelled, "why'd you park that greasy heap on my driveway?"

Moon switched off the ignition. "Why not?" he asked.

"Because of two reasons." Austin had bitten halfway through the black cigar that was clenched between his beautifully capped teeth, "Number one is that them's brand-new slabs, just put down yesterday. The concrete may not be set yet, you could leave tire marks . . . and . . . and . . ."

"Number two?" Moon said helpfully.

"Number two," Austin bellowed, "is that old clunker you drive is probably dripping oil on my clean driveway right now."

"You want me to move it?"

"You got a mind like a steel trap, my boy. Now let's see how fast you
can haul your ass offa my fine new concrete driveway."

Moon nodded genially. He twisted the ignition key, snapped the gear
into reverse, and pressed his boot against the accelerator pedal. The big
Blazer lurched like a bull touched by the electric prod; it roared backwards
down the driveway. Moon turned the steering wheel hard, bumped over
the curb. And kept moving. Toward the powder-blue Cadillac. He barely
heard the chairman's shrill scream.

"No, no . . . lookout there, Charlie . . . my Caddy!" Austin cringed
and slapped a hand over his eyes. "Oh shit," he moaned.

When he was within a yard of Austin's immaculate convertible, Moon
jammed the brake pedal to the floorboard. The brake shoes smoked—
metal surfaces squealed—the big tires laid black rubber globules on the
cool asphalt. The Blazer slid to a stop, the oversized bumper within a
finger's breadth of the Cadillac.

Austin waddled shakily down the lawn—he stood at the passenger-side
window, pounding his white-knuckled fist on the door. "You did that on
purpose, dammit!"

Moon cut the ignition and looked innocently at the man. "Did what?"

The tribal chairman was leaning on the Blazer, sucking in deep breaths,
and exhaling. And counting.

"One . . . two . . . three . . ."

The policeman walked around the car and leaned on the trunk of a
small maple. "You know what I think, Austin?"

"I don't know and I don't care, you overgrown . . . You like to scared
me to death, that's what you did." He restarted the deep-breathing exercise. "Four . . . five . . . six." Got to relax now. Think about something
nice. Little pink clouds. "Seven . . . eight . . . nine . . ." Moon will be
the death of me yet. "Ten . . . eleven . . . Oooh," he groaned, "what's
next . . . ?"

Moon cocked his head and thought about it. "Twelve, I think."

Austin swiveled his fat neck and looked up at the towering man. "I
can count up to twelve, you smart-assed cop. I mean what'll *you* do next?
Dynamite my house?"

Moon thought about it, then shook his head. "No. I don't think so."

The chairman looked as if he might weep.

"Problem is, you've got way too much stress in your life." Moon tapped
the little man on his chest. "It ain't good for the old pump."

Austin leaned over; he reached out with a pudgy finger and touched the gleaming chrome Cadillac bumper. He caressed the ruby-red taillight. "You got any idea how much it cost me to restore this baby, Charlie?"

Moon glanced at his wristwatch. "I'd sure like to hear all about your old car, Austin, but I've got some police business to attend to." I've got to go home. And sleep.

The chairman sighed. "Come on inside, Charlie. We got to talk."

The dining room, where the chairman conducted all his serious business, was as large as Charlie Moon's entire house. The furniture was all polished wood and glass. China dishes and all manner of knickknacks and bric-a-brac were on display everywhere. The fat Guatemalan parrot, Mrs. Sweetwater's precious pet, was housed in an ebony cage that hung from a brass eyebolt mounted in a varnished oak beam in the ceiling.

The bird cocked its blue head sideways, picked up a sunflower seed in its claws, and spoke: "Baby wants a cherry!"

Austin Sweetwater bit on the cigar stub and scowled at the bird. "Shuddup, you stinkin' pest." His wife, who adored the foul creature, was in Durango today. Spending his money at a rate of ten dollars a minute. So he would damn well say what he wanted to the nasty foreign bird. He seated himself at the enormous dining table and, with a nonchalant wave of his arm, invited the policeman to sit.

Austin Sweetwater glared across the glistening oiled surface of the maple table at his reluctant guest. "What I want to know is, what progress are you making on this . . . this Mary Frank killing?"

"Maybe you should talk to the chief of police," Moon said.

"I asked Roy Severo a hunnerd times already. Now I'm askin' you." The chubby man ground the cigar butt in an onyx ashtray.

Mood suspected that it was the election. Austin could be hurt or helped by how this investigation played out. If things went well, there would be the obligatory press conference. He would be flanked by the tribal chairman and Chief of Police Roy Severo while the young lady from the *Southern Ute Drum* took photographs for the newspaper and asked lots of questions. Austin Sweetwater would give a fine speech about how tribal law enforcement was prospering under his capable administration. If the investigation went sour, there would be no news conference. But the chairman would quietly raise questions about Roy Severo's ability to run the Ute cop shop. Severo was supporting Austin's opponent. Moon shrugged. "It's a long story. Kind of complicated."

"Then give me the short version." Austin opened a cedar box filled with aromatic Honduran cigars. "And keep it simple."

Moon folded his hands on the glistening surface of the table. It smelled of lemon. And money. "The Frank family drove up to Wyoming. So Provo could visit Blue Cup, and try and buy his way into some Power."

"What a bunch of superstitious crap," the chairman grumped. "But this don't look like it'll hurt me in the election. Might even help. Knock on wood . . ."

"Provo finally got back to the motel where he'd left his family, and from what their little girl says, her momma wasn't too happy. After they had a shouting match, Provo left his wife and daughter in the motel room. He walked to a bar called the Pynk Garter and had himself a few stiff drinks."

"I already know about that," Austin snapped. "That's where the big mouth was when he called me on the phone. Claimed he'd done something real important for the People, wanted to speak to the tribal elders. Said old Walks Sleeping should be there. One thing I can't stand is a damn drunk callin' me on the phone." Austin looked uncertainly toward his liquor cabinet. "You want a shot of something, Charlie?"

"Coffee, if you got it."

"Oh, that's right . . . you don't drink any hard . . . The missus didn't make no coffee today."

"That's alright." It wasn't. He wanted a cup of coffee.

"Well." Austin waved the cigar impatiently. "Let's get on with it."

"A while after Provo had left the motel room," Moon continued, "Mary Frank told Sarah that her daddy was back, and that she was going outside to talk to him. That was the last time anybody—except the person who killed her—saw Mary alive. It was that same night that Provo skipped without paying his motel bill. Left all his wife's stuff in the room. The next day he told Sarah that her mother had gone to Arizona to take care of her sick father."

"Which was a damn lie."

"When Scott Parris and I got to Wyoming, we found Mary Frank's body on a ridge behind the motel. She died from a blow to the head. A bloody hammer was found a few steps away. It belonged to her husband."

"She was nailed to a tree. And hangin' upside down, from what I heard."

"And it looks like the nails came from a sack Provo had in his old Wagoneer."

"Wonderful," the chairman said glumly. "Provo Frank, who is a Southern Ute boy who drinks a bit too much, nails his sweet Papago wife to a tree."

"And by now you know that we found Provo's body. In a wrecked pickup truck he stole in Granite Creek. After he assaulted a police officer."

"It's been on the radio and the TV. I'm glad the dumb bastard's dead— saves the tribe a lot of embarrassment. And in a couple of months it'll be old news. But one thing I don't understand, Charlie. I know husbands and wives kill each other now and again. But I don't get it. Why didn't he just bury the body? Or haul it off somewheres and dump it?"

"The ground was frozen too hard to bury her, and I guess he didn't want to take her body away in the car. His daughter might have woke up and seen it. Or he might've been stopped by the police. Happens more often than you might think. A taillight goes out . . . they run a stop sign . . . and you stop somebody who doesn't want to be stopped."

"Okay." The chairman gestured impatiently with his eight-dollar cigar. "But why'd he nail her to that damn tree?"

Moon got up from the table and looked longingly toward the front door. "Our best guess is that he was on some kind of drugs he picked up at the Pynk Garter. But crazy as it seems, it might have worked. If Scott Parris hadn't taken me up there on that ridge . . . her body might not have been found for years. Nobody goes up there."

"That's another thing everybody would like to know," the chairman said suspiciously. "How'd that *matukach* cop know just where to look?"

For a moment Moon thought about attempting to explain Scott Parris to Austin Sweetwater. But it would be a waste of time and effort. "I guess he just had a hunch."

The conversation played on until the tribal chairman concluded that there was no political gain to make on this issue. And no likely harm. Not just yet, at least. So he lost interest. Finally the exhausted policeman departed. The politician, who was lost in his own thoughts, sat chewing on his expensive cigar. Austin Sweetwater didn't notice when Charlie Moon closed the front door.

The Ute policeman turned the ignition key. He pulled away from the curb and left it behind. Austin Sweetwater. His fine brick home. And his questions. But the policeman did not leave quite everything behind. Something nagged at his subconscious. Something he'd heard . . . or seen? Or was it something he had *not* seen? Like the carpenter's hammer that should've been in Provo's Wagoneer but wasn't.

Charlie Moon had not driven a mile when the truth came to him. "Well, I'll be . . ." It was less a thought than a revelation. The Ute policeman was certain that he finally understood exactly how it had happened. And why.

Holding sleep at bay, he headed back to the station and removed the thick folder from a desk drawer. It took less than thirty seconds for Moon to find what he thought he remembered reading. Yes. There it was in black and white.

And also, there it wasn't.

Moon got the Wyoming policeman's telephone number from Mountain Bell information. Lieutenant Tommy Schultz, who was about to sit down to a late dinner with his wife, was not particularly happy to be called at home. But after Moon explained his thoughts, the man started to listen carefully. Yes, he allowed, that was damned interesting.

Moon finally said his good-byes to the Wyoming lawman. In a few days he'd know if his hunch was on the mark. But a man can only go so long without sleep. So the Ute policeman drove his old pickup to his home, nestled in a tight bend in the Rio Piños—and fell upon his bed.

✧

Tommy Schultz didn't enjoy his aged T-bone steak; he picked at the baked Idaho spud, turning the sour cream with the prongs of his silver fork. Moreover, he wouldn't sleep well that night. He'd finally get up at 3:00 A.M., brew a small pot of black coffee with chicory, and race his Ford black-and-white down the dark highway at eighty miles an hour. Toward the office where he'd do the planning. There was much to be done. He'd need some help. For a start, a dozen officers with heavy brooms. And he'd need himself a sure-enough crackerjack tracker. There was that Shoshone fellow up by Fort Washakie . . . them Indians said he could track a man across a mile of solid rock.

The tracking job Charlie Moon had suggested wouldn't be nearly that hard.

✧

It was almost noon when Charlie Moon heard the tapping sound at his window. He raised himself on one elbow and squinted at the pane of glass. Scott Parris' face was what he saw. A grinning face. Damned disgusting, that's what it was. More than a man should have to put up with.

Charlie Moon turned over and groaned. "Go 'way," he muttered, and pulled a pillow over his head.

The big SUPD Blazer was lurching down the lane toward *Cañón del Espíritu* before Scott Parris spoke to the taciturn Ute. "You feeling okay, Charlie?"

Moon grunted. He'd intended to tell his partner about his notion . . . but no. He'd wait and see how things turned out. Scott Parris was one fine lawman. Smart enough to notice that a hammer was missing from

Provo Frank's tool kit. But something else was missing. And neither of them had noticed.

Scott Parris was a sworn officer of the law, and what he had in mind was, strictly speaking, illegal. In fact, what he had already done was illegal.

Strictly speaking.

"You didn't sleep so good?"

"Nope." Moon was squinting at the ruts in the dirt road.

Parris leaned forward to stare through the cracked, dusty windshield. The right turn to Daisy Perika's trailer was just over the hill. "Maybe we should've stopped and got us some breakfast." He glanced at the Ute. "Some scrambled eggs sounds good. And sausage." Daisy Perika made a fine breakfast, if you didn't think about the lard in the biscuits. Cholesterol bombs, that's what they were. But delicious. Maybe if they hinted that they'd not even had a cup of coffee yet . . .

Moon made a hard right into Daisy's yard. "I ain't hungry."

"Well, mercy me. You sound like a sick horse."

"Please don't talk to me. If you do, I'll have to shoot you."

"That's not a nice way to treat a fellow that brought you a present."

Charlie Moon cut the ignition and set the brake. He turned to stare at this unpredictable *matukach*.

Parris put his hand in his coat pocket and withdrew a small parcel wrapped in brown paper.

The Ute policeman blinked at the offering. There were grease spots on the paper. Parris had apparently sacrificed a used lunch bag for the wrapping. It was tied with heavy cotton twine. Moon raised an eyebrow. "A present?" He almost smiled. Almost.

"Yeah." Scott Parris was feeling good now. Maybe it really *was* more blessed to give than to receive. Even if you gave someone stolen property.

The Ute pulled gingerly on a loose end of the string. "This ain't one of them spring thingamajigs that'll jump up and scare me out of a year's growth?"

"Sometimes," Parris said, "a man's gotta take a chance." That was, after all, exactly what he'd done. If Doc Simpson noticed it was missing . . . but sometimes a man just had to take a chance.

Moon unwrapped the paper. It was a package of cigarettes. Kools. He turned to smile at his friend. "Well, pardner, you want me to take up smoking?"

"Try the one without a filter."

Moon removed a couple of cigarettes. Then another. His finger touched the object. A polished cylinder. Maybe two inches long. Bone of the wing of the eagle. And fastened around the bone was a metallic circle, blackened with the oxide of ages. A silver ring. Here it was in his hand. An object of theft. Of tribal myth. And superstition. A piece of bone that left death in its wake. But when the Ute closed his fingers over the sacred object, it sang in his palm. He could feel the reverberations moving from his hand to his shoulder. Charlie Moon opened his mouth to say something to this good friend, but he was unable to speak.

Scott Parris had not foreseen the impact his "gift" would have on the big Ute. "Well," he said quickly, "I guess you'd like to know how I got my mitts on this little item."

Moon nodded.

"The way I figured it," Parris continued, "there was an important tradition to keep up."

Moon opened his palm to stare at the treasure. "Tradition?"

"Sure. Provo Frank swiped it from Blue Cup." Scott winked slyly at his best friend. "So I stole it for you, partner."

CHAPTER 21

Daisy stood at the window where the child had once waited, day after day, for her father's return. Now Sarah showed no interest in who might approach the home of the old woman.

The Ute woman had heard Charlie Moon's big black Blazer long before it appeared on the crest in the low ridge. Now he was just sitting in the police car with Scott Parris. Maybe they had something to talk about, before they got out.

Daisy Perika turned and looked at the child, who was seated on the floor with the raggedy little cat. "My nephew Charlie's outside, with his *matukach* friend. You wait here, while I go out and see what they want."

Sarah did not look up. Daisy was certain that the child heard and understood every word she said. Maybe Sarah heard even those words the old shaman did *not* speak. But the child had not uttered a word since Daisy found her in *Cañón del Espíritu* . . . or had the child found her?

Moon had just slammed the Blazer door when Daisy emerged from the trailer. She did not wait for them on the small porch; the old woman climbed down the creaky steps, taking care to keep one trembling hand on the unpainted pine railing.

The policemen waited near the dusty SUPD Blazer.

Scott Parris took his hat off when Daisy was within a couple of yards.

"Hello, young man," she said to the *matukach*.

"Good morning," Scott Parris said. Age, he realized, was a relative condition.

She noticed immediately that these policemen didn't look her straight in the eye. Moon looked over her head, toward the trailer where the child was. The white man looked nervously at the battered hat he was twisting in his hands. This, she knew, was because they had something unpleasant to tell her. They'd probably need some time to get to the point.

"I figured it was best that we talked out here," she said.

Moon nodded.

"I know you're lookin' for Provo," Daisy said. "Well, he was here yesterday. Brought his daughter that birthday pony she'd told us about." The old woman was surprised at the peculiar expressions on the lawmen's faces.

Moon found his voice. "Not yesterday . . . Provo couldn't have . . ."

"Well, he did. Just like his little daughter told us he would. And he brought her a fine pony. I was comin' back from the mailbox when I saw him and Sarah . . . headin' off toward the canyon with that little horse."

Parris turned away and muttered a muffled curse; this puzzled and annoyed the old woman.

Charlie Moon felt a dreadful coldness touch his heart; he clenched his big hands into ham-sized fists. "The little girl . . . she's gone?"

"Oh no," Daisy said with an impatient wave of her hand. "Sarah's back here with me. When I saw 'em leaving, I yelled at Provo, but . . ." She paused to recall how odd it had been. "It was like he didn't hear me. Like he'd gone deaf . . . I guess the wind must've carried my voice away."

"Aunt Daisy," Moon said patiently, "you said that Sarah told 'us' that her father would bring her a horse for her birthday. Who was it she told? You and who else?"

The old woman pulled her shawl tightly around her shoulders and frowned. "Why, Blue Cup. He came all the way down from Wyoming to look for Provo. Said the boy'd stolen something from him."

"When—" Parris began.

"Blue Cup, he came to visit me last week. That's when Sarah told the both of us how her daddy was goin' to bring her a pony for her birthday."

Parris slapped his hat against his thigh; it made the old woman jump. "Damn. We should've guessed he'd come down here to hunt for Provo."

Moon put his hand on his aunt's shoulder. "Was anybody with Blue Cup?"

"No. He was by himself when he came to see me. But when the old man left, he did say something about needin' to get back to his camp. Said he was expecting his Shoshone friend to show up."

"So Blue Cup knew Sarah was expecting her father to bring her a pony for a birthday present," Moon said. "If he wanted to kidnap the child, he could have sent someone with a horse. Someone who'd pass for Provo Frank."

Parris' lips formed the words slowly. Deliberately. "Harry MacFie said Blue Cup's Shoshone sidekick is deaf."

"And we've got a report of a missing horse," Moon said glumly, "not five miles south of here. The Navajo found some footprints by his corral fence; he figures his horse was stolen."

"I don't understand," the old woman said with a hint of exasperation. "I told you it was Provo that brought the horse for Sarah . . ."

"Aunt Daisy, there was a wreck a couple of weeks ago," Moon said. The Ute policeman paused. Provo had died in Parris' jurisdiction. In a stolen pickup that belonged to one of the *matukach* police chief's officers. So let him tell her.

Parris was studying the old hat he held in his hands. As if he'd never seen it before. "Mrs. Perika . . . Provo Frank has been dead for some time now. He couldn't have been here yesterday." He almost choked on the next five words: "Someone else took the child."

Daisy's hand went toward her mouth. "Oh . . . but I was so sure it was Provo." The world seemed to spin around her; she gratefully accepted Scott Parris' hand and steadied herself.

"I expect that's what they wanted you to think," Moon said.

"But I don't see why anyone would want to take the child."

Moon's voice was a low growl. "Maybe Blue Cup thought Sarah knew something about where her father was. Or where he'd hid what he stole from the old man." *Stolen* property. The Ute policeman put his hand over his hip pocket, where the whistle was nestled in a pack of crumpled cigarettes. Damn the "sacred object" anyway. Had Provo died over a sliver of polished bone? How many more would die? The answer came to the policeman. Maybe *two* more. Blue Cup and his Shoshone sidekick.

"Maybe they wanted her just because she's Provo's daughter," Parris said. "They might have figured if they took the girl, it'd smoke her father out." He sighed and felt tired. "The old man must have wanted Provo pretty bad."

Moon looked toward the trailer and saw Sarah's small face framed in the kitchen window. "Blue Cup should've known that I'd find him, no matter where he went."

"Yeah," Parris said, "it was a stupid stunt. Not the sort of thing you'd expect from a smart old fellow like Blue Cup." Of course, if the child went willingly, the Feds might have a hard time making a charge of kidnapping stick. Not that such a formality would matter a whit to this Ute policeman. Parris imagined what could happen to a man who dared kidnap a child off the Ute reservation. Inwardly he shuddered.

Gently Moon put his hand on his aunt's shoulder. "We'll have to talk with Sarah."

A peculiar expression crept over the old woman's wrinkled face. "That'll be a problem." She looked up at her tall nephew. "You could talk *to* her. But that child hasn't said one word since . . . since I brought her back." Daisy stared off into the distance, like she could see someone there. Since she came back, Sarah didn't like to be touched.

The policemen exchanged uneasy glances. They would not speak of such things in front of the old woman. But they both wondered. What had the child experienced that was so awful that she had lost the ability to speak? Moon cleared his throat. "We'll have someone from Social Services come and have a look at Sarah. And she'll need to see the doctor at the clinic in Ignacio. In the meantime, I want to know everything you can remember about . . . about the abduction."

"Well, that's just the problem . . ." Daisy began. She started to speak again, then clamped her mouth shut.

"Mrs. Perika—anything you can recall might be a big help to us," Parris urged gently.

"That's just the thing. I don't remember all that much." The old woman rubbed her hands together, as if they were cold. They were. "See . . . I followed 'em into the Canyon of the Spirits. Then I must've fell down . . . tripped over something. And then—" the shaman made a sweeping movement with her hand "—I was movin' through this fog. I think I talked to some people . . . or maybe they was ghosts. I don't remember for sure. And then I woke up . . . and Sarah . . . she was there with me."

Moon, who had been grinding his teeth at this old woman's foolish dream, turned on his heel and stalked away. I should've picked Sarah up as soon as I knew Provo had left her with Aunt Daisy, put her in protective custody. The child deserved to be protected from this world's predators. Whatever had happened to Sarah, it is my fault. My responsibility.

Now there was a debt to pay.

He opened the Blazer's rear window; the Ute policeman unrolled an old 30-30 Winchester carbine from an oily cloth. A man who'd pretend to be a child's father. Lure a little girl away. Shooting was too damn good for him. Moon loaded several hollow-points into the magazine, then cocked the carbine to inject a round into the firing chamber.

There was, like the Book said, a time to live. A time to die.

Parris, who knew the Ute as a man knew his twin brother, had no doubt of Charlie Moon's intentions. The white man turned to the old woman, who seemed to have shrunk before his eyes. "Mrs. Perika, did Blue Cup tell you where his camp was?"

"No." Her voice quavered. "But I watched him when he left." She pointed toward the southeast. "He went over that way."

Moon walked a hundred-yard circle around the flat site where Daisy's trailer home stood in a grove of stunted trees. Almost immediately the policeman found several hoofprints on a low ridge to the east; a horse had stood here for some time, nervously shifting its weight from one foot to another. Someone who wore a new pair of boots (or boots with new soles, he reminded himself) had evidently sat on the horse, then got off, smoked a Marlboro cigarette (the butt was in a dry clump of grass), then led the horse toward the trailer. The Ute policeman was barely able to follow the prints down the rocky slope, but he picked up clear prints near the propane tank that fueled the old woman's trailer home. He found no tracks at the mouth of *Cañón del Espíritu*. The policeman circled to the south—in a wider arc now—and found a half dozen clear hoofprints leading away from the canyon. The unshod prints were slightly deeper now and spaced much farther apart. The man had ridden the horse away at a gallop. He was in a hurry. He'd been headed toward the southeast; in the same direction where Daisy had thought Blue Cup was camped.

Moon paused in his tracking. It was time for some thinking. For some police work.

Blue Cup must've driven his ancient army-surplus Jeep down from Wyoming. There were only a dozen places within walking distance that an old-fashioned Ute would pick for a campsite. Moon sprinted back toward the trailer, where Scott Parris waited with the old woman and the child. Sarah clutched the wiggling, mewing kitten against her chest. The *matukach* policeman had kneeled by the child, speaking quietly as he stroked the kitten's fur.

Charlie Moon towered over the little girl, who looked up hopefully. There were questions in her dark eyes, if not on her lips.

Moon had his own questions. The Ute policeman wanted to ask her what had happened when the man came with the pony, but the expression on her face told him that questions would be useless. Sarah would not speak.

Scott Parris got to his feet and patted the tiny girl's head. "Find any sign out there, Charlie?"

The Ute policeman nodded. He propped the short barrel of the Winchester carbine on his shoulder. "Let's go do some huntin', pardner."

Daisy wrinkled her brow—this was all so confusing. "Hunting what?"

"Two-legged animals," Charlie Moon said grimly. Then he headed for the Blazer, with his friend close behind.

*   *   *

It took the Ute policeman less than ten minutes to locate the spot where the old Jeep had left the dirt road; the prints in the sand left by the Goodyear Wrangler tires were unmistakable, and indicated several trips in and out. The last trip had been out. Moon shifted into four-wheel drive and eased the big Blazer down a slope strewn with shards of black basalt. When they entered a wide, sandy arroyo, Moon got out and walked ahead while Parris took the wheel and chugged along behind the tracker.

The camp was in a wide, sandy basin where the arroyo had become a shallow, meandering drainage, then finally petered out among a grove of stunted oaks. But it was an abandoned camp. The Ute squatted by the blackened remains of the campfire; the sooty ashes were cold between his fingertips.

Moon inspected the site with meticulous care. He measured the footprints of two men with his hand. One was the fellow who'd rode the horse away from the mouth of *Cañón del Espíritu*. This was probably the Shoshone, the one they called Noah Dancing Crow. The other was an older man, who walked with short, stiff steps. And used some kind of walking stick for support. Blue Cup, of course.

Parris waited patiently, until the Ute had paused to ponder the situation.

"What do you think, Charlie?"

"Well," Moon said as he took one more careful look at the campsite, "a brand-new Cub Scout could figure this one out. Two men've been camped here for about a week. Blue Cup and, most likely, his Shoshone sidekick. They left last night, in the Jeep."

"What about the horse?"

The Ute walked to the edge of the camp, where a gentle rise was dotted with clumps of yucca and yellow-bloomed rabbit brush. He followed the prints of unshod hoofs to the top of the ridge, and shaded his hands with his eyes as he gazed southward.

Parris was coming up behind him.

Moon pointed the barrel of the Winchester carbine with one hand, as if it were a pistol. "By now, that ol' nag is probably all the way home with the rest of that Navajo's horses."

☀ Colorado Route 13 ☀
One mile south of the Wyoming border

Noah Dancing Crow watched a wedge-shaped cloud drift in from the west; dark wisps hung like ghostly stalactites under the misty form. This was what westerners ruefully call "dry rain"; the precious moisture was evaporating before it could reach the thirsty grasslands. Under this gray anvil that teased the parched earth with a sweet promise of moisture, the sun was only six disks above the far horizon. Within minutes, twilight would unfold over the tall-grass prairie like a soft gray blanket. And the wind was still. It was a good omen, the optimistic Shoshone thought. But he was wrong in this assessment. So very wrong.

Noah was now confident that Blue Cup would never know about his plan to lure the child away from the old woman. He had grudgingly admitted to himself that his idea had been a stupid one. The Shoshone promised himself that he would never again entertain such a foolish notion. Never.

But on this very night, before the moon had made its journey halfway across the sky, Noah Dancing Crow would break this promise.

In his duty as camp cook, the Shoshone was twisting the metal key to open a canned Danish ham the old Ute had purchased at a food market in Craig. Noah produced his razor-sharp Buck Knife from a leather sheath under his shirt; he sliced off four thick slabs of the pink meat. He placed these in an iron skillet that was seated on the cherry-red embers of the campfire. After the ham slices had sizzled for a minute—and the frying pan was slick with pork grease—he broke a half dozen fresh eggs onto the smoking iron surface. Dutifully he broke three of the yolks and stirred them. Blue Cup liked his eggs fried well done—but only after the yolks had been broken and stirred. This task done, he turned to his mentor.

"The food smells good."

The elderly Ute merely nodded. Blue Cup seemed to have aged ten years in as many hours.

"I'm sorry," the Shoshone said, "that you did not find the sacred object. But maybe you can get your Power back in some other way . . ."

"The Power," the old shaman said sharply, "has not departed from me. It is deep inside me . . . in the very marrow of my bones." But deep in his marrow, the old man felt cold. And weak.

The Shoshone, thus chastised, went back to his duties.

The old Ute watched his faithful companion prepare their supper; the aroma of the ham touched his nostrils, and this made the old man's stomach growl with anticipation. His bones ached almost as much as his heart. It had been a long, hard journey. First on the big Greyhound bus down to southern Colorado. And now back to Wyoming in the old Jeep.

And all for nothing.

No—not entirely for nothing. There was one small satisfaction. Provo Frank, that thieving weasel, was dead and gone. But the sacred object was also gone . . . forever. With it, much of his share of the Power was also gone.

They ate in silence. Blue Cup picked at his food with a stainless steel fork. Noah speared chunks of ham with the pointed tip of his small hunting knife, and munched happily on the fried eggs.

As the sun settled in the west, the moon came up over a hillock to the east; its silver light bathed the camp in a soft glow.

Noah walked some distance away and relieved his bowels behind a shrub. Then the Shoshone walked alone. And pondered his future.

Blue Cup sat by the small fire, and watched it die. Like all his hopes. But he was warmed by the hatred that burned within him. Hatred against the thief who had stolen his property . . . against his father, who had loved whiskey more than he loved his son . . . against the Southern Utes, who had turned away from him . . . over a trifling incident that had taken place so long ago! The old Ute sat and watched the embers cool. And pondered his future.

The edge of the storm was now barely a mile to the west. It seemed larger now. The cloud, which was edged in scarlet by the waning rays of the nearest star, was illuminated internally by a brief white flash.

The shaman stood up. As was his custom when he wished to call upon the voices of the spirits, he urinated into the fire. Immediately whitish-gray fumes erupted from the coals. He breathed deeply of this smoke, and tried to ignore the searing pain in his throat and lungs. If a man was to have Power . . . he must also accept pain.

This old man, in all his long journey through this barren life, had accepted nothing that was free. He had never received a gift of love. Not once.

Now the shaman saw someone approaching from a great distance. It was a small person. A child?

The Shoshone had returned to a place where he could watch the old man's doings. With that deep awe and admiration that only an adoring disciple can experience, Noah watched intently as Blue Cup gazed at the smoke curling upward from the campfire. The Shoshone strained, but he could see nothing except writhing fumes. He was certain that the old man could see much more.

Blue Cup, who had trained his mind to perceive visions, did indeed see much more. He saw someone walking toward him. But this small figure was not a child. The gait had a strange rocking quality; this was a frame whose joints were tight with age. The figure came near, and the old shaman was awed as he recognized the unmistakable form of a *pitukupf*.

226

It had been more than five decades since he had encountered one of these strange and powerful creatures.

The dwarf-spirit was carrying a yellow wicker basket hooked over one elbow; there was a blue cover on the basket. The *pitukupf*, it seemed, was going to pass by without taking notice of the Ute shaman. But he paused and turned his head, as if noticing the old man for the first time. The dwarf raised his right hand in salute; he spoke to Blue Cup in an archaic version of the Ute tongue that was hard to understand. But the old man understood this much: the *pitukupf* was inquiring whether the shaman would like to see what was in this basket that he carried.

Blue Cup was not short on curiosity; he nodded and leaned close.

The dwarf winked at the old man and, in a dramatic gesture, removed the blue cover from the basket.

Blue Cup looked inside, and was disappointed. The yellow basket was filled with bones. And not even whole bones. All of these bones were broken. And most were burnt a sooty black. "Ahhhh . . . and these are . . . ?"

The *pitukupf* told him. In this basket were not the bones of deer, or badger, or bear. These were very unusual bones.

Blue Cup guessed that these must be the broken, charred bones of someone who had died long ago. He guessed wrong. The little man told the old shaman the truth about the bones.

Sometimes it is hard to hear the truth.

A thin, scarlet arc of the sun was now barely visible on the horizon. As his indistinct shadow grew long, like a dark finger pointing across the prairie toward the east, Noah watched the old *bugahant*. It seemed that the Ute was having a conversation with some invisible presence. Now Blue Cup bent forward, as if to look more closely at something. Noah squatted, his lean arms folded. He would watch the *bugahant* carefully. And maybe learn something.

The thunderstorm continued its relentless approach. Grumbling rumbles of thunder followed the electric discharges inside the cloud; a fresh breeze made rippling waves in the rolling sea of grass. To the west, fat drops of rain fell upon the prairie. The Shoshone imagined that this storm would end its journey in the Never Summer Mountains where the rain would turn to snow. But he was wrong. Its purpose completed, this storm would soon be over.

His eyes unfocused, Blue Cup stared into the remains of the campfire. The embers were now cold. Dead. As he would soon be. The old man had forgotten about the Shoshone. He hardly noticed the few drops of cold rain that pelted his head and shoulders.

It did not matter.

The shaman sat down by the fire, and sighed. Such a long, hard life. An endless quest for the Power. Soon it would all be over. Finished.

Blue Cup began to sing. He sang old Ute songs. Exaggerated epics of great bravery in small wars against Apache and Navajo and Cheyenne, songs of success in the winter's hunt, tales of dauntless men who received mystic power from the spirit of Bear and Coyote and Badger. When he had exhausted the songs of the People, he hummed a few bars from *Ode to Joy.*

The shaman paused in his singing, and blinked. Away in the distance, far to the north, he saw a small light. It moved, and he wondered whether it was a cigarette in some traveler's mouth. But no. The light was moving very fast now . . . and taking on a shape.

The apparition that appeared before him completely astonished the old shaman. It was the form of a man who had once walked upon the earth, his bones clothed in flesh like other men. But this person was now a spirit. It was that Ute herder of sheep who had—if one believed such fanciful tales—been taken up to the heavens in the arms of angels!

The man who stood before Blue Cup—if this could be called a man— was Nahum Yaciiti. It was the old Ute shepherd who had died in a terrific windstorm on the banks of the Animas. He was dressed in a fine deerskin robe that was bleached whiter than fresh snow, and the garment was embroidered with many beads. Glistening beads of colors not seen even in the rainbow. And most wonderful of all to the old Ute's eyes were the eagle feathers that fringed the garment. The shaman could not take his eyes off this beautiful robe.

Nahum spoke: "Blue Cup . . . look upon your own clothing."

The old shaman looked at his shirt, which had been washed in a Steamboat Springs Laundromat only this morning. The cloth was stained with something sticky and repugnant. And he could smell his own body; the stench was like decaying flesh!

"You smell bad," the shepherd observed soberly, "like a corpse too long in the sun."

The old man stood erect, proud, his back straight. "I," the shaman snapped, "am one of the Powerful. Who are you to speak this way to me?"

"I," the apparition said, "am the spirit of the People. I am your grandfather . . . your father . . . your brother."

Blue Cup spat into the fire. "You are nothing to me . . . a mere phantom." The shaman snapped his fingers at the apparition. "If I do not wish to see you, you will vanish like a puff of smoke."

"Take off your garments," Nahum commanded. "There is but little time."

An electric finger of fire touched the grass a few hundred yards away; the shaman heard a sharp report.

"If I take off my clothes," Blue Cup responded stubbornly, "I will be naked. And you can see—" he pointed to the dark cloud, "—that it is raining. And cold."

"I will give you *my* garment." The shepherd lifted his arms, and the white deerskin fringed with eagle feathers was like a pair of great wings. "But you must do this thing quickly . . . hurry," the apparition said with a dreadful urgency. "Take off your shirt . . . throw it into the fire."

The old shaman looked at the wet embers and grunted. "There is no—"

The campfire, which had been dormant, was instantly kindled. The flames wriggled and snapped, the dancing amber lights reflected off Blue Cup's gaunt face. The shaman, who desperately wanted the clean garment, considered the offer . . .

The thundercloud was immediately illuminated by a great surge of ionic lights; the leading edge of the storm sprouted long crooked legs of fire that stood upon the earth. They found a foothold and stepped toward the shaman.

Still the old Ute hesitated . . .

Nahum had one last card to play in this game. "Come quickly," he said to someone who was waiting.

Blue Cup trembled when he saw the two additional visitors. And he experienced three painful emotions that he would not have thought possible.

Guilt.

Shame.

Regret.

Noah, his arms hugging his knees, sat shivering in the cold rain, sniffing the pungent odor of ozone. He trembled before the approaching storm. Noah wanted to fall upon the earth, to crawl into a hole. But frightened as he was, the Shoshone felt compelled to watching the peculiar drama unfold.

The old Ute *bugahant* was talking again. With some unseen visitor. It was more like an argument than a conversation. The campfire, which had been soaked by the rain, suddenly burst into bright yellow flames that were half as high as a man. Blue Cup became quiet, almost reflective . . . as if thinking something over. Now he was taking off his shirt—and dropping it into the fire! Perhaps the old man, having lost his treasure to the thief, had also lost his mind. Now the *bugahant* was taking off his jeans and tossing them into the fire like so much rubbish.

What could this mean?

More than Noah could have imagined.

The astonished Shoshone watched the old *bugahant* stand naked before the campfire. Now Blue Cup lifted his mulberry staff. He pointed it at the cloud. The old man called out to the storm.

Tona-paga-ri . . .

The storm fell silent; the rain stopped. Silence covered the prairie as even the winds fell still.

Noah, in his desire to please his master, had learned a smattering of the Ute tongue. He recognized this word. The strange old *bugahant* was calling to the lightning! But why?

The old shaman called out again; his voice reverberated like thunder across the plain:

Tona-paga-ri . . . *Tona-paga-ri* . . . *Tona-paga-ri* . . .

The lightning answered the shaman's call.

What he saw next may have been a product of the Shoshone's active imagination. Or perhaps his account is accurate. But for the rest of his days, Noah Dancing Crow would remember these few seconds that followed the shaman's last summons to the fire from the heavens. It had been, he would tell his Shoshone friends, unlike the ordinary behavior of a thunderstorm, when such things happen much too fast for a man to comprehend.

Initially the old Ute was bathed in a brilliant flame of blue-white light that encompassed him like a halo. He fairly shimmered in this light, and seemed almost transparent—more like a spirit than a mortal. Then it was as if a long finger reached down to delicately touch the upraised wand in the *bugahant's* hand. Even when the blue fire from heaven consumed him, Blue Cup did not flinch. Neither did he cry out. The Ute shaman stood like the resolute warrior that he was, his mulberry staff raised in defiance . . . or salute? And then the wooden rod burst into flame. The peal of thunder rumbled like ten thousand cannon; the blast of hot wind blew the Shoshone flat on his back.

And it was over.

The storm cloud, its cosmic business completed, had dissipated into thin wisps of vapor. A spray of stars sprinkled the sky. But the outer darkness was not illuminated.

The Shoshone stood over the Ute's pitiful corpse, and wept like an orphaned child.

There was not a cinder left from the mulberry staff. The old man's body had been shattered to flinders by the fire from heaven, and his remains smelled oddly like . . . The Shoshone attempted to push the obscene thought from his consciousness.

Noah Dancing Crow wiped at his eyes with his shirtsleeve and sat down by the shattered corpse. He sat very still and thought very hard. He thought about many things. The Shoshone considered the important lessons he had learned from Blue Cup. If you wanted the jackrabbit's remarkable power to hear, it was not enough to eat just the animal's ears. You must consume the whole body of the leather-tough rodent. Noah remembered the horrible jackrabbit meal, how he had vomited most of it up—the mere memory almost made him gag. But even this had not been enough. He was still deaf. No, if you were to have the Power, first in your skin and hair, and finally deep in your soul, you must do all those things that Blue Cup had told you to do. But now his teacher was gone, nothing but a pile of burned flesh and bones! All was lost. Everything.

Or perhaps . . . if a man was sufficiently clever . . . if a man could understand the hidden meaning behind the *bugahant*'s words . . . "The Power has not departed from me. It is deep inside me . . . in the very marrow of my bones."

A small light, sparked by the electricity of a few thousand neurons, kindled itself in Noah's brain. Now, this was a tiny light indeed. Not enough to jump-start a firefly. But in such a dark place, even a dim light has its effect. Immediately the great darkness of superstition joined itself with the flicker of false light, and together they spoke clearly to the Shoshone.

The moon was not far above the eastern horizon. But already Noah had forgotten his recent promise to himself.

For the first time in his unhappy life, Noah Dancing Crow had (so he believed) entertained an entirely original thought. For the first time in several winters, the Shoshone felt a great sense of pride and exultation! He was, indeed, a clever man. Worthy to carry on in the tradition of Blue Cup.

The great Chief Washakie, that Shoshone who was filled with wisdom in his old age, had made this accurate observation: "Youth does foolish things."

But Noah, sadly, did not have an iota of the wisdom of Washakie. This Shoshone youth had chosen another path; he would follow in the footsteps of his Ute master. And Blue Cup had been a receptacle for the dark Powers. Furthermore, the *bugahant* had told the Shoshone where this Power was: . . . *deep inside me . . . in the very marrow of my bones.*

Noah Dancing Crow blinked warily at the twisted, scrawny carcass of the old Ute. And sniffed. Yes. Even though a man hated to acknowledge such a thought, it smelled much like . . . roast pork. The Shoshone felt a surge of nausea; there was a peculiar gurgling sensation in his gut. This was going to be much worse than the tough old jackrabbit. But if he was to have the Power, it must be done. This unpleasant task was going to take a long time.

And a lot of red pepper.

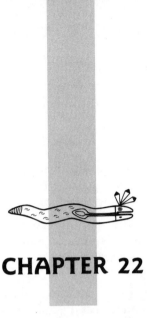

CHAPTER 22

Southern Ute Reservation
Near the mouth of *Cañón del Espíritu*

It was late in the afternoon when Daisy Perika heard his voice. The words came from very far away, but also from inside her. The child was using her crayons to color the funnies in the Durango newspaper, the kitten was lapping at a saucer of milk. Daisy Perika shuffled to the small window, pulled the cotton curtain aside, and squinted into the twilight. A powder-blue mist wafted among the sparse forest of trees around her trailer home; the thin fog drifted toward the mouth of *Cañón del Espíritu*, which inhaled it slowly, as if savoring aromatic smoke from the bowl of a fine pipe.

Daisy knew what she must do, but the old woman hesitated. The child looked up from her coloring with questioning eyes. The old shaman heard the summons again. The call to her was more urgent now.

"You and the cat stay here. I won't be gone a minute."

Sarah did not seem to mind; since her return from . . . from wherever, the child displayed a serenity that one usually saw only in those who were near death. The old woman found this thought somewhat unnerving. She locked the door behind her with a key; if there was an emergency, the child could open the door from the inside. But no intruder could enter.

At the bottom of the porch steps, Daisy paused to get her staff, which was leaning against the aluminum wall of the trailer. Without hesitation, she made her way to the mouth of the Canyon of the Spirits. As she came close, the words she heard were crisp and clear. The shaman was no more than a dozen paces into the shadow of the first of the Three Sisters when she saw him.

✧

Charlie Moon sat across the kitchen table from Scott Parris. The child kneeled in a wooden chair, her chin in her hands, elbows resting against the table. She watched the policemen in silence.

Daisy poured the steaming black liquid into heavy mugs. Each man took a sip of the strongest coffee on the planet, and grimaced. Sarah, in imitation, took a sip of sweet milk from a small plastic cup. And grimaced.

"How d'you like the coffee?" Daisy asked.

"It's absolutely incredible," Parris said with a straight face.

"You've never made better," Moon said grimly. He poured a third of a bowl of sugar into his cup and took another sip. Now the stuff tasted like *sweetened* road tar.

"Glad you like it," the old woman said. It was good to have real men in the house. Men who appreciated a he-man cup of coffee. Just last month, Gorman Sweetwater had pretended to strangle and said that her coffee was worse than goat piss. When she'd snapped: "Well, I expect it takes a lowlife drunk like you to *know* what goat piss tastes like," Gorman had replied with a wink, "I only drink it to get the taste of your coffee out of my mouth, cousin." If he hadn't been a relative, she'd have run him off for sure.

Moon pushed his mug away. The Ute policeman glanced at the child, who was tracing her tiny finger along an irregular crack in the red oilcloth that covered the table. "Me'n Scott," he said to Daisy, "we tracked the fella with the horse to their camp. It was the Shoshone, I expect."

Parris chuckled. "Yeah, I'm some great tracker."

"They were long gone," the Ute policemen said. "Probably headed north. To Wyoming. I've already called in a bulletin on the two of 'em. And the old army Jeep." He was watching the child, but Sarah seemed to have no interest in what he was saying. The child's lips were forming words, but no sounds. Not even a whisper.

Daisy stood by the child; she put her hand on Sarah's head. The child withdrew; she did not wish to be touched. "It's late," the old woman said. "You run off now and get ready for bed."

Sarah slipped off the chair, picked the kitten up, and trotted away toward the bedroom.

"Don't forget to brush your teeth," Daisy called. She sat down in the chair where the child had been and folded her wrinkled hands on the table. "Where Blue Cup has gone," she said evenly, "no policeman will find him." She paused, gauging her next words. How much she should tell them.

The lawmen waited.

"I had a talk with my old friend . . . with Nahum Yaciiti . . . not an hour ago."

Both of the lawmen knew that Nahum was dead. Moon leaned back in his chair and rolled his eyes toward the ceiling. Well, here it comes. Ghosts and goblins and witches and skinwalkers and . . .

Daisy made a point of turning away from her skeptical nephew, who could be such a narrow-minded man. She directed her words to the *matukach*, who understood such things. "Nahum, he told me a lot of things . . . I can only tell you some of them."

Parris leaned forward, his hands clasped around the steaming cup of coffee.

"He told me that you and Charlie—" here she glanced somewhat contemptuously at her nephew "—you should go and find the Shoshone. You . . . you need to talk with him."

There was something else Charlie Moon needed to do, but he'd have to work that out on his own.

In a motherly gesture, she patted Scott Parris' hand. "And Nahum, he told me this: 'when they find the cross on the wall, then they'll understand.' I don't know exactly what he meant by that. Sometimes he likes to talk in riddles."

Moon grunted.

The old woman's eyes snapped at him. "Maybe you don't want to hear none of this."

"Oh no," the Ute policeman replied with thinly veiled sarcasm, "anything a ghost has to tell me about police work, I'm interested in hearing."

"Then," she said, "go find the Shoshone. See what he has to say."

"I expect the Shoshone'll have to wait," Moon said. "Until I've had me a talk with Blue Cup."

Daisy was about to tell Charlie Moon plainly that Blue Cup was dead. But her nephew was such a smart-mouth. The old shaman clamped her lips shut.

Parris put his hand on hers. "Mrs. Perika, where d'you figure we'd find this Shoshone fellow?"

"I don't know where he's at right now," she muttered, "but Nahum said he was on his way to a school somewhere up in Wyoming."

Moon raised an eyebrow? "A school?" Now this was getting good.

"Yes," she said. And told her nephew just what kind of school.

The old woman was outdoing herself. Moon grinned. Then he chuckled. The big Ute's shoulders shook; he laughed until tears ran down his cheeks and Sarah came to peek through the doorway to see what was so funny.

Daisy grabbed the flyswatter and smacked her favorite nephew. Hard.

At the marvelous sight of the big Ute getting swatted by his angry aunt, Parris choked back a laugh.

Daisy uttered dark, vulgar Ute curses. She swatted her insolent nephew again. And again. On the head, on the back, on the shoulders. And it stung.

But Moon, though he put his hands up to protect himself, could not stop laughing. The thought of the deaf Shoshone going to a school where they'd train him to be a . . . No, it was too funny!

The big Ute policeman stumbled from the trailer and down the porch steps—his aunt hot on his heels, wielding her curses and the flyswatter.

Sarah, who had a toothbrush in her hand, looked up at Scott Parris with mild alarm. And a question in her eyes.

He reached out to touch her shoulder; the child did not shrink away.

"One thing a policeman learns," he said gently, "is don't ever get involved in family disputes."

☼ Bitter Springs, Wyoming ☼

Noah Dancing Crow paused on the brick sidewalk and stared glumly at a bevy of fat brown moths dancing around the neon sign suspended above the drugstore entrance. Occasionally a daring celebrant would leave the group and approach the incandescent blue rod. Like a Sun Dancer approaching the sacred tree, to touch the wood with a feather and then retreat.

He was a haunted man. Every night, in his dark dreams . . . he saw it all happen again. The first dream would end when the child was lost in the vaporous mists of *Cañón del Espíritu*. This was the time he dreaded most; because the horrific visions of Blue Cup would begin . . . The old man was missing great chunks of flesh from his body. It was, evidently, not enough that the exhausted Shoshone had made a solemn vow to carry Blue Cup's bones (now carefully stored in a basket) into the Valley of Stinking Waters. Yes, there by the stone with the sacred drawings, it was a fine place for a burial. On the black stone were horned figures of ancient *bugahants*, jagged zigzags of lightning, symbols for stars and Cloud-Spirit. Best of all for the Ute *bugahant's* spirit, the nested circles. The tunnel to other worlds . . .

That promise, the *bugahant's* apprentice reasoned, would surely make the old man happy.

But no.

With a relentless fury, the shaman's gory phantom would chase the Shoshone across dry arroyos and through piñon thickets and across icy rivers. And threaten to burn him with fire and feed his body to the buzzards and magpies. The chase would not end until the red dawn bathed Crowheart Butte.

Noah sighed. He had tried so hard. He had done what no man should have to do, and had suffered terribly. And still, the Power had not come to him. Now the proud Shoshone had to turn to that lesser power of the white race. This was a great disappointment. A stinging humiliation.

He waited outside the drugstore, hesitating.

It was long after dark and almost time to close the store, but there was still a bit of work to do. Theresa Connovan licked the label and fixed it expertly to the brown bottle. She counted twenty green and white capsules of fluoxetine hydrochloride and dropped them into the bottle. She heard the small bell ring as someone came through the front door and interrupted the beam of infrared light. As she twisted the plastic safety lid onto the bottle of twenty-milligram Prozac capsules, the portly woman glanced up from her position behind the druggist's counter. Theresa watched the skinny Indian approach the rear of Connovan's Corner Drugstore. It was her favorite game—to observe customers and deduce the ailment that brought them to her inner sanctum. Decades ago, Theresa had dreamed of being a physician. But there had not been enough money for tuition, and scholarships for women had been scarce.

"Hello there, Noah Dancing Crow." The deaf man was staring at the floor. The pharmacist waited until he looked up, and was close enough to read her lips.

"Hello, Noah."

The Shoshone shoved his hands into his jacket pockets and nodded absently. She noted slight bags under his eyes, an Adam's apple that bobbled as he swallowed, a bluish-yellow cast to the whites of his eyes. She also noticed the transparent plastic parcel under his arm. Ground red pepper. Two, maybe three pounds. Theresa was an observant person and she had an excellent memory. This was the second time this week she'd seen the Shoshone in town, and the first time he'd also had a big bag of red pepper tucked under his arm. Unless the Shoshone had opened a Mexican restaurant on the Wind River reservation, the need for so much red pepper was very curious. And just yesterday, the local sheriff's deputy had told her he was on the lookout for Noah and the old Ute who was a squatter on national forest land. The Feds, he said, were looking for them. For "questioning," the deputy said. Interesting. She wondered what the odd pair had been up to.

"You don't look so good, Noah Dancing Crow."

"No, Tess." His thin voice came from some hollow place inside. "And I don't feel so good neither." He tapped his chest with a grubby finger. "I hurt here when I lay down. My insides ache unless I lay on my left side. I think maybe I got some heart trouble."

"Well," the druggist said with more than a hint of self-assurance, "I'd speculate there ain't nothin' wrong with your heart." She rubbed at the large mole on her chin and closed one eye like the comical Sailor Man. "I can," she announced in a haughty tone that hinted darkly of book learning, "tell by lookin' at you exactly what's wrong."

Noah, who did not doubt the depth of her powers, waited expectantly.

"Firstly, I expect you've got a touch of hiatus hernia." His puzzled look brought her a small surge of satisfaction. The pharmacist did not miss an opportunity to poison communication by using words unfamiliar to the common folk. It was a double-barreled pleasure, actually, because she could also emphasize her superiority by explaining what he could not understand. Theresa spoke very slowly so that it would be easy for the deaf man to read her lips. "A hiatus hernia—" she pointed a finger at the Shoshone's belly "—is a dysfunction of your stomach valve."

She squinted at his belt buckle. It was not fastened to the usual hole in the cowhide strap around his waist, but to a smaller, less worn opening two positions away.

"Secondly, I can see you've put on some weight, maybe six, six and a half pounds. But . . . " She eyed the bag of red pepper. "The extra weight ain't the problem, Noah Dancing Crow, no sir, that's not your problem at all."

The deaf man squinted hopefully at the druggist's lips. "Then what do you figure it is, Tess?"

Theresa leaned over the counter and glared at the Shoshone. "Your problem, young man, is just plain old indigestion. You," she said in grand-motherly fashion, "have got to be lots more careful about what you eat. Stay away from spicy foods. And," she added with a stern air of authority, "especially . . . you stay away from meat."

Noah shuddered; his limbs went limp with guilt. He mouthed the dreaded word without making a sound. "Meat?"

"O'course," she said with the air of an enlightened soul who has tri-umphed over ignorance. "Meat's bad for your insides. Now, your fish and your fowl, they ain't so bad, but what you want to stay away from—" she wagged her finger at the chastened Shoshone "—is *red* meat."

THE SHAMAN'S BONES

Once his connection with the Ute *bugahant* was finally severed, the Shoshone made a life-changing decision. First, he decided that Blue Cup's
religion was too difficult. No matter what hard thing a man was willing
to do, it all came to nothing. The Power evaded him. And his guts just
couldn't take the punishment. He cast aside his desire to become a *bugahant*. A man must take care of his stomach. Let someone else chase after
the Power. After all, what good had it done for Blue Cup?

But when one obsession departs, another must fill the void that is left.
And a far more noble ambition now fired the small furnace of Noah's
imagination. The center of this fantasy was a huge, black Peterbilt chassis.
Big rubber tires, almost as tall as a man. Five hundred thumping diesel
horses. Two hundred pounds of polished chrome. Red leather everywhere.
Two giant air horns, four halogen headlights, a high-powered CB radio . . .
and a sawed-off pump shotgun stashed behind the seat.

In this fantasy, Noah Dancing Crow hauled hard coal from Walsenburg
to Denver, fat sheep from Jasper to Kansas City, pine lumber from Kalis-
pell to Great Falls. And best of all, there would be no need to eat un-
healthy food. No more jackrabbit ears. Most especially, no more . . . But
this grisly memory made him shudder.

From now on it would be cheeseburgers and pork rinds. Slim Jims
spiced with red pepper. And pepperoni pizza seasoned with green chile.
During the long winter, gallons of black coffee. In the summer, Pepsi-
Cola and iced Mexican beer.

Ahhh . . . trucking. This was certainly the proper calling for a man.

✧

On this bright, cloudless morning, Noah Dancing Crow was decked out
in his best duds. The wide-brimmed black felt hat with a band of multicolored beads. The blue checkered shirt and almost new jeans with brass
studs by the pockets. Noah drove Blue Cup's ancient Jeep to Jasper, and
showed up at the Big Mack School for Truck Driving at 8:00 A.M. sharp.
The Shoshone was astonished when the head of admissions refused to
enroll him. Noah simply couldn't understand—this was his chosen calling.

After some hesitation, the kindly man explained slowly, so the young
man could read his lips: "I got nothin' a'tall against you, good buddy. It's
just . . . well, y'see . . . the way it is . . ." He paused and tried to
remember the way one was supposed to say it. Hearing-umpired . . .
hearing-unpaired . . . hearing something or other. Dammit anyway. The
head of admissions could not remember the proper phrase, so he sighed
and spat it out under his bristling mustache: "In these parts, son, we just
don't get much call for truck drivers who's deef as a brass rat!"

So Noah, who was greatly disappointed, decided to have a bottle or two of beer. After that, the prodigal son thought he might return to the Wind River reservation. To his father's house and his mother's good cooking . . . even to his little sister's cruel pranks.

✵ Bar Nunn, Wyoming ✵

Noah emerged from the Woodhen Bar; his boots crunched in the gravel as he made his way to the old Jeep. He climbed in and pushed the starter switch with his left foot. And waited while the energy from the storage battery turned the old engine over. And over. But it didn't start. The Shoshone, who was not mechanically inclined, did not know what to do. So he pumped the accelerator pedal until the engine was well flooded. And held the starter switch down until the electrical charge in the battery was exhausted. Then he got out, cursed, and kicked a front tire three times.

This did not help much.

Slightly sobered, Noah Dancing Crow stood in the parking lot and thought about the Jeep. It must simply be that the car was too old, like an old man. The machine had simply gotten tired—and had died. He would leave it where it sat. It was, after all, not his automobile and not his responsibility. The Shoshone removed his blanket roll from the rear seat of the dead Jeep and slung it over his back. Walking away, he considered his predicament. Because he did not wish to squander his savings on bus fare, it would be necessary to depend upon the kindness of strangers.

Two strangers, who had been shadowing the unfortunate Shoshone, were willing to provide transportation. Eager, in fact. But their intentions toward Noah Dancing Crow could hardly be described as "kind."

One of these strangers had a small automobile part in his jacket pocket. It was a rotor, so called because it rotates. This device spins in the distributor to connect the high-voltage impulse from the auto-transformer coil to the appropriate spark plug. Now, this was an absolutely essential element in the automobile engine. Less than an hour earlier, this particular rotor been removed from the distributor of a very old Jeep.

Noah Dancing Crow turned and squinted into the approaching head-lights; he stuck out his thumb and presented a big smile. The automobile slowed and was dead even with him when it stopped. Someone rolled the window down on the passenger side. The deaf man stuck his head close to the window and shouted one word: "Riverton?"

The man reached over the seat and opened the rear door; this experienced hitchhiker wasted no time—he pitched his blanket roll into the open door, then settled himself into the back seat of the Volvo; the soothing warmth was quite pleasant. The Shoshone was soon drifting toward a heavy, dreamless sleep. As he rested, he counted his blessings. Because he'd caught a ride almost immediately after stumbling onto the rocky shoulder of Wyoming Route 26, the mildly intoxicated Shoshone decided that his luck was changing.

Indeed it was.

Scott Parris took his gaze off the highway long enough to glance over his shoulder at the slight man who snored in the rear seat. "Charlie, you sure this is the right fellow?"

The Ute focused a small penlight on the black-and-white photo they'd picked up from the Shoshone police at Fort Washakie. He turned and used the same light to illuminate the face of the sleeping passenger.

"*Hey, Noah!*" the Ute yelled.

Parris lurched in surprise, swerved the Volvo onto the shoulder and back, and muttered: "Dammit, Charlie . . . at least give a fellow some kind of warning before you bellow out like that."

The deaf man did not stir from his sleep. He did not even twitch.

"Oh yeah," Moon said with a satisfied chuckle. "He's the one."

Parris felt a cold warning in his gut. It was not like they had any hard proof that the man had committed a crime. "You sure you want to do this?" It would be somewhat of an understatement to point out that Moon's plan was about as legal as beating a prisoner with a rubber hose.

The big Ute policeman stared straight ahead. Into the inky darkness that washed across the rolling Wyoming prairie. "He kidnapped a child on the reservation."

"Or attempted to . . . and we don't even know that for certain," Parris said. Uncertainly. And what they had in mind for the Shoshone was . . . well . . . not much different from kidnapping.

The Ute ignored this protest. There was a debt to be paid. A hard lesson to be learned. Moon, of course, expected the Shoshone to learn the lesson. Life has many surprises.

Parris realized that his Ute friend was set on this course. A moaning headwind was flattening tall grass and sage along the broad shoulder of the two-lane road. He swallowed hard and gradually pressed the accelerator to the floorboard to keep the speedometer needle jittering around sixty.

Damn the Wyoming wind!

☼ Central Wyoming, Natrona County ☼

The Volvo droned on westward. Past Natrona. And Powder River. And past the fantastic towers and spires of Hell's Half Acre. The Shoshone slept the sweet sleep of a babe—even drooling on the vinyl seat cover. When Parris left the blacktop at Waltman, the deaf man was almost awakened by the vibrations from rough corduroy patterns left in the unpaved road by graders.

"How far?" Parris muttered. This didn't feel right.

"Not far," the Ute policeman said.

☼

The Shoshone awakened suddenly; a brutally cold rush of air on his face. Someone had opened the rear door of the automobile. This was followed by a big hand on his shoulder, shaking him. Ahhh . . . they must be to Riverton already. He blinked and rubbed at his eyes. It wasn't night anymore. An enormous man towered darkly above him. A broad-shouldered white man stood several paces away, his pale face made pink by the sunrise.

Noah Dancing Crow was almost sober now; he steadied himself on the door as he got out of the Volvo. The hitchhiker was about to thank his benefactors for the ride. But the first light of dawn illuminated this desolate place . . . the jutting ridges of the Rattlesnake Range to the south . . . the meandering yellow banks of Poison Spider Creek to the east. No. This was not Riverton. They were dropping him off way out of town.

The Shoshone, who was still in the process of awakening from his sleep, glanced nervously at the darker and taller of the two men. The big man's face was harder than the granite mountains. A heavy, long-barreled pistol was holstered in beaded buckskin on his hip; the silver buckle on his belt displayed the head of a buffalo—above this tribal symbol were four letters: SUPD. So this was a Southern Ute tribal policeman. Traveling with a tough-looking white man.

Not good news.

The grim expression on the cop's face told the Shoshone that this was not to be an arrest.

Charlie Moon watched his prisoner in silence. The Shoshone police sergeant at Fort Washakie had informed him that the deaf man could read lips. He'd also assured the Ute policeman that Shoshone authorities would bring Noah in for questioning. A representative of the Southern Ute Police Department would be welcome to observe the interrogation, even submit questions. Charlie Moon wasn't interested in such formal proceedings. They would produce nothing.

Moon waited until the deaf man's eyes were focused on his face before he spoke.

"Hello, Noah Dancing Crow."

The Shoshone nodded uncertainly. He quickly summed up his situation. These men knew who he was. They might even know about his attempt to lure the child away from the Perika woman's protection. They were plenty pissed. And they'd brought him to a place where there would be no witnesses. There were two of them, big as buffalo and hard as nails. Noah's dark eyes darted left and right. There was no point in running. They'd just shoot him down like a dog. There was only one thing for a Shoshone warrior to do.

Stand and fight. And die.

The Ute policeman saw the man's hand moving toward an opening in the front of his shirt. Charlie Moon's arms were folded across his chest.

In the blink of an eye, Moon realized that he had underestimated his opponent. The Shoshone—you had to give him credit—was exceptionally fast for a man suffering a hangover. The wiry man's hand moved like the head of a striking rattlesnake—as Moon instinctively threw up his forearm to protect himself, the tip of the Buck Knife clipped a horn button off the cuff of his shirtsleeve. But the Ute, for a large man, was also fast. Before the knife could make another slash, the back of Moon's massive left hand smacked the side of Noah's head; the sound was like a fence post striking an unripe melon. It was as if the Shoshone had been felled by a baseball bat. The hunting knife slipped from his hand, his neck snapped sideways from the impact of the blow, his butt slammed into the Volvo fender, his slack body slid over the trunk and flopped onto the ground like a rag doll.

"Jimminy," Parris yelled, "you don't need to kill him!"

"He cut a button off my shirt," the Ute said.

"Well, hell," Parris said, "that puts it into an altogether different light. If I'd known he caused damage to your shirt, I'd have stomped him to death myself."

"It's a *new* shirt." Moon was squatting, gingerly recovering the dime-sized button between two fingertips. "The button's hand-carved elk horn. Sewed it on myself."

Scott Parris kneeled by the limp body. He put a finger under the man's jaw and felt a weak but rhythmic pulsation from the carotid artery. He pushed back an eyelid and saw that the pupil was not noticeably dilated. The man's ribs occasionally heaved with a breath that reeked of stale beer. Parris got to his feet and glared at his friend. "Well, I expect he'll live."

The Ute seemed unconcerned with this prognosis. He was rubbing the back of his hand; it was sore from the impact with the Shoshone's hard head. "He shouldn't have tried to knife me."

"No," Parris said, "he shouldn't have done that." And two professional lawmen should have made certain the man wasn't armed. "But imagine how you'd feel, Charlie, waking up out here in the wilderness." Parris nodded to indicate the revolver on the Ute's hip. "I expect he saw that horse pistol and thought you were gonna shoot him. It's really no wonder he got nervous."

Moon frowned at the Shoshone's still form. "You know, pardner, I expect you may be right about that." The Ute policeman withdrew the revolver from his holster and offered it to the *matukach*. "Here. You hold onto my sidearm. When he wakes up, it'd be better if he sees that my holster's empty; then maybe he'll calm down a bit. Maybe even talk some."

Parris looked uncertainly at the enormous revolver in his hand; it hefted like it weighed four pounds. "Well, Charlie, I don't know . . ."

"No," the Ute insisted, "when you're right, you're right. From now on, we'll do it your way."

Parris thought he saw a glint of mischief in the Ute's eyes—but he *had* given up his sidearm. Still, with Charlie Moon, you never knew.

✪

The sun was high, its rays sizzling hot, when the Shoshone opened his eyes, but he was in the shade. The shadow across his body was cast by the form of the big Ute. Noah's eyes were not working well. He could barely make out the profile of the tall man's broad shoulders . . . his head under the black Stetson . . . the *empty* holster on his hip. But there was no gun in the Ute's hand. Noah groaned; it seemed impossible to focus his eyes, and there was a high-pitched ringing sound in his head. This was very confusing.

Moon squatted by the Shoshone. When the dazed man seemed to be looking at his face, the policeman spoke slowly. It was important that Noah should have no trouble reading his lips. "I'm Charlie Moon. With the Southern Ute Police Department." He didn't mention that his juris- diction ended about five hundred miles to the south.

"Ahhh . . ." the Shoshone said. This must surely be a dream. Noah Dancing Crow reached up and touched two fingers to the man's face. No. It was real! He should have known. Who had not heard of this aston- ishing policeman? The tales about Charlie Moon were told even among the Shoshone and Bannock. It was said that this man could walk in the snow without making tracks.

"That white feller—" Moon jerked his head to indicate the distant form of Scott Parris "—is the one called Crazy Scotty. I expect you've heard of him."

No, the name was unfamiliar. The Shoshone shook his head.

"Well, I'm surprised you haven't. He's the godfather of Sarah Frank . . . and mighty upset that you kidnapped her."

The Shoshone raised his hand to protest; the Ute ignored this feeble gesture.

"When I told him I didn't necessarily intend to kill you, he knocked me in the head and took my gun." The Ute policeman rubbed at an imaginary bump behind his ear, and winced.

The Shoshone's eyes mirrored his confusion.

"We know you went down to Colorado with Blue Cup," Moon said. "My aunt Daisy, she was there when little Sarah Frank told Blue Cup that she was expecting her father to bring her a horse on her birthday. You stole yourself a horse from the Navajo's ranch down by Arboles." Moon tapped his finger on Noah's boot. "I found your tracks near Aunt Daisy's home. You took the horse there on the little girl's birthday . . . to make Sarah Frank believe her father had showed up with the present he promised. Now, my pardner is mighty offended at you for kidnapping his goddaughter. Crazy Scotty's one mean bastard, wouldn't spit on you if you was on fire. When he's ready to kill somebody, he generally starts to grin. That's why they call him Crazy; his momma give him the name, after he threw his little sister out of a third-floor window."

Noah Dancing Crow raised himself on one elbow to squint at Parris; the awful noise in his head had shifted into a sound like hail on a tin roof. This would not be a good day to die.

Moon turned and shouted. "I told this little weasel that you were holding my gun so I wouldn't shoot him, but he's kind of scared. Show it to him, and smile real friendly."

Parris raised the large revolver so the Shoshone could see it; the white man also smiled to reassure the Shoshone.

Moon turned to Noah Dancing Crow with a look of pity. "Well, I'm sorry. When he grins like that, it means he's got something real special in mind for you. After we picked you up, he was tellin' me what he did to a kidnapper in Chicago a few years ago. First," the Ute said with an expression of barely suppressed distaste, "he broke the man's legs and arms with a ball bat. Then—" Moon hesitated "—he cut out the poor bastard's liver. While he was still alive." He glanced over his shoulder at the *matukach* policeman. "They threw him off the force after that. Even in Chicago," he said by way of explanation, "the police got their limits."

The Shoshone was paying scant attention to the Ute's words. Of course . . . it all made sense now. Tears wetted Noah's eyes.

"I can't make any promises," Moon said, "but if you tell me what you know about Mary Frank's death . . . everything you know about the child's kidnapping . . . he might calm down some, might even give me back my gun, let me turn you over to the Shoshone police. But we already worked out most of what happened, so we'll know if you lie. You've got to tell me everything."

"Yes," the Shoshone whispered. "Everything." Noah Dancing Crow smiled; he reached up and gently touched the big Ute's face. Never in his life had he felt such love for another human being. Such adoration. It was all he could do not to weep openly.

Scott Parris moved a few steps closer. Before he'd agreed to help Charlie Moon find Noah Dancing Crow, he'd pried a promise from the grim Ute policeman. Moon had solemnly promised that *as long as Noah didn't misbehave*, he wouldn't kill the Shoshone kidnapper. He'd just scare a confession out of him and then turn him over to his own people. Charlie Moon was, above all, a man of his word. But the foolish man had tried to knife the Ute. He'd misbehaved. So all promises were off. Parris didn't generally approve of vigilante law, but he remembered how much he'd wanted to get his hands on Provo Frank after the man had smashed the young policewoman's face. The pleasure of beating the bastard into a bloody pulp would have been so sweet. But now Provo Frank's body was cold and dead, and his small daughter had neither mother nor father. When he'd seen the Ute's body in the wreckage of Eddie Knox pickup truck, Parris' anger had also died . . . and its passing was neither missed nor mourned.

He'd only seen Charlie Moon so willing to kill a man on one other occasion . . . when someone the Ute loved had died at the hands of . . . But Parris flung the ugly thought aside, like a filthy rag into a sack of laundry.

Parris watched warily while the Ute interrogated the Shoshone.

Moon's prisoner was chattering excitedly. Noah Dancing Crow was gesturing, pointing to himself, to Charlie Moon, to the heavens. The man was laughing. Now this was odd. Damned odd. Maybe the man was nuts. Or maybe he was pretending.

Then it was over.

Parris was amazed to see Moon offer the Shoshone the return of his sheath knife. He was even more astonished to see the smaller man refuse this offer, and insist that the Ute keep the deadly instrument. Parris slowly made his way toward this odd pair; before he could get within earshot, the Shoshone had embraced the big Ute. Charlie Moon was mortified.

Noah Dancing Crow turned and walked away across the prairie; he was singing. Loud. And off-key. Well, it was done with, and the Shoshone was still alive. Even healthy, judging by the spring in his step. Parris leaned on the hood of the Volvo and grinned at Moon. This Wyoming morning, like all others he'd experienced, was frigid. He rubbed his hands together briskly. "I never knew you was a hugger, Charlie." He chuckled. "But if you should feel the need of another hug comin' on, just don't expect me to oblige you."

A dark look on the Ute's face was sufficient indication that Moon did not wish to recall the Shoshone's embrace.

"So why'd you let him walk, Charlie?"

Charlie Moon shook his head slowly. "I think maybe he's a little crazy." Maybe more than a little.

"He seemed to have a lot to say."

"Well, as usual, you were right, pardner. Once he figured I didn't mean to shoot him, he sure talked a blue streak." Moon grinned sheepishly at his friend. "Just seein' you there holdin' onto my gun . . . and smilin' so nice at him . . . I think that gave him all the confidence he needed." He turned to squint at the departing form of the happy Shoshone. No doubt about it, Noah Dancing Crow was . . . What was the polite term? Unbalanced. Or maybe, Moon thought, the whole universe was a little cockeyed.

Or maybe not.

The Ute policeman quickly dismissed this possibility. If he wasn't careful, he might end up like Aunt Daisy. Dreaming the old dreams. Singing the old songs. Not knowing the difference between substance and mere shadows.

CHAPTER 23

Wyoming
On the ridge

Lieutenant Tommy Schultz stamped his feet in the packed snow. He could have stayed inside the pickup and run the heater. Or in the warm room he'd rented down at the sleazebag motel for a makeshift operations office. But his staff was out here in the snow working like mules, and it wouldn't look right if he stayed warm when they couldn't.

It was being done just like the Ute policeman had suggested. Everybody was wearing snowshoes, so as not to disturb what was underneath. First they'd break up the thick, frozen crust and peel it off. Then they'd use the soft-bristled brooms to brush away the powder . . . ever so gently. When someone found a sign of compression, like a track that'd been made when there wasn't more than an inch or two of snow on the ground, then they'd bring in the portable electric generator and the vacuum cleaners and go to work. There'd been several false alarms on the first two days. Mostly flat rocks and cow pies and such stuff.

But this morning they'd found the tracks! Now it was a matter of making castings with silicone rubber. Yessir, that big Ute cop was one smart cookie. Charlie Moon'd be a good one to hire onto the highway patrol if he was willing to leave the Southern Ute Reservation for Wyoming. Maybe as a replacement for poor old Harry MacFie. Tommy Schultz was playing back happy memories of the ill-tempered Scotsman when he

248

THE SHAMAN'S BONES

heard the crisp sound of footsteps crunching in the snow. He turned to look under the broad brim of his hat. Well—if it wasn't that hotshot Shoshone tracker, who'd been working away to the north. Looking for the other half of what Charlie Moon had predicted would be found.

And the man was wearing a big smile.

☼ Wyoming, Fremont County ☼

Charlie Moon, like most Utes, wasn't a fellow who'd talk your leg off. But Parris found himself intrigued by his friend's silence. The normally lighthearted Moon was more than just quiet, he was damn gloomy.

They were heading west on the shiny blacktop of Wyoming Route 26, not ten minutes from Riverton, when the Ute began to take an interest in the world around him.

"I'm hungry," Moon said. He rubbed the back of his hand on a day-old stubble of beard.

Well, that was a good sign. "You want some cheeseburgers?" Parris asked. "Fries?"

"What I want," the big Ute said with an enormous yawn, "is four fried eggs. Big slab of ham. Hash browns. Slow-cooked grits with real butter. Pot of black coffee. Plate of fat biscuits and brown gravy and . . ." Here his imagination almost failed him. "Oh yeah. And a jar of strawberry jam."

Parris glanced at his wristwatch. "It's half past two. Too late for breakfast."

"Look for a truck stop," the Ute said. "Any time of day, they'll serve a hungry man some eggs."

There was a sign on the roadside.

RIVERTON—5 MI

Parris eased his foot off the accelerator pedal and allowed the Volvo to slow to sixty. He glanced toward his companion, then back at the ribbon of pavement snaking ahead before the Volvo hood. He wondered when the Ute would tell him what he'd learned from the deaf Shoshone. Maybe Moon hadn't learned anything useful . . . or maybe the Ute was just waiting until his *matukach* "pardner" would ask. Well, if that was his game, he'd not satisfy him. He wouldn't show the least interest in what Noah Dancing Crow had said. Moon could wait till hell froze over before he'd ask. And another week after that.

Parris gripped the wheel tightly.

Hell froze over.

A week passed.

"What'd he say, Charlie?" He despised himself.

Moon, who'd been fantasizing about adding waffles and maple syrup as a side order, looked blankly at the *matukach*. "What'd *who* say? . . . Oh, you mean the Shoshone?"

"No," Parris said, "I mean what'd the president of the United States say when he called you on my car phone this morning."

Moon grinned at the man behind the wheel. *My, but the matukach lawman is wound up tight today. Probably because Anne Foster is giving him a hard time.*

"Well, I figured you wasn't interested in what Noah Dancing Crow had to say," Moon said reasonably, "because you never asked."

"Well, I am asking you now." Parris enunciated each syllable.

Moon waited until Parris' neck turned red.

"That man's off in the head," the Ute finally said. "Said he didn't know anything about Mary Frank's murder. Maybe he don't."

"I wouldn't expect the Shoshone to know anything about Mrs. Frank's murder. Provo Frank, drunk or under the influence of drugs . . . he killed his wife. Bashed her head in with the hammer. Nailed her to the tree."

"Hmmph." Moon said.

"What'd he say about kidnapping the child?"

Moon grunted. "Told me a pack o' lies."

Parris grinned; he thought he knew what the Shoshone had said. "I don't mind hearing a good lie now and again."

The Ute folded his arms across his chest and looked out the passenger-side window. "That little peckerwood admitted he'd stole the Navajo's horse. And took it to Aunt Daisy's home, intending to lure the little girl away. But he claims he didn't get a chance to do it."

"No kidding."

"Noah says her daddy . . . her daddy's *ghost* showed up and took the girl away before he had a chance." The Ute wanted to add, "Ha," but he couldn't quite manage it.

"How'd he know it was a ghost?"

"Like in all the ghost stories he's ever seen on the TV, pardner—he could see right through the man. And the pony." Now Moon managed a chuckle.

Parris tried to sound surprised. "Funny . . . his story is a whole lot like your aunt Daisy's account. She was sure it was Provo Frank who took the little girl away. Even though he'd been dead for some time."

The big policeman frowned and muttered something about his aunt Daisy; but it was in the Ute tongue. Something about a wild woman. With a flyswatter.

The driver glanced at the silent man beside him. "I'm surprised you let him go, Charlie. Kinda thought you'd at least break his legs or something."

"There was no point in holdin' on to him." Noah Dancing Crow had said the pony Provo Frank brought for his daughter's birthday had a blue blanket on its back. With white stripes. It was surprising that the man had enough imagination to make up a lie with that kind of detail. Maybe it would be interesting to ask Aunt Daisy whether the horse she saw was coal-black . . . and whether she could describe the saddle. Then, if she said she'd seen a brown-spotted pony with a blue blanket instead of a saddle . . . well . . . No. It didn't bear thinking about.

"What I'd like to do now," the Ute said, "is tie up the last string on Mary Frank's murder." If a man could really call it a murder. Maybe it was something a little bit different. Something worse.

Parris, who was bone-weary, kept his gaze on the highway as he passed an Indiana tourist pulling a trailer. "What's to figure out? Provo Frank went to visit Blue Cup, stole the thingamajig, got stoned on some weird chemical substance at the Pynk Garter Saloon, went nutso, murdered his wife, hightailed it down to Colorado where he left his kid with Daisy Perika, stopped off in Granite Creek long enough to slug my police officer with a beer bottle—" he paused for a breath "—stole Eddie Knox' pickup, headed off into the mountains to hide, drove the truck into a ravine . . . and died."

In spite of a mild headache, Parris smiled. "Blue Cup and his Shoshone sidekick, who don't know that Provo Frank is already dead meat, they motor on down to Colorado to find the thief and get the valuable thing-amajig back. One of these mean-assed sons of bitches, probably the old man, gets the notion that Noah, who is about the same age and build as Provo Frank, can fool the little girl into thinking her daddy is outside with the gift he said he'd bring her. A horse, of course. So Noah, he steals himself a horse and lures the little girl away. Something goes wrong, don't ask me what—maybe the kid bites him, maybe he considers the penalty for kidnapping and gets cold feet. Anyway, Noah and the old man cut loose and head back north. They split up, we find Noah, he tries to knife you, you smack him senseless, he wakes and he tells you a great ghost story so you won't break every bone in his worthless body. He's so pleased with his performance that he actually hugs you before he trots off." He snickered at this friend. The hugging remark was a good parting shot. It would goad the Ute into telling what he knew.

"Well," Moon said, "some of that's pretty close. But I don't figure it happened *exactly* that way."

Parris slowed the Volvo; he turned in to the graveled parking lot of a

JAMES D. DOSS

sprawling log-construction restaurant. A hand-painted sign said TRUCKERS WELCOME. He cut the ignition and stared out the windshield. "So give."

Moon rolled the window down and sniffed. The scent was unmistakable. Chicken-fried steaks. Coffee perking. The Ute's belly growled.

"You tell me a good story," Parris said, "your lunch is on me. And dessert."

Moon's face lit up. "Really?"

"All you can eat, pardner." Considering the big man's appetite, it was a risky offer. But Parris was in a whimsical mood. And he was determined to learn what the Ute policeman knew. Or thought he knew.

Charlie Moon leaned back in the comfortable Volvo seat and sighed. "The first time I knew who'd killed Mary Frank was the other day when I got back to Ignacio." He closed his eyes and remembered what he'd seen. "I went to see the tribal chairman. Austin Sweetwater got all nervous when I parked on his brand-new concrete driveway. He was worried that the Blazer would drop some oil on it."

Parris stared hard at his friend. He wasn't smiling now.

Moon turned to look at his friend. "It was a little while later before it hit me. I went back to the station and read that stuff about Provo's Wagoneer again, just to make sure."

"Leggett's report," Parris whispered. "Dammit, Charlie, I missed it. The old Jeep Wagoneer Provo Frank drove—it leaked oil in puddles."

"Yeah," the Ute policeman said. "I'd read all that stuff. But it didn't seem important at the time."

"That old car was dropping oil by the quart . . . but when we drove on that sandstone road leading up to Blue Cup's cabin—it was clean as a boiled egg."

"Not a spot on it," the Ute agreed.

"So Provo Frank didn't drive the Wagoneer up to the old man's cabin."

"Which could mean," Moon said, "that he hid the old box of bolts somewhere close by. And then walked in."

"Which is not what he'd do if he was paying Blue Cup a friendly visit."

"But," the Ute said, "it's just what he'd do if he'd followed the old man home. Hide his wheels, walk the last mile or so, and wait. And watch."

"For the old guy to lead him to his secret hangout," Parris said. "And do whatever strange things he does there."

"You betcha."

"And when the old geezer left," Parris said, "Provo slipped into the cave, stole the thingamajig, and hotfooted it away." He paused and frowned. "But why would Blue Cup lie about meeting with Provo?"

"It was an opportunity," Moon said slowly, "to convince us . . . to convince me that he had no idea anything had been stolen. That way he

252

didn't have a motive to chase after Provo Frank . . . or search his car for the stolen property . . . or kill Mrs. Frank when she caught him in the act. Blue Cup spins me this big yarn about having a talk with Provo, turning down his offer to 'buy' some Power, and sending the young man away . . . sadder but wiser. When I told Blue Cup about how Provo'd told his wife that he'd got what he went after, he puts on this worried look and takes me to his secret cave, stages the 'discovery' of the theft, and offers to help me find the thief."

"Very slick old fox," Parris said.

"Very." Moon nodded in dismay. "What got me off on the wrong track was what the little girl said . . . that her daddy had 'gone to see' the old man. When I told Blue Cup that we already knew that Provo Frank had come to see him, he picked right up on it and pretended he'd had an ordinary visit. That old man played me like a fiddle. He didn't even know the name of the man who'd stolen his stuff. You should've seen his reaction when I mentioned Provo Frank's name. But the funny thing," Moon said, "was that even though he didn't know who it was who'd stolen the sacred object, he did know what kind of car the man was driving, and which motel near Bitter Springs the man was staying at. Right away he told me what he thought of the Stymes couple."

"So," Parris said, "you figure he spotted Provo after he stole the whistle, then followed him."

"All the way back to the motel," Moon said. "And while Provo was in the Pynk Garter Saloon, Blue Cup must've decided to search the Wagoneer for the whistle."

"And Mary Frank thought it was her husband who'd come back," Parris said, "and went outside to talk to him."

"And she surprised Blue Cup. Probably the old man was searching the toolbox, maybe already had the hammer in his hand. Mary must've come up behind him and realized it wasn't her husband messing around in the family car. Maybe she yelled or something. He hit her with the hammer . . . maybe didn't mean to kill her. But one blow on the head and he figured she was as good as dead."

"Yeah. Maybe it happened like that. Or maybe the old man never got to search the Wagoneer. Maybe it was Provo who was looking for something. Maybe he conked his wife. Just for the hell of it."

Moon shrugged.

Parris' expression was stubborn. "I still think Provo killed his wife. But to be sure, we'll just have to find the old man and get the truth out of him. If he didn't do it, maybe he was a witness."

"According to his Shoshone sidekick, pardner, Blue Cup is dead."

"Dead? How . . . ?"

The Ute's face was deadpan. "Natural causes."

Well, it wasn't surprising. The man looked old as Moses. "Like a heart attack . . . a stroke?"

"Like a stroke of lightning," Moon said.

They were both quiet for a long time.

Parris rubbed his eyes. He wanted to go home. And stay there. "It's hard to believe that old man is dead. Did the Shoshone say where Blue Cup's body is?"

"Noah Dancing Crow . . . he . . . uh . . . disposed of what was left." The Ute's stomach growled again; he felt slightly ill when he remembered the deaf man's bizarre tale. Maybe it was another one of his lies. Or a lunatic's fantasy. But either way, whether he actually did it or made the story up—the Shoshone was a crazy man.

"Your theory about Blue Cup killing Mary Frank—one part still doesn't quite make sense to me," Parris said.

"What part?" To the Ute, none of this made much sense.

"Why would the old man nail the woman's body to the tree? And upside down."

Moon swallowed hard. Blue Cup was a man who never had enough of the Power. It was an ugly throwback to the old days of witches and death spells and demons—a time when a suffocating darkness reigned over the People. Maybe it wasn't something you could explain to a *matukach*. Maybe it wasn't something you could understand yourself.

Parris ran his fingers along the leather-bound steering wheel. Because Moon had once been a drinking buddy of Provo Frank's, he didn't want to believe the young Ute had nailed his wife to a tree. But that was the simple explanation. And in one form or another, it happened every day. Family argument complicated by intoxication. Result: homicide. Killer panics, hides body, flees. In maybe ninety-nine percent of all homicides, the simplest explanation was correct. "My money still says Provo Frank killed his wife."

Ahhh . . . Money. Filthy lucre. This was the cue he'd been waiting for. The Ute tried to sound casual. "You want to place a small bet?"

"Twenty-dollar bill?"

"You betchum, Lone Ranger." Moon was feeling distinctly better.

Parris pushed the door open and got out. "Let's check out this greasy spoon."

Charlie Moon, who had just returned from the restaurant's pay telephone, waved at the waitress and ordered a second helping of peach cobbler.

Scott Parris was stabbing his fork halfheartedly at a large slab of apple pie. Thinking about twenty dollars at risk. He hated to lose a bet to the

Ute. It wasn't just the money. It was the principle of the thing. "Everything all right in Ignacio?"

Moon shrugged. "It generally is." He pretended not to know that Scott Parris was curious about who he'd called. It hadn't been anyone in Ignacio.

The *matukach* policeman regarded his wily Ute friend with a suspicious expression. "Charlie . . . is there any little detail you know about the Mary Frank murder, anything you . . . forgot to tell me about?"

Moon swallowed a mouthful of warm sugared peaches and flaky buttered crust. He paused, as if to consider the question. "Well, nothing special that I can think of, pardner. But if anything comes to me . . ."

Of course, there *was* one small matter. Maybe one or two small matters. Or three or four. Nothing special, though. Hardly worth mentioning.

The Ute tried not to grin.

The same night he'd remembered that the road to Blue Cup's shack didn't have any oil spots, he'd called Lieutenant Tommy Schultz and told him about it. He'd also suggested that Blue Cup would not have attempted to carry the woman's body to the top of the ridge. The old man would have loaded the corpse into his four-wheel-drive Jeep and driven the burden to the top. And from what MacFie had said, the snow had started a little after dark and lasted for most of the night. Somewhere under the icy crust, there should be compressed tire tracks in the early snow. Preserved like fossils. The next morning, Tommy Schultz had taken some officers out to the ridge with brooms and vacuum cleaners.

And Schultz had also sent a Shoshone tracker out to the rainbow-colored canyon.

Just minutes earlier, Moon had called the Wyoming Highway Patrol and gotten the latest word from Tommy Schultz. At three locations on the slope of rocky ridge behind the City Limits Motel, they'd found well-preserved tracks made by Goodyear Wrangler tires.

The Ute policeman had told Schultz where to find the disabled vehicle in Bar Nunn. He had no doubt the prints would be a perfect match to the Goodyear Wrangler tires on Blue Cup's Jeep.

There was more. The Shoshone tracker had found the location where Provo Frank had pulled the Wagoneer off the road; there was a half quart of oil to mark the spot where he'd left the old junker in a juniper thicket. The tracker had easily found Provo's boot prints going and coming from Blue Cup's cave. Child's play, he'd said.

And there was a late development in the investigation of the MacFie homicide. The good news was that Lizzie Pynk had admitted killing Harry MacFie. The bad news was that she'd never serve a day in prison for that offense.

First of all, her expensive Denver attorney argued, the frightened woman had encountered Sergeant MacFie when he had illegally entered Ms. Pynk's place of business. They had a broken lock to prove it, and a pair of bolt cutters. Whether the highway patrolman's intent was to find evidence of alleged drug activities or to steal some booze, it didn't matter. MacFie was a burglar. Therefore, the attorney argued, his client was guilty of nothing more than killing a prowler. She had, the lawyer admitted, acted "unwisely" in disposing of the highway patrolman's body. But this was an "emotional act performed while the distraught lady was under a great deal of stress after discovering the identity of the burglar, whom she'd actually been quite fond of." Lizzie had agreed, said nice things about Harry MacFie, and dabbed at her dry eyes with a silken handkerchief. She'd also claimed to know nothing about any drugs that'd been found in her place. Somebody must have hidden the dreadful stuff in the building before she bought it. And as far as the DEA agent's wild tale about buying cocaine in the Pynk Garter . . . well, that was simply a lie fabricated by a zealous federal employee who wanted a search warrant.

To prove herself a good citizen, Lizzie had offered to give the Wyoming authorities evidence that would lead them to the murderer of Mary Frank. They made no promises about dropping any charges, but the DA knew she was home free on the MacFie homicide. She agreed to listen to whatever Lizzie had to say. The murderer, Ms. Pynk said, was Billy Stymes. Was there any evidence? Indeed there was. The man was carrying around a pocketful of jewelry that he'd stolen from Mr. Frank. Obviously Billy Stymes had been pilfering the automobile, and was surprised by Mrs. Frank.

Billy, confronted with Lizzie's sworn testimony, had grudgingly admitted to having the jewelry, but claimed he'd "found" it in the motel parking lot. Yes, maybe it was near where the Franks' Wagoneer had been parked. When this was greeted by derisive laughter, he told the Cheyenne detectives that he'd heard the woman scream, and had gone outside to see what all the damn commotion was. With no knowledge of the highway patrol's suspicions of Blue Cup's complicity in Mary Frank's death, Billy Stymes had claimed he'd seen the old Ute driving away in his Jeep. But not toward the highway—the old man was headed up the ridge behind the motel. And Billy was willing to swear that Blue Cup had the Frank woman's limp form propped up in the seat beside him. Billy had picked up a pocketful of jewelry off the snow, but then he'd seen the blood. He'd heard Provo Frank coming and had hidden behind his wife's old Cadillac convertible. Provo was walking funny—like a man who'd had one too many. He found the Wagoneer door open, must've seen all the blood. Stymes said Provo stood there by the old car and listened to the awful sounds from up on the ridge. Like someone was hammering nails. And then he'd yelled something and bolted into Unit 11, not even bothering to close the door behind him. It wasn't a minute before the man came out with his little daughter slung over his shoulder like a sack of potatoes. He dumped her in the Wagoneer and drove away fast as that old junker would go, slipping and sliding in the snow.

Neither Blue Cup nor Provo Frank, Billy was certain, had noticed him.

Why hadn't he told the authorities about this earlier? Billy Stymes said at first he didn't know the woman was dead. And he didn't like talking to the po-leece; it always got a man into deep shit. Anyway, if Blue Cup had murdered some tourist, well, that was damn well his business. It wasn't, Billy explained, like he was responsible for the safety of the motel guests. When threatened with charges for withholding evidence, Billy broke down and cried. He said he figured that if he talked about what he'd seen, why, the old Ute witch doctor would just slip away into the Wyoming wilderness. And come back on some dark night and nail him to a tree too.

But the Wyoming lawmen were bothered by another unanswered question. If Provo Frank hadn't murdered his wife, why hadn't he called the police?

Charlie Moon knew that only a Ute would completely understand this. Provo, like Billy Stymes, had been terrified of what the old shaman would do next. To him. And to his daughter. But unlike Billy, Provo's fears were grounded in his firm belief of the shaman's powerful magic. Even if they locked Blue Cup away, the white man's law would never be able to protect him from the shaman's thirst for revenge. So he'd grabbed little Sarah and made a run for it. And once he'd come to his senses—if he ever did—he probably figured it was far too late to tell the police what he suspected. Especially after he assaulted the police officer in Granite Creek. And stole a pickup truck. Who'd believe his story? Certainly not Scott Parris. They'd charge him with his wife's murder. And make it stick.

Charlie Moon sighed. It wasn't all that much. Not really. Later on, he'd tell his pardner all about it. Little by little . . . bit by bit. But only after he had the twenty dollars safely in his pocket. The Ute policeman did have one regret. He should have raised the ante. Forty bucks would have been about right . . . even fifty. For a flickering instant the Ute felt a mild tinge of guilt about fleecing his best friend. This foolish notion was soon dispatched, vanquished by the gambler's sure logic. It was, Moon reminded himself, his bounden duty to take Parris' greenbacks—his bullheaded pardner was practically begging to give his money away. Yes, this educational experience would be a valuable lesson to the man. And a precious gift from his Ute friend. So it wasn't really about money.

It was the principle of the thing.

While Charlie Moon finished his dessert, Scott Parris dropped several quarters into the pay phone coin slot.

The medical examiner answered on the sixth ring. "Yeah," he snapped, "who is it?"

"Hi, Doc. It's me. Scott."

The old man groaned. "You interrupted my afternoon nap. I was dreaming about a warm beach in Tahiti. There was this pretty little woman with a lotus blossom in her hair—but I'm not going to tell you about that part. It's none of your business, so don't ask."

"You need yourself a wife."

The ME's tone was incredulous. "What on earth for?"

"To make you walk the line."

"Bite your tongue."

"Consider it done." Parris glanced toward the table, where Charlie Moon was scraping his pie plate with a fork. "Any results on those tissue samples you took from Provo Frank's body?"

The ME found a sheaf of flimsy papers. "Got a fax from the lab this morning." He adjusted the gold-rimmed spectacles on the bridge of his nose. "Nothing remarkable. Subject suffered from mild anemia, probably because he lived on a diet of beer and pretzels. Other tissue parameters were within normal limits."

"Any sign of drugs?"

"*Nada.* Not a trace."

"Could they have missed something?"

Simpson chuckled. "Not these folks."

"Then when Provo Frank assaulted Officer Alicia Martin, he couldn't have been acting under the influence of drugs?"

"Not unless every last molecule of this hypothetical drug was metabolized into innocuous products before he died."

"What're the chances of that?"

"Considering the fact that Mr. Frank had his fatal accident within hours after he slugged your lady cop, and his corpse stayed very cold up there in that mountain ravine, you can forget about it. Now, stop bugging me."

"Okay, Doc. Talk to you later."

"Not if I can help it. I'm unplugging the telephone." The medical examiner slammed the receiver into its cradle and stomped off toward an overstuffed couch. Maybe he could pick up on the dream where it left off . . .

Parris stood by the pay telephone and stared blankly at the dialing instructions etched on the small aluminum panel. So the Ute hadn't been drugged at the Pynk Garter Saloon. Maybe he'd just been running scared. Damned scared.

✿ Cradle of the Rainbow Lizard ✿

Charlie Moon stood at the hinged side of the locked cabin door, the heel of his right hand resting lightly on the bone grips of the heavy revolver. The Ute policeman was thinking about probabilities. Maybe Blue Cup really *was* dead. Snuffed out by a bolt of lightning. On the other hand, you wouldn't want to bet your life on Noah Dancing Crow's wild tale being the gospel truth. Maybe the Shoshone'd been eating some powerful Mexican mushrooms. That could account for his bizarre hallucinations of ghostly ponies and heavenly lightning and cannibal feasts. Maybe Noah couldn't tell the difference between dreams and reality. And maybe Blue Cup was inside, waiting for the law to show up and arrest him for kidnapping. Sure. The old fox could be sitting there with a shotgun propped on his lap, ready to fire a wad of buckshot into the first idiot who stepped through the door. Maybe, like Noah Dancing Crow, the old *bugahant* was a little bit loco . . . maybe.

Too damn many maybes. Miscalculating a maybe, that's how a man got his last big surprise.

Scott Parris leaned his shoulder against the log wall. What they had in mind was, even for a squatter's cabin, flat-out illegal. Breaking and entering was the technical term. Something the Wyoming Highway Patrol and the Shoshone PD were loath to do. But sometimes, if justice was to be served, you had to stretch the law a bit.

Moon sniffed at the clean air. Except for his partner's aftershave, there was no smell of a human lingering about the cabin. The Ute policeman had a sense that the occupant had not been here for some time.

Parris rapped his knuckles on the door for the third time and shouted, "Hello inside . . . Anybody home?"

A deerfly landed on Moon's neck and took a sharp bite. This annoyance tipped the scales. "Well, pardner," he growled, "I don't intend to stand out here all day."

Moon had the revolver in his hand.

Parris raised an eyebrow. "You gonna shoot the lock?" If the Ute tried any of that cowboy stuff, he was hitting the dirt. Fast.

The Ute policeman grunted. "Shootin' a lock's a good way to get a ricochet bullet up your nose." Moon motioned with the barrel of the pistol. "You want to go in first?"

Parris produced a shiny quarter from his pocket. "Flip you for the honor." He thumbed the coin into a slow arc, caught it, covered it with his hand before Moon could see.

"Heads?"

He looked under his hand at the coin. "Sorry, Charlie."

Moon raised his boot and kicked the door. The lock broke, rusty hinges were ripped from the frame—the door flopped onto the cabin floor. An orange digger wasp flew out through a billow of dust. The Ute moved in quickly, flattening his back against the log wall. But all the policeman's caution was for naught. Blue Cup was not in the cabin. And *dead men rise up never*. In this instance, a most comforting thought. Moon slipped his heavy sidearm into the rawhide holster.

Parris slipped in beside his friend. "Jeepers, it's dark in here."

Moon grinned. "You 'fraid of the dark, pardner?"

"Yeah." He brushed a spiderweb off his face and shuddered. "And bugs too. I hate crawly things." A yellow hornet buzzed by his nose, then droned off toward the rafters.

Moon found a penlight in his jacket pocket. He swept the pencil beam around the musty interior. There wasn't much to see. A heavy wooden table in the center. A few old pots and pans. A Coleman stove. Some kind of makeshift bed. A shelf or two on the walls . . . The beam of light paused.

Parris took three steps toward the peculiar shrine and stopped to stare.

Moon was looking over his shoulder, illuminating the display with his small flashlight.

On the wooden shelf was a yellowed cotton cloth. On the cloth were two lemon-colored candles in brass holders. A hand-carved crucifix was mounted on the wall above the makeshift altar. Moon recalled Aunt Daisy's account of the dead shepherd's prediction: "When they find the cross on the wall—then they'll understand." Around the crucifix were pictures of saints. Small icons. And newspaper photographs of people who were dead. A pope. A former governor of Wyoming. And Mary Frank.

Parris held his breath. It was the same with each item . . . the wooden crucifix . . . the pictures . . . the icons. All were like the body of Mary Frank.

All were mounted upside down.

Not with tape. Not with thumbtacks. Not with staples.

With nails.

Nails that had been hammered hard . . . driven in deep . . . bent over . . . flattened . . . smashed. One could still sense the white-hot fury . . . the terrible anger.

Scott Parris tried not to stare at the perverted altar. He also tried to swallow the dry lump in his throat. Failed at both. "Why are they all . . ."

"It's an old symbol." Moon whispered like he was in a church. Or standing at the open mouth of a grave. "The inverted figure of a human being represents Death. And Power. It was supposed to give Blue Cup power over his enemies . . . and over his own death."

"Looks like it wasn't enough." Noah Dancing Crow's tale about lightning striking the old shaman didn't sound so strange now. No. It seemed a fitting end.

The Ute exhaled a breath he'd been unconsciously holding. No matter what you do . . . swallow bottles of vitamin pills . . . run ten miles a day . . . give up fatty foods—someday the owl calls your name.

A fuzzy spider tiptoed across the altar cloth. It paused and seemed to look at the human beings. With all six optical sensors. Cruel, unblinking eyes.

The sun had been heating the corrugated metal roof for hours. It was suffocatingly hot in the cabin. Parris felt chilled; he shivered. "I don't much like this place, Charlie."

"Let's get some fresh air, pardner."

They sat in the old Volvo, staring at the sinister cabin. Its darkened doorway was a dry, gasping mouth, the dislodged door a parched tongue. Now a light breeze rattled the thirsty leaves of the ancient cottonwood. From a bank of mottled clouds anchored in the lee of the Winds, there was an incessant rumble of dry thunder. Like many hands on many drums.

Scott Parris reached into his hip pocket and removed his wallet. He found a twenty-dollar bill and offered it to the Ute.

Moon accepted the bill without comment, folded it into thirds, and stuffed the greenback into his shirt pocket. This was the first time he'd won a bet and not felt the least bit happy about it. Not a good sign.

"Charlie, I'd rather be somewhere else."

The Ute grunted and turned his face to the south. "Let's ride, pardner."

Parris twisted the key in the ignition switch. The worn Volvo engine coughed once, then sputtered to life. The rubber tires rolled along the shining avenue of sandstone. The spotless road.

The sun was low, throwing crisp yellow beams to illuminate the east face of the Cradle of Rainbow Lizard. The colors on the shimmering canyon wall were gorgeous. Dazzling. Breathtaking. The lawmen never looked back.

This was an ugly place.

CHAPTER 24

Jasper, Wyoming

The head of admissions for the Big Mack School for Truck Driving left the excited young man standing in the entrance foyer by the Formica-topped counter. He closed his office door and sat down at his desk. Now, wasn't this the damnedest thing? He pushed a black button that was mounted in a polished brass disk. Within seconds, his executive assistant appeared in the doorway.

She glanced through the office door at the dark-skinned man who was admiring a $\frac{1}{20}$ scale model of a blue Ford rig hooked to a silver and red Navajo Freight Lines trailer. "Ain't that the guy who was here last week—who wanted to learn how to drive the big trucks?"

The heavy-jowled man nodded and chewed on an unlighted half cigar. "That's him, alright."

"I thought you sent him packing, Larry." She giggled nervously. "I thought he was blind or something."

"He's wasn't blind, Patty-Belle. Last week he was deaf."

She stuck the eraser end of a number 2 lead pencil between her painted lips. "You mean he ain't deaf no more?"

"That's right. Seems he can hear just fine now."

"Did he get one o' them hearin'-aid gadgets?"

"Nope. He says he was cured."

"He go to a doctor? Maybe he just had wax in his ears. My momma lost her hearin' last year, and we spent more'n 'leven hunnerd dollars on a hearin' aid that she didn't even need and then we found out that all she had was this wax jammin' up her ears." Like always, he wasn't half listening to what she was saying.

Larry leaned back in his big leather chair, put his new alligator boots on the desk, and frowned. "He says a Ute Injun cured him of his deef condition. A *powerful* Ute." Larry was gazing out the window at the gathering twilight. There were some mighty strange things going on in this world.

Patty-Belle sighed. "Well, I don't unnerstan' how."

"There's lots of things we don't understand."

"So," she said with a pretty pout, "you want I should sign 'im up?"

"Hell yes, write him up as a full-time student." Larry struck a match and touched it to the tip of the cigar butt. "He's got the makings of one fine truck driver."

He's got the tuition in hard cash.

☼ Ouray, Colorado ☼

When they stopped to fill the Volvo's tank with gasoline, Parris noticed an exceptionally pretty young woman across the street; she was walking a pink poodle. Both wore rhinestone chokers. She was maybe half his age, and very slim. Dark hair fell in waves over her shoulders. The dress under her suede jacket was white cotton. The skirt was pleated. She wore bright red boots with high heels.

She reminded him of someone. Of course. The young Ute woman who took care of her elderly grandfather. Myra Cornstone, that was her name. And she had a baby boy. Cute little fellow.

He watched the attractive young lady until she turned a corner a block away, then went inside to pay for the gas. Moon had a bagful of groceries. Ham-and-cheese sandwiches wrapped in plastic film. Fritos. Orange Hostess cakes with creme filling. Sixteen-ounce colas. Parris frowned.

"Snacks for the road," the Ute explained.

Parris gave his Visa card to a thin blond girl at the cash register; she ripped it through the magnetic reader and chomped on her bubble gum while she waited for the telephone line to connect. He scanned the convenience-store counter. There were candy bars and ninety-nine-cent cigarette lighters and a plastic cylinder filled with Slim Jims. And a pile of fluffy teddy bears from South Korea.

Now, Myra's baby boy might like one of those . . .

James D. Doss

✪ Granite Creek, Colorado ✪

Scott Parris sat in his small parlor and looked out the window. A willow stood perfectly still. The wind wasn't blowing. Hallelujah! More than that, the Mary Frank case was pretty much finished. Funny how Charlie Moon seemed to have some kind of sixth sense about these things. Or maybe the wily Ute knew something and was holding out on his buddy.

But he had a life to get on with.

Parris frowned at the chocolate-brown teddy bear. Idly he scratched the stuffed animal behind a floppy ear. Old dogs liked that sort of thing; maybe bears did too. The bear grinned back at him with a curved mouth of red stitches. Its black button eyes were wide with amusement. *You are a big twerp*, its expression clearly said. *You are a jughead. A dummy.*

"You are a smart-assed bag of stuffing," he retorted. But Chigger Bug will love you. And his mother . . . well, now. Myra Cornstone . . . the slender young woman whose hips moved so easily under the white dress. That was something else again. But she was maybe half his age. Well, maybe just a tad more. But he had no good excuse for calling on Ms. Cornstone. Maybe he'd just mail the thing to the kid.

Or maybe . . .

Impulsively he punched seven buttons on his telephone. After three rings, he heard her voice.

"It's me," he said.

"Well, hello." A pause. "Scott . . . how are you?"

Her voice had a sharp edge of frost. It cut him to the marrow. And what was this "Scott" crap? Whatever happened to the "Scotty" he hated so much?

"Fine. I'm fine." He tried hard to sound casual, but his stomach was fluttering. "How're you?"

Anne didn't want to tell him. "We need to talk." How could she tell him about a foolish girl who'd gotten married in high school? And ended up in a shelter for abused women. And promised herself, after a nasty divorce, that she'd never marry again. Never. Not even to Mr. Perfect.

The line was silent for a long moment that stretched like a taut rubber band.

Parris felt his skin go cold. If he didn't say the right thing . . . and say it quickly . . . He stared blankly at the bear. The bear stared back, taunting him. He grabbed it by the neck. "I bought you something. A present."

"Really?"

He could hear the beginning of a smile in her voice. "Sure." He blinked

264

at her silver-framed picture by the telephone, and swallowed hard. "I've missed you."

"You could drop by sometime." The sharp edges of the frost had melted. "If you bring me my present . . ." Another pause. "Scotty."

Scotty! Spring had come. The frost had melted into warm water, and the water was a rippling stream. And a glistening cutthroat trout swam in that stream. And leaped for joy to be alive and feasting upon all manner of bugs.

"Well," he said, "I think I could find some time to do that." He had the bear in one hand and was reaching for his battered felt hat with the other. "Say, in about five minutes?"

"Make it four," she whispered.

❖ Blind Man's Tale ❖

Myra Cornstone led the big policeman into her grandfather's bedroom, where the old man was sleeping. Charlie Moon, she noticed, had a nice smile . . . broad shoulders . . . forearms like fence posts. And the policeman had a good reputation. Moon was not a man to break his word. Not the sort of man, like the father of her child, who would leave a woman alone.

The policeman sat down by the bed; he would wait patiently until Walks Sleeping awakened.

She moved closer and leaned over her grandfather's bed. So that her glistening black hair barely brushed Moon's face. So this shy man could get a whiff of the nifty new perfume she'd bought in Durango.

"Granddad. Wake up. Charlie's here." Her hand touched Moon's sleeve. Myra was certain that he did not notice. She was mistaken.

The old man grunted and opened milky eyes.

"Charlie Moon . . . Makes No Tracks is in my house?"

Myra turned to smile at the policeman. Her face was now very close to his. "Yes, Grandfather."

Moon did not speak; he removed a beaded deerskin pouch from his shirt pocket and opened it. The policeman placed the eagle-bone whistle in Walks Sleeping's gnarled hand.

The old man closed his fingers around the object and shuddered. The Power was there. His palm buzzed like he'd trapped a bumblebee; his blind eyes immediately saw a bizarre vision. Of a young Shoshone man, who chewed on stringy flesh. Of charred bones, sucked of their marrow. And a wicker basket. Walks Sleeping tried to speak but could find no words; he kept the eagle-bone whistle clenched tightly in his fist.

"I must get out of this bed." He spoke in a voice that had surprising strength. The voice of a younger man. A man touched by the Power.

He steadied himself on the Ute policeman's arm as he settled into the rocking chair. And then he found his voice again. "Now that you have found the sacred object, I will answer your questions."

Moon stared at the blind man. "I'd like to know how Blue Cup came to have it."

Walks Sleeping cocked his head to one side; he rocked back and forth and coughed into a red handkerchief. He cleared his throat and began:

"It happened back in nineteen and thirty-eight. We had an important visitor that year. He was a Sioux, one of the Miniconjou band in the Dakota Territory who'd married a Ute woman from the White River band. Her name was Pearl Drum. This Miniconjou, he was called Pierced Nose. He brought a treasure all the way from the Pine Ridge reservation, where the government had put the Sioux. It was a sacred whistle that his father, or maybe it was his grandfather, had carried in the fight at the Greasy Grass against Yellow Hair, the soldier the bluecoats called Custer. That sacred whistle had very strong medicine. Pierced Nose brought it here as a gift for the Ute." He paused and nodded wisely. "It would have been better if the Sioux had kept the thing at Pine Ridge, but we didn't know that then." He offered the whistle to Moon, who put it back in the pouch. "I think maybe his Ute wife, Pearl Drum, she made him bring that medicine down to Ignacio. Women," he sighed, "they can make us do anything if they keep after us long enough."

Myra Cornstone, who stole a glance at Moon's face, wondered whether this was so.

Walks Sleeping searched a small drawer in the lamp table by his bed until he found an old brier pipe and a U.S. Marines cigarette lighter. He touched a flame to the bowl of his pipe and continued. "Anyway, Pierced Nose, him and his wife, they drive down to Ignacio in a big black Packard automobile, so everybody here figures this Sioux has found a pile of money somewhere. Because I am acting chairman of the tribe that year, Pierced Nose, he comes to see me in my office. With a little cedar box in his hand. He tells me a story about this sacred object which has much strong spirit medicine, and how he is going to give it to the Southern Ute tribe." The old man paused to remember Pierced Nose's face, then cleared his throat and continued. "I told him I was pleased to accept the sacred object, and that I would take good care of it for the People. But no, that wouldn't do. There had to be a big secret ceremony. The Sioux," he said thoughtfully, "are sometimes a tiresome people. They got to have a big ceremony for everything, and Pierced Nose, he tells me just how the thing has to be done. It sounds strange to me, but because he has brought the People a gift, I must do just what this Sioux fellow says. Not only that, it is also because his wife is a Ute and she has a lot of relatives who live in Ignacio. And all of them vote in the election for chairman. Hah—maybe some of them vote twice."

"Well, when Pierced Nose told me what must be done, I sent word out for four young men, Peter Frank and Blue Cup and Stewart Sweetwater and Bruce Tonompicket. We couldn't find Bruce Tonompicket because he was sick or maybe he was over in Towaoc to a funeral, I don't remember for sure. But Blue Cup, he had this Cheyenne friend, I think his name was Black Arm, so he came instead of Bruce Tonompicket. The five of us, along with Pierced Nose, we drove out to the foot of Shellhammer Ridge. We rode in that big black Packard automobile. Up on the top of that ridge, we made a big circle of twelve black rocks, like that Miniconjou Sioux told us to do—and he put a granite metate in the center of this circle. Pierced Nose, he took out a little cotton tobacco sack and spread something—I think it was corn pollen—on the metate. Then he said some secret words over the metate in that funny Sioux language. You know how peculiar these Sioux are, a very superstitious people."

The old man looked vacantly toward the ceiling where the steel blades of an electric fan were rotating slowly. "Well, we did some singing and we would have done some drumming, except no one remembered to bring a drum, and this made Pierced Nose unhappy. You know how those Sioux are, they get unhappy about the least thing. Well, finally Pierced Nose got over being unhappy and we did some more loud singing and drank a little because somebody did remember to bring some beer. Then Pierced Nose, he got this little cedar box out of his coat pocket, and inside it there was a shiny leather pouch. Inside this pouch there was this little piece of bone. It was a whistle, but it wasn't no regular whistle like we use at the Sun Dance. It didn't have no eagle plume on it and it was very short. And it had a silver ring around it. This Miniconjou Sioux, he told us that this was the very first eagle wing-bone whistle that was ever made and that the Great Spirit told an eagle to give it to this Paiute man a long time ago. I don't know what his name was. This happened so long ago that nobody remembers his name anymore. Anyway, when that Paiute went without any food or water for eight days, he went yonder to the world of the spirits and talked with Eagle, who told him about the future and gave him the whistle. Then he came back to this world. He still had the whistle when he got back, and so I guess that proves it was a true story. That Paiute, he gave the whistle to his son, who gave it to his son. A long time later, a Shoshone man, somehow he got ahold of the whistle. When he was old, he took it up to the Dakota Territory and gave it to a Lakota friend of his. This was during the times when everybody was doing the Ghost Dance to drive away the *matukach*. The Lakota, they called the whites *wasi-chu*. Well, them Sioux, they kept the whistle there for a long time, and I guess it was good medicine for the Lakota, although they were mostly very poor and hadn't killed any bluecoats or eaten any buffalo for a long time. Then the Lakota gave this sacred whistle to the Miniconjous, but I don't think it changed their luck either. Maybe it is good for a man's soul for him to be poor . . . at least for a while. And this Miniconjou Sioux, I mean Pierced Nose, he ended up with the whistle after his father died. Pierced Nose's wife, that's Pearl Drum, she thought it was a good idea to bring the whistle to the Utes." He grinned a toothless grin. "Maybe so we could learn how to be as poor as the Sioux."

"Anyway, when the sun was going down, Pierced Nose, he stood up in front of us four Utes and the Cheyenne. He made a big speech up there on Shellhammer Ridge—I don't remember anything he said—and presented the sacred whistle to the Ute people. He put the whistle on the metate that already had the yellow pollen on it. It was supposed to stay there until the sun came up, then I would accept it for the tribe and bury it in a secret place after all the others had left."

Memories were now flooding back to the old man. Walks Sleeping closed his eyes. "The thing was, this whistle had very strong medicine. If we did everything just like the Sioux told us to, it would bring lots of good luck to the Southern Utes. Anyway, that is what Pierced Nose said. I was worried that it might make us as poor as the Lakota and the Miniconjous, but you can't turn down such a gift. So we sang some more old songs, and Pierced Nose, he put more pollen onto that metate with the whistle. He took those four young men, that was Blue Cup and Peter Frank and the Cheyenne, he was Black Arm, and Stewart Sweetwater . . . he put them on the four sides of the metate and told them to sleep in a circle around the sacred whistle. They were not to move until the sun came up over the far mountains. Yes . . . that was how it was."

Walks Sleeping closed his eyes and nodded. "Ahhh . . . it was such a long time ago."

Charlie Moon noticed that Myra was smiling at him. He also noticed the fragrance of her perfume.

Walks Sleeping opened his milky eyes. "When the sun came up, the sacred eagle whistle was gone. Stewart Sweetwater was very excited. He thought that Eagle had taken the sacred object back, maybe because the Utes were not ready to receive it. Pierced Nose was very unhappy and he stomped around a lot and said plenty of nasty things in that funny Sioux language. You know how they jabber and mutter when they're upset. I was also very unhappy, because I was acting tribal chairman and had some responsibilities for not losing gifts that were brought to the People. But—" he shook his finger at Moon "—I did not believe Eagle took the sacred object. I figured the Cheyenne, the one called Black Arm, had stolen the whistle, because the Cheyennes back then didn't much like the Utes and would steal anything from the People that wasn't nailed down." The old man's opaque eyes became dreamy. "Of course, when I was a young man I stole some fine young horses from a band of Cheyenne—" he pointed toward the north "—that was camped away up there by the Smoking Earth River. But," he added in a tone that did not invite dispute, "that was different."

Walks Sleeping blinked toward the afternoon light flooding through a broad window. "They tell me that the Cheyennes are not like that now, that they are almost as good as the Utes. Hah!" He tapped the pipe on the arm of the rocking chair. "Anyway, things got worse when Blue Cup came forward to speak. I can still remember what he said, just like it happened yesterday:

> "Friends, the whistle, the sacred gift from our brother Pierced Nose, was not taken by Eagle. It has been stolen. I had to get up during the night to pass water. In the moonlight I saw the thief taking the sacred whistle. I would have stopped him from doing this bad thing, but I thought he was only making a prayer, and that was why he had his hand on the metate. Now I know that he was stealing the sacred object."

The old man was silent for some time, the sound of Blue Cup's accusation still ringing in his ears. "There was not a word from the rest of us . . . but we all wanted to know who had stolen the sacred eagle wingbone whistle from the metate. Blue Cup, he pointed to Peter Frank, who would become the father of Provo Frank. —That man,' Blue Cup said, — he is the thief.' Well, Peter Frank's mouth fell open when he heard this. He said he had slept all night, that Blue Cup was a liar and probably took the whistle himself. But Blue Cup, he had himself a witness. That Cheyenne called Black Arm, got up and made a speech. He said that he had also seen Peter Frank take the whistle. Well, Peter Frank became like a wild man. He tried to break the Cheyenne's head with a big stone, but a Cheyenne's head is very hard and Peter only made a little crack in Black Arm's head-bone. That Cheyenne, he left right away to get his head doctored up in Durango. Peter Frank also tried to kill Blue Cup by cutting him with a knife, but we stopped him because Blue Cup was one of the People. Well, after that, there was lots of talk. Some of the people said that Peter Frank must have taken the sacred whistle, because two men had said they seen him do it, even if one of them was a Cheyenne. Others said that Peter Frank was an honest man and that a Cheyenne's word didn't count for nothing and that Blue Cup must have paid the Cheyenne to lie. I think—" the old man paused to relight his pipe "—you would not have to pay a Cheyenne to lie. He would do it for nothing."

Walks Sleeping felt a momentary pang of shame. "I guess I should not say such things because they tell me that the Cheyennes are friends of the People now." The world had changed in ways that puzzled him. When he had been a young man, it was a Ute's duty to kill Cheyenne and Apache and Navajo and steal their horses and women. Now all the tribes were having joint powwows and dancing together. And here was Charlie Moon, whose best friend was a pale-skinned *matukach*!

Moon leaned forward. "Grandfather . . . did you try to find the sacred whistle?"

The old man smiled at this question. "Hah. I almost forget that you are a policeman. You would have searched everybody's pockets to see who had stolen the sacred object." He pointed the pipe stem at the shadowy form of the young Ute. "Charlie Moon, listen to me speak. I tell you this: Our life is like a circle." He traced an orb in the air with his pipe stem. "One who does something bad will have something bad happen to him. That is the way it is in this world. And in the next."

He paused, hoping the young man would understand this important lesson.

"I believe Blue Cup left the reservation because he knew that Peter Frank would kill him if he stayed around Ignacio. Blue Cup moved first to Montana, where he went to a white man's school. After that, I heard that he went to kill some Japanese out there in the great ocean. But I hear that the Japanese shoot him instead and the military doctors have to dig a lot of metal out of his ass."

The old man paused to chuckle.

"Then after the big war, he goes somewhere else, maybe down to California. Then, I think it was sometime after that peanut farmer was president of America, Blue Cup went over to Wyoming."

The old man tapped the pipe on the chair; fragments of tobacco fell onto the floor, and Myra scowled at him.

"Peter Frank, he went off to fight the Germans, and got shell-shock from those big guns. He came back to Ignacio after V-E Day. But he never danced at a Bear Dance or a Sun Dance after that. Except for going to the Catholic church on Sundays, Peter Frank mostly kept himself apart from the People. But not too long ago, after Peter Frank died of the trouble in his stomach, his son came to see me. Provo Frank wanted to hear about the gift from the Miniconjou Sioux . . . the stolen whistle made from the hollow bone of the eagle's wing. I think his father must have told him something about it, and I also told him what I could remember. What the sacred whistle looked like. I told him the gossip about Blue Cup, those stories about how he kept some sacred object hidden in the center of a cave somewhere not far from his house in Wyoming. And how he goes to visit it every day and get his Power from it. I am very old now and not so clever. I thought the boy only wanted to hear some old stories. Didn't know he would try to steal it."

The old man puffed on the pipe before he asked the important question. "Charlie Moon, what will you do with this sacred object?"

Moon glanced at the pretty girl, then at the old man. "You may decide, Grandfather. Keep it, if you wish."

There was a noticeable hesitation. "No. It is not mine to keep." His sightless eyes seemed to look through Moon. The old man licked at his dry lips. He complained of a great thirst. His granddaughter left the bedroom to get him a cold Dr. Pepper from the refrigerator. While Myra was busy with her errand, Walks Sleeping told Charlie Moon precisely what must be done with the sacred object.

☼ Remedies ☼

A week passed, then ten days. Still the child remained silent.

Sarah was sitting cross-legged on the kitchen linoleum, coloring pictures in a book the woman from Social Services had brought. The kindly *matukach* psychologist had visited the remote trailer home three times. She had talked, and cajoled, and talked some more. She had given the child tests. Sarah had obligingly put little round pegs into little round holes. And little square pegs into little square holes. She had, by pointing, correctly identified the pictures of dogs and cats and elephants. The child had been patient when the social worker took her to the clinic, where her throat had been examined, her ears probed with a pencil beam of light, her little knees gently tapped with a small hammer.

It had, of course, not helped.

Once the white man's medicine had failed to even determine the cause of the malady, the old shaman had attempted older remedies to restore the child's power of speech. She had applied mild ointments of grindelia and maidenhair fern and hound's-tongue to Sarah's throat. To no avail. She had repeated the application with a bayberry-mallow poultice. Still the child did not speak. Daisy made Sarah a cup of blood tea, from the root the Navajos call *bike tlool lichiigigii*. This is mainly used for stopping nosebleeds and preventing blood clots, but the old woman was desperate. After one sip, the child made an ugly face and spat it out.

The Ute woman tried several Navajo tobaccos. First she used *hozhooji natoh*, the "beauty way" smoke. Then *atsa azee*, which is "eagle smoke." And *dzil natoh*, the smoke that comes from the mountains. She would light these tobaccos in her second husband's old brier pipe, suck in a lungful, and blow the smoke in the face of the child. The smoke made Daisy cough and her eyes to water. The kitten meowed loudly, even left the room in protest. The smoke did not bother Sarah, but the child uttered not one word.

As a last resort, Daisy applied a pinch of the valuable *ajilee natoh*, the one the Navajos call "the powerful smoke." Alas, even this remedy failed. Surely it was a powerful magic that had taken away Sarah's ability to speak.

Daisy was sitting on her porch steps, pondering her next move, when she heard the approach of an automobile. The Ute woman recognized the rumble of Louise Marie LaForte's old car, and so was not unduly alarmed when the black car turned sharply into her lane. Daisy did retreat up the steps to the relative safety of her porch.

Louise Marie climbed out with many grunts and puffs; she waddled uncertainly toward the trailer. She carried a yellow plastic grocery bag.

More used cosmetics, Daisy thought. Well, I ain't buyin' none this time.

The tiny woman stood at the bottom of the steps, breathing heavily from the exertion of walking. She raised the bag for Daisy to see. "I brought some ice cream and sweets," she said.

The Ute woman nodded with appreciation as her visitor used one hand to grip the pine railing and made her way up the steps. Ice cream was a rare treat out here. "Is it sugar-free and fat-free?"

Louise Marie paused at the top step, gasping for breath. "Oh no, I don't think so," she said apologetically.

"Well, good," Daisy cackled. "That healthy stuff tastes like wallpaper paste."

The French-Canadian woman, who had never tasted wallpaper paste—or had the least desire to—thought this observation to be quite odd.

Daisy was about to invite Louise Marie inside when Sarah emerged from the trailer, the kitten cradled in her arms.

Louise Marie bent over and smiled sweetly. "Ahhh . . . *de jeune fille* . . . See? I bring you some ice cream. And cookies." She touched the tip of her little finger to the kitten's nose. "And your little *chatte* can have some too."

Sarah reached out to feel the coldness of the ice cream cartons. The child looked up at the visitor, and spoke: "I like ice cream. Is it chocolate?"

Daisy caught her breath.

Louise Marie's eyes goggled. "But I thought she couldn't . . ."

"She couldn't," Daisy muttered, "until now." The Ute woman put her hand on the child's head; tears wetted the shaman's eyes. It must have been the *ajilee natoh*. That Navajo tobacco was slow-working, but it was powerful medicine.

Almost an hour later, as Louise Marie departed, the old woman and the child watched the blue smoke belch from the black rattletrap. The French-Canadian woman had solved the problem with the out-of-date license plate. She had removed it. Daisy sat down on the porch step.

Sarah sat down beside her, munching happily on a yellow half-moon of sugar cookie. "Aunt Daisy . . . ?"

"Yes?"

"Where does ice cream come from?"

"From half-froze cows that live up in Alaska."

"Then where does cookies come from?"

"Why, anybody knows that—from the big bakery down in Pietown."

"Pietown?"

"Sure. It's down in New Mexico, out west of Socorro. That's where all the pies come from, too. Cherry, apple, peach, lemon . . . They bake nothin' but pies Monday through Friday. But every Saturday, why, they bake loads of cookies. Them Pietown folks ships pies and cookies everywhere. In big trucks that say PIE on the side."

"Oh." Sarah stared at the cookie, then back at the clever old woman. There was one really hard question, which had always made Daddy laugh and pull on his collar and say, "Ask your mother, she's lots older than me and knows all about stuff like that." But the hard question made Mommy sigh and say, "Sarah, why *do* you ask such questions?" But this old woman knew everything. Yes, she'd know for sure.

"Aunt Daisy—where does little babies come from?"

The old woman cut her eyes at the child. "Someday . . . when you're all grown-up . . . then maybe we'll talk about such things." Or maybe not.

"But I want to know *now*."

Daisy patted the child's head. "Sometimes people ask questions about things they ain't supposed to know nothin' about. Especially young people." She looked toward the yawning mouth of the canyon. Slyly she said: "Let's talk about something else. Maybe you'd like to tell me all about what happened on your birthday . . . when you rode off into the Canyon of the Spirits. On that pretty little spotted pony."

Sarah thought about this; a frown made tiny wrinkles on her forehead. It was true. Sometimes people *do* ask questions about things they aren't supposed to know about. Especially old people. The child licked cookie crumbs off her lips; she smiled innocently at the old woman. "Someday . . . when I'm all growed-up . . . then maybe we'll talk about such things."

Or maybe not.

☼ On Shellhammer Ridge ☼

The granite metate is long gone, carried away by a collector of such stone artifacts. But the crude circle of twelve black basalt stones has not been touched by the decades that have passed. The policeman uses his fingers to smooth the sandy ground in the center of the circle. He has done precisely as Walks Sleeping directed; the sacred object is buried in this place. Here it will remain, at the very spot where it was stolen from the People. Perhaps . . . until the end of the ages. Charlie Moon stands upright and brushes the earth from his palms.

Now it is finished. Like the sacred whistle, all the bodies are buried. Mary, of the Tohono O'otam. Provo, of the People. And, of course, Blue Cup . . . Perhaps his soul is restored to the circle of the People.

On this night, the circle is closed.

The policeman should have a sense of peace, but Charlie Moon is a man divided. The Ute warrior feels the humming presence of the eagle-bone whistle. As if it is still in his hand. And he feels the delicate presence of the slender young woman. That accidental brush of her dark hair on his face, the casual touch of her hand on his arm. It had, of course, meant nothing to her. This woman has no idea of her powers.

The tall man called Makes No Tracks turns and gazes to the northwest; the night spits fine grains of sleet into his face. Moon buttons the collar of his sheepskin jacket and tugs the black Stetson down across his forehead. The Moon of Dead Leaves falling has come to the piñon-dotted mesas and serpentine canyons; it will be a long time until the Moon of Grass Is Tender. A man needs someone to keep him warm when the frigid winds rattle the windowpanes. And someone to whisper to him on summer nights. Upon the sharp breeze, he imagines that he catches the sweet scent of her perfume.

He takes a final look at the circle of basalt stones. Charlie Moon had questioned the old man's directions—was it the right thing to do, burying the sacred object in this desolate place? If Walks Sleeping did not want this treasure, would it not be better to present the whistle to the Council of Elders, so that it might be preserved as a significant artifact of tribal history?

Walks Sleeping had simply repeated his instructions—and promised the young man that there would be an omen from the heavens . . . a sign that he had, indeed, done the right thing for the People.

In the clear light of day, the policeman is an entirely rational man. But on this night, this son of the Utes will wait for the promised sign. At least for a little while . . . until he becomes embarrassed by this nod to the old superstitions.

The sleet-spitting cloud has drifted to the southeast. The midnight sky is crystal-clear over the gently rounded, almost feminine profiles of the San Juans. Every star is brilliant. . . countless diamonds strewn on a velvet shawl by a wildly extravagant Creator. Presently the sigh of wind is stilled; a heavy silence moves across the rocky summit of Shellhammer Ridge.

The Ute senses *something* approaching. He raises his face to the heavens. No . . . this is a twilight fantasy called forth by Walks Sleeping's tale. An old man's superstition is tickling at your insides . . . Its icy fingers will take hold and never release you. Unless you resist. Go away now. Hurry!

Another voice whispers to him: wait . . . wait . . . wait and see.

It happens suddenly. The stillness is broken by the raspy whistle of a shooting star. The cosmic missile penetrates the thin shroud of earth's atmosphere—it blazes into a white-hot needle that pulls a glistening silver thread across the velvet sky. Now the iron-nickel meteorite fractures and is broken into a half dozen fiery embers. One fragment glows an iridescent cobalt-blue, another is yellow-orange, others are dull red fireflies. But one by one, like the six men who stood on this ridge decades ago . . . four Utes . . . the Sioux . . . the Cheyenne . . . all the flames are extinguished. It is finished. The cosmos is serenely unperturbed by this brief display of fire in the night.

Now the Ute cocks his head. He hears something . . . the wind rolling off the mountains? Or a chorus of faraway voices . . . singing in angelic symphony? If these are the voices of souls immortal, they speak not the language of the Ute . . . or of the *matukach* . . . or of any earthly people. Yet their words sigh in the pines; they caress his face.

His mind warns him: *This is an illusion, a fantasy. It is merely the wind— a swarm of molecules, driven by differences in pressure. Nothing more.*

But in his ear there is a gentle, persistent whisper: *Listen . . . listen to the voices of those who sing the song eternal.*

The Ute warrior listens . . . The voices sing an old, sweet song. They sing of the Beloved. Of that which is passing away . . . and of that which is yet to be. This life . . . and the life to come. Now the man hears both the winds and the voices . . . the atoms and the spirits. Deep calls unto deep . . . they sing together. It is a perfect resonance; an exquisite harmony.

For an instant he has an inkling . . . he almost understands. *Almost*. The stars wink slyly at the man—as if they share some sweet secret. Charlie Moon laughs; he winks back at the stars.

James D. Doss works at the University of California's Los Alamos National Laboratory. Both of his previous novels—*The Shaman Sings* and *The Shaman Laughs*—were selections of the Mystery Guild, and each was named one of the Best Books of the year by *Publishers Weekly*. Originally from Kentucky, Mr. Doss now divides his time between Los Alamos and Taos, New Mexico.